D1016367

Praise for *Memories of a Pure Spring*

"Darkly poetic . . . Duong . . . deftly employs flashbacks, multiple points of view and a haunting interplay of narrative and interior voices to construct her sadly beautiful tale."

—*The New York Times Book Review*

"Powerful . . . a novel about what happened when war and the music stopped."

—*The Boston Globe*

"A work of exceptional lyricism, psychological acumen, and high drama [that] boldly explores the interface between totalitarian politics and art. . . . Huong, a brilliant storyteller, skillfully illuminates the human spirit's capacity for brutality and compassion, betrayal and beauty in each elegantly drawn and profoundly poignant scene in this complex and timeless novel of conscience, which will take its rightful place beside the works of Nina Berberova and Anchee Min."

—*Booklist* (starred review)

PENGUIN BOOKS

MEMORIES OF A PURE SPRING

Duong Thu Huong, one of Vietnam's most popular writers, was born in 1947. At the age of twenty, she led a Communist Youth Brigade sent to the front to entertain troops during the war in Vietnam. Of her volunteer group of forty, she was one of three survivors. During China's 1979 attack on Vietnam, she became the first woman combatant present on the front lines to chronicle the conflict. A vocal advocate of human rights and democratic political reform, she was expelled from the Communist party in 1989. She was imprisoned without trial for seven months in 1991 for her political beliefs. Duong Thu Huong is the author of *Paradise of the Blind* (shortlisted for the Prix Femina), the first Vietnamese novel ever translated into English and published in the United States, and *Novel Without a Name* (shortlisted for the IMPAC Dublin Award). Both are available from Penguin. All of Duong Thu Huong's work has been effectively banned by the Vietnamese government. She lives in Hanoi.

Nina McPherson and Phan Huy Duong translated *Paradise of the Blind* and *Novel Without a Name*. They live in Paris.

Memories of a Pure Spring

Duong Thu Huong

Translated from the Vietnamese by
Nina McPherson and Phan Huy Duong

PENGUIN BOOKS

Nina McPherson wishes to thank the author for all her generous help
in discussing the work and answering questions regarding the translations.
The translation is from the original Vietnamese manuscript
and has been edited with the author's permission.

PENGUIN BOOKS
Published by the Penguin Group
Penguin Putnam Inc., 375 Hudson Street,
New York, New York 10014, U.S.A.
Penguin Books Ltd, 27 Wrights Lane, London W8 5TZ, England
Penguin Books Australia Ltd, Ringwood, Victoria, Australia
Penguin Books Canada Ltd, 10 Alcorn Avenue,
Toronto, Ontario, Canada M4V 3B2
Penguin Books (N.Z.) Ltd, 182–190 Wairau Road,
Auckland 10, New Zealand

Penguin Books Ltd, Registered Offices: Harmondsworth, Middlesex, England

First published in the United States of America by Hyperion 2000
Reprinted by arrangement with Hyperion
Published by Penguin Books 2001

1 3 5 7 9 10 8 6 4 2

PUBLISHER'S NOTE
This is a work of fiction. Names, characters, places, and incidents either are the
product of the author's imagination or are used fictitiously, and any resemblance to actual
persons, living or dead, business establishments, events, or locales is entirely coincidental.

THE LIBRARY OF CONGRESS HAS CATALOGED THE HARDCOVER EDITION AS FOLLOWS:
Duong, Thu Huong.
Memories of a pure spring/Duong Thu Huong; translated
from Vietnamese by Nina McPherson and Phan Huy Duong.
p. cm.
ISBN 0-7868-6581-4 (hc.)
ISBN 0 14 02.9843 6 (pbk.)
I. Title.
PL4378.9.D79 2000
895.9'22334—dc21   99–41340

Printed in the United States of America
Set in Centaur

Memories of a
Pure Spring

I

Vinh stood motionless, his heart pounding. The pale gray of his elder sister's face deepened by the minute, turning to violet. The rustle of white uniforms, the antiseptic smell mingled with the pungent stench of sick people lying around him; this suffocating atmosphere transfixed him. Vinh could barely breathe. His temples pounded, a relentless cadence, like the beating of a drum that transported him back, twelve years earlier, to his father's funeral.

"Who is the patient's family here?"

"I am."

"Brother . . . or husband?"

Two opaque eyes, as cold as those of a fish, looked up from under a pair of glasses. The long, frail face of the nurse reminded Vinh of someone he had once met but couldn't recall.

"Younger brother."

"Where is the patient's father?"

"My father is dead."

"And the husband?"

"He's . . . also dead."

The nurse looked at him again, suspicion flashing across her silvery eyes. Then she stood up. "That's all. Sign here. The next of kin has to confirm the state of the patient."

Vinh pressed his hand against the table, signed his name for the first time in his life. Eighteen years old, and all he had done was scrawl doodles of animals on the backs of his school buddies' T-shirts. On his exam papers, he used to trace a big letter V with a curly line under it, like the tail of an earthworm. Today, he really signed. He stared at his sister's deathly pale face against the bed; the inky black lines of her eyebrows seemed to tremble, like the life and death in the trace of his signature.

"There, underneath, write the day and the month, then your family name. You may leave now." The voice seemed to rise from the tomb. The young man fled, weaving through a crowd of admirers that had gathered outside the door to the hospital corridor.

"Who's that?"

"Her little brother, apparently."

"Oh? I thought it was her husband."

"I heard he was dead."

"Oh, no he's not. He spends his days drinking like a fish. He's drunk from dawn to midnight."

"A beautiful woman's destiny is always tragic."

Their whispers pursued Vinh. As he turned down a corridor, he bumped into a pot at the foot of a wall.

"Idiot! Are you blind?" An old woman's high-pitched voice pierced his eardrums. He didn't dare turn around, he walked faster, striding past the examination rooms, the contagious disease section, the venereal disease section, the morgue, and out the door to the cemetery behind the hospital.

Night was falling, and the tombs, newly dusted with joss-paper gold, glistened oddly in the sunlight. Bushes of heliotrope, mint, and cherry faded in the evening light. Wild chrysanthemums glowed in the dusk. Vinh knelt down on the grass between two tombs. Huge hedges of cactus encircled the cemetery, looming in front of him. In the distance, the lush green of rice paddies. The sun melted over the fields. Vastness. A melancholy beauty.

Vinh began to sob.

"Oh Papa, oh Mama, why did you abandon me like this?

His tears overflowed, sudden, hot.

It was the first time in twelve years he had cried like this; with each breath the tears came harder, faster, choking him: tears like a squall, a flood that carried him into a delirium, not just of pain but of release. Something gentle, too, something like happiness glistened in the tears; he wailed like a six-year-old boy.

For more than a decade, the memory of his father had been absent from his mind. If there was a spirit that flickered for him in the shadows of the night, a perfume that still reached him, it was his mother's. But now, across the empty desert of the last twelve years of his life, the old man had suddenly come back, following the call of his son's voice. Vinh could smell the acrid sweat of his father's black pajamas, the aroma of fish grilled over a campfire at the base of a casuarina tree.

They had buried him on a blazing July afternoon. Funeral banners fluttered above the heads of the cortege that advanced, zigzagging, cloaked in a swirling cloud of red dust. A flaming halo around the sun, like a ripe fruit hanging in the sky, spilled a searing light onto the earth. Space seemed warped, bent under the waves of dizzying light, in the deafening buzz of the flies. A crowd plodded in silence, weaving its way through tall reeds bleached white by heat, ripped and tattered by the salty sea wind. Dazed, they walked as if numbed, as if hypnotized by the sun and the salt carried on the wind, by the funeral dirge and the sound of trumpets, flutes, two-string lutes that wailed through the hills of reeds, echoing over the white dunes along the sea.

Oh Papa, why did you abandon us? His two sisters wailed, their sobs piercing his young heart.

Vinh wore the white tunic of mourning, the straw hat. He moved through the crowd, leaning on a bamboo cane. He had stopped weeping, but tears still stained his cheeks, mixing with the dust, stinging his face. He didn't dare raise his hand to scratch; as the only son, Vinh had to walk backward in front of his father's coffin, maintain a dignified, solemn bearing until they returned to the house.

Oh Papa, why did you abandon us like this?

Their wails sounded like the cries of wounded birds. They were just a few miles from Trang Nguyen Lake. How many times had his father taken him there to hunt birds? Father and son had woken before dawn, when fog still cloaked the treetops. Vinh had huddled against his father; though he felt like clutching his father's shirt, he didn't dare.

You're the only son, the pillar of the family.

His father had taught him this lesson when he was three years old. That sentence hung around his neck like an invisible whip ready, at any moment, to strike his back. Sometimes, it brought him a kind of satisfaction; it was a vague, but nevertheless real sensation. One stormy night at the age of four, Vinh had practiced being a man, the pillar of the family. It was pouring rain. The sea howled like a starving animal. Vinh stood trembling outside in the courtyard. His father had ordered him to stand there, while he sat inside and glared out at his son. His mother, in a corner of the room, begged him to let Vinh back inside.

"Please . . . please . . . he's too little."

"No."

"Please, do it for me . . . let him in . . . please."

"No."

His father's charcoal eyes flashed rays of inky black light. Vinh clenched his fists, forced himself to stand straight. With each crack of thunder, his heart stopped, his blood seemed to freeze over. He looked away from his father, avoiding his gaze, imagining his own heaven: the silky panels of his mother's *ao dai* tunic that always smelled of lemongrass and jasmine. In her pockets, he could always find a few coins to buy sweets or caramel-coated peanuts.

Lightning flashed, blinding, turning the clouds to silver. Thunder, like an earthquake above his head. Vinh let out a sob, but remained glued to the spot. His father suddenly got up and went out, scooping the boy up in his arms.

"Not bad, my son."

Vinh burst into jagged sobs, choked with hatred. He squirmed out of the grip of those iron hands and ran headlong into his mother's arms. She covered him with her perfume of faded flowers, wiped his tears. Vinh nuzzled his head under her armpit, falling into agitated, turbulent sleep. He saw birds fluttering over water, a rain of tiny blossoms. Suddenly the storm burst over the garden of honey locust trees; Vinh dreamed he had tied his father to the trunk of an old tree with cord they used to lash together planks of wood. His father's back was covered with welts from a whip . . .

Now the old man lay in a red lacquer coffin, hoisted on the shoulders of eight of the strongest timber men in the guild, the same men who had carried his body back from the forest. They had found him there: his face a ghostly shade of gray, eyelids as puffy as if he had drowned. He must have wept a long time before dying. His mouth was swollen too, as if his last words, imprisoned between his teeth, had burned it.

For three months he had exhausted himself felling trees, binding the trunks into rafts. Going down the river he was caught in an icy storm that had chilled him. In the middle of the jungle it was impossible to find a doctor and the medicine they had brought along had already been used up by other members of the guild. Vinh's father was the leader, and a leader had to make sacrifices for his men. His death was part of his job, his duty in those circumstances. His eyes wouldn't close, revealing pupils the color of lead, a look of stupefaction and doubt.

That year Vinh was just six years old. Mien, his eldest sister, was fifteen, and Suong—the future "nightingale with the crystal voice"—was twelve. The two sisters walked behind the coffin; Vinh walked ahead, a little man at age six. On the road through the village, he had overheard the murmurs of the crowd.

"Where is his wife?"

"At home. When they told her the old man was dead, she collapsed. Fainted."

"That man's fate was as black as a dog's. A wife as frail as a slug. When he was alive, he bent over backward to support her. Now that he's dead, she's not even here to mourn him, to roll in the dust and open the road to death."

Vinh ran back behind the coffin, whispering to his sisters: "Roll in the dust . . . roll in the dust . . . roll in it or people are going to insult our mother!"

His sisters looked up at him, uncomprehending, their faces streaked with tears. The six-year-old man furrowed his dark eyebrows and screamed at them: "I told you to roll in the dust, did you hear me?"

After he finished speaking, Vinh strode back to the front of the cortege, leaned on the bamboo cane and continued walking backward, his back hunched over like a real old man. The two sisters ran past Vinh, far ahead of the cortege, and then threw themselves on the ground, rolling in the dust and sand, sobbing:

> *Father, why have you abandoned us?*
> *The earth is vast, its roads countless,*
> *How will we know to find you?*

The wild birds, hit by bullets, used to cry like this before they fell into the lake, Vinh thought. He wiped his face with his hands. Sweat and red dust stuck to his palms. His sisters' faces were also filthy. Their long hair cascaded down their backs, a dense, black flood. Vinh's hair was thick too. Brothers and sisters had been cast in the same mold. Their father had left them the same dark legacy: black hair, black eyes, black eyebrows. It was as if a thousand nights had been distilled in them.

The shrill wail of a trumpet, like a bird's cry, rose, then suddenly fell. The funeral banners unfurled, held taut for a moment in a gust of salt wind.

"Stop, stop here," boomed the voice of the funeral director. They placed the coffin on two ropes held parallel, then lowered it into the grave. Each gesture was slow, silent. No one said a word. Everything sunk into a numbing sadness.

O lost soul, o lost soul . . .
If you hear our prayers . . . Find the way, the path home to your father's village,
Don't ever stay far from your mother's village . . .
If you hear our prayers . . . Find the source of the wind
Find the foot of the wave . . .
Like the white kite, like the wise sail . . . find the way home . . .

This song to bear the soul rose first on the rasping voice of an old drunkard, then swelled as the crowd joined in chorus. Every time the cry "O lost soul!" rose, the orb of the sky seemed to tremble fitfully in a red halo of light. Waves of light rippled and danced in space like thousands of crystal boats chasing each other on the sea. Only the cluster of flies wasn't swept up by the mournful song; they still stuck to the coffin, swirling up in a cloud of filthy, black dust. A swarm of them tried to poke their way through a crack in the casket, their taut bellies tipped upward. Vinh couldn't take his eyes off them, these flies were eating his father's flesh, the first man in the family. Now that he was the man in the family, would they eat his too?

"Oh, Father!" wailed Suong, jumping down into the grave. She threw herself on the coffin, oblivious to the disgusting swarms of flies that stuck to her neck and face.

Her tiny fingers clenched the lid of the coffin as if she could pull her father back, as if he wasn't a corpse that had already begun to reek.

"Pull her out . . . pull the child up!" cried an old woman.

Two men, woodcutters, jumped down into the grave at the same time. They pulled her off the coffin and pushed her up onto the ground. Another grabbed Suong and dragged her away from the grave. Then they hurriedly filled it, since gusts of sea wind were gathering now, making the stench stronger.

Vinh felt tears sting his cheeks again. He rubbed his eyes. Standing there, just three paces away on the patch of dry grass he saw a wraith, pants lightly fluttering like silk clouds: It was his father. The figure laughed, his eyes flickering mischievously, casting rays of black light. "My son . . . I've gone already. From now on, you're the only man in the family, the pillar . . ."

Vinh opened his mouth to speak, but the words choked in his dry throat. He watched, mute, as his father gently waved, then skimmed over the reeds, the rippling white dunes, moving out toward the sea. Vinh's heart raced, full of fear, full of envy . . .

Twelve years had passed. He knew now what he had wanted then.

Evening fell. Vinh got up, ready to return to the hospital. Cherry trees hung low across his path, thorn bushes scratched his legs, as if to block his way. Once his mother had told him that handsome boys and girls who strolled in the cemeteries often met the souls of dead youth, who would lure them into their embrace. *Perhaps a young virgin has transformed herself into a thorn bush to hold me back? An old legend, just an old legend . . . but why does it call my name?*

"Vinh, Vinh . . ."

The young man ripped a thorny branch that had hooked the leg of his pants; his face burned. When he looked up, the voice called again.

"Vinh, Vinh . . ."

It wasn't the ghost of a young virgin, but a young man; Tan, a student Vinh had just met on the municipal volleyball court.

"Hi Vinh, I've been looking for you."

"What for?"

Vinh looked Tan over. *The only son of one of the richest families in town. He's probably never wept in his life.*

Tan furrowed his eyebrows. "I heard about your sister's accident. I just came to see you."

"Thanks," Vinh replied coldly.

The two young men walked toward the hospital. The rice paddies, the houses, the streets, even the horizon seemed heavier, fading to a leaden gray, then sinking under a tide of dark shadow. Sea wind blew across the fields of casuarina trees, a shrill, piercing whistle, like the sound of fabric tearing. The sky exhaled smoke that unfurled over the towns, heavy veils of it that fell on the rows of yellow lanterns.

"Your sister . . . Is it serious?" Tan asked, as they reached the hospital.

Vinh sighed. "I don't know."

They reached the hospital, walked down the corridors, past the rooms. Behind the windows, patients watched them with a distracted gaze. There was light in the recovery room. Vinh pushed open a white door stained with sweaty fingerprints.

"Come in."

A gigantic back blocked Vinh's passage, it was the nurse on duty, seated in the middle of the room, shelling peanuts. The glare of the ceiling light illuminated her hair, her huge head.

"How is my sister, doctor?"

The woman wheeled around. "I'm not a doctor, I'm a nurse. She's better . . . but we've got to keep an eye on her." She bent back over her peanuts, pinching them nimbly between her fingers.

Suong lay motionless on the bed, strapped down by a tangle of tubes and IVs linked to bottles of liquid arranged on a table by her side. The star singer of central Vietnam was now just a little girl buried under white covers, a pale child that they had barely saved from drowning. Only her black eyebrows still glistened like two deft strokes of China ink.

Vinh stood silent, watching her, forgetting the young man by his side. He remembered a distant hill covered with rose myrtle, a place she used to take him. The way she led him by the hand, consoled him, her voice like a thin wisp of smoke.

Sleep my child, sleep.

Suddenly the door opened. A man appeared, pressed his face against the glass door panel, almost fell down. But he caught himself in time, staggered, then stood swaying in the middle of the room. He looked drunk; his eyes were bloodshot. His face must once have been handsome, with that straight nose, large, finely drawn mouth. His thick, wavy hair, flecked with gray, fell across his forehead. His breath reeked of alcohol. The nurse noticed, threw down her handful of peanuts, and stood up.

"What do you want?"

"I'm looking for my wife."

The nurse stood in front of the man, staring him down. He stared back at the woman, who loomed in front of him like a temple guard.

"I'm looking for my wife," he repeated, then stepped forward, gesturing. "I'm looking for Mai Suong, the famous singer. You tell her this. You tell her she can't run away from me. As long as I'm alive, Suong, you have no right to die!"

Distracted by her curiosity the nurse suddenly remembered her duty. "I must ask you to leave!" She snapped, pointing to the door.

The man tilted his head, tossed his hair. "What did you say?" At that moment, he spotted Suong. His haggard, drunken face suddenly lit up and he rushed toward the bed.

"Ah, Mai Suong, I found you!"

"Stop him!" the nurse shouted.

Vinh jumped on the man, grabbed his arm, and twisted it behind his back. The man winced from pain. He leaned over Vinh.

"Vinh . . . how dare you?" He stared, wide-eyed, in surprise.

"I'm going to strangle you, I'll kill you, I'll *kill* you!" Vinh screamed. He wrenched the man's wrist with all his strength, so hard that the man couldn't speak from the pain.

"Throw him out!" the nurse ordered.

Vinh dragged him out of the room, down the corridor, across the courtyard, arriving in front of the iron gate. He shouted to the guard: "Don't let this drunk guy back in! He's making trouble." Then he returned to the recovery room. Tan was standing by the foot of Suong's bed, staring at the transparent tubes that poured all sorts of liquids into her veins. From the back he looked to Vinh like a film star.

He's a head taller than I am. He's handsome. He still has a father, a mother, and he's rich to boot. Heaven has truly given him a lot . . . why is he so concerned about my sister? When did they meet?

"That . . . that was the first time you hit someone, wasn't it?" Tan said without turning around.

After a moment, Vinh nodded. "How did you know?"

"I watched you."

"You're very observant."

"What if you had been stronger, taller?"

"It's not because I'm small or weak . . . it's because . . . he's the father of my nieces."

Vinh gazed at the woman lying on the bed. As if he could see himself, a madman bent over at the river's edge, searching the waves for an image of himself that the months and years had carried away on the current.

One July day, who knows whether it was an angel or a devil who sent a buffalo-drawn wagon through the mountain hamlet where the three orphans lived together. Vinh was ten years old, Suong just sixteen. Sister Mien was nineteen and married already, but only six months after the wedding, her husband had been mobilized for the army. Mien had taken her sister and brother into her own home, to care for them. A godforsaken mountain village, a few sparse rice paddies, here people made a living off the pepper trees and the timber.

That morning, Mien had gone into the forest with the other village women to look for wood. Suong and Vinh stayed back to weed the pepper garden. That afternoon, they both took refuge in the shade to rest, stretched out on a dry straw mat at the foot of a tree. As Vinh slept, Suong sang to herself. Suddenly, the dry, rhythmic creaking of the wagon echoed at the top of the hill. Vinh sat up, opened his eyes. Buffalo-drawn wagons rarely passed through their region, though trucks and tanks packed with soldiers crisscrossed the neighboring village just ten miles from their hamlet. The wagon shuddered to a halt at the top of the hill. The old driver, a huge guy with dark, glistening skin and a black turban wrapped around his head, shouted at the top of his lungs. "Calm down you, calm down."

His voice echoed through the valley. "Calm down or I'm going to bring out the whip."

Behind the old man, two men sat perched on top of bundles of wood. As the water buffalo spread its legs and planted its hooves in the ground to brake the wagon, which was about to slide down the hill, one of the two men leaned forward and whispered something into the old man's ear. Immediately, the man sat straight up and brought his whip down on the buffalo's head.

"Vruu, vruu . . ."

The poor animal hunched its back, pulling the shafts of the wagon right down to the ground, its back as pointy as a termite's mound. There was a grating screech and then the wagon came to a halt. The man who had whispered in the driver's ear jumped down and strode toward Vinh and his sister. He wore a dusty flowered shirt and washed out soldier's pants; he didn't look anything like the mountain people, nor like the soldiers who passed through these parts. He walked slowly, arms swinging, relaxed, tossing his wavy hair as he went, like a well-fed cow returning to the stable. Suong still hadn't noticed anything; she kept singing.

"Some people are coming . . ." Vinh said.

Suong stopped abruptly and sat up. Just at that moment, the man reached them. He sat down naturally, right next to them.

"Why don't you keep singing?"

Neither Vinh nor Suong replied. The man wasn't offended, he just laughed.

"You sing very well . . . please continue."

"No." Suong replied coldly, which pleased Vinh. But he saw his sister blush, lower her eyes, and stare at the holes in the sleeve of her blouse. Furtively, she hid the torn fabric by putting her hands under her armpits. Vinh suddenly felt a wave of hatred for this stranger. What right did this man have to embarrass his sister? The man looked straight at Vinh, amused. Vinh turned away. But he had spotted a badge pinned to the man's shirt collar: a tiny guitar on a half sun. The enamel glistened like fish scales. Vinh had never seen such a beautiful object. Once, when his father was alive, he had taken all the kids into town, treated them to cakes, ice cream, coconut juice. They had ridden on carousels, shot down prizes in the carnival stands. But he had never thought to buy them a souvenir. For the first time in his life, Vinh glimpsed something like the sparkling pins of gold and jade that had filled the legends of his childhood.

The man noticed the look of awe on Vinh's face. He pulled off the pin and handed it to the boy. "It's yours."

"No!" Vinh shouted. He pulled his hand back abruptly and nestled against his sister.

The man burst out laughing. A gay, booming, slightly mocking laugh. He held out his hand. "Here, you're not going to die from it. If you like it, I give it to you."

In the palm of the man's hand, the pin shimmered like a star fallen from the firmament. Vinh's heart raced, his ears burned. This magical object fascinated him. He clenched his fists violently to resist. The man laughed again. His laugh echoed through the valley.

"Come on, take it. I'm a grown-up and this kind of thing doesn't interest me anymore." His eyes shone tenderly. Vinh looked up, stared at the man. He wasn't old, but his temples were specked with a few gray hairs. Somehow this touched the child. Vinh took the pin from the palm of the man's outstretched hand, like a souvenir from a fairy tale.

The man watched the child pin it to his chest, then turned to the boy's sister.

"Little sister, I heard you singing. You sing very, very well."

"No, I don't. I don't know how to sing."

"Have you ever been to a performance by our town's artistic troupe?"

"Yes, once."

"You sing as well as their star singer . . . no, you sing a thousand times better, I'm sure of it, and if we train you . . ." He fell silent, gazing at the small valley, the path that wound down the hill, the wagon that patiently waited for him, the plantations of pepper trees on the other side of the road, the wild hills that undulated as far as the eye could see. Suong, her head lowered, contemplated the straw on the ground, her hands still thrust under her armpits to hide the holes in her old blouse. After a long silence, the man glanced at his watch and said: "Do you want to become a singer?"

"I don't know . . . I'd have to ask Mien."

"Who is Mien?"

"My older sister."

"Why do you have to ask?"

"My parents are dead. I live with her."

"Oh, I see." He nodded, pulled a pad out of his pocket. "What grade are you in?"

"I'm in the fifth grade . . . I mean, no . . . I left school during the sixth."

"To help your sister with the pepper trees?"

"Yes."

The man rapidly scribbled something in his notebook, tore off the sheet of paper, and handed it to Suong. "Here's my address. I can give you lessons. If your sister allows you to join the provincial artistic troupe, come find me. I can help you become a singer."

The man didn't wait for her answer. He got up, turned, and walked toward the wagon. Brother and sister watched, mesmerized by this strange visitor, as the sun fell low on the horizon.

That night, planes bombed the road on the other side of the mountain. The gas lamp clogged their shelter with smoke, its flames dancing in the darkness. Suong pulled the piece of paper out of her pocket, handed it to her elder sister. They whispered and cried in the night. Vinh tried to hear what they were saying but sleep overcame him and he drifted off on the wood planks that served as their bed.

A few days later, Suong gathered her clothes in a cloth knapsack and left.

"You be good, little brother."

"When are you coming back?"

"As soon as I can."

"I don't want you to go. I'm not going to let you go!"

Suong's eyes brimmed with tears, which then streamed down her face. "Oh, but I have to go . . . please, make me happy."

Mien leaned toward the boy, took his hand. "Let her go. With luck, she'll be able to study. If she stays here, I won't have the means to help her continue her studies."

Side by side, the three orphans wept.

Suong had found a buffalo-drawn wagon to take her to the coastal region. Mien and Vinh followed her with their eyes as the wagon disappeared in the distance. The red dust swirled on the steep hills, blurring Vinh's vision.

For seven years, that red dust would sting his eyes. Vinh regretted it, reproached himself. *If only I hadn't yielded to him, if only I had refused that pin . . . if only . . . would Suong's life have been better?*

2

Outside, behind the hospital gate, the drunken man refused to go. He clung violently to the iron bar that blocked the gate.

"Open up! Open up for me! I want to see my wife . . . I must see her!"

He begged, patient, didn't shout, didn't try and break anything like the other drunks. Inside a guardhouse, a man counted out numbered aluminum tags, which he distributed to visitors who wanted him to watch their bicycles or their motor scooters. He had the right to do what he wanted with the money; usually he made five times his salary off this every month. "Five hundred seventeen, five hundred eighteen, five hundred nineteen . . . damn it, what is that guy mumbling about? Shut up and let me count in peace, will you? Hundred . . . ah, five hundred twenty, five hundred twenty-one . . . five hundred . . . oh, to hell with your mother, shut up! Oh now I'm confused . . . because of that bastard!"

The guard threw the tags into a tin mess kit and stood up, glowering. He turned back into his booth, searching for a bucket of water. Unable to find one, he ran out to a snack stand on the other side of the street, came back with a washbasin full of dirty water and dumped it on the drunkard's head. Dripping with dirty water from head to toe, flat on his back, the man wriggled like a fish on a slick tile floor and finally stopped howling. A large, stocky woman walked into the hospital courtyard.

"Open up! Why is this gate locked? It's not time yet!" she shouted.

"It's closed because of this drunkard," the guard replied.

The woman crossed the gate and approached the man seated in the puddle of water, scrutinizing him. She threw down the empty tin pan she was holding, grabbed the man, and pulled him up. "Hung! Hung! What's happened to you? How did you get into this state?"

Hung gradually came to, pulling his hair back to dry it out. "What are you doing here?"

"My father had an operation on his stomach and I brought him some rice porridge."

"Do you know what's happened?"

"Don't worry, I just visited Suong. She's regained consciousness."

"Miss Hue, you and the others, you despise me, don't you?"

The woman undid a thin silk scarf from her neck and handed it to him.

"Dry your hair, Hung, I'm taking you home, okay?"

Hung slowly dried his hair, handed the scarf back to Hue, a star who specialized in masculine roles. Heaven had endowed her with a particularly masculine voice and appearance. Hue waited until he had finished. "I'm taking you home now."

They walked in silence side by side. They were almost the same size. From a distance, you would have said two men were walking, chatting together. At the intersection, Hung turned to her.

"Thanks. I can walk alone now. You go on home."

"Hung, you're still the same person to me. My parents taught me that anyone who teaches you, even a few words, is always your master. A child must honor his parents, a student must never forget his debt toward his master. You hired me, taught me the trade . . ."

"That's nothing. Is Dam still giving you parts to play?"

"Yeah. He's a good man. He has a lot of respect and affection for you. He's always telling people you're his friend."

"We were colleagues."

They remained silent for a moment. Then Hung took Hue's hand, squeezed it instead of saying good-bye, and turned down the street leading to his house.

The gate was wide open. Dead leaves littered the courtyard. The door to the house was also ajar. Hung's artist friends were still there, still dead drunk after their wild drinking party. The poet Truc Son was lying faceup in the courtyard, his feet and hands splayed like a frog, a saliva stain spreading on the tiles. The playwright Trong Cang was lying on the bed, his two hands under the nape of his neck. The electric light beamed right into his face, exposing large beads of sweat on his forehead and the two sides of his nose. On the plastic-covered long chair, the bearded painter Doan lay on his back, naked except for his underpants. His penis was erect, vigilant, like an animal caught in the act. Hung stepped back. He looked slowly around at the group of men who had once been close friends, who had once discussed lofty subjects, once chased bewitching melodies, fantastic rhythms and visions that only the muses bestowed in rare moments of inspiration. Were these men, who had shared the same dreams, who once considered themselves the essence of culture, the elite of their people, now just disgusting pieces of flesh lying scattered around the room? Hung felt dizzy: *Is this real or just an illusion, the result of too much wine?* He staggered past them, could hear their panting, smell the wine on their breath, their bad teeth. *God, am I just a piece of rotting flesh too? Miss Hue must have had to strain to hide her disgust. So I too have become someone people pity.*

Lucid now, Hung felt his knees go weak, no longer able to support his body. He sat down on a chair, clasped his two trembling hands. He remembered their lunch, then their lively late-afternoon drinking party. What had happened between those two bouts of drinking? Some literary games, a challenge, a recitation of a few poems by Rimbaud, and then his wife's pale, white face. After that a long, heavy sleep, a dream in which he saw his mother lift him from the cradle onto a boat without a sail, then push him from the bank out to sea. He implored her. But she shook her head, hard, determined. "I can't live forever. Cross the ocean alone, find your own oar, my son."

He screamed to her, "But I have no oar."

She called to him, "It's under the boat, reach for it."

Hung bent over the water at the place his mother had pointed to with her finger. He saw an oar floating, linked to the boat by a transparent nylon string. He reached out his hand to grab it, but each time he touched it a wave pulled him farther out and the oar danced on the waves as if to mock him. Losing patience, he screamed: "Mama, give me the oar, Mama, I'm going crazy . . ."

He had never imagined he could be so angry. Never had his mother seemed so strange. In his memory she was a meek, obedient woman. He thrashed about, screamed for a long time, then a real woman's arm pulled him from his dream; their neighbor, Auntie Tuong, a single woman who took care of their children, told him that Suong had just tried to kill herself by jumping into the river. He ran all the way to the hospital, dashing across streets, in front of cars, bicycles. But when he arrived at the recovery room, he stopped, self-conscious, distraught. People were crowded outside her door. All healthy young people, fans of hers, gawking adolescents, gossipy women, the fishermen who had pulled Suong out of the river and followed the stretcher to the hospital. They all had the right to come visit her, to ask how she was. Every time he tried to push his way through the crowd, they pushed him back with an elbow to the stomach.

"Are you crazy? Where do you think you're going like that?"

"Line up, just like everyone else. Don't try to jump your turn."

No one knew who he was. And yet they were all talking about him.

"Where's her husband?"

"He fled with the boat people. Didn't you hear it on the radio?" They announced it all the time a while ago. He's on the list of boat people: Hoang Hung's the name."

"No, they nabbed him. He's probably planting manioc in one of the camps."

"I heard he'd been freed last year."

"Impossible. He's the kind to get at least seven years of forced labor."

"Oh stop. Who cares whether he's free or not. The man's a loser."

True. I'm just a loser. . . . I don't know why Suong threw herself in the river. It wasn't me who pulled her out and brought her here. I'm an outcast. My wife belongs to these people who worried, suffered for her, who pulled her from the water and brought her back to life . . .

Hung mumbled to himself and turned to go home. He was calm now, and yet he felt as if something had slipped through his hands, escaped him. A deep sadness tugged at his heart.

Back at the house, his artist friends now woke up and they were busily preparing to drink again. Suong was a devoted wife: Food was never lacking, and the bottles of spirits filled with medicinal plants were always full. The four men were seated on the floor around a large platter piled with food.

"Come on, Hung, don't be sad. How can a man of your age be fooled by a childish game like that? A famous singer pretends to commit suicide at a place in the river teeming with fisherman. Now that's a badly acted play isn't it? Anybody can guess the ending to that little drama." The playwright tried to console Hung. His confidence seemed to calm him.

"Suong is threatening you; that's what women do. She's holding out a thermometer to test the heat of your love. Such a famous woman— she must have tons of suitors. And yet she's worried about your love, and she wants to claim it. Now that's a real woman!"

They poured another round of the amber liquid that fueled their conversation. Doan spoke up. "You two have your theories. Allow me to contribute another one, brutal, but more realistic: It's a wife's act of rebellion against her husband, a way of denouncing him in public. In that case, how would gentlemen react?"

Everyone remained silent. Then Trong Cang spoke. "I don't have time for ridiculous theories."

Doan snickered. "Because you're a coward. You don't dare face the truth."

"As far as cowardice goes, everybody seated here is about equal," the playwright replied.

"Now, now, friends," the poet intervened. "Please . . . Suong is a good woman. We don't need to consider that hypothesis."

"All truth starts with a hypothesis," Doan continued. "Even if it is the truth, this method of blackmail, fake suicide, doesn't impress me. This kind of drama shouldn't fool artists like us. When I get married, I'll educate my wife in the traditional Asian way . . ."

They had kept drinking. And after the party was over, they had all passed out and had gone to sleep.

Now Hung was back at home. He looked around at the men. Stinking piles of flesh. He felt overcome by terror—of himself, of those around him, of life. He was lucid now, but empty, weak. Weak in both senses of the word: He didn't have the strength to remember or judge himself with clarity.

I've got to go, go, go . . . at any price.

He pushed past the gate, went out. Where to? Left, right? He couldn't remember. He closed his eyes, walked blindly in a direction. It was past ten at night. He wasn't heading in any direction; he just went where his feet carried him. By midnight, he had reached the beach. The same beach where he had left with the boat people. Now it was deserted. No one would try to flee the country from this place a second time. Only the waves danced gaily, calmly, lapping at the sandy shore. Hung gazed listlessly out at them, thinking of nothing, his head empty, like a dried-out coconut shell. He felt cold. The moon rose as tiny gray clouds, like a bunch of lizards, crawled slowly across the sky. And the waves, flickering in the hazy light, seemed to exude a chill mist. Hung shivered, then went looking for the shack where the fishermen stored their nets. He walked in circles for almost half an hour before he found it, hidden low between the shore and the edge of the field. He crawled under the door, into a tangle of nets, wriggled about to warm himself up, then fell off to sleep.

Around noon the next day, when the sun blazed down on Hung's face, he finally woke up. Still buried in the middle of the nets, in the shack covered with mangrove leaves and slats of rough wood, he looked around. The low door was barely high enough for a kid to crawl under, even bent over. How had he done that without hitting his head? Was it the instinct that the heavens gave to the disciples of the god of drink? If it wasn't for them, wouldn't all the good, virtuous people lack people to mock? But this bitter thought didn't cheer him up. He was completely empty. As empty as if he had no body. He wasn't hungry. He was no longer anxious or tortured, like he had been the previous last night. Suong was lying in the hospital. She would get better, if heaven willed it. There were so many people to worry about her, especially her little brother. Whether she liked it or not, she was still the most famous singer in central Vietnam; no one was going to let her waste away. That 110-pound piece of flesh had brought people glory and fortune, and pleasure to her fans. Did she still think of him? He, who was just a superfluous thing in her life now? In any case, it was hopeless. She didn't belong to him anymore. Had she asked him before she jumped into the river? And why had she done it? He didn't know. But one thing was certain: He was just a castoff; if there wasn't any other legitimate reason, then her jumping in the river was the last straw, the full stop, the end to what she could bear from him.

Hung's sadness was right in front of him, as close as the waves. Just a few feet lay between the shack filled with fishing nets where he had slept and the sea. He could see the foam fly off the waves, the seaweed drying on the green sand, that bewitching froth from the depths, the crabs scuttling along the beach, brandishing their tiny claws in defiance.

He let out a long sigh.

And to think that after the war, I looked to the cities with such hope.

That first day of peace, he hadn't been the only one. Everyone had looked to the cities and the towns, ready to turn the page, waiting for the light of the electric lamps to illuminate the horizon.

The war had gone on for a long time, too long. No one imagined the end would come so suddenly. People emptied their guns into the sky, ushering in peace. Gunfire everywhere. From mortars, machine guns, rifles, cannons, B40, and -41 antitank pistols. The sky blazed from dawn to dusk. No one slept.

About six o'clock, a thin wisp of jade-colored cloud rose from the sea. The gunfire ceased. A few seconds later, the clouds turned to pearly white, then a scarlet, fiery red. The sun rose, flooding the earth with light. Everywhere, people who had been evacuated and dispersed received the order to return to their hometowns. The artistic troupe and the Cultural Services were transferred to one of the new towns. The former town, razed by bombs, had to be rebuilt. The new town, in fact, merged three former towns and it needed a suitable cultural center. It had become a large seaside town, five times the size of the provincial capital, and wealthier too, set on the splendid tongue of earth that spanned central Vietnam, between the sea to the east and the mountains to the west, where the echo of the waves and the roar of tigers only stopped at the doorsteps of the houses.

Everyone went crazy with joy. They bustled about, running here and there, excitable, shouting, laughing, jumping up and down like a bunch of madmen. A long line of trucks waited on the roads. From the mouths of the underground bomb shelters, people swarmed out like termites. They dragged a motley assortment of objects: theater backdrops, clothes, musical instruments, makeup kits, personal belongings, pots and pans, bowls, spoons, and ladles. Some of the cooking instruments were earthenware, but most had been fashioned out of tin cans or cluster bombs.

Someone cried out, "It's peacetime. Throw those horrible things out!"

"Wait until we've got new utensils. How do you propose to eat, with our hands?"

Looong coong, loooc cooc, leeng keeng . . . All the bowls and cluster bombs, the dried-out coconut shells, the manioc, the oil lamps, the wash basins, bathtubs made out of airplane fuel tanks. This clanging sound of all the riches created during the long years of underground existence accompanied the troupe. Women refused to throw out even the smallest object. They would scream at their husbands and children, ordering them to pick up tiny packets of sesame seeds, peanuts, a dried-out calabash filled with salt, a half-empty bottle of fish sauce, a sack of wizened potatoes. In the light of day, their faces shone, happy and yet drained, ragged from years of hunger, childbirth without painkillers, the lack of sleep.

Suong was the youngest and the most beautiful, and neither time nor misery had succeeded in sullying her. Youth and happiness had helped her triumph. Like other women, she busied herself gathering her pitiful fortune. Her husband paced about, their daughter in his arms. The man that had picked her out of the mountains had become her lover the first day they met again; he had married her a year later. Right before their wedding, he had been named head of the troupe, replacing a musician who had died of chronic dysentery. He had choreographed numerous shows, trained a new generation of actors. Suong was his best student, his lover, his wife. They had nothing to complain about.

When the end of war came, they waited, expectant, for a new life. They would return to the town, they imagined, live with electric lights. At least this was the Party's slogan: a new life, in a new light.

One of those lights had just appeared on the horizon. A jeep slowly climbed the hill, heading in their direction. Hung squinted, scrutinizing it for a long time before recognizing it as an American-made jeep. This was the embodiment of victory after their grandiose war.

A face trembled with excitement behind the window. Hung turned his back. He didn't want to gaze at this symbol of victory: It was too ordinary, too cheap. The patriotic feelings that had filled his heart all those years, all the sacrifice—none of this had prepared him to imagine that the glory of their sacred resistance would take such a shameless form. The strength of that feeling, which had helped him get through the endless months and years, overflowed like floodwaters in his music, demanding a purer, nobler reward. Even just a flower trembling in the night fog. Or a stranger's hand, hesitant, beckoning. If nothing else, an old woman's gaze suddenly brightening. Hung didn't know what it would look like, but he had dreamed of a moment of grace, when all the melodies and shapes would melt into the halo of light out there in front of him, the vision that had called him to forge ahead all those long years, underground, during the war. Never had he imagined victory would come dressed as an American jeep, with no more than a sheet-metal body, a moldy old tarpaulin for a roof, and a dust-coated windshield behind which he could see the teeth of a driver who cackled too loudly.

Hung turned away, protecting the poetic feelings he had nurtured in his soul these last ten years. The jeep stopped right at his back, as if to mock him, and the driver honked the horn loudly.

Hung wheeled around. Not one, but two people with gleaming teeth were laughing at him behind the windshield. *They don't mean to mock me. He's just carried away by the joy of victory. He doesn't ask complicated questions. He doesn't worry about anything. I should welcome him.*

And yet Hung couldn't manage a smile to respond to the eager greetings of the deputy chief of the Cultural Service.

"Oh, yes, you're the composer . . . your daughter is adorable!"

"Hello. Is there something urgent that brings you."

"No. I've just come to take a look at the troupe before the big move. The provincial committee gave us three days to put together a show in honor of the victory."

"We'll need at least two days to put up the personnel. That leaves only one day for rehearsals, not counting the time we need to get used to a new stage in a real theater. Could you ask the authorities for a few more days?"

"No. The program for the festivities is already set. It's tight, but we've got to try and meet the deadline."

"Okay then."

"Tomorrow night, come work with me."

The deputy chief pinched Hung's daughter's cheek, rattled off a few more compliments, and walked toward the group of actors. He had the strut of a rooster. Suddenly he was greeted with laughter and mocking voices.

"How are you ladies and gentlemen? What joy, isn't it? In a few days, you'll all be back in town. And then everything's going to be just great, nothing more to worry about. Here, let me help you carry that sack of rice. A frugal woman is a husband's treasure. My, my, Madame Hue, you're as green as a banana leaf. Another abortion? That makes four. The next time, we're going to have to do a self-criticism in front of the troupe, you know. No sense of responsibility! You should take care of your health to serve the revolution!"

"My husband doesn't see it like that. As soon as he climbs on my belly, he forgets his revolutionary duty."

"That's because you aren't educating him properly. If you can't do it, find another method."

The sun blazed. The engines of the trucks piled with instruments and set backdrops roared. The deputy chief returned to his jeep after another round of jokes and laughter.

His face is beaming. The others too. They're happy. They're right to be. Life is simple. For the deputy chief, victory was an American jeep. Before, he used to ride a Chinese Phoenix bicycle, once in a while borrowing the rundown car from the Cultural Service. Now, he's got a jeep all to himself. And it's the same for the others. They all hoped to return to the town, get allocated an apartment, a salary, eat fresh fish, vegetables grown in a garden. And me, what do I want? A roof over my head, a salary to support my wife, my children, just like everyone else, naturally. But not just that. Just that wouldn't be worth all those years of inhuman existence.

Hung felt overcome by sadness. What did he want? He didn't know. Something was missing. The jeep was already far down the road. In the billowing cloud of dust and light, the dreams that he had cherished all those years fell apart, like so many planks of wood, adrift, bobbing on the waves.

"Hung, everyone is ready. We're waiting for the signal," said Suong.

He lowered his eyes, surprised by the radiant gaze of his wife.

From now on, you are everything for me, my love. A modest dream, but real. Something to fill the emptiness.

Suong probably had no idea what he was thinking. She waited for the signal to take to the road. She too was waiting impatiently, eager to see the town.

Crystal chandeliers lit the town theater. That night was the premiere of the show to celebrate the victory. For ten years, the troupe had performed in hiding, wandering from underground shelters to trenches, through the mountain gorges and the jungles. The actors had forgotten even the memory of electric lights. Today, this happiness surprised them. All day they had rehearsed their lines, running around the theater, excitedly stroking the leather chairs, the windows, the velvet curtains, the multicolored backdrops; this was a heritage they hadn't even been able to imagine existed. Carpenters had been hired to repair the broken beams on one side of the theater. The curtains and the backdrops still carried traces of gunfire, knife stabs, cigarette burns, but the spectators wouldn't be able to see them. The enemy army, as it fled, hadn't had the time to destroy the theater. Only two windows had been broken. There hadn't been time to change them.

It was a solemn, extraordinary evening for them all. Hung reminded the actors to pay attention to their costumes and their makeup. They were all used to the simple, ragged costumes of a wartime traveling theater troupe. They had gotten used to putting on makeup by the light of oil lamps or torches. The effect of electric light on makeup was totally different. The troupe ate dinner early and was dressed by six o'clock, but after inspection, they had to redo their makeup entirely. The old costumes couldn't be used either. Made out of rough fabric, parachute silk, decorated with pieces of metal-colored paper, sequins, and silver thread, they rustled every time the actors moved. Sometimes they ripped and fell and the actor had to improvise a scene, invent a reason for leaving the stage.

Hung had been able to contact the female cadres of the town's Student Union. All the troupe needed was a half hour to borrow more than a hundred costumes. *Everyone is happy to help you.* Hung knew that they were sincere; the women of this town sometimes had dozens of changes of clothing. All they had to do was donate a few outdated outfits to make the actors happy. The actresses jumped on these piles of clothes, sifting through for an outfit their size.

Hung left the room, went out into the corridor, and lit a cigarette. In the darkness, he watched the troupe through the harshly lit window. The women came and went, admiring themselves in the mirrors. A bit more lipstick, a bit less powder on the cheeks. They gazed at each other, nervous, fascinated. Suong stood out among them. The older women were wearing more shimmering clothes, but Suong just wore a mauve *ao dai*, embroidered with a few white flowers at the shoulder. The simplicity of her dress only heightened the curves of her body. Her long hair tumbled down her back. A hint of violet makeup brought out the deep night in her velvety eyes. Her lips were full, red. Suong was wearing new shoes and their tight new leather made her wince, but even grimacing she was still beautiful.

Hung stood transfixed. From the day he had met her until now, this was the first time he had watched her from afar. She seemed like a gift of fate, an apparition out of some fairy tale. *I chose her like a child takes a piece of candy, without even taking time to look at her.*

"Comrade Hung, Comrade Hung . . ." a frantic voice shouted. The deputy chief strutted into the room.

"Ladies, where is the head of the troupe?"

Irritated, Hung took a long drag on his cigarette, then left the corridor and entered the room. "Yes, here I am."

"Is everything ready? It's almost time to raise the curtain. All the leading cadres of the province have arrived."

"As you see, everything is ready."

"Well done. Let's do a final inspection. We begin in ten minutes. I've got to go and check the flowers."

The deputy chief ran toward the stage, then stopped abruptly, froze for a few seconds, and turned his head.

"Ah, Comrade Hung, come see me at my office, next Monday."

"What's the problem?"

"Something . . . well, I've got to be going," he replied abruptly and lunged toward the stage, as if he were fleeing. Against the left wall of the room a huge table was piled with bouquets of flowers: peonies, dahlias, eggplant flowers, red and white roses, pansies. The deputy chief approached the table, weighed each bouquet like a fishmonger, and proceeded meticulously to count the flowers in each of them. Hung watched as he pulled a tiny notebook out of his pocket, the size of two matchboxes, bent over the table, and wrote one line on each piece of paper with the concentrated, deliberate air of a schoolboy. Names followed by titles, Hung guessed.

The largest, most grandiose bouquet of peonies was reserved for the provincial first secretary of the Party. The next smaller bouquet of roses and purple nightingalespur would be for the deputy secretary. The bouquet of dahlias wrapped in transparent paper with a silver ribbon would no doubt go to the secretary of the Party standing committee. And the bouquets without bows would go to the lowly members of the secretariat. During the war, Hung had participated in the cultural congresses. He had seen how the deputy chief bowed low before the jars of ginseng candy, the candied apples, and bonbons from China, how expertly he divided the loot into portions according to the importance of the mandarins of the province. He was a professional.

You know nothing about culture, about theater, about music or painting . . . nothing, nothing. You don't even know how to organize activities for amateurs. But to compensate, you do know how to be a servant, to do their bidding . . . and you've become the legal representative of the cultural authorities. All in all, it's good this way. Society

needs men like you. If someone had offered me three promotions in exchange for my obe-
dience, a job dividing up gifts and counting out flowers, I would have thrown my cup
of tea in his face.

Hung felt lighter, remembering their confrontation, when they first met. He had been very young at the time. The deputy chief, then a demobilized lieutenant, had just been assigned to the Cultural Service. The war hadn't broken out yet, and the province's cultural activities were managed by the Bureau of Arts.

Having barely taken up his new job, the lieutenant called a plenary assembly of the artistic troupe to "launch a campaign" on the cultural front, an area that "the Party wouldn't think of leaving without appropriate guidance."

In opening the meeting, he introduced himself like an officer during military training. Everyone sat stunned, in silence. The former lieutenant didn't deign to look his colleagues in the eye and, reading their silence as the rapt devotion of the believers, continued his long sermon on the political and historic significance of their mission and their civic duty. He concluded by exhorting them to "create model activities worthy of the great celebration of our homeland, the four-thousand-year-old patriotic tradition of our people, and the trust of the Party and Uncle Ho . . ."

While he was feverishly lecturing, more than twenty people—both young and old—lay on the floor of the meeting hall. Some stared at the ceiling, their backs on the ground. One twisted his neck, pulling hairs out of his chin. Another yawned, then noisily sipped some tea. One man even pulled some cotton out of his pocket, wrapped it around a stick and began cleaning his ears. At the end of his speech, the former lieutenant finally took the time to survey his troops. He was stunned, as if someone had hit him on the head with a hammer. His face slowly turned scarlet: "Comrades!" he almost screamed, the echo of his voice bouncing off the walls. "Comrades! Do you understand what I'm saying?!" He continued to shout. Who knows whether it had been to impress his subordinates or to regain confidence in himself?

But apparently everyone was deaf; in fact, they had all silently agreed to treat the man with contempt.

Hung looked up, saw the deputy chief's scarlet face turn purple, then gray-green. *This man is choking from hatred. Maybe he's dreaming of emptying an AK-47 on our heads. Or a grenade. He certainly wouldn't hesitate to throw it into this room. A single explosion and then just a bloody mess of flesh and bone. I'd better help them bring this little game to a close.*

Hung pitied the deputy chief. He had flaunted his power recklessly, awkwardly. Now the man had to confront their hatred, and he didn't know how to get out of it, how to extend a bridge between himself and these people lying on the floor. Despite his rage, the man couldn't ignore the fact that these people were meant to be his future colleagues. Hung looked straight at the new deputy chief. The man met his gaze, hanging on like a drowning man. "Comrade, Comrade composer, what do you think?" he stammered, staring at Hung, trying to avoid the icy, contemptuous gaze of the others.

"I think it's a shame our first working session had to take place in this kind of atmosphere," Hung replied, then glanced at his notebook. "In your speech, by my count, you repeat the word 'duty' eighty-seven times." He turned the pages, pointing to some heavily underlined words, and then continued. "I understand that you're used to commanding as a military officer, that you're not aware of what you're doing. Nobody wants to offend their colleagues or incur their hostility. So I don't blame you. But I don't approve of the military-barracks atmosphere you created during today's meeting. Dear Comrade Deputy Chief . . ." Hung lowered his voice and winked in the direction of his colleagues, a familiar, almost seductive gesture. He didn't know when he had picked up the habit; sometimes it made him attractive, sometimes it betrayed him. At that moment, it made his half-serious, half-mocking "Dear Comrade Deputy Chief" seem a bit derisive, triggering hilarity among his colleagues. Laughter exploded, as if the dynamite compressed in everyone's thorax for the last two hours had suddenly been given a chance to ignite. Without meaning to, Hung was drawn into the fit of hilarity. When it had subsided, he wiped his eyes and concluded. "It's unfortunate. We just can't stand this kind of barracks education. We're not elementary school kids who need a monitor to help them go to the bathroom, or wash their hands before lunch."

Another wave of laughter rippled through the room. Then, without warning, the crowd got up, as if they themselves had declared an end to the meeting. Someone shouted, "The World Cup is on the radio this afternoon!"

A dozen other voices chimed in: "God, we'd almost forgotten!"

"Hurry, we still have time for a few beers before the match."

Hung walked up to the deputy chief to console him. "Comrade, just learn from the experience. The next time, they'll behave differently."

The deputy chief didn't respond. His droopy, wrinkled eyelids were like an elephant's, masking his pupils.

Anger or shame? After all, I've been sincere with you. if I hadn't said anything, it would have been even more of a nightmare. Not a word of thanks. I guess that's another military habit.

How many years had gone by since then? Suddenly he remembered that morning and felt the vast emptiness of time. A war was ending and now they were going to put on the first show in celebration of the return of peacetime, amidst the perfume of new makeup, under a strange, yet familiar light, like some long-lost love suddenly found.

The office was opulent with its painted walls, fake leather sofa, and rows of terra-cotta urns. The windows and doors were covered with pearly white curtains. No paintings adorned the walls, just a large frame around the Chinese ideogram for "Happiness," written in the running stroke on a pure white background. Just opposite was a chandelier. The light reflected off the glass of the frame, rainbowlike, creating a dreamy poetic atmosphere.

In this setting, the deputy chief seemed like a superfluous object, a lost machine, but invested with power and conscious of it. Sprawled on the sofa, head tipped back against the thick cushion, he gazed at the ceiling. He had propped his legs on a glass table that was already smeared with dirty handprints. Next to his feet lay a cracked porcelain ashtray and a vase filled with roses and forget-me-nots. The maid who had arranged the flowers knew what she was doing: The frail stems of the forget-me-nots rose artfully above the roses, like autumn grass. The Cultural Service had set up its offices in a villa that had once belonged to one of the town's richest and most powerful families. The owners had fled, probably died fleeing by boat, devoured by fish. Or with a bit of luck they were wandering in exile in some foreign country. At the suggestion of the organization cadres, the Service had kept the maid.

"Ah, Comrade Hung . . . welcome, composer, I've been waiting for you. Come in," the deputy chief said warmly. Seeing Hung, he pulled his feet off the table. He was still wearing the old black rubber house slippers and they stood out against the carpet like two proud charcoal stains. Hung sat down and felt himself slipping into a strange feeling of space and softness. He wasn't the kind of person who cared about material things, but this was the most comfortable chair he had ever sat in. The deputy chief was facing him, his hair sticky with the sweat and dust that had smeared the soft, light-colored cushion.

My God, if this continues, in ten days the thing is going to be gray. This guy probably washes his hair every full moon.

After the struggle he had during the first meeting with the artists of Hung's troupe, the deputy chief had beat a retreat, undertaking only administrative tasks; he didn't dare touch anything to do with theater. Then the war had broken out, and the difficult, challenging life of wartime swept away order, institutions. The deputy chief wasn't cowardly like the others who loitered back in the underground shelters, stinking of fish sauce; so he chose to accompany the entertainment troupes during their shows in the civilian zone. He participated in the activities for the active soldiers and for the wounded. Once, when the Cultural Service was bombed, the treasurer was killed, and the deputy chief had joined his colleagues in scouring the surrounding area for the body, gathering pieces of arms and legs, the intestines, even the flesh, and packing them in a plastic body bag. He had also helped with the burial. Everyone was very moved. Once, when the chief of service left for a two-month study session in Hanoi, the deputy chief took charge of the troupe's administrative bureau. Something like this would never have happened before the war, but everyone accepted it in silence. During the war, all values changed. Hung still remembered the day the deputy chief had appointed him head of the troupe, replacing a musician who had died of chronic diarrhea. It was a sweltering day and the underground shelter had been like a furnace. Hung felt as if his head were on fire. Sweat poured down the deputy chief's face, and he wiped his face and neck with a dirty handkerchief.

"How are you?"

"Not bad," Hung replied, scrutinizing the deputy chief seated across from him, straining to make a link between the man who had wiped his face with a dirty handkerchief back in the underground shelter and the one here now.

"The performance was a huge success. I congratulate you," the deputy chief said in a booming voice.

"No better than usual."

"How is Suong?"

"Well, thank you."

"It's great to be back in town, isn't it? Did you know, Comrade, that we've reserved the most beautiful quarter here for the troupe and the most beautiful apartment for you and your wife?"

"Thank you."

"After all those years of sleeping in bunkers, it's good to see the glow of electric light, isn't it? Let's drink to that, Comrade. This tea isn't bad, eh?"

Hung mumbled something, starting to feel ill at ease after this flood of unctuous words. The deputy chief had suddenly become overly attentive, and Hung detested this kind of behavior.

"What business do you have with me, Comrade?" Hung asked abruptly.

"Oh, uh, ah . . . nothing urgent. It's peacetime. There's no rush," the deputy chief replied. He pressed on a buzzer.

A few minutes later the door opened and a woman of about forty, dressed in an embroidered *ao dai* entered, nodding her head gracefully. "What can I do for you?"

Ah, so this is the beauty! She's not as young as they say, but she is elegant. Perfect, that way of fluttering her eyelashes to show obedience.

"Bring me a pack of cigarettes," the deputy chief said coldly.

The woman nodded again, bowing low this time. With a slight, barely noticeable gesture, she pushed back the panel of her *ao dai*, prolonged the movement, then turned to go out, as graceful as a reed. Still slumped against the back of his chair, the deputy chief followed the woman with his eyes.

Where did he learn this distant, severe, contemptuous look? And this dry, condescending tone of a man burdened with huge responsibilities, weary of pleasure, a sated man indifferent to the beauty of women?

Sometimes, when Hung returned to the Cultural Service for meetings, he had slept in the underground shelter, in a room right next to the deputy chief's. In fact, the "rooms" were only partitions, separated by a thin curtain, and stories had flowed freely across those partitions; there were all kinds, from ancient legends to modern fables, but of course the salacious ones were the most appreciated. The deputy chief never told them, but he always urged others to while he hid behind his curtain to indulge in solitary pleasure. One holiday evening, one of the deputies to the administrative bureau, drunk on a kind of wine brewed from manioc, suddenly said in a loud voice: "Chief, oh Chief, give me another jar of that wine and I'll tell stories for you all night. You can jack off to your heart's content."

Light taps against the door, like a signal, then the maid entered the room. "Your cigarettes, Chief. If you need anything else, please call me."

"That's fine, thank you. I'll call for you."

The woman bowed and withdrew, the panel of her *ao dai* tracing a half-circle as it floated in the air. *What self-confidence, what grace! This kind of woman always gets what she wants. She has beautiful hands and feet! It would be hard to find hands like that among our actresses. This old guy's wife doesn't even deserve to be a maid to this woman.*

Hung remembered the deputy chief's wife, a short communal cadre with bad skin and pale lips that never seemed to cover her buck teeth. She seemed to eat for three, burping loudly at the end of each meal.

"Have a cigarette. I'm not used to this brand, but it'll do," the deputy chief said.

Hung took a cigarette, trying to decipher the face of this man who he had known for more than a decade. *How people change. This metamorphosis into a boss has given him self-confidence. Victory has put him above everyone. But at night, when he climbs into his bed, he must dream of undressing the servant woman.*

"Our Vietnamese rolling tobacco is still the best," the deputy chief proclaimed.

It's always the same refrain. Our country, eternally beautiful, richly endowed.

Hung kept his silence, inhaling his cigarette, waiting. The squinty brown, elephantine eyelids of the deputy chief masked his pupils. He looked like a man fighting off sleep. He contemplated the ashtray, then said in a weary voice, "After the war, after the sky stopped raining bombs and bullets, I thought we might be able to rest. But I'm just drowning in work. I'd like to go back to my home village, but I can't seem to get out of here. What village are you from, Comrade Hung?"

Hung hated this way of talking, deliberately using village slang, the regional accent. He had always trained his actors to speak correctly.

"What village are you from, Comrade Hung?" the deputy chief repeated.

Hung was suddenly struck by a thought: *Whenever we're about to kill each other, we start to speak in the old language.*

"I come from Dong Hoi, the village of roses. Now it's just a field of rubble."

"And your father, your mother?"

"My mother left the house for the cemetery, twenty years ago. My father joined her the day they razed Dong Hoi."

"Ah, I remember now . . . yes, I remember. He died in the August twentieth bombing . . . I was in the mountains that day."

Hung snuffed out his cigarette, stared at the porcelain ashtray; the tiny veins made it look like a rice field in the dry season.

From the bottom of my heart, I hate and love music with the same passion. Some unfathomable love forces me to sacrifice everything to it and all it gives me are hateful illusions.

Where had he read that passage? It had been a long time ago, when he was taking courses at the conservatory. He remembered those days: a bed in winter in a student dormitory; a coverlet that stank of fuel; all Sunday's silence and loneliness; the first hesitant piano notes of a freshman.

"How the years go by, don't they?"

This banal line pulled Hung out of his reverie, only irritating him more.

"Is there a problem, Chief?"

"Yes." This time, the man replied dryly. His face hardened and froze. The polite smile had vanished without a trace.

"Today, in the name of the Cultural Service, I summoned you here, Comrade, to announce the decision of the Service to transfer you to your former post at the Bureau of Arts. The troupe will be led by a cadre sent from the Ministry of Culture. We greatly appreciate your contribution these past years. The performances that you directed were a great success during the resistance against the Americans, to defend our country. But the revolution has entered a new stage. Our town merges three towns into one. One part of the town was led by the Party, but another fell under the influence of the American puppets for almost twenty years. The ideology, the lifestyle, the political level of that population are extremely complex. To re-educate, we need cadres who are competent and resolutely revolutionary. Faced with this situation, the leadership of the Service has decided to ask the Ministry to send as a reinforcement a highly competent cadre, a man who has been with the Party for years.

My God, he has never spoken with so much ease. He must have practiced this speech. Not bad, from barracks officer to orator.

"Do you have anything to say, Comrade?" the deputy chief asked.

"What do you expect me to say?" Hung replied. Stupefied by the deputy chief's oratorical skills, he hadn't really grasped the question.

"I asked your opinion about this decision."

"What decision?"

The man furrowed his thick, stubby eyebrows. His deeply wrinkled eyelids fell over his eyes. He smiled contemptuously and repeated in a condescending voice: "I know artists often have a weak grip on real life. But this decision concerns you personally. We have decided to transfer you to the Bureau of Arts, to give your current job to another cadre that the Ministry has been kind enough to send us."

Ah, I see . . . I understand . . . the unexpected blow.

The man's booming voice echoed, jeering, in his brain, but inside there was pain. And there was also a strange, new feeling of fear, of panic. He heard his voice tremble and stutter something in an anxious tone that was totally different from his normal voice.

"What, what did you say, Comrade?"

"I repeat," the deputy chief replied in a slow voice, slowly savoring each of his words like he would tear off a piece of grilled dried squid. "The leaders of the Cultural Service have decided . . ."

Hung stood up. "I understand."

The elephant eyelids opened for the space of an instant, then lowered, hiding his pupils, hiding any deeper feelings that Hung had noticed in the eyes of the man during their first encounter, some ten years earlier. The memories that had come back to him of the evening of the victory celebration flooded back again. The old mule had taken fourteen years to deliver the kick. But what would bring a man to react like this? His reputation had been built on the sweat and talent of people like Hung. Who had given him this power? Even in a dream, Hung would never have imagined such a situation.

I understand. The war is over, the country reunified. I see, you've crossed the river and now the time has come for you to spit on the waves. But . . . it's not going to be easy . . . I won't let you push me out so easily.

Hung glared at the man's expressionless face: It was like a dried-out hide. As he stared at the thick, wrinkled eyelids, he felt like plunging a spear into the man's chest like a fisherman harpoons a fish, wanted to see his blood spurt like water from a hose, shower the room.

The deputy chief remained seated, frozen. He set his half-smoked cigarette down in the ashtray, observing Hung with a fixed stare. He remained that way until the composer left, with a slam of the door.

3

A clear river. Jade green, translucent water. She slips down, lightly, like a kite gliding in the sky over her village. *There is no river back there, just a lake, Lake Trang Nguyen. My father used to go hunting there when winter came. Am I back there in the middle of this river?* Algae shaped like dogs' tails whir and eddy, caressing, their leaves icy. Fish flip by, circle back. A new world. She sinks into the soft mud, in the middle of the reeds and algae. No more worries, no more humiliation. Suddenly rough grains of sand scratch her throat, pain shoots through her brain as a wave pulls her down in its whirlpool. Sand crystals stream down her throat, choking her lungs. *Heavens, what have I done to suffer such a death?* Suong screams through her sand-choked vocal cords. Suffocating, she vomits.

The first image she saw was the nape of a neck, above a shirt collar. Then the whole neck, shoulders barely muscled. A young man, just out of adolescence. Her little brother. Her own blood. How many days had he been keeping watch over her bedside? She tried to move her icy hands, groping for her brother's shirttail.

"Vinh?"

The young man turned around. "You're awake?" He squeezed Suong's hand in his, tenderly, warmly. She closed her eyes, letting herself taste the sweet feeling of happiness, then opened them. Her brother was watching her, his eyes brimming with tears.

"How do you feel?"

"I see you clearly, little brother."

"You can't eat anything yet. Not even rice or bouillon. They told me they still have to give you blood transfusions."

"I'm not hungry. How are the girls?"

"I left them with Auntie Tuong. They're fine. Don't worry about them."

Suong fell silent, gazed at her brother. He seemed to have grown older. His cheeks were covered with a vigorous beard. He looked like their father. The timber men used to mock him, saying he must have Indian or Western ancestors. Vinh wiped back his tears, squeezing his sister's hand again.

"Your hand is icy. Let me warm it up."

They both kept silent for a long time. The nurse entered the room. She took Suong's temperature, checked the tubes connected to her hands and legs.

"Rest. In an hour I'll hook up another vial of medicine."

Before leaving the room, she turned. "She can't have any other visitors. Don't let anyone in here. You'll remember?"

"Yes, I'll remember." Vinh closed the door, tidied the empty bottles by Suong's bedside. "The other day, there was a crowd out there waiting to see how you were."

"Who were they?"

"All admirers. But no one was allowed in except for two guys. I knew one of them and the other was that bastard husband of yours. He was drunk. I had to hit him."

"My God, was he okay?"

Vinh turned to glare at his sister. "Even after all this, you still worry about him? You still love him?"

Suong said nothing; she didn't dare reply. She avoided the violent look that flashed in her brother's eyes, eyes that had always terrified her;

they too resembled their father's, but there seemed to be something missing. Hands on his hips, Vinh stared at her for a long time, then left the room.

Suong groped for a towel, covered her face with it. Tears flooded down her cheeks, running over her temples. They were still warm when she heard Vinh's footsteps.

"Elder sister, listen to me, are you awake or asleep?" He spoke to her in the heavy farmer's accent of the central provinces, exaggerating every word. He started to shout. Afraid of attracting the nurse's attention, Suong finally spoke. "I hear you, little brother."

"I forbid you to think about that bastard. It doesn't make sense. You should hate him . . . Do you hear me?"

"I hear you."

She heard the nurse's footsteps approach and Vinh's recede. She tried not to breathe too heavily under the towel that hid her face. She didn't want the nurse to see her crying. The nurse changed the vial of medicine on the IV. Suong tried to trace the vague warmth that traveled through her body. Her eyes felt heavy. She heard an icy voice echoing in the distance: *You should hate him!* Hatred. It seemed that she had felt this, at times, like the sting of lemon on a cut, the invisible claws that sink into your heart, but at that moment it seemed faraway. Beyond that hatred, there was something else, a vast sky ringed with hills.

"Here's the thermometer. Don't forget to take the temperature regularly and write it on the chart."

"Yes."

"You've got to let her sleep. Not too much conversation."

"Yes."

"And it's forbidden to give her anything to eat. You can give her some milk diluted with a bit of hot water. You'll remember? I've got to be going," the nurse said, giving her last orders. Vinh left behind her, closing the door with a loud screech. Suong felt waves of warmth flow through her body. Her tears dried, cooling her cheeks. The wind from the hills of her past, her village, rippled through her hair.

• • •

Mountain winds blew, heavy with scent. The buffalo-drawn cart teetered as it carried the young woman through devastated villages, entire towns in ruin. *Ipomoea* vines climbed lazily over windows shattered by bombings. They traveled along a deserted sand beach. A seventy-two-year-old man with dark, leathery skin, as thin as a hungry devil, was her driver. All he had for food was a bottle of rice spirits, which he swigged while chewing slices of dried potato. Soldiers had given him two rations of dried food when they stopped at a guard post along the way.

"Take them," he said, handing both to Suong.

"No, I don't want any. You have almost nothing left to eat."

"I told you to take them. I've got another sack of dried potatoes back at the house. Take them, a girl like you will never dare ask for help from anyone when she's hungry."

And he left. With her two rations of dried food in hand, Suong searched for an underground shelter to sleep in. All night, starving rats scuttled and chased each other around, jumping on her body. Their claws pierced her shirt, scratching her skin. She had hidden the two rations of food under her back along with the piece of paper with the man's name, so she could only wriggle, waving her hands and feet to shoo the rats away. But whenever she fell asleep, they attacked. At dawn, Suong dragged herself out of the bunker, sat down at the foot of a poplar tree on a bed of dead leaves, and fell asleep. She woke up to the blistering sun on her face, and the rumbling of bombs on the horizon. She sat up, looking at the vast space around her. Suddenly, she felt afraid. She was alone. What if she couldn't find the place where the Cultural Service had taken refuge when they fled the town? Or what if she did find them, but the man didn't remember her? She was paralyzed, just thinking about it. She pulled the tattered, sweat-stained sheet of paper out of her blouse, reading and rereading the name of the stranger who had appeared to her like a guardian angel, praying that he would remember her.

She finally found Con Hamlet, where the artistic troupe had set up headquarters. It was a miserably poor hamlet, scattered over barren hills. On each hill there were a few underground A-shaped shelters. The hills were linked by valleys shrouded with a tangle of vines, ferns, and thorn bushes covered with tiny yellow fruit. Hung's shelter was on the last hill. The old woman who was guiding Suong shouted at the top of her lungs at least seven times before Hung emerged. His hair standing on end, his shirt untucked, hanging out of his pants, Hung blinked his eyes at the two women, laughing. "My bunker is as cool as marble. I fell asleep."

"Well, here's a visitor for you," said the old woman. "I had to lead her here from the lower hamlet. My mission is accomplished, I'll be going."

"Thanks a million!"

"Now, now, no need to be so polite!" the old woman exclaimed, and she was off. Her voice, though reproachful, was full of tenderness. The man followed her with his eyes, then lowered them. Suong froze, petrified with fear. She was afraid that he had forgotten her, that the tiny piece of paper had been some kind of joke, and that she had fallen into a trap. Unable to speak, she held her breath, waited, her head low, eyes riveted on her feet, her rubber sandals covered with the dust of the road. She was so anxious she could see her breasts heaving like palm nuts under the faded black fabric of her blouse. Seconds passed, interminable. He bent over her, looked deep into her eyes, laughing, full of warmth.

"Hello little sister from the mountains."

Suong felt lighter, relieved, as if she were waking from a nightmare. Hung looked her over from head to toe. Suong was dirty after three days on the road without anywhere to wash; her face, hands, and feet were caked with dirt and sweat. Her hair must stink, she thought, and she flushed with shame.

"You're really tired, aren't you?"

She nodded. Hung smiled. "You've got to get rid of the dirt of the roads. Come with me, I'll show you to the river."

Gently, he picked up her bundle of clothes and steered her toward a path that led to the foot of the hill. As she turned, Suong happened to glance inside his shelter. A woman emerged and walked toward a stand of bamboo in front of a neighboring bunker. She was tall and thin, like a pole. Her shadow slipped quickly between the trees in the flickering light of dusk. Suong couldn't make out her face, only her hair gathered in a chignon at the back of her neck.

Hung turned around. "Why are you stopping? Come along..."

Suddenly, Suong felt a wave of anger, a kind she had never felt before. She pulled her hand away from his. "I'm comin', can't ya see?" she snapped in a thick, peasant slang.

Hung stared at the girl, stunned, but suddenly he understood. "Listen, little sister..." His voice was tender, cajoling. His eyes sparkled. "Don't be jealous so fast, little sister. And from now on, don't use that country accent. We don't say 'comin'' here, but 'coming,' and don't say 'ya.'"

He stroked her hair, pulling her toward him. Never had Suong felt such a soft touch on her body. She felt herself swoon. Her heart burst like a jungle cavern whose walls suddenly collapsed. In an instant, she forgot who she was: the village she had left; the dusty, sun-baked roads littered with artillery, crisscrossed with trenches; the nights underground filled with sweat and bitterness. She forgot the dark rat-filled bunker, her childish terror leaving. She forgot the artistic troupe she had dreamed of, the promises to her brother and sister, their tears as they watched her and a buffalo-drawn cart disappear in a cloud of dust. All she could see was this man who bent over her, murmuring: "I knew you would come, little girl of the mountains... I knew from the first moment."

To the west, clouds dissipated in a violet haze. A few minutes later the bamboo groves and star fruit trees, the spiny grapefruit bushes all faded into darkness. The sixteen-year-old girl, no longer fearful or hesitant, melted under the first kisses of her life. They forgot where they were, until they were startled by the sound of footsteps heading in the direction of the river. "I'll take you to the spring," Hung said, taking her hand, leading her quickly through the darkness. They climbed a remote bank covered with a thick stand of bamboo. He undid the buttons to her shirt one by one. It was the first time, but Suong felt no fear as this strange man touched her body. His touch was like her mother's, and she closed her eyes, dreaming of a bronze basin her mother used to place her in to scrub her down with steaming, fragrant water scented with lemongrass. And she had sat silently, waiting, trusting in the fresh sensation of the spring water and the warm perfume of childhood.

"Am I hurting you?" Hung asked softly.

She didn't reply. Her mother's hand had also been soft and nimble like his.

Hung washed Suong's blouse, then doused her with water, scrubbing her neck, arms, and shoulders. Meticulous, careful, he pressed the fabric down her slender back.

"Am I hurting you? If I am, tell me," he repeated.

She still didn't reply. Her flesh came alive, like grass, the wild reeds that grew at the edge of the swamps, the kind that turned green as if by magic, that grew, not over months, but every day, every hour, every second. She was mute, motionless.

He rubbed the damp blouse over her breasts. Suong let out a cry of fear as her nipples suddenly hardened.

"Did I hurt you?" Hung bent down and covered her with kisses.

A group of swimmers arrived at the stream. Their jokes and laughter echoed in the darkness.

"Let's go home, little sister," Hung said.

He put her clothes back on, brought her back to the shelter. Floating in a strange limbo between child and woman, Suong wasn't hungry or tired. The grass had sunk its roots into each pore of her skin, and now it flooded her blood with its intoxicating sap. She followed him, her hand in his, oblivious to all the turns in the winding path, the thorn bushes that caught at the leg of her pants and which Hung deftly removed. By the time they reached the shelter it was cloaked in darkness.

"Give me your bundle of clothes."

She handed them to him.

"Put your arm around my neck."

And she did, just as she once had with her father when he came back from the jungle and carried her on walks through the village. The entrance to the shelter wasn't very big, but Hung managed to slide in with her on his back. He carefully climbed down stairs, step by step, set her down on a wood plank, and announced happily: "We're here."

Suong didn't have time to stand up. He took her head in his hands. "Are you dizzy?"

"No."

"That's good. I was afraid, because you must be exhausted by that long trip."

The shelter was thick with shadows. Suong nestled her head on his warm chest the way a bird nestles in winter in the warmth and security of its nest. He sheltered her with his own body. She couldn't do without him now. He was something nameless but vast; if she lost him, she would fall into a life that left no trace, like a feather carried by the wind. She suddenly clutched him tighter.

"I love you, little girl, I loved you the instant I heard you singing, stretched out on that bed of straw."

She nodded. "I love you too, I love you," she replied feverishly, her eyes brimming with tears.

Hung hesitated. He didn't understand these tears, but he wiped them away with a handkerchief, consoled her. "Sleep a bit, little sister, the road must have been exhausting."

"No, no, I'm not tired," she said.

"I'll sing you a lullaby, okay?"

"No, no, no."

"Do you want some light?"

"No." She didn't know why she had answered that way. She wanted to hold onto the warmth that he had wrapped her in, to press her hair against his chest, keep his tender hand on her body always.

Hung said nothing. Their caresses became faster and more rhythmic, like sea waves sculpting the shore. Suong stopped trembling. She fell into another kind of sobbing, another world.

The next morning, Hung woke up first. He cooked rice and then woke Suong for breakfast. He brought her to the Cultural Service to attend to formalities and sign her up as a trainee. He brought her back to the troupe's camp, found her lodging near his shelter. In the months that followed, he taught her how to fix her hair, restyle her peasant clothes. And because she was a woman now, he even sent someone to Hanoi to buy her bras made of blue-checked fabric. He taught her to speak correctly, to sing, to compose her first scales by the smoky, flickering light of the oil lamp.

Hung had kept a few books in his wartime knapsack. Every volume of *A Quiet River in Winter*. A collection of short stories by Chekhov. *The Gilded Rose* by Patovsky, Gogol's *Tarass Boulba*. That was all he possessed of world culture. And he opened this world to her, patiently, passionately.

4

Ah, they're just bastards, they piss on the waves after they've crossed the river. Illiterate bastards. I'm not going to let you get away with this so easily.

This thought boiled in Hung's brain as he left the deputy chief's office. That bunch of bastards included the chief and his three deputies. They must have all agreed, given the speed of his dismissal as head of the troupe. But why? He was blinded by rage. His arms and legs tensed, trembled.

If I go home in this state, I won't be able to hide the truth. Suong will panic. She's too young to go through this. She's still a child.

He remembered how he had felt the other night when he watched her from backstage, at the theater, how he had been struck yet again by her beauty. How it had dizzied him. The little girl had grown up. He hadn't noticed. That first night in the underground, she had given herself to him. Blinded by passion, unaware of her own body. A woman's heart in a girl's body. He had been stunned, moved by this love, had accepted it with all the tenderness heaven had endowed him with.

His love for this mountain girl had become a love suffused with pain, not as sacred as a saint's for his God, but a hundred times more generous, more ardent, since it was the love of the sky for the earth, of the stronger for the weak.

What will become of her? What will become of her?

Suddenly, fearful of being seen, he went into a café.

There was no one there. Hung sat down on a wicker chair in a corner of the room in front of a low varnished wood table. Behind the table, there was a huge vase of bamboo. Other customers, passersby, would have difficulty seeing him in this corner.

"Is there anyone here?"

No reply.

"Is anyone serving?"

Still no reply.

Hung sat down, lit a cigarette. He found a pink glass ashtray at the foot of the pot of bamboo and set his cigarette down. The glow of it tinted the crystal violet, then dark red.

If only I'd listened to my friends, I'd have studied electricity and stayed in Hanoi. Life would have been very different.

He sighed. Behind this sigh appeared the faces of his wife, his daughter. His daughter thrashed in her mother's arms, waving her hands as if to call to him. Pain shot through him. A naive young woman and a tiny child lived in the protective shadow of his arms. What would become of them? He wasn't going to give up the fight so easily; after all, he was one of the most confident and ambitious cadres in the province. Two of the three deputy chiefs were newcomers from the smaller towns that had just been integrated and they were ignorant, easily manipulated. But one of them was educated, lived an austere life, according to his principles. A bit dogmatic, but no idiot. Moreover, he knew how to be loyal, humane. He had been one of the first to discover Hung's talent, to give him responsibility. Hung had responded with his trust. In the past, the Bureau of Arts was a major asset in the power struggles. Now, it was just an impoverished public service for cadres who were either incompetent, crazy, or corrupt, and who hadn't reached retirement age. Hung had contributed to this evolution; as soon as he had been named head of the artistic troupe, he had allied himself with two particularly competent friends. The three of them had rapidly consolidated their position and promoted a number of policies that concentrated power in their hands. During the war years, the services they directed grew in size and scope. They had an autonomous budget and had complete decision-making power over their programs. All they had left behind at the Bureau of Arts and Culture was a bunch of lazy, proud old men who, realizing they had lost their power, had retreated to the shadows, resigned. They forgot the golden age when the head of the artistic troupe and the other directors had to shower them with gifts to ensure their support. A few years later, the Party organization department of the Cultural Service no longer felt the need to respect these dethroned experts, and they merely rusticated incompetent or troublesome cadres to this department. And now this is where they were sending Hung. It was a way of liquidating him, and he knew it. The person who had the final say in this decision was the chief.

I seem incapable of detecting human treachery. His face was radiant with goodness, culture. More than once he publicly acknowledged my competence, my devotion to our common cause. Not a hint of flattery, or hypocrisy. He's been criticized for his dogmatism, but no one ever accused him of cruelty or lack of integrity. And now, suddenly, he changes. Has he forgotten all the nights we spent during the war in the shelters, discussing every detail of the performances in Huong Hoa, Canh Duong, An Thuy?

The deputy chief of service had taken music classes in secondary school. In his youth, he had strummed a banjo like many of his generation. They even said he could dance a few waltzes. But Hung, respectful of people's private lives, had never asked him about his past. He noticed that the man spoke with prudence, moderation. He seemed more like a schoolteacher than a mandarin. He discreetly withdrew when his colleagues started to eat and drink or tell dirty stories. Some people said he was a fake. Hung guessed that he was just trying to hide his disgust, and this reserve had raised the man in Hung's esteem. But now he was behaving like a traitor.

"Ah." A woman's frightened cry cut short Hung's thoughts. He looked up. The shop owner was standing, frozen, in the frame of a back door that opened onto a tiny garden filled with rubble and a few faded chrysanthemums. The owner stared at him for a few seconds, her face white. Suddenly she came to her wits and stammered, "Hello sir, what will you have?"

"A coffee. I've been waiting for you for a long time."

"Sorry . . . please excuse me." She moved toward the counter. When she turned to the side, you could see huge freckles on her cheeks despite the rose-colored powder she used to cover them. Her eyes seemed alarmed.

"I was looking for a quiet corner, to think," said Hung. "I'm not an intruder. You can check the register to see if there's anything missing."

"No, no, sir, of course not."

She composed herself and began to prepare the coffee with precise, graceful gestures that fascinated Hung. He watched the way she measured the coffee, poured it into the filter, then rinsed the cup and the finely made silver spoon with boiling water. The cup and saucer were of porcelain the color of white jade, without flowers or decoration, the coffee in the glass jar tightly sealed by a thick cork—everything was so clean, so elegant, not as coldly professional as other cafés he knew.

"Here you go." The owner set the cup in front of Hung, glancing at him discreetly.

She's got a cutting look. I wonder if some kind of ruin forced her to open this café.

Then, the glow in the woman's eyes reminded him of the wrinkled elephant skin of the deputy chief's eyelids. This image brought him back to reality.

Hung emptied the cup of coffee in one gulp, almost like a heavy drinker. He walked swiftly to the Cultural Service offices, but midway he remembered that the chief had been mysteriously absent these last few weeks.

I'm just a hopeless dreamer. A practical man would have asked why the chief was absent at such an important occasion. Who can I turn to now?

Hung stopped, confused, in the middle of the street. His cigarette burned his fingers, and he flung it on the sidewalk. A young man who had been walking behind him, bent down, picked up the cigarette butt, and threw it in a public wastebasket a few steps away.

"I'm sorry, I was . . ."

"I know, you were thinking," the young man replied, his voice clear, confident. With his finely drawn face and hair neatly parted, he was cute, like a pet dog. His searing gaze reminded Hung of someone. He nodded to the young man and turned to go. He decided to go to the Cultural Service Cadres Residence. His best friend, the director of the municipal library, lived there.

The sun beat down. A cyclo driver pedaled toward him, in hopes of a passenger. Hung had never dared take a cyclo. The idea of relaxing, letting himself be served by another man, disgusted him. But anger had drained him. The cyclo driver hovered, pedaling close at his heels.

"Oh Mr. Cadre, please, come on in, help me earn some rice. I don't have any passengers these days. We're liberated and that's a great happiness, but we don't have anything to eat, so I don't know how to survive. Please, get in."

Hung stepped into the cyclo and asked the young man to unfold the roof, to pull down the cover to hide him. The cyclo driver sighed: "Cadres don't take cyclos, so people don't dare take them either. They're afraid of being called arrogant bourgeois. And in the end, who suffers? We do, the little people."

Hung said nothing, depression tugging at his heart. *Another totally illogical situation. Is it more shameless, more cruel than my own?* When they got to the residence, he pulled out a wad of worn bills from his pocket and counted out money to pay the cyclo driver.

"You're still young."

"Yes."

"How old are you?"

"Twenty-two. But I've got three kids," the man replied proudly. Hung waved good-bye, stepped onto the sidewalk, and walked toward the residence. Sweat broke out on his neck, as the ruthless sun of central Vietnam stung his skin like salt. He found his friend at home with his wife and son, busy tidying the apartment. They were washing it down, polishing the furniture—the bed, the table, the chairs, the curtains, the rugs, even the kitchen utensils belonged to the former owners. When they fled for their lives, they hadn't missed these household objects. But for the newcomers, this was a bounty they hadn't even dared dream of. Hung waited a long time, time enough for the couple to polish off an old armoire.

"Please don't think badly of us," his friend said, as he washed his hands. "I couldn't leave this work unfinished. Why not stay and have lunch? It's been a long time since we've seen you, not since we lived like cavemen." The man laughed softly. "My, such changes, all in the space of a full moon."

There's satisfaction in his laugh. The satisfaction of the victor. A vulgar happiness. Exactly like the beaming vulgar smile of the deputy chief behind the windshield of that jeep. People are all alike, and they're the ones who make up the majority. I'm outside all that. I must be a madman. I invested everything, bet everything on that romantic war! The honor of the nation. The meaning of life. All my youthful ideals. And how does it end? Watching people ecstatic with joy, over a jeep, an apartment, an old armoire.

"Come, sit down, I'm going to serve you something. People in this town have great appetizers. Nothing like the peasants back in our village with their green bananas and pickled shrimp."

His wife set the dishes on the table. She wore a blue silk blouse, which was too short. Rolls of fatty flesh from her stomach and back overflowed every time she leaned down to serve him.

"To your health."

"To the Liberation!"

"And peace."

"And in honor of our new life."

"Bottoms up. The new life is always better than the past. Unfortunately, I can't seem to find my place. Did you hear that they've pushed me out of the troupe?"

"Yes," his friend sighed. "The head of the Services organization department told me last night. Did you know he's my wife's cousin?"

Hung said nothing.

"I'm so sorry. He couldn't do anything for you in this situation. According to him, the deputy chief wanted to push you out right after Liberation but he couldn't find anyone to replace you. Now he's found the replacement and a good excuse."

"I'm an idiot. I didn't believe it."

"Technical cadres are not as stupid as Party leaders and organization cadres. They're more savvy about life than we are. The deputy chief had enough power to convince his two colleagues. No one could go against the current."

"And where's the chief himself?"

His friend stared at him, wide-eyed. "You mean you don't know?"

Hung shook his head: "I've been up to my ears preparing for the show."

"The Party committee discovered that the chief had a brother who was a colonel in the American-puppet army. He didn't mention it in his dossier. He still hasn't been officially stripped of his post, but he had to stop working and stay home to draft his self-criticism."

Hung was stunned. A real catastrophe. Under this regime, the worst of crimes was "lacking political purity." This man, who was so cultured, was in grave danger. Now Hung understood why the man used to hide his reactions, his contempt for their crudeness and vulgarity, under a mask of indifference; he must have lived in constant fear. Hung had suspected the man too quickly, and he had been wrong. Now, Hung was alone in his struggle. He couldn't rely on anyone. But he had to fight, even if it was hopeless.

"Elder brother Hung, try some of this *chè* pudding. The townspeople here make it really well," the man's wife said, returning from the kitchen with two bowls of corn *chè*. His friend placed a spoon in Hung's hand. "Eat up, dear friend, let them do what they will. Who cares? At the Bureau of Arts, you'll have lots of free time. Why not use it to raise chickens, make some money?"

Hung ate in silence. He couldn't tell whether the *chè* was sweet or salty. He set the bowl back on the table, got out his handkerchief, and wiped his hands. His host poured him some water. He drank it like an automaton. His friend kept silent, then rose to see him out, accompanying Hung all the way down to the street.

The corridors leading to the Party's provincial offices were long, interminably long, and heavy with the limey smell of whitewashed walls, of paper and ink, and cut flowers. All these smells mixed with the cheap aftershave that wafted off the shirt collars of these officials who had left the jungles to set up in town. For Hung, this was the smell of power. He sat down on a bench along the corridor, waiting his turn to see the chairman of the Party organization committee. He felt anxious, frightened. It seemed to him that he had changed, been diminished, shrunken, crushed by the walls of the city. His heart raced under the weight of some unfathomable fear, besieged by anarchic hopes, suppositions, jumbled, hot-headed resolutions. Behind the heavy, black ironwood door across from him sat the man who would decide his fate. Hung had chatted and joked with this man many times back in the jungle, during meetings and the troupe's performances for the provincial Party committee, The old man was unpretentious and badly dressed. He still wore the same Mao-style Chinese jacket, the collar ringed a grimy black. How distant he seemed now, as if a wall had risen between them. The vague feeling that he had felt in the deputy chief's office was growing in him.

Why do I feel this way? Like a man who has lost confidence in himself and knows it. Yesterday, I was a free man. Now I'm fearful, jumpy as a fish on a chopping board, I'm afraid of people I thought I knew like the lines of my palm: the life line, the heart line, the head line. I know their enthusiasm, their ignorance, their spirit of self-sacrifice, their vulgarity, their baseness . . . everything. Then why does my heart race like this? The man behind that door has the power to decide my fate, and that of those I love. It's for them I'm afraid. Will I one day become a coward, some obsequious, fawning flatterer for their sake?

Hung imagined different ways he could curry favor with the old man. There were a million. All too familiar to him. But he was incapable of doing it.

To see the cowardice of a certain behavior and do it anyway, now that was lowering yourself to an animal level. In the fight for its life, an animal wins or loses, survives or dies; it doesn't know how to fawn or flatter. It only knows fear, but that's not cowardice. Why should I flatter a man who is worthless, in whose eyes I'm nothing, just someone with whom he once shared a long journey, all those years surviving underground. Now, he's forgotten the old solidarity, but I'm still hanging on, begging a little pity in hopes I can save my life from ruin! The free man in me is dead. That was the man of the past, the underground man. Back then, they knew they needed me. Now, the winds have changed. It's like the legend about Thach Sanh and the evil boa constrictor, now that the boa is dead, they can throw the hero in jail. Gone is the voice of solidarity, of human feeling. Success belongs to the usurpers. It's been like that since time immemorial, and it will always be like this.

"Comrade Hung?" A head popped out from behind a half-opened door.

"Yes, I'm here, yes," Hung stammered, his throat tight. Even in those brief, stammering words, he could hear his fear, his cowardice, and he felt his face flush as he stood up and entered the office. His graceful, nonchalant stride and lithe figure, made him look carefree, but his heart raced as he sat down on the nearest chair.

The chairman of the organization committee smiled warmly, baring teeth blackened by cigarette smoke. "Well, well, hello Mr. Composer! How's it going Comrade? It's been a long time since I've had a chance to meet a friend from culture and the arts."

Hung hadn't had time to gather his thoughts when the chairman added: "I just received a report about you. You must be asking yourself a lot of questions."

"Does that mean you've made a decision?"

"No, and I'm not the one who proposed your transfer. I just ratified a proposal by the Cultural Service's organization department."

Oh that voice. I've heard it so many times. Unctuous, overly familiar, yet sometimes harsh, ruthless. That heavy central accent that weighs every vowel, I'd know it anywhere. He's from Quang Ngai province . . . That's it, he's from the same region as the deputy chief. Someone told me, a long time ago . . . I'd forgotten . . . They're part of the same clan, he and the deputy.

Hung felt a chill run down his spine, sweat beading at the nape of his neck, on his forehead, streaming down his back. Clan solidarity, regional loyalties—ignorant, irrational, peasant feelings that Hung had never been able to stand—had enslaved the country. And now he was getting the backlash.

"Please understand the difficulties the provincial Party leadership is facing. Our revolutionary duties have never been so heavy. The bombs, the bullets may have subsided, but the people's mentality is complicated, and political consciousness is still uneven, unwholesome. Not to mention the economic reconstruction, which is causing us a number of particularly thorny problems . . ."

Bunch of idiots! They don't even know how to talk. They never finished primary school but they move their tongues faster than a serpent snaps its tail. To think that a few minutes ago I waited anxiously for this meeting, that I hoped to convince this old man by reminding him of our camaraderie in combat, the long years of communal life underground, that I was ready to humor him . . . What a ridiculous thought. All you have to do is look at his face, the food stuck in his rotting, tobacco-stained teeth, the bit of duckweed caught in his lower jaw. Leftover breakfast no doubt. And then in the lower right jaw, the piece of pickled cabbage. Yesterday's dinner. He must eat three meals every day and not less than five bowls of rice.

"We recognize your great contribution to the training of the artistic troupe. That troupe was forged in your hands. But each of us is only a cog in the wheel of the revolution. We must put the interests of the revolution above our own personal considerations. We have to sacrifice ourselves to achieve our great mission. As you can see, I myself have lived far from my wife, my children for more than a decade."

There, the old guy speaks the truth. He had to leave his wife and kids for at least ten years, back in Quang Ngai on the other side of the seventeenth parallel, to come here. And for ten years he lived alone, gritting his teeth, faithful. He was the only man who dared discipline the militia commander and the Party vice-secretary for seducing young, virginal women in their underground shelters. Is he trying to use his virtue to convince me? What virtue? Behind these lofty words, there's just an unconscious nostalgia for his wife and children, his hometown in Quang Ngai. And now that love has bound them, all these men from the same place. The deputy chief must have convinced him with this same appeal to sentiment. It's like some blind, mysterious force that transcends them.

Hung noticed the spittle gathered on the old man's flabby lips as he rambled on, saliva spraying from his mouth, trying to convince Hung with a bravado and self-confidence that should have commanded respect. Distraught, Hung realized his fight would be in vain and he got up abruptly to go. "Good-bye, Comrade," he said simply, striding out the room.

The chairman watched him and his jaw dropped. No one had ever dared turn their back on him, or leave while he was still speaking. For a long time afterward, the man stood there, listening to the click of Hung's footsteps fade down the corridor. *They say artists are unpredictable, that trauma can make them crazy. I've got to tell the Service to raise his salary so he gets a grip on himself. If we let this man go mad, people will blame the Party leadership.* He promptly wrote up a brief report and ordered his secretary to bring it to the Service's organization department.

When the deputy chief received the chairman's report, he was sipping tea in the company of some administrative cadres. He grabbed the letter, brought it into his office, read it, and threw it in a drawer. And that's where it stayed.

One day, some weeks later, the committee called for a conference on the vertical organization of cultural and artistic activities. The chairman remembered the composer, the former head of the artistic troupe, who had once surprised him with his indifferent attitude.

"What has become of Hung?" he asked. "Did you give him that salary raise?"

The head of the Service's organization department froze, confused. "No collective decision was ever made regarding that sir. And . . ."

"What do you mean? I wrote you about this matter a long time ago" the chairman replied.

"Uh, er, yes, sir."

"Don't waste your breath. You've got to be flexible when you head up an organization. If we waited every time for collective decisions it would be too late."

"Yes, yes sir," the man stammered.

Irate that one of his orders had been disregarded, the chairman called for an investigation of the Service. A frenzied search ensued, and ultimately the letter was found buried in a drawer of the deputy chief's desk. In the end, the Service decided to raise Hung's salary by two grades. But by that time, Hung was already drifting on the open sea, huddled on a boat with 102 other unhappy souls with whom his destiny had been linked.

5

Suong woke up when evening fell. As the sun slanted through the window, it illuminated Vinh's back. He was seated by her side, as motionless as a statue. Her little brother, those rough familiar features. The light shimmered on his hair. She wasn't angry anymore; there was only tenderness. Her heart overflowed with it, like a rice field brimming with water; the same feeling that had overcome her when she saw him again, after seven years of separation. She remembered how she had missed him and her family the day they had summoned her, informing her that Hung had "plotted to flee by boat with one hundred and two other counterrevolutionaries who oppose the regime and thereby sully the reputation of the state. But thanks to border guards in Vietnam's heroic marine corps and their round-the-clock vigilance, the boat was captured at zero miles off the coast. The one hundred and three fugitives have been imprisoned in a camp while they await sentencing."

The young officer who had read her the decision had a handsome, tanned, icy face. He didn't look at her; he was contemplating something else in the distance. As he spoke, he tapped the glass that covered his desk with a red pencil. "Take her outside," he ordered a subordinate, as soon as he had finished.

"Out, out," barked the young soldier, shoving Suong with a rough push to her back. After this gesture, she understood: To them, she was an accomplice, an accessory to her husband's crime. She lowered her head, followed the soldier across the vast courtyard of the police headquarters toward the gate. On the road back home, she didn't dare look at anyone. From every street in town, public loudspeakers bellowed the officer's verdict, reciting the list of guilty runaways. People recognized her; Suong knew it. "Our nightingale from the mountain valleys," they had once called her. People crowded around, whispering, pointing at her. A few curious ones ran after her, trying to catch a glimpse of the famous singer, "that traitor's wife." Finally, she arrived at the troupe's headquarters. Fortunately, rehearsal was over and the performers and troupe leader had already gone home. Only the union secretary remained. Suong asked for permission to go and visit her husband.

"All right," he said coldly. "In the name of the union, I give you permission. But you have to swear in writing that you're not going to go and flee on some boat like your husband."

"I'll sign," she said, lowering her head. It seemed like just yesterday that this same man had set aside cigarettes for Hung, gone out of his way to get her a bunch of water spinach, a few shrimp for a soup. Now, as he thrust a sheet of paper in front of her, Suong stared at his familiar, bony, rugged hands. She felt like weeping, but she knew she no longer even had the right to do that. She picked up the sheet of paper and nodded in thanks. On the way back, she covered her tear-drenched face with her hat.

When she reached their house, Auntie Tuong was waiting for her at the door.

"So sorry I'm late," Suong stammered.

Seeing her tears, the woman said loudly, "Don't cry. Hung's no criminal. He didn't steal, he didn't pillage. He didn't lie to anyone. He's not a drug dealer. Don't be afraid. Men are like birds; they make their nests where they're welcome and fly off when it's hostile. That's as natural as eating when you're hungry." The woman's voice echoed through the streets: She was deliberately speaking to everyone. Sung saw shadows flit behind windows. They were peering at her.

The woman lowered her voice. "Your daughter's asleep. Leave her with me. You go and visit your husband. A prison run by those Communists isn't going to be up to the same standards as the Nationalists, you know."

Suong stepped into her house. It seemed huge, cold. Each leaf on the tree in the garden seemed to hide some ghostly, furtive gaze that followed her. She quickly turned on a lamp and a shaft of light cast her own, long shadow on the tiles of the empty room. She sat down at the desk, took out a piece of paper, a pen, and began to write.

Dear Mien, dear Vinh . . .
It's been a long time since I've written . . .

Tears fell, dripping down her face. Her own sister and brother, her only two close relatives—she had abandoned them in a godforsaken hole in the mountains, at the end of a winding road swirling in red dust. She remembered how they had stood watching her until she disappeared from sight. How many times had they returned to that place, scouring the horizon, waiting for her return? She had forgotten them, lost herself in happiness, in the pleasures of the flesh, carried away by the blinding swirl of stage lights. From time to time, she had written to them, but then the letters became fewer and farther between. Now that she was in trouble she realized that they were now the only people to whom she could turn.

Please understand, my sister, let Vinh come and join me. I'm waiting for you . . .

Early the next day, Suong went to the bus station. The sky was thick with fog. Her head and face covered by a scarf, she edged through the milling crowd, weaving her way past the sticky rice vendors, the people selling sandwiches, the men offering their services as porters. As she crossed the taxi stand, moving toward the horse-drawn wagons, a young man who had been seated munching a sandwich spotted her and jumped down to run after her. Suong pulled the scarf tighter over her face, hunching over and stepping up the pace. He was one of her most passionate fans, the one who always brought her flowers after each performance. Did he know what had happened to her? She walked faster, head lowered, toward the wagons. She didn't know the number of the wagon that belonged to Lam, the clown in their troupe. He was the only man in the whole troupe she trusted. During the war years, he had been a familiar visitor to their shelter, sharing meals with them, stopping by for tea. When peace returned, and everyone was eager to return to town, Lam had declared: "I'm going back to the village. When the country was in danger, people joined the army. Me, I've got no talent for guns, so I sang for people. That's another way of doing one's duty, isn't it? Now I'm going home, back to my old job as a carter."

Hung had begged him to stay with the troupe. But Lam had refused. "I've always done what I wanted to do. I miss the long trips. The rhythm of those roads has beat in my blood since my childhood. My father was a carter, and my mother spent her life on a wagon hauling merchandise." And he left. Suong had never asked for the number of his wagon. Now she searched for it, at random. She approached each wagon, trying to make out something that might belong to Lam. She would recognize his hat anywhere, his shirts, even the cotton towel he used to wrap around his neck.

A thick, firm hand settled on her shoulder. Suong froze. She didn't need to turn around to know who it was. She burst into tears.

"Don't cry," Lam murmured softly.

"You know?"

"Yes, I know."

"How did you find out so quickly?" Suong asked.

"Nothing happens here that isn't discussed at the bus station. Where did they imprison him?"

"K41."

"I know the place well. It's not comfortable. Have you prepared some supplies for him?"

"Yes, I've got everything. But first help me bring this letter to my sister. Here, read it."

Lam read the letter, nodded. "I understand. I'll bring your little brother back. How old is he now? I remember vaguely, he must have been . . ."

"Ten. He was ten years old when I left. Now he's almost seventeen."

"Yes, I met you seven years ago. My God, time has gone fast. Okay, you head home now. I'll do my best to be back soon."

That night, about three in the morning, Suong was sleeping with her daughter, when the bell rang. Lam's wagon stood outside the gate. She didn't have time to see anyone clearly when a voice rang out: "Sister Suong!"

A silhouette bounded out of the darkness, opened its arms to embrace her, then suddenly froze right in front of her. A tanned face, long eyebrows over liquid, sparkling eyes, a nose identical to her father's. Her mouth quivering, Suong hugged her brother to her. His dark, dusty body was like some wave from the core of the earth, from the painful depths of memory and separation.

Vinh turned toward the hospital bed where his sister lay, sensing she was awake.

"Sorry, do you want some water?" Vinh stammered, searching awkwardly for words to console her. Country folk often began speaking by apologizing, and he had only been in town for a short while, not enough time to lose the habit. "You can have some orange juice . . . I forgot."

"I'm not thirsty. Have you eaten, little brother?"

"Yes."

"At the market?"

"No, in a café."

"It's expensive and not very good. Why didn't you go to the market?"

"I couldn't leave you alone for too long."

"I'm better. Would you go by the house to see if everything is okay?"

"Why? The girls are sleeping at Auntie Tuong's."

"I'm so worried."

"About what?"

"The house, the cleaning, the clothes."

"Hung's friends devoured everything, and you didn't have the nerve to throw them out."

Suong was silent. Her brother was right; she couldn't deny it. But now she was worried about the money; there was so little, but it was the fruit of much sweat and hard work. To supplement her income from the troupe's official performances, Suong had also sung for official congresses and conferences. Toiling away like a farm laborer doing overtime in the rice paddies, she had sung her throat raw to feed her children. And in a fit of anger, she had been careless enough to throw the keys at Hung's feet! Her entire savings was hidden in that closet. Had her husband been sober enough to keep that money to feed their children?

Suong took her brother's hand: "Vinh . . . I'm afraid . . . where did Hung put the keys?"

"Which keys?"

"To the closet, where I keep my savings."

Vinh started. "You gave that bastard the keys? How could you be so stupid! He's never sober."

"I wanted to die. I wasn't thinking."

"You *gave* them to him?"

"I threw them at him."

"Oh, my God." Vinh moaned. No one could survive without money in this town. Streets all over, not a patch of land where you could dig up a potato or gather some wild vegetables. Of all their neighbors, only Auntie Tuong dared visit them; since Hung had been imprisoned as a counterrevolutionary, people had shunned them. Since then, they had lived in fear. Vinh slumped down at the end of his sister's bed. "Suong," he said in a sad, low voice. "How can I help you earn a living in this town? I've got no education. People wouldn't even hire me as a servant."

"Go back to the house, run, find those keys and open the closet, see if the money is still there. It's in the tea caddy, in the black bag I used to wear. Pray to the heavens and to our parents' souls, may they protect us and that money. Without it, I have nothing left."

Vinh ran out of the room. When he reached the house, he found the big gate wide open. Hung's guests were still in the same position, one slumped on the ground, the other asleep, and the third curled up on Suong's bed. The painter, the one Vinh hated most, lay faceup, his penis erect, exposed. But Hung was gone. Stunned at first, Vinh then felt as if a weight had been lifted. The only man who could have forced him to control his rage wasn't there: The absence was a wonderful surprise.

Parasites! I'm going to show you a thing or two . . . but before I do, let's find those keys. Vinh pulled on the doors to the closet. Locked. He fumbled through Hung's pants and shirts. The keys weren't there either. He rummaged through the drawers, the bookshelves, an old trunk. Nothing. He was sweating hard. The poverty they had lived through after their father died flashed into his memory.

But that was in the countryside. There, you could always get help from your neighbors. Poverty here in the towns is like poverty in the middle of the desert. No one to turn to. Keep calm. Sit down and think. She threw the keys at his feet. He was drunk. He might have seen them. If he did, he would have grabbed them to throw them back at her, or out the window. But he might not have seen anything, kicked them into a corner. Let's hope these guys have drunk themselves unconscious. Start with the garden, then search under the windows . . .

Vinh rushed outside, inspecting the ground under the windows. The light of the street lamp wove dancing shadows through the branches.

It was impossible to see clearly. He groped for his flashlight, a familiar object he had brought from the mountains, examined the foot of each tree, every inch of the garden. Drenched in sweat, he went back into the house with one last hope: to find the keys in a corner under one of the closets. In the end, luck was with him: The keys were right under the bed. All he had to do was reach out his hand. He grabbed them like a wild beast pounces on its prey, squeezed them hard, as if to reassure himself that they were real. Then he rushed to open the closet: The money was all there, intact. The drunken bastards hadn't even noticed the keys on the ground.

"Bless you mother and father, for protecting us!" Vinh murmured. Somehow, this prayer couldn't express all that was in his heart. He went outside, stood in the middle of the courtyard, looked up to the sky, and spoke aloud, distinctly: "Mother, watch over Suong and me. Protect us, do something so that we may eat our fill, know peace, security."

Dead souls always follow the steps of their loved ones, but Vinh didn't want to lie to his father, even if he was dead. He wanted to tell his father, frankly, with dignity that his love belonged exclusively to his mother.

"Mother, I pray that you know peace and serenity in the Land of the Nine Springs. If you have the power, come back to us, accompany us."

After praying, Vinh felt as if the ground were firmer under his feet, as if he had finally become a man now that he had the power to force others to obey him. Suddenly, he glimpsed his own shadow on the ground.

Vinh contemplated his shadow, content. The street lamp's magical light had transformed him into a giant, flattering his wounded soul. For more than a year, since he had turned sixteen, Vinh had often secretly admired his shadow on the walls, his silhouette in mirrors, reflected in the streams, on the sides of the mountains. He knew he had inherited his pitifully short stature from his mother; he was just five feet two inches; though his father had been five feet ten inches. And this made him unhappy, envious, and jealous of his father.

Vinh stood for a long time in the middle of the courtyard contemplating his shadow until he heard his niece shout from inside the neighbor's house. He woke up. The keys in the bottom of his pocket were proof of his victory. *Okay, now what do I do?* He shoved his hands deep into his pockets. *Go see the girls? Not worth it, Auntie Tuong will look after them. I've got to go back and watch over Suong. But before I do, I'm going to kick these parasites out and lock the door. Her bastard of a husband isn't there, but if he came back it'd do him good to sleep on the sidewalk for a few nights.*

Just thinking about it filled him with glee. All those nights he and his sister had retreated to the kitchen for a frugal dinner while those dogs ate and drank around a table piled with expensive food.

Vinh strode back into the living room, surveyed the three men sprawled on the furniture.

Should I pull them up, one by one, and slap them around, or just smash their heads against the wall? Or maybe a good thrashing with a whip before I throw them out? But they would take revenge, and when Suong came back, they'd make her pay. Who's going to defend the wife of a counterrevolutionary?

In the end, Vinh resisted his desire for vengeance. He went out into the courtyard and returned with a bucket of water, which he threw in their faces, one after the other, sparing no one. The slumbering men woke up with a start, jerking their heads forward under the splash of icy water. Gasping, they opened their mouths, but were unable to cry out. It took a few minutes before they realized what had happened: The master of ceremonies was absent and facing them was a young man, his eyes flashing with rage, a bucket in one hand, a bamboo rod in the other. He seemed to be just waiting for an excuse to smash it on their heads. The playwright looked at the poet. The poet looked at the painter. They knew they were in trouble—and booze and poetic inspiration always yield to the instinct for self-preservation. Trembling, his hair drenched, Doan the painter was the first to get dressed. The others followed. Barely able to conceal their fear, they slipped silently out into the courtyard.

Vinh waited until they had moved past the gate, then put away the bucket and the rod and tidied the room, sweeping away the filth and mess the visitors had left behind.

6

Hung had spent two days and two nights in the fisherman's shack, enjoying the happiness of feeling utterly empty. It had been longer than he could remember, long before his prison days, that he had felt this way. He wasn't hungry, or thirsty, and he didn't have to face anyone, or speak to anyone. At that time of year, the fishermen didn't use the nets left in the shack. It would be another two months before the winds changed and the new fishing season started. Stretched out under the nets all through the sweltering heat of the afternoon and then the long, foggy night, Hung had felt neither warmth nor cold. He had become used to the nauseating fish smell that clung to the nets, like a beast to the smell of its den.

Hours passed. His eyes half-closed, Hung was content just to smell the salty, stormy sea breeze, to listen to the roar of the waves whipping at rocks somewhere in the distance. These wild, violent sounds soothed his soul more than all the classical melodies he had ever heard as a student. Even the strains of Beethoven, those dull blows that his music professor had worshipped, could have been no more than the sound of rocks shattering, of the bricks hooligans hurled onto the rooftops, or the rumbling of the carts piled with sugar that he and the other prisoners had been forced to drag through the mountain ravines. All you had to do was put a microphone on the back of a detained man in the throes of a fit of chronic malaria, or a prisoner pushing a millstone to grind corn to come up with sounds like that. As for romantic music, like the *Moonlight Sonata*, how alien it all seemed to him now: the beautiful love of princes in velvet gloves, the nostalgia of souls as frail as crystal; the tenuous light of the December dawns shrouded in fog.

How it disgusts me, and yet how I long for it, the past, the two-story bunk bed at the university dormitory, the sooty old kerosene lamp, the soups we used to make, the piano music, Sundays, all the pages of all those books. Were those the happiest years of my life?

Outside, the sea bellowed, whipping violently against the shores. Somewhere, in the distance, the waves subsided. All Hung could see was a vast surface quivering in a metallic reflection. On this space, shimmering rays of light merged with the currents, and the mist rose, churning their reflections in a thousand flickering paths.

Roads paved with illusions crisscross the world, laying traps in all directions. And these traps are more numerous than all the roads and all the human footsteps over the earth. I threw myself into that Holy War like a bird taking flight. And it was all just another Moonlight Sonata, *a beautiful, romantic composition that ended up reeking of corpses and blood, full of the bellowing of bombs. And then the crescendo, a symphony of mortars, rifles, and arms celebrating Liberation, a magnificent velvet curtain slowly rising over a stage flooded with dazzling spotlights.*

In that shadowy fool's game everything had seemed easy and yet now everything was impossible. The provincial organization committee never revoked its decisions, not even for the sake of coherence or practicality, not even for some higher goal, for the good of society. And all this out of pride, to save face, a mask more fragile than an eggshell.

Hung looked out over the concrete buildings that loomed in the distance, past the walls and gardens, the urns filled with cotton flowers, the guard post, the newly installed soldier there. The power of the apparatus. Once, they had held their meetings and congresses in the jungle, stumbling on roots at every step. There had been no walls, or gardens, or vases, or guard posts; the war was a place where it had been impossible to rule by building cement fortresses. But life had changed. That was obvious to him. The curtain had fallen on those memories, those loyalties. No one felt they had the duty to remember a traveling theater troupe, its peregrinations through the jungles and trenches and ravines, the actors dripping with sweat under their amateur makeup who once performed in caves thick with torch smoke, on barren, devastated hills stinking of rotting flesh.

Hung remembered how once the troupe had received orders to perform for a unit of nearly three hundred young women volunteers who lived on the opposite side of the mountain. They lived in the jungle, far from their homes, their villages, without a shadow of a man, and they were known to go into fits of mass hysteria. The troupe's scout had already been to this part of the jungle twice. And both times he had been scared out of his wits when the entire horde of women had swooped down on him like a swarm of bees, teasing and flirting with him. Once, running for dear life, he had hidden in a crevice in the mountain and looking back he had seen them seated, hugging their knees, weeping and sniffling on one anothers' shoulders, huddled together in one sobbing mass. It was a sight that could make your skin crawl. And the sound of them, hundreds of women, their moans echoing through the jungle, still haunted him. When the scout told the story, his face went pale. Hung comforted him, but his male actors dismissed the lugubrious story with a few dirty jokes, taunting the scout, calling him "a virgin" whose fear and shame proved he was still a child who hadn't been weaned from his mother's breast. They, on the other hand, old hands when it came to the battlefield of love, were only eager to serve young women and to follow the slogan "ready to die for the country so the country may live again." That was, on the condition that the young women line up in order, not jostle or elbow each other, or scream, so that the men could concentrate on "fulfilling their civic duty." This plan, half-joking, half-serious, seemed to reassure the scout and put the entire troupe at ease. But the troupe had only gotten halfway to the women's encampment when a flood stopped them in their tracks. Torrential, continuous rain for two weeks, and there was nothing to eat except a few handfuls of corn that they ground into porridge, or that the scout bartered with the locals for coveted goods like flashlights, anti-malaria medicine, salt, or MSG. When the flood subsided, the troupe was called back to the Red River Delta to perform for some antiaircraft units. The messenger who brought the news carried a sausage-shaped rice-belt, and they emptied it to make rice they ate with fried salt. At that moment, Hung asked the same group of actors: "How about one of you male heroes climbing over the mountain to serve those three hundred women trapped in the jungle?" They all clasped their hands and pretended to kowtow feverishly, as if they were sending prayers to the sky. "Oh Chief, spare us, right now all we want is to stagger back without falling apart, before we reach the delta." Then they had all left the cave where they had taken shelter from the storm, the stream still rushing and gurgling behind them, wisps of heavy clouds drifting over the mountain peaks flitting in and out of the rain-drenched trees.

Why have these images, these smells suddenly flooded back? My inspiration sprang from that time, the melody from all the hardship, tragedy, and suffering. But that time also reeked of sacrifice. Along with the sacred scent of all the temples and shrines, sheltered in my heart, in the soul of the "masses," or what they used to call "the nation." We didn't distill that from flowers, but from our own illusions, from the delirium of an entire people. We once bathed in its nectar, like a master Zen hermit, soaring into space in a qi gong exercise, rising up and drawing away from the earth, out of body. And like that, we left normal life behind, reincarnated as some magical bird in flight across unending mountain ranges, all those months, all those years. But the flight was too long too magical, too grandiose. And look how it ended. In such vulgar images: grinning jaws behind the windshield of a jeep, a couple ecstatic over a few old pieces of furniture, the lousy junk booty of the war.

Hung suddenly realized that he was standing in front of the same café: So his wandering had brought him here, as to a rendezvous. He entered, looking for the same table in the back, between the two pots of bamboo. This time, the owner standing behind the counter recognized him. "Will you be having a cup of coffee, sir?"

"Yes."

"Do you need any cigarettes?"

"Yes, give me a pack."

A couple of lovers were sitting in the opposite corner, their heads together, whispering, as if they were the only ones in the world. Hung stared at the sparkling drops of coffee as they dripped from the filter.

What am I going to do now? Open a café? It seems easy but it's not that simple. I'd be a café owner without the capital or the skills, and certainly not the patience. After a long flight through a sky of illusions, at the end of the game we're all left empty-handed. A pitiful salary, just barely enough to assure the life of an ascetic. If they take back the apartment they've allocated to me, I'll be on the street.

Hung shivered at the thought, suddenly imagining Suong wandering in the street, their daughter in her arms, how totally helpless he would be to support them.

My childhood home was razed by the bombs; my parents are dead, there's no one to lend me a hand. It's my parents' fault; they spoiled me, invested too much hope in my talent. They only taught me love, lofty emotions, but they never taught me how to be realistic, practical, calculating.

Hung remembered his childhood, how the mornings had followed each other as smoothly as silk threads woven into the same cloth. Calm, oddly calm, and peaceful, the scent of red roses and yellow ylang-ylang flowers, the chirping of birds in the garden, the bubbling of the earthenware pot his father used for boiling water for tea, and his father's voice reciting poems with all the passion of a failed poet. His mother, a resourceful, energetic woman, had somehow always known how to navigate, to steer the family vessel through storms, wars, revolutions. She was one of those people who, whatever the times, always managed to find shelter, a role for herself. And somehow she had always ensured that her husband and son had a comfortable life. Worshipping her husband just as devoutly as he worshipped art, she could spend entire evenings serving him tea, listening to him discourse on the sublime powers of the classical Chinese poet Li Bai. And this love had filled Hung's young soul like pure springwater, as intoxicating as opium, inspiring dreams that had dissolved his brain into so many atoms when he had to actually face life's barbs and walls. In fact, he had never really had to confront real life. After his mother's death, his father had supported him, paid his way through university. With the fortune his wife had left him, Hung's father had more than enough to live on until the day his son bore him grandchildren. Every morning, seated on the low wooden bed, savoring the perfume of his orchids and roses, he had taught Hung the art of preparing lotus or chrysanthemum tea, how to identify different bird calls, or appreciate the poetic sensibility of his favorite classical Chinese poets. Every time Hung came back to spend his vacation in Hanoi, his father would sell a "leaf" of gold—that was the word he used for the precious metals—in exchange for a wad of bank notes. Father and son would chat over a cup of tea or rice wine.

For the true, classical gentleman, the mandarin, life was only a dream. By day, he had to comport himself according to the rituals of the imperial court. But at night, he could retreat to the mountains, till the land, look up at the sky and admire the moon, sing an ode to serenity. His heart was untainted by fame or ambition, his destiny as vast as the ocean.

Later, after he had met many scholars of ancient literature, Hung realized that his father was a faithful slave of literature. The rhyming prose, the poems he read, didn't respect the classical canons, and they were often awkward, or superficial. But he used to trace the ideograms on paper with such passion, such sincerity. And what was most important was that he had lived lovingly, generously, faithful to both his wife and son. Hung didn't let his father down: He graduated from the Hanoi Music Conservatory with honors and won numerous awards at the student music and dance competitions. His father had proudly stored Hung's diploma in a precious antique wood urn and placed it on the altar to the ancestors. His son's early success had satisfied the old man's aspiration in life. But those moments of happiness were short-lived. The war broke out, and his father died when their house was bombed, in the company of the diploma delivered by the Hanoi Music Conservatory. When they pulled his father out of the rubble, the old man was vomiting blood and didn't have time to utter his final wishes to his son, or reveal the spot where his mother had hid their fortune. In his grief, Hung didn't think of it, though his aunts had often urged him to ask his father. Instead, he threw himself into the war, joining the nation's glorious, heroic struggle to avenge his father. And all those long years people didn't think of themselves, nor had they ever imagined that after victory the day would come when they would be cast out, left helpless by the side of the road.

My God, if only I had been shrewder, more hard-headed. If only I had thought a bit, like everyone else, preparing for the day when I too would have a wife and children and I'd have to trade "leaves of metal for a wad of bills." Then I could have given Suong and Da Hai a life at least comparable to what I knew.

Once again, anxiety seized his heart, the way it had the first time he had entered this café during the dark days after they pushed him out of the troupe. He puffed deeply on his cigarette, oblivious to its flavor, the cigarette butt glowing at the edge of his lips. He had finished the pack a long time ago, but the owner had discreetly placed another pack in front of him, then retreated behind the counter. The ashtray overflowed with butts and ash, and when someone came over to empty it, Hung looked up and recognized the young man who had picked up his cigarette butt off the ground.

"Why, thank you," Hung said.

The young man placed the ashtray back in front of him. "Care for something to drink?" he asked, tossing back the long locks that fell over his forehead.

"You have alcohol here?" Hung asked.

After all, why not drink? I'd forgotten the consoling brew. And during this unhappiness, I need to. Not the rice wine that inspired Li Bai's poetry, but fire that burns away sadness and fear. It's true, I've started to fear life and all the wolves out there. I don't know how to face it anymore . . . I need something to lift me up.

The young man smiled. "We don't serve alcohol, but I'll offer you

a drink. It's on me." He disappeared into a back room off the tiny back-
yard garden strewn with rocks and pots of faded chrysanthemums that
no one had bothered to water. The young man returned, a carafe in
hand. He noticed Hung contemplating the faded flowers.

"Nothing sadder, is there?" he said, and sat down across from
Hung. He had large, dark eyes, like the café owner.

"Are you her son?" Hung asked.

The young man laughed and turned to his mother. "Yes, I'm my
mother's son." She laughed too. The young man poured a clear, amber-
colored wine into the cups. Tiny bubbles rose to the surface, reminding
Hung of the foam of the mountain springs, where the water spurted
forth from clean rocks, reflecting the sun like facets of a diamond.
They drank together. The wine was delicious. It was a pure wine, not
the medicinal spirits that his father used to drink. When Hung was a
little boy, his mother kept three shelves in her shed stocked with huge
jars of spirits. On the bottom shelf, there were eight jars filled with
liqueur made from snake, seahorse, wild goat's blood, and tiger gelatin.
In the middle, there were eight other jars of spirits made with medicinal herbs for winter and summer. His father had never been able to
remember which herbs had been used to flavor the spirits. But his
mother knew exactly which herbs were in which jar, when you were supposed to drink it, in what season, and which vital forces it strengthened
or weakened. On the highest shelf, there were eight jars of brandies
made with all sorts of fruits: Vietnamese and Chinese apples, kumquats
and grapes, apricots from the Perfume Pagoda, persimmons from
Dalat, peaches and plums. Hung was allowed to drink the fruit spirits.
His mother used to distill her mysterious mixtures with great concen-
tration. And Hung liked to tease her, saying that the wine she gave him
was an elixir of youth.

"Would you like some snacks?" the young man asked him. Hung
looked up in surprise, startled from his reverie. Without waiting for his
reply, the young man turned to his mother: "Mother, could you bring
us something to eat with the wine?"

The owner went back into the adjoining room, returning with a plate of fried chicken. Her son looked up. "Come on, have a drink with us. Just for fun."

"No thanks, I don't feel like it at the moment. You go ahead and drink with your guest." She turned to Hung. "You can't drink a good wine alone. That's a family tradition. Make yourself at home."

Hung lifted the glass to his lips and felt a trickle of warmth spread through his veins. Beyond the window, through the bamboo, he could see a corner of sky, a road, the shadow of a few passersby. These images shrank and dissipated, fading in the distance.

Everything disappears in the dust. Everything fades. What song is that from? Our childhood, our dreams, our family . . . melodies from the void return one day to the void. Human happiness grows in the heart, then shrivels and rots there. Why am I so unhappy? The revolution, my ideals, my wife, my daughter, everything: They're all like these shadows that recede, then disappear over the horizon, annihilated in a game that leaves no traces. It's useless to suffer like this, to worry . . .

He had emptied three, four cups.

You should never have more than three cups. That had been his father's rule and his principle, the family tradition. Three tiny china cups, each the size of a jackfruit pit, were what Hung was allowed when he was just a boy. But he was a man now, and three tiny cups weren't enough to soothe his soul.

Hung woke up in complete darkness, on the bed of the owner's son. He apologized, embarrassed. There was compassion and dignity in their understanding smiles. In the vague words of consolation they offered, he guessed that they knew his story, the unhappiness that had befallen him, and that they were ready to lend a hand if he needed it. Hung had never allowed himself to accept the pity of others. That, too, had been his father's principle, and he had been right. Hung felt his face burn with shame. The icy blue neon light of the café seemed to sting his flesh.

Suong still knew nothing. When Hung arrived home, she was singing gaily to herself, still basking in the glow of their "life under the new lights," busy altering an *ao dai* that she had just bought. Deeply concentrating on her task—trying to make the tunic more fashionable—she didn't notice her husband's face.

"We waited a long time for you. So we went ahead and ate. Where did you eat tonight?"

"At . . . at a friend's house."

"You can go and wash up. No one came to see you tonight."

Hung went into the bathroom. *From now on no one will come to see me. So you won't have to play the role of personal secretary anymore.* The cold water made him shiver. He felt a flash of terror and plunged his head into the washbasin for a long time, as if to cool the burning skin of his face, trying to overcome the fear of water that haunts a drinker. He returned without drying his hair. Suong was trying on a new shirt, raising a neckline. She had resisted the new urban fashion of low necklines; she hadn't had time to adjust. A hint of naiveté lit her concentrated face, her eyebrows drawn together like two brush strokes. That way of looking, of furrowing her brow—everything about her seemed to marry the spontaneity of a mountain girl and the sophistication of the theater.

How am I going to bring up the subject? She's still too young, too fragile to handle this disaster. Ever since she's known me, she's been like a well-behaved girl, fulfilling all my dreams, executing my orders. It's only now that I realize that every family needs a pillar, each vessel a pilot. How is she, my small, obedient student, going to navigate the family boat? Suong is so different from my mother; she's still just the-girl-I-love-who-bore-me-a-child. She still hasn't become a traditional Vietnamese woman, the warrior who watches over the clan and their territory, who raises and educates the younger generations, a flower with nerves of steel.

Hung remembered watching the ceremonies in honor of the ancestors as a child, how all the relatives had been there, the maternal line, the paternal line. His mother used to fill baskets for them with all sorts of delicacies: bamboo shoots, angel hair vermicelli, mushrooms, and salty and sweet dried Chinese sausages, all kinds of cakes. Then she would pile them all on a big table to distribute to each relative. Hung remembered the lively but orderly atmosphere in the house on those days, how his mother used to bustle about, darting out of the main house across the courtyard, flitting back and forth, from one room to the other, disappearing and reappearing, watching everything vigilantly from the corner of her eye. As gentle as a silk veil, as silent as a shadow, as imperious as a marshal, she rarely raised her voice to give orders or explanations. With her gaze alone she ruled a compact army of several dozen servants who ran about from dawn to dusk, serving platters of food, cooking, without the slightest quarrel. She entertained hundreds of guests, relatives, neighbors, friends, business contacts, and local officials—all with the same soft voice, the same welcoming smile. Meanwhile, Hung's father would sit in the main room, praising the refinement of poetry, priming the souls of their guests, searching for new territory to sow the seeds of his passion for literature.

Suong's voice interrupted Hung's thoughts. "Sweetheart, come see if this blouse suits me."

"Ah . . . yeah, looks great."

"But you see the collar in the back? I tightened it a bit."

"Hmm, let me see. It looks fine. You're so good with your hands."

She's just a spring flower that's going to snap in the first wind. And soon she's going to have to take the helm. I'm no longer head of the troupe, and the burden is going to fall on her. I've got to break the news to her. Sooner or later she's going to learn the truth.

"Sweetheart, sister Hue has an aunt who lives right nearby."

"Really?"

"She's got this big silk shop."

"Yeah?"

"She just gave Hue a beautiful gold necklace and some jade earrings! When we're rich, will you buy me some earrings like that?"

"Yes."

She's dreaming of jade earrings. My mother once had a chest full of them. She would stick her hand in and pull it out covered with gold and precious gems. Poor Suong. She's never had a chance to indulge in such pleasures. She dreams of earrings like a child dreams of a new shirt for Tet Lunar New Year. I can't bring up my sordid news now. Tonight she's too happy, her face is radiant.

Hung set his cup of tea back on the table, walked toward his wife, and kissed her on the back of her neck, on the down beneath her ears. Intense, light, sad kisses. These weren't a husband's kisses, but those of a man still passionately in love, the inspired, anxious kiss of a sculptor for his most perfect creation, a statue that he sensed would someday leave his atelier to become the centerpiece in a museum, or the town park.

The next morning, while Hung was still asleep, a visitor arrived to see him. He woke to feel Suong shaking him as if the house were on fire.

"Darling, wake up. There's a friend who wants to see you, from Hanoi."

"A friend?"

All night he had stared at the ceiling, the mosquito netting strung above the bed. He had finally fallen asleep to the radio playing calisthenics music at about five o'clock in the morning. In his stupor, he couldn't think of a single friend who would have made the trek all the way down from the north to come visit him. He got up, asked Suong to serve the visitor some tea while he washed up. He heard Suong greet the visitor, offer him a drink. The man replied cheerfully, softly, in the pure, precise accent of the north, an accent only people from Hanoi had. Who could he be? Probably one of his classmates from the Music Conservatory, since Hung didn't know anyone else from the north. Which clan had he belonged to, Hung wondered? Maybe it was Phuc, the trumpetist, or Tao, the folk musician. No, more likely it was Kien, the monocord player, that young man with the high-pitched voice who adored other beautiful young men. One Sunday, he had made a pass at Hung, hugged him in the public baths. Hung had genuinely liked Kien, and ever since he had often worried about what had happened to the young Hanoian who loved the sound of the monocord and lived his days in loneliness and desire. If not Kien, then who was it? Hung couldn't guess. He finally hung up his towel and entered the living room.

"Hello, Hung," the visitor said, rising to greet him. Hung recognized the man, but he was not someone he had ever expected to see again.

"Hello, Dam. Weren't you Professor Han's favorite disciple?"

"Good memory. It's been more than ten years," Dam said, extending a hand.

"Yes, it's been more than a decade since I left Hanoi."

"You've lost weight," Dam said, still holding Hung's hand in his. He looked Hung straight in the eye. "You've lost weight, but you're still the same," he added, his voice slightly tremulous.

They sat down, side by side, silent, and let the time pass, time enough to light a stick of incense and watch it burn on the tomb of their youth. Each of them had spent it in his own way, but at that moment, it was as if they had buried the same corpse, watched it decompose with the same sadness and regret. At the conservatory, they had seen each other from time to time. Hung lived in the student dormitory, while Dam lived with his family in the old quarter of Hanoi, right in the center of town in the area known as the "Hanoi of 36 Streets and Guilds." A slight, unspoken inferiority complex separated the provincial students from the Hanoians like Dam, and this complex was especially strong for people from the central provinces. Hung lived in the dormitory, but he lived well. The other students were envious of his clothes and his lifestyle. Dam was one of the more brilliant students in theory and art criticism, while Hung was the most talented student in the artistic creation course. Outside of the Communist Youth League meetings, the plays, and the annual retreats, they had also met twice in the vacation camps in the Bac hills outside of Hanoi. The youthful campfires often lit the souls of men for the rest of their lives. Their faces and voices, the sound of their laughter had bloomed in their undying glow. And now, these two men, both of them more than forty years old, were passionate about rekindling those fires.

Dam stayed for lunch and the two of them spent the afternoon reminiscing. Suddenly, Hung came to his senses. "Are you here as a tourist, or on business?"

"To work," Dam replied. His happy, enthusiastic face suddenly froze, embarrassed. He cleared his throat and said in a slow voice. "That, unfortunately, is the horrible reason that brought me here to see you."

"What's so horrible between us? We may not have seen each other for ten years, but it's not like we're in love with the same woman, or something?" Hung joked. He was so busy savoring their conversation, the tea, reliving the memories that Dam's visit had rekindled that he hadn't even noticed the anxious, unhappy look in his eyes. Dam cleared his throat again.

"Hung, do you know when I arrived here?"

"No."

"Yesterday morning."

"Why, did an earthquake happen between now and then?"

"No, but something very unfortunate. Something that concerns you. That's why I came here first, instead of looking for a place to live, or exploring the town. The man who greeted me at the airport was a cadre from the provincial organization committee and he drove me straight to their offices. As soon as we got there, he handed me an 'important dossier'—with your name on it! Now do you understand?"

"Quite clearly."

"Well, you explain it to me then. Why?"

"On this tiny strip of land, I'm the only one who has a university degree in music, the only one who has a passion for this ephemeral product in the market of life. If you had come as a tourist, that would be another story. But if you're here on business, it could only be to do what I used to do. Nothing else would match your qualifications."

"I've read their dossier on you. I was stunned. I just can't accept that they pushed you out. I refuse to. Even if we weren't close friends, we were classmates. We've lived fair, honest lives, respected justice. There's no reason for me to accept a decision like this. It's illogical, it's dishonest, and its simply base. We have the same qualifications, the same diploma. And this troupe is your creation, you put it together, trained it, forged it. I'm not the kind of man to pilfer my neighbor's rice crop, especially when the neighbor is you." Dam stopped to catch his breath and light a cigarette.

Hung said nothing.

"I've told the organization committee exactly what I think," Dam continued. "They listened, but didn't say a word. When I asked them to send me to the Bureau of Arts and keep you as the head of the troupe, the chairman said, 'Comrade, please understand. The provincial leadership is currently inundated with urgent, important tasks, and it can't cater to the personal desires of each cadre. Like me, it's your duty to put the interests of the revolution above everything, to sacrifice your personal feelings.' I laid out my arguments again. He patiently listened, but then he gave me the same reply."

"It's useless to protest . . ." Hung replied, and he saw Dam wince, his brow furrowed with deep wrinkles. "Did you notice anything?" Hung said in a slow, deliberate voice, "I mean, about the chairman of the organization committee, while you were talking with him?"

"He's a complete peasant, but with unbelievable patience."

"What else?"

Dam shrugged.

"He speaks with a Quang Ngai accent," Hung continued. "Dam, that's the heartland, the hometown of the deputy chief of the Service, the man who hates me. So any decisions or explanations can only serve one purpose: to prove that he's right. In fact, this kind of man is a creature of habit, an old dog who repeats the same tricks, bends to the rules, follows his gut. I'm telling you, the man you saw is from a place that belongs to the deputy chief. You live in the north, Dam, so you don't know what that means down here. It's the strongest, most instinctive peasant feeling. I've observed it so many times. That old bastard is trying to concentrate all the power over the cultural sphere in his hands by using a hierarchical superior who is more competent, and who has more integrity than he does. The chief's luck is my misfortune. What can I do?"

"No . . . I'm not a blind optimist, but I never forget the saying: There's always a way up the mountain."

"What way? There's only one way, that's to kowtow at the guy's feet, to beg his forgiveness for having made him lose face more than ten years ago, to swear blind loyalty to him, to bend over, lick his boots, and eat his shit like King Cau Tien did to trick the Chinese. But I've never been a king, and I don't have the courage to taste other people's shit to get what I want. I've never known the supreme joy of power, but I'm not going to sell my soul. I've only ever had one dream in my life, a crazy dream, which is to create. It's a drug my father virtually injected into my blood."

Hung slowly recounted the conflict of ten years earlier, the catastrophic meeting when he had held out a hand to the deputy chief, and then unwittingly become the focus of all his enmity.

Dam sighed. "Now I understand the chairman's intransigence. He kept the same line from start to finish. No argument could sway him. And at one point, I just declared that I had no ambition to make a career here, that my home was in the North, that I was only here on business. For me, a job is a job. They can rusticate me to the Bureau of Arts, or leave me in peace—it's all the same. As for the troupe, they should put that back in your hands. You're the man who created it." Dam paused, shook his head. "Do you know what else he said? He told me that my salary was higher than the deputy chiefs and that he couldn't place me anywhere else. I told him that you and I graduated from the same conservatory, the same class, that we got our degrees the same day, that you had had better grades on the finals. He just replied coldly: 'That's the conservatory's business. As for the provincial organization committee we place cadres in function of their salary.'"

"I told you. It's useless to argue. Utterly hopeless. The root of the problem lies elsewhere. If I threw myself at that bastard's feet, I'd give him the satisfaction of victory, just like the Chinese king felt when Cau Tien bowed to him. He would change his mind and the organization committee would tell you: 'Despite your high salary, despite your incomparable qualifications, you lack, Comrade, the essential qualification needed to succeed in this position, love of your home territory. For us, this feeling is the engine of the revolution, the indispensable key to our success. You don't really understand this province, the psychology of people here. You won't be able to lead the artistic work here. For these reasons, Comrade, I ask you to accept the position of consultant to the Bureau of Arts' . . . or something like that, you get it? We used to say once that in this country there are no laws, and I didn't believe it. But now, since this disaster has struck, I do."

Dam sighed, looked at Hung. "So we have to surrender? You'll become an outcast, and me a man without honor?"

"Neither of us can change our fate."

"Let's try one more time, Hung. Let's ask to meet the provincial Party secretary. Maybe he'll find a solution. I'm telling you frankly, I didn't lie to the chairman. I've got no vested interest in this thing. I actually prefer the Bureau of Arts; it's better for me, gives me time for my research. And as for money, my aunt sends me plenty of that every month. Aside from coffee and cigarettes, I don't have expenses."

Hung shook his head. "You're deluding yourself. The provincial Party secretary doesn't have time to waste on folks like us. He's the top dog in the province and he's got more important matters to deal with. Remember what Prof. Han used to say about artists in a feudal society? In this hierarchical society there are four classes: mandarins, peasants, artisans, and merchants. And the artists are at the bottom of the ladder, just above the beggars. You'd hoped our society would be more progressive? No, it's still the same, just under a different guise."

"Aren't you a bit too pessimistic?"

"Perhaps. But in my situation, it's easy to fall into that. Since they pushed me out, I've had time to do a lot of thinking. There's no way out."

"What a cruel joke this is! Here I am, just a lazy Northern boy who thought by coming to this isolated town in the center of Vietnam I'd finally have time to read, do research, finally finish my book on folk music. Of course, being head of the troupe brings fame and a nice salary, and other perks. But it's a job for a creative person, someone with the wealth of experience you have. I'm not cut out for this, and I take no pleasure in it." Dam got up and paced around the room for a long time, then said: "Listen Hung, if we can't turn this situation around, let's find a compromise that suits both of us. I'm going to propose to the deputy chief that you stay on with the troupe as my assistant. I'll be the front man for the officials at the Service. As for the rest, the shows, the budget, managing the actors—that'll be your job. In short, you do what you want to do, only under my name. We're friends, that's what counts. What do you say?"

"I . . . I accept . . ." Hung replied, his mouth quivering slightly. His eyes flashed for a moment, then he added, his voice choked, moved: "You know that I have only one dream. I want to create, compose a real body of work. It just flows in my blood."

"And me, all I aspire to is the peace and quiet to do my research. I want to read and write—a passion as dreamy and impractical as your own, though it's in a different sphere." Dam glanced at his watch. "It's time. I'm going to see that old guy right away at his residence, behind the offices." And he left.

Hung continued to sip his tea. Suong appeared from her room. Her eyes were red, puffy. "Why didn't you tell me?"

"Sit down, my girl."

"Why did you hide this from me?"

"You would have known, sooner or later. I didn't dare tell you. I was afraid of hurting you. Other husbands would do the same in my situation."

"That old deputy chief is so cruel! How can he be so vindictive? What a snake!" Suong's eyes filled with tears. "Is Dam going to be able to keep you with the troupe?"

Hung shook his head. "I don't know. I hope that aside from his desire to humiliate me and get his revenge, the deputy chief will be motivated by another goal—keeping the troupe and all its talent together. During the war, we were his secret weapon, the ultimate bait. Remember how he used us to attract the attention of the high-ranking officials, to create his aura? And now that his reputation needs a boost, he may just have to meet Dam's conditions."

Suong sighed. Hung realized that now she was just as terrified as he was, filled with the same anxiety, the same hope. They both fell silent, tried to busy themselves tidying the house, playing with their daughter. They finished dinner quickly, and Hung barely ate at all. Just a few mouthfuls of rice, a few vegetables, a piece of fish stewed in *nuoc mam* and chilies, his favorite dish. He drank more tea, flipped through a book. But he couldn't read a single line. His eyes just slid down the text as he turned the pages mechanically. His heart, his brain, each cell in his body was as taut as an antenna, waiting. In bed, Suong held their daughter in her arms. She didn't dare sing to her, like she usually did, so she just murmured, frantic with anxiety, waiting.

Slowly, night fell. The seconds and minutes passed, echoing through the room with the tick tock of the clock. Just past ten o'clock, Dam returned. As soon as he got past the door, he slumped down in a chair, avoiding their eyes.

Suong and Hung knew they had lost. All three of them kept silent. Suong began to cry, gasping for breath like a child unfairly whipped. The two men kept silent. The clock continued its tick tock, punctuating time in the empty space, its rhythm like blows of a hammer. Finally, Hung spoke up: "Well, the game is over. This is my fate. I must thank you, Dam, all the same. You've been a real friend."

"Hung, please. I'm partly responsible for this defeat."

"That's a strange thing to say."

"No, entirely accurate. On the way back, I kept thinking that if only I hadn't been so naive, so frank, we might have worked things out. If I hadn't told them that we were classmates, that we respected each other . . . if I had been more calculating, if I had invented some tale of hatred. If I had told them that you were arrogant, contemptuous, that you had delivered some low blows to your colleagues and that this was a perfect opportunity for me to reeducate you . . . Yes, if I had been able to trick them, we would have succeeded. But I was too stupid to think of the ruse in time."

Hung paled, looked at Dam. "You're right. If you had pretended to hate me, they would have yielded. Everything depends on that man."

"It was only on the way back here that it occurred to me. Too late.

Much too late. He's determined to get his revenge, and there I was, trying to convince him with my sincere arguments! Like they say, you don't go meet the Devil in a monk's habit."

"You're forgetting that the troupe reports to the Cultural Service, which reports to the provincial authority. And at both levels, he's the winner. You forget the principle of democratic centralism. The Party's leading role depends on it. How long have you been a Party member?"

"Five years."

"That's three and a half years less than I've got in seniority," Hung said, shaking his head. "And yet when they dismissed me as head of the troupe, they told me it was because in this new phase of the Revolution the troupe needed to be led by a cadre who was more competent . . . more 'red.'"

"What do you mean more 'red'?"

"More political seniority, more years in the Party organization."

"Shit! Red, pink, what is this shit? Do those old bastards really believe that crap?"

"That's the way it is."

"The most important thing now is . . . what are you going to do?"

"The most important thing is that no one gives a shit about me, or my work. This is the donkey's kick in the ass. The deputy chief is the instigator and the chairman of the provincial organization committee is playing the role of accomplice. It's hopeless. All your good intentions, all your hopes for me are futile. You can't win against them. It's not just that they've got the power: They've got infinite patience. There's nothing more patient than a bunch of old resentful mules waiting in ambush." Hung said, smiling contemptuously. But his lips were as pale as a dead man's.

"So we just let our hands be tied?" Dam asked, staring at him.

No one said anything. The two men looked at each other in silence. Suong sobbed softly. It was midnight. A wild sea wind, heavy with fog and salt, swept through the garden and the house, more and more violent as the night deepened. Trees thrashed about continuously.

"I'm going home," Dam said.

"Why not stay the night? The streets aren't dangerous, but the wind is like ice."

"Not for northerners like me. Try and get some sleep. Whatever happens, keep your spirits up. If not, you won't be able to create . . . and if you can't do that, live for your wife and kids. Happiness weighs the same on God's altar."

"I forgot to ask, where are your wife and kids?"

"I'm not lucky enough to have such treasures."

"You're joking?"

"No, it's the truth." Dam looked at Hung. Then it was his turn to smile. "You, you love art, me I loved a woman. I don't know which of us is the greater fool, but every passion has its price. I waited fifteen years for her. And the ending wasn't like the *Tale of Kieu:* The beautiful Kieu didn't rejoin the pious Kim; instead, she wrote a self-criticism and submitted it to the rich Thuc Sinh, who continued to keep her as his mistress."

"I don't understand."

"I loved a married woman. I waited, believed in her for fifteen years. After fifteen years of happiness with me, she denounced me to her husband, said I had seduced her, lured her down the road to hell." Dam paused, then turned to Hung: "Do you know why I'm here?"

"They told me they asked the Ministry to send a competent cadre to the province as a reinforcement."

Dam almost choked laughing. Finally he wiped his eyes and spoke. "That was after a disciplinary sanction. Being posted to central Vietnam is a form of exile. Because . . . the love of my life is the wife of a vice minister."

And with that, he left.

The first morning Hung tasted the feeling of "being superfluous" it was pouring rain. After a week of absence from the rehearsals, Suong had to attend a meeting with the troupe leadership. It was composed of four members: the troupe leader, the Party cell secretary, the union secretary, and the head of the Communist Youth League. Ordinarily, the troupe leader was also the Party secretary, so that the leadership would be unified. But Dam had obstinately refused to take up this post, saying that he was "naturally lazy, and that technical responsibilities were already tiring enough," so he couldn't possibly assume those of the Party secretary. They arranged for the union secretary to fill this position. So that was how a man with callused hands who used to be a stage manager became the political soul of the troupe. When he noticed Suong's absence, he alerted the deputy chief, who then called Dam to inquire about her health, using the opportunity to ask more about Suong: "The nightingale with the crystal voice as her admirers call her, the jewel of our province. You must watch over her health, Comrade make sure she follows a special gymnastic program." Dam immediately understood the deputy chief's insinuation.

"Tomorrow, you've got to go back to rehearsals," he told Suong. "The old mule's spies are meticulous. Hung is right. They are all in league to torture and take revenge on people."

The next day, Suong got up early to prepare lunch and took Da Hai over to Auntie Tuong's house, since she intended to work with the troupe all day. After Suong had dropped off her daughter, she returned to the house to prepare breakfast for Hung.

"I've got to leave now, don't forget to fill the teapot when the water boils. The tea is on your desk," Suong said.

"You go on ahead to work," Hung answered. Then, according to his habit, he sat down at his desk looking out over the trees in the garden. A few pens in a white ceramic pot. An eraser. A crystal paperweight with a lotus flower inside. Suong had arranged everything. She wasn't like his mother, but she was a devoted, obedient wife. With what little money they had, she had bought all these objects for him in the street markets, so nothing really matched. The boiling water let off a thick cloud of steam over the electric burner, set up right beside his desk. He pulled out the plug, poured the water into a Thermos bottle and then, also out of habit, set up his tiny bachelor's tea set on the desk. Suong had bought the teapot, too, in an old antique store. It must have been worth something, since it had belonged to a noble family before they sold it and fled town. The brown earthenware glistened, polished by years of use, decorated with Chinese ideograms. It was rare to find antiques with such beautiful calligraphy. The tea set went well with the dark, smooth amboyna wood table. The perfection of its color reminded him of the elegant, dreamy atmosphere of his parents' home, his childhood. As he prepared the tea, pouring it into a tiny cup the size of a water buffalo's eye, he contemplated this clear liquid that exuded the warm, sweet scent of the hills. Suddenly he shuddered.

Drink your tea and get to work. What can I do now aside from watching the steam float up from a cup of tea? And even this can't go on forever. And yet all those years during the war, I used to drink tea from a cracked tin mug from some factory in Hai Phong. The enamel cover had been chipped away, exposing the metal. I didn't have a cup as tiny as a buffalo's eye, or a beautiful table made of amboyna wood, or peaceful dawns spent by a window overlooking a garden of ylang-ylang trees. There wasn't time to smell the flowers, or gaze at the sky, or listen to the birds sing. Now I have every-thing, but I have nothing to write about. All my efforts would be a waste. Life under "the new lights" will bring profits to the others, and losses to me.

He drank the tea without tasting it. He lifted up the tea canister, shook it for a long time, listening to the swish of dry leaves, then slowly set it back on the table. He stared at the pile of music paper on which he had carefully traced scores, contemplated its whiteness; vast, infinite, like a desert covering the earth, the trees, the rivers, the streams, engulfing his past and future.

All that's left is the desert, for years to come. All that's left, facing me, is death. How I long to live the life of the esthete, like my father. All his life, he was the host to literature, to the beauty of the world of art, a vine curled around an ancient oak tree, lucky to lead a life of leisure. Elegant, noble. He was free. Me, I'm just a worker in an assembly line, making bolts, pounding a hammer.

"Who wants copper pots, aluminum tins? Anyone selling alu-minum, or iron?" The scrap metal vendor shouted up, standing in front of their door. From the window, Hung could see the old man's dirty beard quiver with each shout, as if to mask a smile.

I wonder if he's an emissary of the deputy chief, come to mock me? Because I really am a reject, a piece of scrap metal. No, I'm imagining things. The vendor is going to stand in front of every house with the same patience . . . I'm slipping. This is sick. I'm pessimistic about everything. I'm not going to let this storm beat me down. I must compose . . . I will compose something, anything. If they refuse to use my music here I'll send it to Hanoi. Who knows, maybe I'll push my work to a new level.

He pulled the pile of music paper toward him, took out a pen and put a black stroke to the scale.

My destiny is in the minor key. This loving, painful key has haunted me since my first composition, when I was only eighteen.

Hung kept pressing the tip of the pen on the note, letting the ink seep and spread on the paper, transforming the note into a blurry asterisk the size of a kernel of corn. He threw the pen on the table and got up, realizing he couldn't do it: There was no echo in reply. And the first note you put on paper was like the first brick in an edifice: It made way for the rest. The first sound had to awaken thousands and thousands of sounds, the first melody calling to others. Otherwise it was just a rotten sprout, a bad grain of paddy rice, an unrequited love.

He drank the cold tea. Outside, the rain suddenly came pouring down. That evening, when Suong returned, she wanted to go pick up Da Hai at Auntie Tuong's, but she hesitated. She went into the kitchen, prepared dinner, and called Hung to come help wash the vegetables. "Are you okay?"

"Yes."

"I was afraid the rain would make you sad," she stammered, awkward.

Hung smiled. "Don't worry about me, I'm not a child like Da Hai . . . I'm ten years older than you are," he said, his heart twisting.

My own wife worries about me as if I were a sick child. Next she'll be taking my pulse, feeling my forehead. I'm not just redundant; I'm already infirm. When she rehearses she must pity me, once her respectable husband, now just a useless guy biting his nails in front of a pile of blank scores.

"Look Suong, this cabbage has an extra branch, like a hand with six fingers. Odd, isn't it?" Hung lifted up the strange branch, showing it to his wife. She laughed gaily, like a child playing with a toy, unaware of the dark thoughts that haunted him.

Today's my first day as court jester. My wife goes off to work, provides for the family, and I, the husband, stay at home racking my brain for ways to amuse her when she comes home. The days will go by, life will go on, the funny tricks will grow old, and this husband's face is going to become more humdrum by the day.

It was pouring rain, the endless, rotting rain of the central provinces. A rain that crushed the land, reduced gardens to mud, that churned and swelled the rivers. Thick, heavy clouds screened off the sky. Then, it would stop, and the sun, like a rotting orange, would appear for an instant, then vanish. Night and day the garden hummed with the ceaseless drumming of the rain and its odd, damp, musty scent. For seventeen days straight, seated in his room, Hung counted the storms. He felt his blood thicken in his veins as if he were dying, uttering his last gasp before turning into a piece of frozen meat. He hadn't even written a single musical phrase. Little by little, he lost awareness of his state. All he could feel was the interminable rain that poured down on his soul, leaving it soggy, rotten. All day he sat motionless at his smooth wood desk, knowing his ideas would slide across the white pages, the score sheets, and that the white desert of death strewn with the bones of lost travelers, the skins of poisonous snakes, would gape wider and wider in front of him with each passing day. He paced in circles in his room, brooding, breathing the stench of corpses that seemed to waft from the four walls.

On the eighteenth day, the rain stopped. The sun spread a blazing light, mixing with sudden, tempestuous gusts of sea wind. Rain-soaked flowers lay rotting in the sun. Steam rose from the gardens. Everywhere the chattering of birds. And from the markets to the suburbs, the streets were filled with yellow butterflies that flapped at the eyes and faces of the pedestrians, making space swirl. A mysterious call rang from the sky, hovering in the heady atmosphere of sunlight and butterfly wings. And this call resonated in Hung's heart, like the sound of a church bell in some faraway place, beckoning, promising sustenance and shelter.

He waited until Suong had left for work, then locked the door behind him and headed off in a random direction.

Go, go, go, go, go . . .

All he could hear was a rat-a-tat-tat, the roll of a drum in his head. As a music student, he had only studied revolutionary marches, like the *Marseillese*, like those written by Shostakovitch. He had only composed to a steady beat, on the musical scale of a great people on the road to great truths. *Farewell, grandiose symphonies. Now, this nearly forty-year-old man only wants to follow the symphony of escape. . . . Go, go, go, go, go, go, go! You have to go; if you don't, you'll die seated here, stiff and staring at these four walls, in your own house.*

He ran down to the beach. Enough distance so he wouldn't have to see anyone, face anyone anymore. There on the white sand, gazing at the fragile waves in front of him, he took a deep breath, as if he were emerging from a bomb shelter, like coming up for air.

I'm happy.

It was a small, modest happiness, like a drop of honey that you spread on the tongue of a newborn babe. After a cramped, fetid time staring at those dank four walls, at last he faced the open sea. "Our country lies on the edge of the Pacific Ocean," as his old geography teacher used to say, sowing this pride and painful love in his soul.

But the sea would always be the sea. Not just here, in his country, this curving S-shaped land of those familiar ballads. In any country, the sea would be as salty, have those same cresting, foaming waves. In any country, a storm tide could crush everything in its wake, concealing gold and silver treasure, the wrecks of ships. And it was because it had no country, no fatherland, no nationality that the sea was free. Azure blue waves would glisten whether here or on the other side. The sea was still enchanting, still like an amulet that would always have the power to lure ships away from the shores. The surface of the water shimmered with the furrows of a million illusory paths, beckoning to the human spirit with the promise of adventure.

Suddenly, he understood something that he never had. He discovered the sea—not the sea of this S-shaped country, but the sea of the sea: the free, unbridled sea that belonged to no one, that answered to no one, that was no one's slave. Mesmerized, he gazed into the vast expanse of water as if he too could vanish into its endless churning. In the mysterious light, he heard a thousand voices, saw countless visions behind each scale fused into the most perfect polyphony he had ever imagined. From the deep, foggy valleys he heard a bassoon rise: A deep, bass note that hadn't faded from the rows of pines that ran lengthwise down the mountain slopes. Then the frail, tinny wail of a clarinet, like the thinnest sprig of violet orchid. And from the deepest, remotest distant ravines, a piano unfurled its tide, flooding the streams and forests he had once led the troupe through. The poor, yet noble life they had led during the war: He *must* immortalize it, record it on the scales. The souls of dead soldiers still wandered here, as if waiting for some final rite, an answer to all the times they had waited and never received a reply. To capture the light that beamed from their frantic, anguished, glowering eyes after a convoy of trucks tumbled into a ravine, after the thunder of a B52 bombing raid, after artillery fire lobbed from the sea. The light that had flickered for the last time in the eyes of the dead, an expression of surprise frozen there; they had been like children who didn't understand that the game had suddenly ended. And there was the stammering from the lips of the dying, the stagnant melodies, the trickle of congealing blood, the cracking of water freezing into ice, mountains crumbling . . .

Yes, his life was over. His comrades were dead; his compatriots had fled. Now he would have to write in a different light, in the howl of the sea, of freedom.

The sun set. The surface of the waves was a shimmering purple, the faded color of lotus blossoms in August. Dusk trickled down over the sea, flooding the horizon. And at the point where the water met the clouds, the fishing boats were no more than tiny, bobbing dots in the fading shadows. But Hung hadn't noticed the shadows at his back, behind the fields of casuarina trees, the dunes, the plots of land filled with rocks and wild morning glories. When he finally emerged from his trance, the night had engulfed the sea. The wind howled through the rocky gorges.

My God, it's night already, maybe even past seven o'clock. Suong must have already made dinner, and will be waiting for me. Time to go . . . . but why? I'm going to suffocate to death between those walls. This is the first time I've felt alive since they kicked me out. Why go home? To sit at the family dinner table, across from my wife, to be the father figure? Suong needs to see me across the table just like she needs to see the coatrack or the set of keys hanging on the wall.

Hung imagined her face. In his mind, she was still just his student, his lover, his little wife. Her gaze always shone with trust, respect. He was taller than she was; she had to lift her head to look at him. In this position, her round, clear eyes always filled him with a tenderness that was hard to describe.

His tears overflowed, streamed down his cheeks, cooling in the evening wind. He didn't want to return home, but he didn't know where to go.

The last frail glow of dusk flickered out over the steep rock cliffs. Even the shadow of Venus had faded. Hung felt cold, tired. All around him, the sea. He slipped under an overturned boat, a few steps away, to take refuge from the fog and mist. Chaotic dreams drew him down into a narrow, suffocating world, where people scrambled and fought, murdering each other for mysterious reasons. These brief, anarchic dreams came and went, leaving him exhausted, before he fell into a deep, peaceful sleep. He awoke to the sound of heavy footsteps, murmuring. Someone must have tripped over the boat; he froze, vigilant, completely awake.

There are people out there . . . where are they running like that? Fishermen preparing to go out to sea? Or maybe a hamlet caught fire?

Hung groped his way out from under the boat.

"My God, there's a guy under there!"

"Oh, it's all over . . . quick, run."

Two women shot past him, letting out frightened cries. Hung didn't have time to make out their faces.

"Stop! I order you to stop! And be quiet!" a rasping voice shouted, right near him. The two women stopped in their tracks.

Hands like steel clenched Hung's neck and began to strangle him. A huge black figure, like a bear, rose in front of him. Hung sunk his nails into the man's wrists, shaking him with all his strength, but to no avail. While he thrashed about, he saw a dagger flash out of the man's other hand toward the sky.

"Wait, wait, brother Hai! Stop!" someone shouted, panting, from behind him. "Stop . . . he's with us . . . with my family."

The hands loosened their grip. Hung touched his neck, not knowing whether it had been broken. It took him a long time to catch his breath, before the pounding in his ears finally subsided. The younger man moved in front of the bearlike figure, pointed toward Hung.

"He's my cousin . . . he's family."

The bearlike man wheeled around, revealing a rough, sinister face. "Yeah, what now?"

"I forbid you to kill him."

"Then we're taking him with us."

The women, standing just a few feet away, started to wail. "That's impossible. No, no, the boat will be too heavy!"

The bearlike man roared. "You want me to kill him? Is that what you want? He's Quang's family, and it's Quang's uncle who is going to meet you in California."

The women fell silent.

The bearlike man grabbed Hung by the shirt collar, shoved him hard. "Get out of here!"

The younger man, his hair parted in the middle, held out a hand to help him up and Hung immediately recognized him as the café owner's son. "Look, either you come on the boat with us, or he's going to kill you . . . quick, I'll explain later."

Hung didn't have time to think, didn't realize what was happening to him. The bearlike man grabbed him by his shirt collar, and the café owner's son took him by the arm, pulling him along with a group of complete strangers.

It's impossible to cry out, or escape. There's no way out.

Hung suddenly had a vision out of the legend: a woman clutching a child in her arms, waiting so long for her husband to return from war that she turned to stone, petrified. And the vision broke his heart. But he said nothing.

As the sea wind whipped his face, a boat appeared from behind the rocks, moving toward them.

7

The doctor had given Suong permission to have a bit of weak rice porridge. The smell of young rice reminded her of the harvests. Her father had been a woodcutter, but he had also cultivated a few acres of rice. During the harvest season, he would take her out to the fields, set her down on a dike, and let her run along the harvested paddies, play amidst their spiky stalks. Suong used to stroll along the grassy dikes, gathering heliotrope flowers, chasing dragonflies and crickets, weaving necklaces of tiny wildflowers that she strung around her neck. The smell of porridge rekindled the memory of those rice paddies; the blue sky speckled with tiny, pearly white clouds; the Truong Son Cordillera rising against the horizon like a purple curtain. Against this landscape, a tall, tanned man in faded clothes with charcoal eyes and finely drawn eyebrows harvested rice with rapid slashes of a sickle, bending and straightening, tossing bunches of rice onto the dikes. In her memory, she could still see him wipe the sweat with the back of his hand, then turn to her with a toothy smile, his face glowing.

The nurse noticed Suong sniff the bowl of rice without eating. "Eat before it gets cold."

Suong composed herself and lifted a spoonful obediently to her lips. Satisfied, the nurse continued knitting. Constantly busy, she never took a break from her peanut-shelling or knitting, despite the doctor's admonishments. She did exactly as she pleased. Her enormous fingers patiently and laboriously clicked the knitting needles. Fascinated by the nurse's hands, Suong was still eating when Lam arrived. He knocked at the door with an elegant, ceremonial air, greeted the nurse with the politesse of a diplomat, and entered the room.

"Eat while it's hot," Lam said, putting the bowl back in Suong's hand. Water trickled down the clown's face; no doubt he had just washed in the public faucet. He waited for her to finish, then served tea. "So you've been here sixteen days?" he asked.

"Yes."

"No one told me. I've been stuck in the village for these last three weeks trying to settle my paternal uncle's inheritance dispute. I just got here by today's bus."

"How did you find out?"

"People . . . in the train stations. Nothing escapes the rumor mill."

He fell silent, looked out the window to avoid Suong's pale face. Suong too kept silent. The nurse rolled up her wool, got up, stretched, and yawned loudly. "You keep her company. I'm going out for a bit."

She tossed her unfinished knitting on a corner of the table against the wall and went out. Only after the sound of her clogs had faded down the corridor did Lam speak: "I never thought you'd end up here."

"Neither did I," Suong said, lowering her eyes to hold back her tears.

"Is Hung still at home?" Lam asked.

"No, Vinh told me he hasn't been back since the first night."

"Where did he go?"

"I don't know. Vinh doesn't want to go look for him. He hates him."

"I understand."

"I've got to stay here, I can't . . ."

"I understand. How long has Hung been gone?"

"It's been two weeks now."

Lam froze like a statue, his thick eyebrows furrowing tight over his nose. His gaze stared somewhere in the void, as if the light in his eyes had concentrated in an effort to understand the distant past, something vague, shadowy, that he only dimly remembered. He got up. "I'll go look for him. Vinh will take good care of you, right?"

"Oh yes."

"When's he coming back?"

"In a half hour. He's gone for lunch."

"Good, then I'm off." He put his hat on his head and left. From the back, he looked more like a farmer than a carter or a clown who made people roar with laughter. His silhouette had become familiar and dear to Suong. Without Lam's help, she would never have been able to feed Hung while he was in prison. Thinking back on that time, Suong barely recognized herself, it seemed like a previous life.

Coming back from the bus station that icy morning, Suong had had to prepare "provisions for the prisoner"—a job that she had never heard of, let alone knew how to do. She ran over to Auntie Tuong's house, embraced her daughter, covering her with kisses, as if she were asking for the intercession of some all-powerful God before crossing a desert. Da Hai was deep asleep, as rosy as a cherub in a painting. Suong wanted to take her in her arms, but Auntie Tuong stopped her. "You've just come in from the cold, you're going to wake her."

Suong resigned herself to just gazing at her daughter from the edge of the bed.

"Have you ever carried supplies to a prisoner?" Auntie Tuong asked as she served Suong some ginger tea.

"No."

"Well it's no easy job, let me tell you. That's something you've got to learn how to do. This morning you should go see the Prisoner Mama."

"Who's the Prisoner Mama?"

"You've never heard of her? She's a legend around here. She lives at the end of the street, down an alley to the left, right before the intersection. In this season, all you have to do is follow the smell of the ripe guavas." She opened the safety pin that held her blouse pocket closed, pulled out a wad of bills, and handed them to Suong.

"No, I can't take this," Suong said, shaking her head.

"Take it. I'm not rich, but I'm alone. In life I provide for myself and in death I have no heirs."

"You've already been so good to me and my daughter. I couldn't . . ."

"Take it. It's the same as if I gave to the pagoda or the orphanage. Don't worry."

The old woman pushed the bills, still warm from her bosom, back into Suong's hand, led her to the door and showed her the way to the woman they only knew by her nickname "Prisoner Mama."

Following Auntie Tuong's instructions, Suong arrived at the end of the street. Two houses from the intersection, she turned left down a narrow alley, typical of those found in seaside hamlets like this one. On both sides, wooden doors, all closed. Houses without voices. The doors were crumbling, gnawed by termites, some had basket-sized holes through which an old, hairless dog would poke its lazy head. Behind the doors, a few peeling walls covered with moss, or a courtyard shielded by a thick hedge of hibiscus or acanthus that no one ever bothered to trim. The alley was very long, and the farther Suong went, the stronger the smell of ripe guavas became. At the end stood a large arched bamboo gate with panels that swung open. Behind it, opening onto a dirt courtyard, was a house made of old bricks with low walls and a roof covered with moss. The door was wide open. Not the shadow of a human presence, or even of a guard dog; it looked more like a small pagoda than a house. Hesitant, Suong entered silently, on tiptoe, then stopped in the middle of the courtyard, surveying the empty space. Except for the slow rustle of falling jackfruit leaves, all was silent. Golden leaves littered the courtyard. In a corner, on a tiny table made of jackfruit wood, a few sticks of incense—stuck upright in a bowl of sticky rice—burned slowly, surrounded by a few roses. The heady scent of incense hung around the house. Suong waited for a long time. Still seeing no one, she called, then stopped, then called again, waiting for a reply amid the echoes of her own voice and the swish of the jackfruit leaves. Just when she was about to leave, the mistress of the house appeared.

"I'm here." A brusque voice answered behind Suong's back. Before she could reply, an old woman with murky eyes walked in front of her, looking her over suspiciously. "You're looking for me?"

"Yes, I came to, to ask you about . . ."

"I know . . ." the woman interrupted, setting down the two baskets she was carrying filled with custard apples and ripe guavas. "Please sit down," she continued, pulling a wooden stump toward her for a stool and gently pushing another toward Suong, as if her first impression had made her more trusting. Suong sat down facing her.

"What village are you from?" she asked, as if she were conducting a professional interview. "Who are you? What's your family name? Who are you supplying? What crime is the poor man accused of?" And while she asked these questions, she kept plucking old leaves off the stems of the guavas and the custard apples, the veins in her bony hands pulsing under the spotted skin. She must have been very old, but she had maintained her health, because she obviously had no intention of dying before her poor imprisoned child. She told Suong that for the last eighteen years she had visited her only son, a thief condemned for life. The skin on her neck was wrinkled and her eyes were clouded over, but they still flashed hard and icy, without the slightest trace of fear. Suong shivered, thinking how you would have to have eyes like that to scale mountains and wade through the mud of rivers for eighteen years, to be known only as "Prisoner Mama" instead of the name her parents had given her.

"Have some guavas. In this alley, only mine are sweet," she said, as if to conclude her interrogation, and handed Suong a few. She stood up and retreated back into the house, reappearing a few minutes later with a pitcher of water and a cracked earthenware bowl. Sitting back down on the tree stump, she poured herself some water, which she drank in long gulps, like a worker. When she had emptied the bowl and set the pitcher down at the foot of the jackfruit tree, she spoke again. "For the moment, forget about what you need to buy. First, you've got to learn the formalities to get you past the various doors, how to do the paperwork, how to behave with all their excellencies in the prison bureaucracy, with all the official "reeducators"—since there are several different kinds—what they like, how they think . . ." She spoke for a long time, without stopping.

The woman was like a living encyclopedia of prisons and reeducation camps, a world that Suong had never imagined. It was as if the old woman wasn't speaking as much as reciting a book that had long since been engraved into her heart. Her hands continued to work, mechanically, her fingers as rough and gnarled as tree roots.

"You know, thousands of people come to ask me for advice. Not just the townspeople. They come all the way from the suburbs and the surrounding districts. And there are more and more of them every day," she said. And the lesson was over.

Suong thanked the old woman and left for the market. When she got back home, she went straight to the kitchen to prepare the food that the Prisoner Mama had recommended: pork and shrimp salted and dried in a pan, then pounded into threads; ground, salted meat mixed with galangale ginger, pastes made of salted shrimp, peanuts, and sesame seeds. She had also bought various medicines for malaria, diarrhea, and typhoid; and for the prison guards, some of the most expensive cigarettes and lotus tea that they could drink with green bean cakes. Finally, some cheap tobacco for Hung and his friends. The Prisoner Mama had told her that in prison no one survives without their friends, and those who didn't join a "clan" would face a kind of double blackmail. That the jailers and administrators would threaten them was a given, but there was also the intimidation of the gangs that pillaged the other prisoners' supplies, beating them and torturing them like animals for their pleasure. Suong had also been instructed to bring

Hung a few old wool scarves; the mountain air was harsh; vegetables were scarce, and the prisoners usually ate just rice and rotten fish pastes, so they could easily come down with lung diseases. She also had to remember to bring Hung a few sacks of rice and dried beans so he could make some porridge if he got sick.

By the time she had finished all the preparations for the trip, it was early morning. The cock crowed, signaling the first watch. Suong collapsed on the bed, too tired to even put up the mosquito netting, and fell into a deep sleep. After about two hours, Lam rang at the gate. He had brought her little brother back. Lam let them chat a few minutes and then said, "That's enough . . . you'll have time to talk, but right now I'm starving and I'm going to have a soup to calm my stomach. I've also got to feed the horse." Lam hitched the horse to the foot of a jasmine tree. The horse whinnied and Lam patted him on the cheek. "Don't be fussy . . . I haven't forgotten your food. Have I ever eaten before you? Calm down." Lam took out a basket of paddy rice in sugar cane juice, then turned to Vinh and asked him to bring the horse a bucket of water. The horse plunged his head into the feed bin. Lam returned to the wagon, lifted out a mess tin that he had brought along for the trip full of salt-poached shrimp, a handful of angel hair vermicelli, and vegetables wrapped in a banana leaf.

"Come on, Suong, put a pot on the fire."

"I don't have any onions or any lard at home. Yesterday, I spent all day preparing food for Hung."

"I don't need it. A shrimp soup with angel-hair is better without fat. All I need are some *hao* leaves to season it," Lam said as he washed the vegetables and cut them into strips, as thin and fine as tobacco. He brought the soup to a boil, waited until the crabmeat rose to the surface in a reddish foam, then tossed the herbs in and lowered the heat. The herbs simmered, turning from dark green to emerald, in the steamy broth.

"Do you have any chilies?" he asked Suong.

I forgot to buy some."

"It's okay," he said, then ran out to the wagon and opened a jar full of chilies marinated in oil, just tiny, thin, red chilies like wild banana flowers—the kind that burned and shredded your tongue.

"Let's eat while it's hot," he said, glancing at Suong. "You look a bit pale. You probably haven't eaten anything since last night, right? You've got to be ready for the trip tomorrow. The paved road only lasts for a short stretch. After that it's all boulders and mountain roads. The horse's back is going to make you dizzy."

Lam dished the vermicelli soup into three bowls. They ate in silence. Suong felt pangs of hunger wrench her gut. Lam had guessed right. Yesterday, she'd only had a bowl of tea. The hot vermicelli soup was like food out of some fairy tale, just like Lam's devotion to her family. Once, Lam had been just one of six friends who came to their underground shelter for tea and the caramelized peanut Cu Do candy. During the war, Cu Do candy from Duc Tho district in Ha Tinh province was a gift people often offered in the villages and provinces of central Vietnam. You could make that caramel candy yourself, all you needed was a bit of charcoal and a metal pot.

Everyone in the troupe loved Lam. It wasn't just his talent on stage, but also his sense of humor. On their free nights, when the troupe was between shows, Hung's shelter became a gathering place. Everyone liked to come by, even the provincial officials. All they had was a makeshift lamp that ran on kerosene and salt, a teapot, and a few pieces of Cu Do candy. But an essential accompaniment to their poor snacks was the rambling story, and Lam was among the best storytellers, so fine that Hung had affectionately given him the title "His Excellency, Mr. Humor." The friendships that had bloomed in the depths of the undergrounds, that they had believed would last forever, vanished like smoke when Hung lost his position, and especially after he became "the accomplice of counterrevolutionaries who organize escapes by boat." The only person who came back to see him, to offer a hand in sympathy, was Mr. Humor.

Lam finished eating first. He poured himself a glass of water, rinsed his mouth, and lay down on the sofa. "I'm going to sleep."

Before anyone could utter a word, he was snoring. Suong was familiar with Lam's miraculous gift from their war days. Their road trips had lasted months, and they had crossed thousands of miles on foot, moving between regions. There often wasn't time to rest before their performances, and the troupe was tortured by lack of sleep. Their faces went pale, their cheeks hollowed; only Lam seemed untouched. His clown act and his solo usually opened and closed the show, so between curtains he would slip into the corner of an underground or the stage and announce: "I'm going to sleep." Then he would cover his face with his papier-mâché clown hat and fall into a deep sleep. Lam also used to snore, but luckily it was drowned out by the singing and music. When the actor who preceded him was preparing to leave the stage, Lam would somehow snap awake—no one woke him, not even an alarm clock—and slip out of whatever corner he was sleeping in, dust off his costume, and walk on stage, wiggling his long nose in a way that made the audience explode with laughter.

"He sleeps easily, doesn't he?" Vinh murmured.

"You get some sleep, too, little brother."

"No, you go ahead. I'll watch the wagon and the horse. I'm not going on the trip, so I can sleep as much as I like tomorrow," Vinh said. At five o'clock, Lam sat up and went to wake Suong. "Let's go! You've got fifteen minutes to wash up while I pump some water and harness the horse. We'll leave as soon as the radio begins the last set of calisthenics." He walked out into the courtyard, stretching and cracking a few joints. Suong ran into the bathroom to change after first handing Vinh the supplies to load into the wagon. She realized her brother was just her height; it was a pity he hadn't inherited their father's stature.

As the wagon left, Vinh stood watching, following it with his eyes until it turned the corner and disappeared.

The long, gray solitary road unfurled to the horizon; it was the only paved stretch of road in the whole province. Later, after the turn in the road, it would all be long paths through barren mountains, then hills littered with jagged boulders. Space cloaked the dunes, the wild hills seemed to stand stiff in the bewitching silence. The sun blazed, as if consuming itself, leaving only a gnarled block of molten silver that threw off arrows of blinding, metallic light, a prism of dazzling shards. Some were as clear as crystal, revealing the watery vapors that rose from the scorched earth, others like malevolent shooting stars presaging battles among the spirit world.

Suong clutched the shawl, pulled it over her head to shield her eyes from the light. In front of her, Lam's shadow filled the arched door to the wagon; he had changed from the black sweater and soldier's fatigues he had worn the night before into white khakis. In his new clothes he seemed taller and his wide-brimmed hat made him look like a jockey or a hotel porter.

As if sensing her gaze, Lam turned around. "See how fast a man can change his appearance?" Suong said nothing.

"A man has many sides . . . Life too," Lam continued. "Think of what has happened as part of life, and then don't think at all anymore. Fate . . . Men may sometimes escape it, though just barely, but for women . . . that's for heaven to decide. . . .

> *"Those meant to roll in dust shall roll in dust,*
> *Those meant to reign on high shall reign on high"*

The famous verse from the *Tale of Kieu;* now, finally, Suong understood. She stretched her numbed legs onto the rattan sacks packed with food, remembering another star-filled sky on another windy autumn night, her father lying on his back in the courtyard, gazing up at the stars. She must have been only three years old; she would climb like a kitten onto his chest. All around them, trees swayed in the wind; fish scales stuck to the nets hung on wooden poles, glittering like fireflies; bats darted through space. Suong would nestle against her father and stare, fascinated, at the world around her. That bare chest had been a refuge, a vantage point from which she saw the universe as a familiar, reassuring presence. Without his soothing voice, his breathing, the familiar tickle of his beard when she rubbed her face against his, she might never have felt this way. Those trees swaying in the night, the fishing nets draped in space, the flight of bats—all of this would have been a world filled with dark mysteries and ghosts. Now she feared life, this life without Hung.

> *Where have you gone on this foggy day?*
> *Leaving me alone,*
> *Under the empty sky, at the crossroads?*

Even this song, Hung had taught her. When she first sang it, her heart had raced; she trembled under his gaze, giddy with tenderness. She had sung it without understanding, like a bird heralds the dawn. Absence, solitude; now, she understood these emotions, and the old melody came back to her, note by note. Yes, her life had been like one long journey with neither a starting point nor a destination, an endless road that had no known source, no end in sight. Everything seemed to float, weightless around her. She had never needed to think before, to calculate; Hung had been the one who decided everything, for their art as well as for their life. His voice still echoed in her brain:

Let it go for twelve beats, then begin the first note after the silence of the thirteenth beat. Let's take it again. Don't turn this into opera. Trust your instincts.

Interpreting a new song, choosing a new dress—she had relied on his judgment for everything. His gaze was her center, her anchor, the familiar sun that illuminated her eyes and face. She had created an entire universe in that light. Now, even in that sweltering afternoon, the world seemed lonely and cold, and she, torn from its orbit, frantically whirling, weightless, directionless. A shiver ran up her spine, and Suong hurriedly pulled the shawl back over her head so she wouldn't see the windswept reeds, the endless sand dunes, the stagnant coppery blue ponds, and their reflections, the ravens that flew up from abandoned graves. Under the canopy of her shawl, she could almost see the dense, starry sky of her past, her lost world. But the harsh sunlight blazed through the cloth, stinging her eyes. She felt feverish, as if her veins had swollen in the stifling heat. The horse's jerky rhythms made her gut churn, and with each plodding step the bile rose from her stomach, making her nauseous. She hadn't had her period in over two months. Now she felt the pangs . . .

"Brother Lam!" She clapped her hand to her mouth, but the vomit had risen. Suong grabbed her throat to stop herself Lam pulled the wagon to the side of the road, lifted her down, and waited until she had emptied her stomach. Then he brought out a canteen he had kept under the hay, out of the heat, and offered it to her. "Here, drink something. And wash your face. Then you should get some sleep so you can regain your strength."

She took a gulp of water. Tears sprang to her eyes.

"Oh, Brother Lam, I must have done something in a previous life to suffer like this!"

He helped her back up into the wagon, pulled a cover over her. "Oh, Suong, please spare me. Just like a woman. Get some sleep. We've still got a long ways to go."

Suong cried to herself. The thin shawl couldn't shield her heart from dread. Her body went hot and cold; the memory of her daughter, who she had left with Auntie Tuong, tormented her. Now that tiny, pretty face haunted her: *Da Hai*, born on the beach, in the middle of a stormy night, as they were fleeing, during a military operation. Hung had helped bring Da Hai into the world and he was the one who had given her the name "Sea Night" in remembrance.

"Stop, stop!" Lam shouted, reigning in the horse. The wagon rocked and swayed a moment, then shuddered to a halt. He drew in his breath and let his whip down hard on the horse's head. "Stop idiot, are you deaf!?" he shrieked. The horse balked and shivered, shook its mane, then stilled.

Suong threw the shawl off her head and grasped the side of the wagon, trying to gain her balance. Space seemed to sway around her, bursting with tiny gold and silver stars. But these were not the familiar stars of her safe, familiar world. She shuddered from fear, a fear of the unknown that ran in the sweat that streamed from her pores, leaving her body wet, icy. She clung tightly to the edge of the wagon with both hands now, bracing herself against the jolts and bumps of the road.

"Suong! Careful!" It was Lam's voice. His two hands massaged her shoulders, their warmth penetrating her skin, soothing her nerves, like a breath of life passing through her. She opened her eyes. Lam was looking down at her, frantic.

"You must be careful, Suong! You're going to get sick. And you simply can't right now . . . you've got to go on . . . We've got work to do . . . please, try to keep going."

Lam waited until she was lucid before he jumped down off the wagon.

"You stay and rest," Lam said. "I'm going to give the horse some water, a few handfuls of paddy. You see that turn ahead of us? After that pass, it's all mountains. If the horse is hungry going into that he's going to weep tears of blood." Then he picked up two buckets and hauled them over to a bog clogged with reeds by the side of the road, rolled up his pants, and waded in up to his knees. He swung the bucket into the deepest part, but only came up with half a bucketful. When he stepped out, his calves were covered with leeches. He set the bucket down, spat into his palms, and started to pull them off, hurling them onto the road. Starved for blood, the leeches clung to him; every time he pulled one off, blood spurted and streamed down his legs.

"Wash your legs, Lam. It's horrible to look at!"

"No, I've got to let it dry. Imprisoned water is dangerous."

Imprisoned. The word reminded her of Hung. He was a prisoner now, living among other prisoners somewhere along this deserted road clogged with wild grasses and reeds, somewhere in the middle of those steep mountains beyond. Her husband, her love, her entire world, was imprisoned there.

• • •

They arrived about two o'clock . . . or had it been three? She couldn't remember clearly. The rocky, bumpy road had been torture, leaving her mute with pain. Her gut wrenched, twisting with each jolt of the horse, every time it stepped in a pothole, or the wheel of the wagon crashed against a rock. She had already vomited everything in her. Her throat and tongue were bitter. The sky was a dull, sallow yellow, like the bile and saliva she had spat out. One hand on her stomach, the other gripping the side of the wagon, she repeated her mantra: *You can't get sick; Lam says you can't get sick.*

She had lost all sense of time and space. All she could remember was a flock of wild game hens flying up over the wagon. Then, Lam saying that he liked to hunt, that when it was all over he would take her and Hung hunting back in his mountain village; how they would go walking, visit the forests where they had once entertained the troops, how he would teach her to roast chickens and make chicken porridge with wild herbs.

Lam suddenly pulled the wagon to a halt: In the distance, two men, their heads shaved, slipped furtively through the field of reeds at the edge of the road. At first, he had thought they were bandits. Then, he realized they were fugitives from the prison camp: These men weren't attacking, they were fleeing. The wagon returned to its regular rhythm. Suong didn't hear anything anymore, just clutched the side, slipping into a deep sleep, a netherworld of dark shadows. She vaguely remembered the wagon stopping, Lam saying something; she couldn't hear what, couldn't open her mouth to speak. Then Lam spreading a mat out for her in the bottom of the wagon, how she had fallen onto it like a sack of rice.

When she awoke, she found herself huddled in a ball in the bottom of the wagon, covered with a thin blanket. Outside, a milk white sky, and fog that hung over the fields of reeds, tumbling like an avalanche of clouds into the ravines. She shivered. This was a godforsaken place out of a horror story, nothing like the peaceful mountain hamlet of her childhood. The landscape was wild, desolate, filled with dense stands of reeds; huge slugs that clung to the branches of the trees; gnarled, ancient tree roots so strong they broke rocks in their grip. The lush emerald green of leaves mixed with the indigo blue shadows of the forest, turning to black. Dwarfed by the parasols of trees as tall as buildings, their horse stood nibbling grass, looking like a small, lost goat. At the edge of the clearing, looming like giant cacti, were thorn bushes with bulging, hoary gray trunks, fringed with orchid-shaped blooms, their petals swollen, as if gorged with blood. Suong trembled, pulled off her shawl, and stepped down from the wagon. Lam was seated on the ground, under the wagon, scraping dried blood off his legs with a pocketknife. Without his hat, in the eery, green light of dawn, he looked suddenly aged.

"Why don't you get some sleep?" Suong asked.

"And have them steal our food? No thanks. When we get there, I'll try and catch some." Lam shook his head.

"You're too cautious. Who would steal these lousy provisions?"

"Listen, Suong, I know more about all this than you do. We don't need to be paranoid, but you've got to be on your guard, all the same." He pointed to a huge gate about a hundred yards from them, made from planks of wood that had been meticulously sanded and polished. Above it was a sign with letters scrawled in lime, blurred by rain and wind: REEDUCATION CAMP K41. To the right of the gate, four wagons had been parked head to head, and two pairs of horses grazed nearby. Their riders lay slumped on the grass, sleeping. There must have been about thirty people, their plastic mats laid out on the ground, held down with bowls. The men were snoring loudly, mouths agape. The women were curled up under their shawls to protect themselves from the chill of fog and dew. At the edge of the clearing, two old women were huddled together, preparing breakfast. They had piled stones up to make a hearth and were shredding up old newspapers that they had kept inside their clothes. Then they lit the fire, their cheeks pressed to the ground as they blew on branches still damp from the fog.

They toiled with unusual patience, as silently and stealthily as ghosts. Suong felt her bitterness subside: She was not alone, not the only one suffering in this world. She stared at the white-haired old women: What if Hung were to spend his whole life in prison? Would she be able to make it through the years, her hair going white, her skin covered with dark spots? Her life would ebb away, punctuated by the long road trips, nights spent sleeping on the grass like this, a shawl wrapped around her head. Other people would count the years in Lunar New Year parties, and she by the number of signatures in a prison guest-book.

"Brother Lam, how long are they going to keep him in there?"

"I don't know. Who would ever have imagined that one day Hung would land himself in prison? But I think he'll be luckier than the others."

"Luckier? What do you mean?"

"Because of you. You see, in the middle of the night, when you were asleep, I had time to do a lot of thinking. This is a pit, and who-ever enters it either rots away or dies. Not just the prisoners, but the jailers too. They are also in a kind of prison. But thanks to their unhap-piness, we can achieve our ends."

Puzzled, Suong looked at him, her eyes questioning. Lam's face, usually so comic, had turned oddly severe. He stared off into the dis-tance where the fog was lifting to reveal small thatch huts clustered under the trees.

"It's not so hard to figure out. Your singing can save Hung. Here in the jungle, there's no law higher than the hearts of men. They're just people, and they have a heart there, somewhere. If you sing for them, make them happy, they will help you free your husband."

"Sing for them? These jailers, these . . ." Suong remembered Pris-oner Mama's words: *They beat them every day in prison; that's their daily fare, like a bowl of rice. The truth is never what the officials say . . .*

Lam ignored the revolt in her question and kept staring, calmly, into the distance. "I know," he said softly. "That's precisely why you must sing for them." He looked at her, the wrinkles and worry lines on his face deepening. She studied his eyes, waited. Then, after a long moment, he continued.

"I've thought a long time. Heaven gave us ten years on the stage during the war, singing for the people. Why shouldn't we use this talent to save ourselves? You'll sing, I'll do my one-man comic show. Between the two of us, we've got enough strength to make it through a few nights. We've got to get Hung out of here—whatever the price. It's no paradise in there, Suong; in fact, it's not far from hell."

People had begun to stir in the clearing near the prison gate. They were pulling their bags and belongings off the wagons, dividing them up. An old man brought water back from the stream in a tin cup. His family crowded around him, all of them dipping in a towel to wash their faces. Then they gathered around the pots of rice the two old women had gotten up early to cook. A young woman, about thirty years old, unfurled a banana leaf shriveled by the heat of the fire, tossing out a pile of food and seasonings: dried meat, salt, sesame powder. After she had finished, she returned to the wagon and pulled out a pile of plastic bowls and spoons, and distributed them. Then they all sat down and began to eat. These people's every gesture was disciplined, familiar: They must have known each other for a long time, from previous visits. Over time they had become like a clan, an association.

Lam returned to the wagon to get the gas stove and a can of oil. As he poured oil into the stove, he asked Suong: "Do you know what kind of prisoners those people there have come to visit? Boat people. All boat people. Most of them have probably come all the way from the southern cities and towns. The reeducation camps there are full, overflowing, so the authorities have had to send some of the prisoners here." Lam set a pot on the tiny gas stove and began to make a soup out of rice vermicelli and strips of dried meat. He didn't have fresh onions, but he had brought dried onions and some pepper. As she watched his agile hands, Suong thought to herself. *What would I have done without him these last few days?*

It was daylight by the time they finished eating. Suddenly, from inside the prison camp, a gong sounded, reverberating through the mountains. Lam told Suong to follow the other people into the camp; he would wait outside. When she got permission for the visit, he would carry the provisions into the camp.

Suong pulled her scarf tightly over her face and walked toward the gate, merging with the crowd of people laden with sacks and bags who pushed and pressed each other toward the two opening doors. They all craned their necks, their eyes fixed on the widening crack between the gates, as if they could make out the silhouette, or the face of their loved ones on the other side, in that sad, cold, empty space. No one spoke. Everyone was orderly, disciplined, like kids doing penance for some misdemeanor. After a few minutes, a guard climbed laboriously up the guard tower, flipped a latch, and the gate swung open, the doors creaking on their hinges. The guard looked away as he pushed them open; the dull, sad, boring faces of the visitors were of no interest to him. He fastened the doors open, climbed listlessly back into the watchtower, and sat down on a high stool. A leaden face, rough, pimply cheeks, narrow, vacant eyes. Who knew what he thought about from dawn to dusk, day after day, month after month, year after year?

A voice out of nowhere: "First time you've come here?"

Suong turned around. It was one of the old women she had seen cooking rice at dawn. The woman asked the question without meeting Suong's eyes, looking straight ahead, one hand clutching a basket, the other a heavy sack slung over her tiny shoulder. She was almost as old as the Prisoner Mama; her temples were covered with dark age spots, her gray hair was gathered back into a tight chignon fastened with a wooden stick. She seemed brave, clever, without the severity of the Prisoner Mama, but Suong could tell she was forged from the same steel, the kind they used to cool three times in horse's blood.

"Yes, this is the first time," Suong replied gently, admiration in her voice. "Can I help you with that sack?"

"No thanks. You're as green as a leaf, if you aren't sick then you must be pregnant. Just worry about yourself. Hurry up, we're almost at the door." Suong looked in the direction of the woman's gaze: a long, narrow shed with a thatch roof; the kind of house she had seen a lot during the war, like soldiers' barracks or shelters for young volunteers. These houses were built with wood pillars and beams and covered with bamboo leaves. They were grouped—not in threes or fives according to tradition—but in seven or eight, even twelve houses. They came to the first room; it had a sign that read: VISITORS' RECEPTION. The crude, painted wooden door to the room was smeared with sweaty finger-prints. A rifle had been slung carelessly on the back of the door, its owner probably nearby. Visitors streamed in, taking turns sitting on rows of low wooden benches, piling their sacks and bags filled with provisions at the foot of the cement walls. Facing the first row of benches, about two yards away, was a desk, only half varnished, as if someone had lost interest halfway through the job. A beer bottle cap lay in the middle of the desk, belly up.

The old woman, seated next to Suong, fumbled in her satchel and pulled out a ready-made betel quid.

"Will they let us see our relatives?" Suong whispered.

The old woman popped the quid in her mouth. "Depends. If there's no particular problem, they let you." Then, she pointed. "Over there . . . after all the forms are finished, if they give you permission, you go to the next room." Then she stopped, because the prison official was coming.

Wearing a green security police uniform, meeting no one's eyes, he walked straight to the table, set down a thick pile of dossiers, pulled out the chair, and flipped open his list of names. Without once lifting his bald head to the anxious crowd gathered in front of him, he began tapping his pen down the columns of names.

"Now, what's today?" He flung this question into the void. The crowd of visitors, their pleading eyes riveted on his every gesture, com-peted to reply: "Yes, sir, officer, yes, today's the fifteenth of July, West-ern calendar, third day of the sixth month, our Lunar calendar."

"Lunar, Western, bullshit . . . whatever," he grumbled, then pulled a pale blue dossier out of his pile and snapped. "Now, get your papers out and come up here, in order."

The old woman turned to Suong: "Where are your papers? Give them to me. I'll submit them with mine." Suong handed the woman the authorizations from the police, the Communist Youth League, and her identity papers.

A door slammed. A rustling sound. A young man, about twenty-five, entered the room, pulled the rifle down from the door. He wore a black-striped shirt over army pants, and hunting boots caked with mud. A slight moustache over his lips, he was obviously some provincial hotshot. He chewed peanuts, spitting out the shells as he paced around the room. He slung the rifle over his shoulder and, instead of going out, walked up to the desk: "Want some peanuts?"

The bald man didn't look up. "Not for me thanks. Hurts my throat."

"Uh-huh," the young man agreed, but continued spitting and spraying peanut shells around the room.

"We were out all night. Not a single animal. As soon as we got back to the camp, the commander crashed out. Fast asleep. I had to go to the kitchen to find something to eat. All I found was this bag of peanuts."

"Last time you guys shot a monkey, didn't you? Wasn't it ten pounds or something?"

"Ten pounds? You're tired again. *Sixteen* pounds, my monkey. Enough to make a huge salad and a pot of porridge. The whole camp got to chow down on that."

"Yeah, monkey meat is delicious, but that pimpled skin . . . horrible to look at . . . like a badly burned baby . . . Next, Mr. Tran Van Dan."

"Yes, present!"

"Permission granted. Last time was the eleventh of January, right?"

"Correct sir."

"Sign here."

"Yes sir."

"Go to the next room."

The guard closed the folder, got up, and opened the door from the visitors' room to the next one. Through the open door, Suong could see a huge room, the size of seven or eight rooms—it could easily hold a hundred people.

"Oh, thank you sir, I'm so grateful sir," Old Tran Dan, bowed, his beard glistening with beads of sweat. Keeping his back hunched over, obsequious, he dragged his sack of provisions into the next room. The muscles in his chin quivered with happiness.

"Mrs. Do Thi Thu . . ."

"Yes sir, present."

"Mrs. Le Thi Tham . . ."

"Yes sir, present."

The people took turns carrying their goods into the next room. Little by little, the rows of benches emptied.

"Mrs. Nguyen Thi Han . . ."

"Present." The old woman with the gray hair stood up, as alert as a chipmunk, her eyes glistening. She had waited six months for this moment. She had imagined it every evening when she tore the page with the day's date off the wall calendar, throwing the day that had just ended into her past. Under her heavy load of sacks and bags, her shoulders were emaciated, her bones pointy, her neck as thin as a sparrow's, crisscrossed with veins. Teetering, a bag in one hand, the other gripping the sack slung over her back, she advanced step by step, trying to keep it all from falling, like a tightrope walker.

Suong wasn't thinking of anything, aware of anything, except this fierce, tiny old woman.

"Pham Mai Suong . . ."

She stood up. She didn't have time to finish her sentence when the man in the black-striped shirt walked up to her.

"You're Pham Mai Suong?" he asked brusquely.

"Yes."

The man didn't wait to hear the rest of her answer; he strode back to the desk and grabbed the papers from the bald man's hands.

"So you're with the provincial artistic troupe? The famous singer?"

He stared at her, partly stunned, partly curious. So this woman, floating in all these layers of clothes like some kind of Buddhist nun, was the most famous singer of the five central provinces? He struggled to regain his composure. "Wait here for a moment," he told her. The bald official looked up, surprised.

"You handle the other cases. I'll be back right away." The young man said, grabbing his rifle as he ran out the door.

The sun was setting. Patches of golden sunlight filtered through the leaves, dappling the walls of the room. A group of prisoners marching in single file across the courtyard outside trudged past the window, pale and gaunt. A few of them seemed overweight, but the heavier they were, the sicker they looked. Here, men lost the look of human beings: Those vacant eyes, faces as shriveled as dried fruit, hands that swung limply, heads silently bent over—there was something rotten in them. Two stiff, hulking guards armed with machine guns kept watch, their hands on the triggers.

Suong watched, petrified, until the last prisoner had disappeared behind the barracks. Would the plan Lam had imagined unfold like some comic play arranged by heaven and hell? Was this luck or humiliation for her? She couldn't say. Hung's face, his gentle, laughing eyes, haunted her. How he used to kiss her at the oddest moments, when she was rehearsing, or singing a lullaby to the baby, or cooking a meal. Like a cat, he would lick the nape of her neck, making her hair stick to her skin: *There, look, there's a string of notes on your neck.* With that naturally flirtatious voice.

The hotshot in the black-striped shirt returned. Without the rifle. He kicked his mud-coated boots on the steps to clean them off and then turned to Suong. "Follow me, miss," he announced enthusiastically.

Seeing her silent, hesitant, he continued warmly. "Please, follow me. My boss is going to receive you personally."

Panicked, desperately trying to recall Lam's plan, Suong didn't have time to reply when the man insisted: "Let's go . . . is there some problem?"

"I've come with someone."

"He'll have to wait!"

She shook her head. "It's not possible."

"Everything is possible here. I'll order him to wait."

"No . . . he's my colleague."

"Colleague?"

"He's the soloist of the troupe."

"You mean Lam, the clown?"

"Yes."

"Why that's great!" the man roared with joy, "I'll invite him in. He's the man seated on the wagon, right?" Without even waiting for her reply, he ran straight out into the prison courtyard. A moment later, Lam's wagon rolled past the gates. Lam hitched the horse to a tree and followed the young man. There wasn't a trace of worry or anxiety on his face; his eyebrows and long nose twitched. Seeing Suong's surprise, his eyes twinkled, stretching to his temples in a wide grin. "Shall we go, Miss Suong?" His voice was calm, neutral, his face guileless, as if he happened to be escorting her into a game that fate had prepared for them.

Night fell. The rumbling of motors rose suddenly from the deep shadows of the jungle, near the foot of the mountain. This was a special night for the reeducation camp. More than a hundred employees and guards raced about to set up a generator run by a forty-horsepower gas engine. There was no electricity in the camp. Every year, they had permission to use the generator for a few special occasions—Tet Lunar New Year, National Day, visits from international delegations or some high-ranking dignitary who came to inspect the camp, award one of the officials, or amnesty one of the prisoners. Tonight was extraordinary; this visit was an unexpected pleasure, and now the commander of the camp had promised to extend it for three or four nights running.

They lifted the canvas cover off the generator: It was covered with a thick coat of greasy dust, tough as a water buffalo hide. They had to drag it far away before spreading it on the ground so people wouldn't choke from the dust. The generator hadn't been used for ages, and it sputtered and spat like a drowning man. The light it projected varied between scarlet red and murky yellow. A few prisoners requisitioned for the occasion huddled around the machine. A guard, standing near, hands on his buttocks, watched the crowd.

"Reporting sir, the machine is too dirty."

"What can we do?"

"We've got to clean all the parts, oil them, then reassemble it."

"How much time do you need?"

"About three hours."

"That's impossible; it'll be too late for the show."

"Uh, yes sir."

"Find a way!" he barked. "What do you have, a bunch of stones in your brains? Do whatever you want, but get me light by six o'clock!"

"Yes, but . . ."

Standing behind the curtain on a makeshift stage, Suong watched the prisoners huddled around the generator. In their faces, their eyes, their way of speaking, there was a strange terror. Human terror, fear of man. Birds, wild beasts, domestic animals, never show this kind of fear. Hung, had he felt this since he had been here? She couldn't imagine him in this wretched role.

Light streamed forth amidst cries of joy from the crowd. Suong was suddenly in a room bathed with dazzling light. She closed her eyes, waited a minute until she was used to the glare, then let out a long sigh and opened them slowly. She was going to sing tonight whether she liked it or not. And she would have to sing gloriously because that was the only way up the mountain.

"Let's start . . ." Lam's voice suddenly rose behind her back. He had been chatting with the guards and had just arrived.

"Go ahead and put on your makeup. And make you sure you put it on carefully . . . for me, it's simple, just a few strokes of greasepaint and that's it."

He pulled out a stool for Suong. The room was tiny, there was only space for a table and a stool. This room was also reserved for the electricians who manned the projectors and spotlights on festival nights. On the table, there was a mirror in a silver frame and an open makeup case—these were from the warehouse. Among the boat people imprisoned here there were lots of students and young women from the towns. Their personal effects had become like war booty for the prison, but the loot was hard to use. This evening was a precious opportunity to bring out all sorts of luxury goods that had been moldering away in a corner of their warehouse. When Suong opened a shell-shaped powder case, a heady perfume wafted through the room. Lam bent over it, inhaling deeply.

Suong spread the base makeup on her face, lightly powdering her forehead. In the mirror, two red eyes stared back at her, distraught. How she had aged, grown thinner in just a few days! Her pale, dazed face seemed to belong to someone else. This wasn't the face of a woman but of a child abandoned along the roadside.

"Finish up," Lam murmured softly. "Hurry, the crowd is waiting." He seemed to read her thoughts. "Tonight, in this godforsaken reeducation camp lost in the jungle, we've got to rival the town theater."

Suong didn't reply. She spread a final veil of pink powder over her eyelids, examined herself one last time in the mirror. The pale young nun in baggy clothes was dead. Now the woman facing her was *the queen of the stage, the nightingale from the lands of exile.* She knew that she would become a stranger the moment she emerged from the shadow of the curtains, and the harsh light of the spots was on her, as soon as the applause and laughter and tears of the audience washed over her in a magical veil of fog that would transport her, like a boat, out to sea.

"Don't worry Lam, I know what to do under the stage lights."

Lam didn't say anything. He looked her over. "You're very beautiful. Now it's my turn."

Suong got up, turning over the makeup table to Lam. The clown's face slowly took shape in a few strokes of his nimble fingers. He covered his face with base makeup and powder with the quick, precise, experienced gestures of a caramel maker stirring his chopsticks in a pot of sugar, as if it wasn't a face he was painting but an inanimate paste that he kneaded as he liked.

Suong cried out "My God, what are you doing to your face, pounding it like that?"

Lain laughed. "Clowns have thick skin, not like you princesses."

Suong hesitated a moment. "Lam?"

"Yes?"

"Do you think they'll let us see Hung?"

"Our sack of provisions got through without inspection. They even sent someone to deliver it to Hung directly."

"But I want . . ."

"Don't ask that question. I don't want to ask questions that they don't like or don't want to answer. Listen, Suong, why can't you understand? Do you think they'd enjoy seeing you embrace a prisoner while they're wasting away, frustrated, because they're not getting it? I want to see Hung too, he's my friend. So I can imagine what you, his wife must . . . But it would serve no purpose. Grit your teeth and let's try to spoil them so we can get Hung out of here." Lam tossed the powder puff on the table, took Suong's hand, squeezed it a moment, then let it go. "When I was a little boy, my mother took me to visit . . ."

But Suong wasn't listening anymore. Her nostrils quivered and stung. She looked at the ground, trying to forget everything, holding back her tears. They were going to go on stage, so they didn't have the right to blur their makeup. Through the dirty red curtains she could see the crowd standing, packed into the prison courtyard. The administrators, the guards, the "progressive" prisoners who were rewarded with the perks of the camp. The courtyard was dark with people, all the way to the walls of the enclosure, not an empty space. Some of the spectators were seated on high platforms that they used inside the building. Suong watched them, curious, haunted by the Prisoner Mama's words. There were shadowy, lackluster faces; hard, brutal faces; sluggish, dull faces; sad, resentful faces, like those of a spurned lover forced to bide his time in a monastery. Why were they doing this job? To spend their lives counting the grim, joyless days in this godforsaken jungle? To bring their whip down on the heads of prisoners? To humiliate other men, out of habit or for sadistic pleasure, to die sometimes, battered and broken in some deep ravine, killed by prisoners in search of revenge, to . . . ? She couldn't possibly understand what the Prisoner Mama had recounted, but seeing the crowd on the other side of the curtain, she knew that their world wasn't just violent, barbarous, it was also sad, an infinite, torturous, unbearable sadness. She suddenly felt a wave of pity . . . but for whom? The prisoners, or their jailers? She didn't know anymore.

The bell rang, piercing, strident, long, insistent, as if it wasn't just to announce the beginning of the show but to take revenge on the silence that had shrouded the mountains and the jungle for so long now. The curtains parted, pulled by old ropes on squeaking wheels. Lam placed a hand on Suong's shoulder. "Now, Comrade . . . onto the battlefield."

The national anthem, half ironic from the lips of this clown, gave Suong a start. She stepped out onto the stage. Applause exploded from all sides like firecrackers, and it was oddly warm, lasting too long, as if they wanted it to last all night, as if, long deprived of this habit, they had waited for her arrival to quench their thirst. Suong stood straight and tall, a reed in the halo of light. She didn't know why they had called her "the queen of the stage," but she knew that this shimmering space gave her an extraordinary power over them. Out of habit, she looked straight ahead into the distance, there where the crowd melted into a dark, shapeless mass. This was a trick Hung had taught her early on, a way to focus the attention of the audience. But at the edge of the stage, a face stood out of the crowd, attracting her gaze. A dark, hardened face, with nostrils dilated, that froze, mesmerized. The face split into two: one, ferocious, used to whipping until it drew blood, ripping into the flesh of the prisoners; the other paralyzed with terror under the avenging flash of a knife. She suddenly felt her knees go weak, as if she would faint. But a professional reflex made her stretch her hand forward to regain her balance and the gesture was like a signal, calling for the mad outpouring of applause to stop. Her stage instincts had pulled her from the brink of her nightmarish vision, and she straightened and moved forward, step by step, into the dazzling light.

She knew the moment had come to forget the crowd. She was adrift now on the open sea, tossed by infinite waves. She was empty, and yet from this emptiness sprang a faraway music, a melody that inspired a thousand others, and suddenly, out of the depths of her soul, a voice thick with fog, rose as if from a lake, lost in the endless whisper of reeds, from the deserted hills, as frail and melancholy as the wail of a monochord.

From the wings of the theater, Lam watched, motionless, moved by this voice. For years now, the theater, dance, folk songs had all bored him—everything except this voice. He remembered Suong's first performance, one icy winter night during the war when a cape of salty sea mist hung over the mountains, ravines, and forests. They were performing in a cave for three engineering platoons. Torches burned in place of oil lamps, wind swirled in gusts down into the caverns, like the icy breath of some hellish monster. The spectators were riveted, mesmerized by the haunting voice of this young woman. From that moment, Lam knew that this voice would survive time. Now, again, the crowd assembled here in the prison courtyard listened, breathless, to every sound that fell from her lips. As if they could cast off their bodies of flesh and blood into the shadows of jungle, take flight toward another image of themselves. Suong's lips slaked some thirst in their desiccated, wizened hearts. A childlike voice, a cry into a lonely soul that reminded them of home: a roof over their heads, a hearth, covers to be pulled back, a lamp waiting to be lit. Like a flame from the center of the earth, her voice licked at these unsteady souls that were just waiting to be set on fire. Suong's eyes were immense: sometimes shimmering with stars, sometimes shrouded in fog and mist, they tortured these souls, fascinated them. Every time she took a breath, Lam could see the veins on her neck pulse violently.

She's exhausted . . . but she's never sung this well. Despair, like happiness, can sometimes make people extremely seductive. So here we are: a pregnant woman and a clown come to visit a prisoner, and we end up gritting our teeth as we entertain his jailers. Heaven is the worst old bastard of all . . .

Lam stepped back behind the curtain, picked up a pot of black greasepaint and daubed a beauty spot the size of a coin on his left cheek. It was his hallmark, the sign of the cynical jester, a clown in the service of Fate.

The next day Lam woke at about eight-thirty. The performance had lasted until one o'clock in the morning. Suong had gone ahead to sleep, but Lam stayed up to eat *cháo* rice porridge and chat with the guards until almost three in the morning. Still, he felt fresh when he woke. He went to Suong's room. She was awake, pensive, watching the prisoners as they filed past her window. They were carrying sugar cane through the courtyard. About twenty wheelbarrows screeched across the gravel path, a prisoner pulling each one. Following them, drawn by oxen, were five wagons heaped with sugar cane. They all moved toward the west, where the ovens spat out fumes from the bottom of ravines.

"Were you able to sleep?" Lam asked her.

"Yes."

"Do you feel less tired?"

"Yes, I'm better."

"Try to bear it for a few days. Then, everything will pass. I'm going to get some breakfast for you."

"There's no need. I'm not hungry."

"Even fermented rice rots if you don't replenish it. Don't forget you've still got a heavy debt with this world."

Lam got up and walked toward the kitchen. They hadn't even been there a whole day, but already he knew every corner of the camp, as if he had once lived there. The prisoner employees, from the cook to the educators, all greeted him warmly, joking with him as if he were an old friend. Ten minutes later, he returned with a plate of sticky rice and an omelet.

"Here Suong, pick up your chopsticks. The omelet is slightly burned, isn't it? But the sticky rice is still hot. The cook must have kept it warm by the stove. This is enough to make us happy, right? People here are fed on rotten fish paste while we eat omelets with sticky rice. Bless the Heavens, bless the Buddha! Your children bow their heads to the ground in thanks."

The mountain fog drifted into the room, cooling their breakfast. Lam made himself a filter coffee and then went to get a glass of hot water for Suong. The reception room, reserved for officials who came to visit the camp, was well equipped. The armoires, the tea chest, and the bed were all made of fine ebony wood, beautifully carved. The cabinet was filled with rows of tea, coffee, cups, and spoons of all sizes, earthenware candy jars filled with candied lotus seeds. But everything was moldy, unmatching, vulgar. Lam opened a few tins of tea and coffee. The odor of mold wafted out.

"People rarely come here. We're among the rare guests. Or are we just miserable beggars? Whatever we are, we're housed in the most luxurious building in the entire camp. All the same, no one can drink moldy coffee. I should've asked for some from the kitchen."

He savored the coffee in tiny sips, like he used to savor the lotus tea during the war, with Suong and Hung in their underground. After a long silence, he looked up. "Drink up, and try to act cheerful. Today they're giving us a tour of the camp. Don't say a word that might offend them. Act as if you're going to see an exhibit in town. You know, our stage is just a tiny space in this world. We play with wooden rifles and swords. But here they don't just use props. This theater of theirs is much more terrifying."

At that moment, a man entered. Lam promptly rose and shook his hand warmly, turning to Suong. "Suong, allow me to introduce the deputy commander in chief of the camp. He leads the troops that patrol the forests and the coastline. Today he's doing us the honor of taking us on a visit of the camp."

Suong nodded in greeting, not knowing what to say. The man bowed, smiling uneasily. He was over fifty, thin, with a squat neck and beady, birdlike eyes—not the eyes of a falcon or a buzzard, but those of a warbler or a woodpecker from the countryside, always on the look-out, frightened. He went outside to wait for them, as if he wanted to give Suong time to change or put on new shoes before going out. When he saw that Suong wasn't doing this, he turned to Lam and whispered in his ear. "You should tell her to put on more clothes. It's really cold down in the ravines."

Lam urged Suong to do this and they left, following the deputy commander. The man walked ahead, saying almost nothing, leading them through workshops where they made wood products, repaired cars, cut stone. They visited a livestock farm and an agricultural plantation.

Once, along the road, Lam dropped back and murmured to Suong: "You see, it's like the old saying: water from rivers, riches from prisons." He quickly rejoined the deputy commander, walking close to him, shoulder to shoulder. A few minutes later they stopped in front of a group of prisoners hauling sugar cane.

"Get a cart ready for our visitors," the deputy commander ordered.

The prisoner who was leading the group laid down his bundle of sugar cane, wiped off the floor of a cart with his scarf, and spread out a piece of sheet plastic.

"There, please step in, cadre." The man crossed his arms, obsequious, and added: "I'll go back on foot. If you please, Mr. Cadre, you can just leave the cart by the sugar cane factory." They stepped into the cart. A young prisoner, about seventeen or eighteen years old, drove them. The ox was robust, pulling the cart rapidly. They drove by a large shed covered with bamboo—it had a sign indicating that it was an infirmary. Suong saw prisoners leaving with two stretchers of corpses covered with torn reed mats. The mats hid the faces, but they were too short to cover the feet. Suong recoiled at the sight of the yellow, wizened feet. She almost cried out, but held back. The sky and the road ahead of her seemed to pitch and sway. The thin horns of the ox seemed to rise out of the shoulders of the prisoner who drove the cart. She thought she was going to faint and fall onto the gravel road.

"Hey, Suong . . ." Lam's warm hand took her arm, pulled him toward her. "Suong, look at the oxen pulling that sugar cane. They're two times the size of the oxen you see down south."

Suong closed her eyes. The ox's four yellow hooves and sharp horns flashed and swirled in her brain. She clutched Lam's hand, hoping some of its warmth and calm would spread to her. "When I was little, I just loved sugar cane factories," Lam continued, his voice booming. "My aunt's sugar cane factory was huge. That charcoal stove burned day and night. I used to hang around, sometimes fall asleep on a pile of sugar cane, waiting for the third watch to taste a bowl of *chè* made with the second water."

That night, the performance began a half hour earlier.

And on the third night, it was the same. The prisoners thronged to hear Suong's voice blasting from the loudspeakers that ringed the camp. Only those prisoners who wasted away in cells—the life sentences and those waiting for execution on death row—couldn't hear them. They were locked into caverns dug out of the rock face of a ravine on the other side of the mountain, facing the sugar cane factory. Suong remembered how, at one point, she had asked the deputy commander why they couldn't visit the other side. Terror had flashed through the man's eyes, and he had replied, almost breathless: "No, no, you can't go over there. It's impossible."

Now she shuddered as she watched the steam rise in jagged zigzags from these undergrounds, thinking that her husband must be there, with the prisoners kept apart from the others.

The performances lasted until one in the morning. Afterward, they would turn off the lights and light the Manson lamps and eat *cháo* and *chè* while talking. Everyone, the commander, the deputy, the educators, the administrators, the cooks, flocked to Lam. They sang, they recited poetry, they listened to him tell dirty stories.

Suong would sleep for a bit, then peep through the half-open door, see the lights, hear the bursts of laughter rise like waves in the night. She knew Lam was an extraordinary storyteller, but she didn't know he had such a large repertoire. She imagined the scene, the men with their jaws dropped, their eyes riveted on Lam.

"Once in a rich province, there was a mandarin famous for his fortune and his talents as a seducer of women. All the great ladies of the neighboring provinces, the duchesses and princesses of the court tried to find excuses—festivals, ceremonies, various events—to meet him on the sly. No one knew how, but a rumor that should have stayed within the red lacquer pavilions leaked out to the people. Soon, everyone knew that the mandarin's 'treasure' wasn't just *five times* as big as an ordinary man's, but was also barbed with *spines!*"

Suong and Lam's performances lasted four nights. On the fifth, there was no show. The commander butchered a cow to celebrate and bid them farewell. They lit three Manson lamps in the courtyard, and the chairs made way for long tables. All afternoon the prisoners received orders to go into the mountains and gather peonies, wild orchids, daisies, and banana flowers to decorate the courtyard. These flowers brightened the space, and even the prisoners' faces, normally so strained and sad, seemed to glow. The head cook demonstrated his talent by making twelve kinds of beef: raw beef marinated in lemon juice and vinegar, stewed with herbs, curried, grilled, wrapped in bacon, simmered with ginger and soybean paste, barbecued with caramel and ginger, marinated with sesame seeds, and so on. And they brought three huge jars of rice wine, twenty-five quarts each.

"You are my guests of honor, so I've ordered that these jars be brought up from the cellars. The best alcohol is reserved for the best of friends." The commander's voice boomed, echoing over the other voices, haughty, ebullient: "This wine, made with tiger gelatin, was brewed right here in the camp. A while ago, we killed three tigers, five bears, and a rhinoceros."

Every word made Suong shiver. It was the first time, since their brief meeting, that she had seen the commander. She noticed how tall, young, and attractive he was. His gestures were controlled and discrete, but every time he looked at her an ocean of male desire seemed to flood his gaze. Every time he laughed, the bricks and tiles around them seemed to shake. This was the booming laugh of an adventurer or a man with a mission. He had bushy eyebrows, flashing eyes, a wide mouth, and a jaw that could have crushed iron. Despite his serene, relaxed bearing, the tense muscles of his neck and massive chest made him look like a heavyweight wrestler.

"In three years, we've emptied fifteen jars of alcohol kept under three yards of stone in our undergrounds. Tonight, I give everyone permission to get drunk."

He strode up and down with long, steady steps, like a wild beast prowls its territory in the jungle. His employees burst out laughing. He laughed too. His eyes stretched to the temples, sparkling with delight, flickering with life. Suong shivered again. She didn't know why, but she was terrified of him. The corners of those eyes, that gaze, those strangely white teeth, that powerful body, as agile as a leopard's . . . everything about him. She didn't remember what Lam had told her, or how he led her to the table, or when he had served her some food. She tried to listen, answer questions, swallow the food Lam and the deputy commander placed in her bowl, but as soon as she could she excused herself and left the banquet table.

The deputy commander accompanied Suong back to the guest room, lit a candle in a bronze candelabra, then prepared tea and withdrew in silence. This man was like a shadow: omnipresent, constantly attentive, mute.

The night was thick, black as charcoal. Not a star. Not a firefly. Not even a will-o'-the-wisp flickering over the rotting grass. In the vast darkness, the courtyard shimmered like the arc of a flare during wartime. Voices, laughter, shouts—happy, boisterous toasts. Yet somewhere here, in the midst of these dark shadows, there were thousands of prisoners. Where was Hung? During the visits, and later on her own walks, she had searched for him with her eyes, but in vain. They had said that half of the prisoners were sent to fell trees in the forests and then transport them back to the camp. They lived in small huts in the middle of the jungle. Was Hung among them? What was he doing now? Felling trees? Harvesting sugar cane and corn? Making charcoal? She didn't dare imagine.

He's a Communist Party member, a cadre, but he "betrayed the country, joined the reactionaries, and tried to flee by sea to oppose socialism. He sullied the honor the Party and the State, damaged their prestige."

That was the verdict that had been read over the radio, blasted over the loudspeakers, through the streets. She knew that it was only because Dam had defended her, and because they still needed her voice, that they hadn't expelled her from the troupe and driven her from their home.

The candle dripped onto the table, staining it with red, waxy tears. Suong stretched out on the bed, pulled the covers over her face. She felt like crying out to someone to help soothe the pain that tortured her. *Who? Who? Who?* Her body went limp, exhausted. She longed to sleep but couldn't seem to close her eyes. *Father, Father, oh, Father* . . . Finally, the tears streamed down her cheeks.

The next day Lam woke her at five o'clock. His face glowed, even though he had stayed up drinking with the camp managers until three o'clock in the morning. He urged her to wash her face and change, then brought her a steaming bowl of chicken rice soup.

"The cook didn't sleep at all last night. He went to get the hen to make you this soup just when I was going off to sleep. Only princesses like you get this kind of attention," Lam said, gathering his belongings.

After a while, when she went out into the courtyard, Suong saw

Lam in the middle of the people who waited to see them off: the deputy commander, the elegant young man with the striped shirt, the head cook, the administrators, the reeducators. The wagon was heaped with gifts. Wooden objects, embroidered pillows, tablets of raw sugar, tiger and bear gelatin, wild honey. And mountains of boxes, packages wrapped in plastic or sycamore leaves. It was as if they had just visited a rich agricultural plantation. Suong stepped into the wagon but Lam continued to chat with everyone, as if he didn't want to leave. Shaking hands with some, patting others affectionately on the back, Lam flattered and joked, promising to come back and see them. It was a long time before their wagon finally pulled out of the camp. As they slowly crossed the courtyard, Suong happened to glance up at the commander's window. The man stood behind a thin curtain, following her with his gaze. Suong felt her heart race, and again, the inexplicable terror washed over her.

"Let's go, he, he, heh!" Lam nudged the horse. He waved good-bye to people one more time with a flick of his whip, and the wagon lurched through the gate. The doors squeaked closed behind them. Four days and five nights of festivities had come to an end. Now everything would fall into a dreamlike sleep, a dull, plodding rhythm.

The wagon had covered a long stretch of road, but Suong could still see the crowd gathered outside the prison gate, silent, motionless. Fog floated over their heads, swirling over the grass.

"Brother Lam, where is Hung?" Suong asked.

I discussed it last night with the commander. He's got five years ahead of him, at least. The commander promised to do everything he could to reduce his sentence."

"Can we trust him?"

I think we can . . . watch out, a hole!" Lam shouted. The wagon pitched to one side. Suong didn't have time to grab the iron beam under the roof, she tumbled down like a sack in the middle of an avalanche of gifts and packages.

"Get, get!" Lam shouted at the horse. The horse leapt forward, crossing a ditch that the rain had made in the middle of the road. Lam turned around: "Are you okay?"

"I'm fine, I'm fine," she said, getting up painfully, dizzied by the shock. Once she was seated she felt a sharp pain in her hips. She didn't dare say anything to Lam. He was already too worried about her, she didn't have the right to bother him about yet another thing. The fog was still thick, and the road appeared and disappeared ahead of them. Lam swore to himself "Bitch of a road, damnation!"

After a long silence, he said: "You know, Suong, Hung will definitely get out sooner, but we're going to have to come back and perform for them again. This is no one-time contract; it's a long-term debt. And it's one we can't afford to leave unpaid."

After Suong's suicide attempt, Hung had been alone with the sea for three days and three nights. The bracing wind of the freedom of those first few moments had become an icy tempest that swept over the surface of the water, raking it with dust and sand that pounded his flesh and skin, drenching him in cold and loneliness. He knew that nothing was as generous as the sea, nor as indifferent. The sea was free, so it didn't make distinctions between people. He was just like a tiny, anonymous grain of sand, his sufferings like the cry of a gull drowned out in the infinite roar of the ocean. He remembered the face of the woman he loved. The laughter and babbling of children. The cool shade of the yellow and white ylang-ylang flowers framed in their window, how the seductive scent of the yellow blossoms mingled with the bewitching perfume of the white. He remembered everything. He missed everything. And he didn't understand why, after Suong's fit of madness, he had abandoned it all to lose himself in the middle of these fishing nets. Why had she tried to take her life? After all, he was the one who deserved to drown, the one who had lost everything, that life had cast out.

You have honor, respect. When you step on stage, thousands of pairs of eyes follow your every gesture, thousands of people hold their breath to hear you, thousands of men secretly long for you, the nightingale with the crystal voice. No one, not even the highest ranking officials in the province, are worshipped like you are. Every step you make they watch, whispering and dreaming about you. And when you come back from the hospital, you'll be the mistress of the house. Me, the children, your little brother—we all love you, dream only of serving you. Why this insane act?

The high waves tossed against each other, crashing and foaming on the beach, hurling their debris on the sand—seaweed, dead jellyfish, bloated fish. Wave after wave, the sea kept playing the same malicious, brutal game, erasing the holes dug in the sand by the crabs, erasing all trace of life. His wife, might she too have a bit of the sea's indifference, its coldness? He had loved her more than a man can love a woman. He felt it again, the excitement, the anxiety that had gripped him seated in Lam's wagon when he left the jungle to return to the town. It was the happiness of a fanatic, the rapture of a pilgrim as he approaches the holy land.

I trusted you more than anyone in the world. I repressed all my doubts, my jealousy, the hatred, the rage that poisoned my soul as I huddled in the shadows of the camp, as I listened to you sing over the loudspeakers while we ate moldy rice and fished for a few lousy slices of pumpkin in their insipid broth. I tried to ignore the insinuations, the lewd remarks of my comrades, the other prisoners, who watched the glow of the Manson lamp out there, where you were fêted by my jailers, where your smile, your looks, your perfume were all for them, while I, your husband, hugged my knees to my chest, silent. All I needed was a single word from Lam and I forgot everything. I loved you in so many ways, and I was so grateful to you. We were so happy.

When Hung was released from prison and returned home, Dam gave Suong two weeks vacation, which he justified by the two weeks of extra performances she had given.

After the long trip to the camp, Suong had miscarried, but she quickly regained her strength, never missing a rehearsal. Whether they liked it or not, all the troupe members had to agree that Suong was an outstanding actress, talented and hardworking, so no one said anything when Dam proposed to raise her salary by two grades. Her entire family depended on the money she earned. Three days after Hung's arrest in the company of the boat people, his name was erased from the salary list and he was expelled from the state organization. He became, in short, the lowest class of citizen, the type whose names filled the black-lists of the provincial public security police: no more ration tickets for rice or basic foodstuffs; no more fuel coupons; nothing at all to ensure his survival except the roof over his head. But these losses didn't haunt Hung for long after Suong's long, tear-drenched kiss their first night together after their reunion. Suong was more tender than she had ever been, and he was more in love than he had ever been during all their years together.

No, no, nothing is as important as happiness. I hold the most precious thing in the world in my hand. Forget the music, the lure of the stage lights, your crazy artist's dreams. Now, the most noble work, the most sacred, is my child.

It was now just like during the war, when they were first reunited, when he had caressed Suong as innocently as he would a child, washed her hair, bathed her. And as in the past, she gazed adoringly at him with her soft, trusting, velvety-black eyes. They forgot the outside world, the stage, even their own feelings. The past and the future dissolved in the fog on the steps of their door, and their lovemaking was unending, as if they could erase the barriers between night and day, drown their memories and their worries in the present. These days, Suong barely went out except to shop a bit. She gave Hung all her time, and he show-ered her with love, with all his repressed desire. The yellow ylang-ylang flowers bloomed, night after night, week after week, their disquieting perfume wafting through space. *I love you, I love you . . . we'll always be together, we're going to have lots of children. And when they grow up I'll tell them about the day I met you, little girl of the mountains.* Hung must have whispered it a hundred times. And she answered his dream a hundred times, her lips wet with tears.

A month later, when Suong announced that she had missed her period, Hung's knees went weak from happiness.

Another baby's babbling, like more flames to beat the winter, new fans to cool the summer. In life you can desire, seek, and find a thousand things, but there's one thing no one can make. A child is a gift from the Heavens, from the Buddha.

His mother used to say that to him when he began to learn to read. His parents had only one son—for them, children were the only things worth wanting in this world. Hung didn't have their wealth, nor could he lead a life of leisure; he was unemployed, excluded from society, living off his wife, but he was ecstatic because he was having a second child.

"We'll give the baby a peaceful, good-natured name, like a prayer to heaven and earth: Phuoc Hanh . . . whether it's a girl or a boy, our child will bear this name," he told Suong.

"All the names you choose are beautiful," she replied. "That's a choice for someone like you, with your education." She threw her arms around his neck and they wrapped around each other, making love feverishly, like two people gone mad. But often, during these crazy bouts of lovemaking, Hung would look out past the window at the sky. Sometimes foggy, sometimes flickering with street lamps, sometimes an intense blue, the sky reminded him that he could no longer flee into the emotion. He knew that he had given the woman he loved a child to chain her to him; in his heart he already feared their love would break.

No, you can't try to be happy. No lasting happiness is built on the mad coupling of the body and the soul. These crazy moments are only embellishments, secondary notes, not the melody; they can't build a song.

Hung was experienced in love. Before he married Suong, many women had offered themselves to him. He understood. He read the cowardice and fear in his heart as if he were watching pebbles in a dry streambed.

These brief moments of clarity, of honesty with himself, were painful, ruthless, almost inhuman. Hung saw everything, and yet he deluded himself so he could continue. He kept drawing his frail, obedient wife into the passions of the flesh. He never said it aloud, but someone inside him, a being without a name or a face, formless, never stopped repeating: *Forget, forget, forget, forget, forget . . .*

And then the rainy season came. Rain like waterfalls, like wine poured recklessly from a bottle, as if the universe were melting. Every day, Suong went to work—despite her nausea, her vomiting. She couldn't miss a rehearsal or a performance. Heaven had endowed her tiny body with the resistance of a water buffalo.

Facing the window, seated at the amboyna wood table where he no longer dared to place a pile of music paper, Hung watched as sheets of rain fell from the sky. Some dark premonition echoed inside him: *After this rainy season, what's going to happen?*

The last rainy season, the previous year, after three weeks of uninterrupted, suffocating rain, he had run to the edge of the sea to breathe, to live, and then had found himself dragged along with a crowd of boat people. That disaster had plunged him into the hell of the prison camp. During this rainy season would he be able to escape the unhappiness that lurked behind that dense curtain of rain? The fear made him suddenly stand up. He grabbed his raincoat and ran over to Auntie Tuong's house to play with his daughter. Da Hai was eating her lunch, snuggled up against the old woman. She reached out and touched his cheek instead of running into his arms. Hung waited until she had finished eating, then had to cajole her for a long time before she agreed to let him pick her up and take her out for a walk. But as soon as she saw Auntie Tuong emerge from the kitchen with a steaming bowl of mung bean *chè*, the little girl wriggled out of his arms, shrieked with joy, her eyes twinkling, attracted by the sweet perfume of her favorite pudding.

Auntie Tuong burst out laughing. "You little darling, what you wouldn't do for this pudding!" She turned to Hung. "Set her down, you can't hold her back now."

The little girl ran to the old woman, her eyes riveted on the pudding, completely forgetting her father. Hung laughed, but felt a heavy sadness. "She's just a child," Auntie Tuong said, as if to console him. "Children are attached to the smell of those who carry them. Your wife works all day, and you're often away from the house . . . you've got to spend a lot of time with kids before they miss you. Would you like some tea? I'll make some."

"Thanks, I've just had some at home."

"I've got chrysanthemum tea, really fragrant . . . my tea is straight from the Nga Mi Mountain, the flowers are from my garden. I picked them myself."

"Thanks, Auntie, but I'm not thirsty."

"Well then, have a bowl of *chè*. I made it for her, but there's still some left in the pot."

"Thanks, I'm not hungry."

"Don't be polite, take some, here, feed her. I'm going to serve you a bowl of *chè* with some roast sesame seeds on it."

She pushed Da Hai from her arms and handed him a bowl of *chè* to feed her. Three or four times he ended up smearing *chè* on Da Hai's chin. It wasn't until the fifth that he got the hang of it, his gestures becoming more natural. Auntie Tuong returned with another steaming bowl of *chè*. The surface of the clear, yellow mung bean pudding was covered with grilled sesame seeds. She picked up Da Hai, wiped the traces of pudding off her chin and cheeks, and kissed her, hugging her like a real mother and not some old woman watching a neighbor's child.

Hung lifted the bowl of *chè* to his lips.

I'm eating this so as not to offend her and then I'm going home. I have no place here. I'm a bother, I make her uneasy because she pities me, and so I destroy the familiar, peaceful atmosphere between her and Da Hai. In a year, Da Hai has already left her mother and father's orbit for the arms and the affection of this old woman. She only remembers Suong and me when the sun sets and the smell of her mother comes back with the shadows of the night.

Hung finished the *chè*, said good-bye to his neighbor and left, giving her no time to invite him to eat anything more. When he reached their house, he lifted off his raincoat, entered his room, and looked at himself in the mirror.

What is it in this face that betrays my misery, the poverty of my spirit? Is there some sign that inspires people's pity? Why can't I seem to see my own true face?

He could see all the wrinkles at the corners of his eyes, on his cheekbones, how the handsome, wavy hair that had once charmed so many women was turning gray. His temples looked wan, hollow. A few age spots had appeared under his eyes. The laughing, dancing eyes of Hoang Hung, the composer, were now webbed with thin red veins. Since his release from prison, this was the first time he had really looked at himself in the mirror.

The rain fell, extinguishing his illusions. Hung contemplated the deep wrinkles under his eyes. Was it the six months in prison that had destroyed him like this? He remembered his first meal in the camp. He and fifteen of the men, squatted around a big pot filled with a vile black liquid they called "water spinach and broth"; a withered bunch of leaves, stems, and roots still coated with dirt and human excrement. Each prisoner had an aluminum bowl, a spoon without a handle. The cold, stale rice smelled moldy; the grains were mixed with bits of chaff, pebbles, and insect droppings. A tin dish was filled with a nauseating brown shrimp sauce. The men looked at each other; the hair on their skulls had been shaved intentionally jagged. They all understood; they were considered animals who had to eat animal feed and eat it like animals. They had been forced to understand this. Famished, whimpering, they shoveled the cold rice into their mouths.

Enough. Enough. Why these dark memories now? I'm under my own roof, with my wife, my child, a happiness that's the envy of thousands of other men. The past is a shadow. No one wants to live with shadows, breathe the stench of corpses, eat the ash and dust of life.

Tears blurred his vision. His heart reared in hate and humiliation. He saw his comrades back in prison, these men linked to him by horrible images. Human shit in the roots of the water spinach. The putrid shrimp sauce, the rusty bowl, the spoons without handles. These weren't just symbols of their wretched existence; they were like props in a play the prisoners were forced to act out.

Boat people. Traitors who sully the honor of the Party, the State. So we had to be treated like animals. God! Even farmers washed water spinach before giving it to their pigs, so they won't get diarrhea. The shit we were forced to eat is proof that the boat people are less to them than livestock.

These men who claim to represent this country now, weren't they out there once, back in the crowds that we entertained those long years, during the war?

Thousands of images pressed up against that question. Hung relived the days, the months on the front. In his mind, he walked down the paths that crisscrossed the land, the roads that dropped off the horizon under the bombs. His eyes blurred again with tears.

That night, when Suong came home, he tried to be cheerful, tender. He had hastily dried his tears and greeted her, hung up her coat, served the evening meal. After they had finished eating together in the golden light, she persuaded him to help her rearrange the house.

"I'm going to throw this old army backpack out, honey. Is there anything in it you want to keep?"

"No. No, don't throw it out," he snapped. "Leave it for me," he added in a dull, troubled voice she hadn't heard before. His face was white.

She stared at him, petrified. He walked quickly to the window, staring up at the sky over the town.

In his mind, he remembered a song he had been taught in high school: *"Don't forget the hate, never, never, through the thousands of generations, never forget."* The song was about the poisoning of Communist prisoners by the American-sponsored south Vietnamese regime. In the north, in the 1950s, thirteen million Vietnamese had screamed this song of hatred. He and his high school buddies, filled with pain, their hearts on fire, had screamed it too: *"Thousands of generations will preserve this, carved in our flesh, this unforgettable hatred."*

Now that same melody echoed in his head, not for the prisoners of Phu Loi, but for himself, for the boat people who had shared that wretched soup of water spinach and human shit: *Never forget, never forget, even after a thousand generations.*

Blood didn't just run through his veins anymore; it boiled and turned to smoke. Hung knew his face was changing. It wasn't the face he used to have; it was a face of hate. He was afraid Suong would notice, so he stood there in the window for a long time, pretending to contemplate some musical scale in the dark, unfathomable sky.

Suong waited a long time, until she didn't see him turn around. Silently, she came down to the ground floor. That night Hung slept alone. He told her that since she was pregnant he didn't want their lovemaking to affect the baby. He sat in the darkness, staring silently. He couldn't delude himself anymore. That vision of happiness had flickered out. Now, he had to settle his own fate, accept this new life, its new limits.

Hung sat there like that until the sky turned white. He only came down when Vinh and Suong began rummaging in the kitchen to make breakfast. Suong stared at him, her voice cracking as she spoke: "You're as pale as a ghost. Are you sick?"

"Ah, no . . . I just couldn't sleep last night . . . I remembered . . ."

"What?"

"The days when we first met."

"Today you should try and catch up on sleep," Suong muttered, then went into the room to change. As she left, he followed her with his eyes, gazed sadly at her slender back, as she guided the motorcycle out the gate.

You're going to your theater. Tonight the lights will dim and you will come out on stage to act. Like every night they will applaud until their hands burn; they'll buy you huge bouquets of flowers even though it's the rainy season and the prices are high.

You don't know that my imagination no longer holds flowers, or music, just pieces of shit floating in water spinach . . .

Hung sat and watched the rain fall, and fall. Everything was like the prisoners' faces—deformed, rotten. At that moment the rain poured, crashing down as if to threaten and intimidate him. And from somewhere behind the rain, frail notes sang out from a dim, shuddering place that wouldn't release him, or his foolish dreams about music, and which only added a kind of poison to his blood.

He listened to the fragile scales as if he were watching the writhing of a fetus expelled from the womb but that refuses to die, that thrashes furiously, unable to understand why it has been banished from its mother's soft belly. Just like the sounds that sprang from the rain's mournful lament. Hung called to them, strained to capture them, but they were drowned out under the rush of the rain, carried away by the floodwaters. As soon as he touched them, they seemed to slip away.

He heard someone calling to him, then felt someone hitting his shoulder, pulling his hand, his hair. Not just once but twice, three, five, seven times. It had been ages since anyone had shouted his name with such insistence. When he woke, his head, face, and neck were drenched in sweat.

"Hung, Hung, wake up, open your eyes, it's me, Lam, open your eyes."

He felt a hand touch his and he opened his eyes. Lam was standing in front of him. Next to him, a fisherman, short and dwarflike, with skin the color of burnt rice, held a Thermos in one hand and an earthenware pot in the other. Seeing Hung open his eyes, the man exclaimed: "There you go . . . what luck. Give him some rice porridge."

"Yes, please give me some, Uncle," Lam replied, as the man handed him a bamboo basket. Lam pulled off a hot compress that covered Hung's head. "Can you sit up straight?"

"Yes." Hung was still caught in a tangle of fishing nets. His limbs felt as if they were floating, as if they hung from the body of a mannequin. But he couldn't seem to move. Lam pushed Hung forward and helped him sit up. "Eat directly from the pot. I didn't bring a bowl." Lam lifted the cover off the soup, and the steam flew up into Hung's eyes. The strong smell of young rice and fresh fish that had once pleased him now filled him with disgust.

"I can't," he said, turning to Lam.

"Eat, you have to eat," Lam said with a stern, fatherly voice. "Eat so you'll have the strength to drag yourself off this beach. I'm not going to carry you. You're not little Da Hai. You weigh almost as much as I do."

Lam plunged his hand into the basket and pulled out a green chili, broke it in two and threw it into the pot. The strong, acrid scent of the chili blocked out the fish smell. Hung felt less nauseous. He began to eat, spoonful by spoonful.

"Eat up. Remember what our ancestors taught us: Rice comforts, porridge comforts, but don't expect comfort from anyone. You're no match for those heavy drinkers. You've got to eat."

Hung didn't reply, didn't think anymore, just shoveled down the *cháo,* spoonful after spoonful, under Lam's stern gaze. Finally, he emptied the pot, and Lam took it and handed it back to the old fisherman. "Could you take this back to the stall for me?"

"Yes, would you like anything to drink?"

"Of course."

"Well, I'll leave you the Thermos bottle. You can use this as a cup," the old man said, turning over the bottle cap. He pulled a tiny packet of paper out of his pocket and handed it to Lam. "Here's some tea. I'm going home now." The fisherman put his cap on his head and walked down the length of the beach, his bamboo basket in hand.

Lam and Hung sat and sipped the tea, reminiscing about the long years they had lived side by side, sharing the same half-stick of dried rations, the last can of water. In the distance, the sea thundered, hurling waves against the beach and the rocks. And the sound of the wind mixed with the howl of the sea was a long, thin wail. They sat there like that a long time, pouring water again and again over the tea leaves, until the leaves had lost all taste. When the Thermos was empty, Lam turned to Hung, looked him straight in the eye: "Now, tell me. Why are you behaving like this?"

Hung was disoriented, exhausted, but he had heard Lam clearly and the restrained anger underlying the question.

"What have I done?" Hung asked.

"You don't understand?"

"No."

"Okay, let's say you don't know. Then what made Suong throw herself in the river, a stone tied around her? Don't tell me that you don't know she almost died?"

"I know . . . but I don't understand why. Because I'm a counterrevolutionary? Well, then she should have done it while I was in the prison camp. Because I'm a parasite? She should have thrown me out long ago . . . and if it's because I'm a drunkard, she should have hanged herself before Phuoc Hanh was born."

"And if she didn't do it for any of those reasons, then she must be crazy? Is that what you're saying?"

"No, that's not what I'm saying. Maybe she did it in a kind of wild, impulsive gesture, like famous women who need constant adulation."

"So you're jealous of your own wife?"

"No, I'm not jealous. It's the truth. In fact, the one who should have thrown himself to the bottom of the river is me."

"You? Well why don't you, then?" Lam retorted.

Hung stared at the clown, stunned, then after a moment his face turned dreamy, and he managed a weak smile: "Yes, maybe, one of these days."

Now it was Lam's turn to be stunned. "Listen, forgive me . . . I lost my temper."

"How can I be angry with you? You're the only one, among all of our friends, who has helped both of us during hard times."

"You don't need to say that. Listen to me, Hung." Lam fell silent, swallowed hard, his Adam's apple bobbing up and then falling, his two bushy eyebrows furrowed over the arch of his nose. He focused his gaze on a broken buoy next to one of the fishing nets. Only after a silence did he speak: "I'm your friend, but I'm also Suong's friend. She's like a little sister to me. I'm not on anybody's side; I just need to know what happened. Not for me, but for the two of you. I can't stand by and watch her waste away in that hospital, and then come here and find you in this state."

"How did you know I was here?"

"I've been looking for you for two days. The first day, in the inns in the suburbs. The second, all the way down the beach. Today's the third day . . ."

"Why didn't you think I was dead? After all, I've got no reason to live anymore."

"It's not easy to live, but it's just as hard to die. Hung, you've got so much still ahead of you."

"Oh yeah? Like what?"

"You know what, but you're an ingrate. You have Suong. She loves you, and she is totally devoted to you. You have your daughters. You have talent. And you can pick up your pen and compose, even write."

"Write! You're crazy . . ."

"I'm not crazy yet, and I know what I'm talking about even though I've never picked up a pen in place of my horsewhip. Once you told me the story of a writer named Fusik. His book was called *Written under the Gallows*."

"He was a Communist. He wrote to oppose fascism. If I wrote like him, who would I be writing against?"

"If anyone is going to hang you, write against them. That would be logical. For the moment, no one is planning to hang you. So write like our great poet Nguyen Du did."

"So you think people would use my music, with all my pain, my sadness, my hatred, my despair?"

"You were lucky enough to study in the capital, you're well educated, cultured. I didn't have that luck, so I can't argue with you. But I'm capable of using my brain. For example, I'm a carter. To earn money? Yeah, that's one reason. But there are many ways to make a living. Hung, I could have stayed with the troupe; I'd have had one of the best salaries in the profession by now. I could have gone into business with my elder brother in the salt trade, or gone home to raise goats with my uncle. Goat meat sells for a high price. And you can drink the milk. It would have been a peaceful, relaxing life. But, I left the troupe to go back to my old job, because my blood is full of the sun and wind of the open road, the opium of travel. I can't live day after day, for months and years, on a plot of land that's only a few dozen yards wide. I have a house, a garden I've left to my wife and two girls. Me, I live in the wagon, I dream of dying there, so that my faithful horse will pull me down all the familiar roads. It's a kind of madness, isn't it, Hung? And yet the madmen are the happiest in this life. They do what they please; who cares whether others approve or criticize them. All in all, the man who follows his own star is a happy man, a free man . . ."

"You speak well, but it's all theory."

"I didn't study theory like you, Hung. I'm a clown, a driver."

"You forget that I don't share your passion for traveling."

"Oh you can travel on other roads, not necessarily those paved with stones or asphalt that I'm used to taking."

"That's difficult."

"Whether it's difficult or not depends on you."

"You can't lock music in a drawer for future generations like you can a literary work. Music has its own demands."

Lam burst out laughing, his eyebrows dancing and wriggling, clownish. "So you need to put it on stage, show it off to everyone? Then you're even weaker than I am. Don't forget that I was once an actor under your direction, and I was quite successful. Audiences used to shower me with applause that paled only by comparison to the applause they gave your wife. To tell the truth, I was flattered by my celebrity, by the affection and admiration of the audiences. But I left all that to go back to my parents' wagon. In the end, I prefer the happiness I make to the kind other people give me. I wish you that kind of happiness. If only, every time you finished a song, you felt the same pleasure I feel pushing my wagon through the valleys at dawn, without hurrying to deliver some merchandise, or worrying about profits and losses, but just for the sheer pleasure of wandering, and because these places make my heart lighter, my spirit clearer, make me feel life is worth living! Hung, I don't pretend to have the talent to debate with you. But I'm your friend, and I'm Suong's friend. I want you two to be happy."

"Lam, I'll always be grateful to you."

"You don't need to talk about gratitude, even if it's sincere. That's friendship. But friends have the right to ask, to make demands. I'm only asking you for one thing: Tell me sincerely, don't you know why Suong tried to take her life?"

"I don't know . . . or maybe I don't know all that burdens her, in our family life, that would drive her to . . . maybe she hid something from me."

"That's true. She's had to bear a lot, for a long time, in silence—not just from you but from your drinking buddies too."

"You know about all that?"

"Suong didn't say anything, but Vinh did. After you got out of prison, you two were happy. But a few months later you brought a bunch of lazy artist types home who sang your praises all day long. At the beginning, they just came by from time to time. Then, they seemed to hang around all day, every day, for months on end. Drinking. And demanding more and more every day: more food, different kinds of spirits, cigarettes, a game of chess to pass the time. And your wife paid for all that out of her own pocket. She had to sing extra hours until she was as thin as a cicada to pay for those expenses. She tried to please you, so you could find some peace of mind, tried to convince Vinh to put up with everything. All to please you, so you wouldn't lose face in front of that bunch of drunkards. Isn't that right?"

"Yes, it's true. I thought Suong wanted it that way too."

"Hung . . . as intelligent as you are, do you think your wife really wanted to become a water buffalo pulling the only plow?"

"Lam, my father lived his whole life under my mother's protection. He was just a literature student, and he didn't even pass his exams. He spent his entire life reciting poems by Li Bai and Du Fu, or commenting on *Lament of a Soldier's Wife* and *The Pavilion of the Golden Stork*. And whenever he had his literary friends over, my mother would have the servants prepare five or seven trays for a banquet, and she would even drop her business to sit and keep them company."

"Those were your ancestors, Hung, but they lived in another age. Have you forgotten the saying: Different waters at each bend in the river?"

"I know. My mother was as solid as cypress or pine wood, and my own wife is made of a much more fragile species. She's like a flowering vine."

Lam laughed. "Why do you force her to carry such a heavy load?"

"She's a Vietnamese woman, born in a land where women are ready to bear any burden, make any sacrifice. Suong can carry a heavy burden, just like my mother did."

"Oh how you can talk, Hung. Tell me then, did you ever hear your father's literary friends mock your mother, or treat her with contempt?"

"My drinking buddies only praised Suong. No one dared . . ."

"You're wrong, Hung. Here's my second question. While your father made merry with his friends in the family living room, did he let your mother eat in the kitchen with the servants, like Suong and Vinh? While you and your drunken friends were knocking back the booze until you vomited, Suong and Vinh were eating the leftovers of your banquet."

Hung said nothing.

"Did you not know that?" Lam continued. "Or didn't you want to know? You use alcohol to numb yourself, to plug your ears and blind your eyes, to live unconsciously. That's the most cowardly thing we men do, that we've always done. You say your friends just shower praise on Suong. That doesn't surprise me. What man wouldn't flatter his host's wife when she allows him to drink and eat without spending a single *dong*, without having to move a single, rotten finger on his lazy body? But after all the sweet talk, who was it who pointed at Suong and said, 'Without Hung you'd still be just another peasant girl in a godforsaken mountain hamlet, and you should serve him with devotion because you'll never even pay half your debt of gratitude to the man who made you who you are.' Who said that? And who said it more than once?"

"I don't know, I wasn't paying attention . . . I . . ."

"You know who it was. Vinh told me that you yourself once told this person to shut up. And then a few days later, drunk, he started to insult Suong again when she left without making a sweet-and-sour salad for your drinking party.

Hung lowered his head, murmured. "Doan. I know it must have been Doan."

"Yes, the painter. Vinh told me. He also told me why Suong tried to commit suicide."

Hung remained silent.

"Suong would go to work while you and your friends stayed home and drank. Once, when she came back, you were fairly drunk, shouting, singing, arguing like a bunch of madmen. Doan declared that if you were a real man you first had to prove your authority with your wife. And he doubted that... You cursed him, bragging that obviously Suong loved you, that if she had been like other women she would have left you when you became a pariah, and that she would always be your faithful little wife. Then Doan challenged you to prove it, told you to call Suong in and ask her to let each of them kiss her, one after the other. Only under these 'conditions' would they believe that she loved you, that her fidelity was absolute."

Lam stopped talking, seeing Hung's face stiffen. His words had worked like the brush of an expert painter bringing back to life an old canvas damaged by too long a storage underground. Yes, Hung had been drunk, completely drunk that afternoon, and it had been so hot that the sweat from the heat mixed with the sweat from the alcohol. Except for him, they had all been in shorts. Doan had taken his off, keeping only his underwear on. He was obsessed with sex and didn't hide it, as if he considered that part of his talent. They had only discussed lofty subjects—like the spirit of Tang dynasty ink paintings, or China, the birthplace of martial arts and great love stories between humans and demons. They talked about Taoist monks who channeled their vital energy to make their bodies as light as swans. And then suddenly the conversation had turned to love. Hung's friends commented on the love between Suong and Hung, a subject that they had covered a thousand times without ever tiring of it. Maybe because that love was the only thing holding Hung to life, and his guests liked to remind him of it, to make him happy. But also because lazy, useless people can never get beyond their own orbit. That afternoon, the discussion was more heated and more vehement than ever. And in the end, it had become a challenge. Hung remembered that he had staggered down the stairs and called to Suong as she arrived at the gate, pushing her bicycle.

"So you've come home, my faithful wife, come here."

She looked at him, her eyes patient. "You keep drinking . . . I'm going to rest a bit."

He took her by the hand, pleading with her. "Just a minute, come up and see us."

Vinh was standing in the kitchen, waiting for Suong, his face grave. Suong turned to her brother. "Okay, you start dinner without me."

She followed Hung up the stairs, stopping a minute in front of the door as she noticed all the half-naked men. She tried to wrench away and go down the stairs, but Hung begged her. "Please, honey, just a moment."

He turned to his friends. "You guys aren't showing any respect . . . come on, dress correctly."

The men hurriedly threw on their pants, staggering around a platter piled with their debris: banana leaves that had wrapped spring rolls, pieces of dried squid, peanut shells, and crumbs from crab fritters. Hung pulled Suong into the room. She turned to Hung: "What do you want from me?"

"Nothing, just stand there, like a statue, my devoted wife," he said, steering her toward the wall. The men applauded like madmen. "Long live the queen of the stage! Bravo, muse of the art, she hasn't let us down. She is indeed the ideal wife." And they ran over and grabbed at her, one pulling at her blouse, the other fondling her hair. Hung shouted at them. "Sit down! On the mats! Order!"

Suong looked up at him. "What is this all about, Hung?"

Hung turned to her. "My friends want to kiss you. They want to have the honor, just once. I've given them my permission."

Suong cried out. "No . . . Hung, you can't do that. . . . you can't!"

He laughed, still holding her tightly by the arms. "Come on, honey, in the West people kiss each other every time they meet, just like we shake hands or nod to greet people in Asia. It's convention. These gestures have no meaning in themselves."

Suong shook her head, struggled to free herself from Hung's grasp: "No! You have no right, I don't want to!"

He didn't reply and turned toward the drinkers. "I give you my permission, one after the other, in order. I won't accept chaos in this house."

Suong, on the edge of tears, begged him. "No, Hung, I can't, I just can't."

Someone, maybe it had been the playwright, spoke up. "Obey Hung. Without him you'd still be just a shepherd girl humming some sappy praise of the mountains. Your life is like the greatest of the twentieth-century revolutions."

The unkempt poet, Truc Son, joined in. "The water buffalo wagon has stepped onto the stage, once a mountain girl, now queen of the stage, the nightingale with the crystal voice."

Suong didn't reply. She stood straight, as motionless as a statue, against the wall while Hung allowed them, one by one, to kiss her—first it was Trong Cang, then Doan, then finally Truc Son. Everyone laughed, shouted bravos, delighted with this game.

"Hung, is it over now?" Suong asked, looking straight at him, without pleading or trembling, her eyes cold, enraged. Even now, Hung remembered that look, how at that moment, his brain reeling in their dizzy laughter, in the flickering haze of alcohol, he had felt happy and had even bent down to kiss her hand and said: "Thank you my darling, my devoted wife. You helped me win my bet."

There was no reply. Suong ran out of the room and down the stairs.

"Well, now do you remember?" Lam's voice echoed, bringing Hung back to the present. Hung didn't dare reply, horrified. He had just understood Lam's anger: His crime had been unforgivable.

"Do you know why Vinh knows everything? Instead of eating dinner that night, he followed Suong, heard everything."

Hung was silent. He had read Vinh's hatred a long time ago in the young man's eyes, his threatening gestures. The young man hated him passionately, but he took out his hatred on Suong. Sometimes, when Hung went out to the courtyard to the toilet, he overheard their arguments in the kitchen.

"I'm leaving! I'm going back home, to our mountains, with Mien."

"Vinh, listen to me, you have to study, become a man. Your father went all the way through secondary school. Then when our grandparents died in a cholera epidemic, he was forced to abandon his studies, to become a woodcutter. He always said that if the Heavens kept him in good health he would try and send us off to study in town, but they didn't spare him. Now I've got to take his place, provide for you, pay for your studies. To console our parents' souls."

"How can I study when you're so unhappy?"

"How am I unhappy? I earn enough to feed you and . . ."

"Auntie Tuong says that you're selling your lungs, singing yourself hoarse, that you have to slave away to feed that bunch of old drunken bastards."

"Don't speak like that! Those are Hung's friends."

Lam continued: "So while Suong was fleeing, Vinh picked up an ax to split your skull. Suong stopped him and forced him to swear on the souls of their parents that he would never do such a thing. As you see, she was still worried about your life right before she put a stone around her neck and threw herself in the river."

Hung said nothing.

"What were you thinking, at that moment, my dear intellectual?" Lam asked.

"Don't be cruel . . . I know, I don't deserve to live."

"Oh come on! Stop your tragic whining. You sound like the ancients with their long fingernails. Come with me. Go back home, ask Suong for her forgiveness, try and lead a normal life, throw those drunken pigs out of your house. As for me, I'm going to teach that painter a lesson. Your intelligence hasn't helped you one bit in this whole mess."

Hung kept silent.

Lam got up, lowered his voice and spat out his words: "Get up and follow me! I'm not going to carry you on my back. Stop dreaming!"

Lam singlehandedly helped reconcile Hung's broken family. He brought Hung back home, then he went to get Suong at the hospital. He forced them to make peace in front of him, light incense, and swear on the souls of their parents that they would henceforth live with dignity, like human beings. Lam knew that they still loved each other, didn't want to separate. And yet, during the reunion meal, behind the husband's plea for forgiveness, the wife's bitter tears, the little brother's contemptuous, vengeful gaze, even after his own words of conciliation and congratulations, Lam sensed unhappiness lurking, like some shapeless shadow that milled about the courtyard, spying on the doorway, flitting in and out of the yellow and white ylang-ylang flowers.

Is this a premonition or some mirage created by all the legends that haunted me when I was a child, wandering with my father all those summer afternoons, those long winter evenings, the nights spent in the rhythm of the waves? Why do those ylang-ylang blossoms in the garden frighten me? My father used to tell me that white ylang-ylang should only be planted in the pagodas, mausoleums, or altars—places protected by the spirits of pure men, masters of their fate, free of the mud of the world. He who is tempted by flesh is still chained to the infernal cycle of ambition, anger, passion. If you cultivate white ylang-ylang you attract demons and create your own downfall.

When he was a little boy, Lam had often heard these superstitious legends about the ylang-ylangs. Remembering them now stirred premonitions of disaster. "Why don't you plant some fruit trees in the garden?" Lam asked the couple. "As they grow, the kids will need to eat fruit. In this town lots of families plant persimmons, star apples, and avocados. If I were you, I'd chop those ylang-ylang trees down immediately and plant some persimmon trees."

"I've already asked Hung, but he doesn't want to," Suong said.

Hung laughed. "She believes the stories the old women who come here to buy flowers tell her."

"What do they say?" Lam asked.

"They say that the heavy-scented ylang-ylang has evil blossoms, that whoever grows them will die or be divorced, that their pillow will be drenched with tears. Those who make the mistake of planting them must offer these unlucky, diabolical-smelling flowers to the temples and pagodas. They mustn't let the perfume waft around their gardens, and they can't make money by selling them," Suong said.

Hung laughed. "That's a businessman's mind. They invent stories so they can buy flowers on the cheap, or get them for free. But you know that the same old women who tell you to get rid of these flowers sell the unlucky blossoms in front of the pagodas and temples to all kinds of visitors. And they don't give them away; they barter them for hard cash."

"Of course, but prudence is the mother of security . . . I'm scared," Suong said. She didn't dare say another word after Hung's mocking.

Lam spoke up. "I'm not a woman, but I agree with Suong. There's got to be something useful in what the ancestors taught us. Cut down a few of those ylang-ylang trees and plant some persimmons, or some other kind of fruit tree."

"Oh no! Of all the scents, the white and yellow ylang-ylangs' is the most romantic. How could I banish such a precious fragrance from my life? You've got the sun and the wind and the open road. Me, I'm stuck between these four walls. Aside from the ylang-ylang flowers, what else do I have?" Hung shook his head.

Lam decided not to discuss the ylang-ylangs anymore. He asked Hung: "I've got to settle a certain matter before I leave this town. Where does your friend the painter live?"

"Doan? I have no idea. They say he lives in a residence at the liquor factory. His mother is a worker in the wine-packaging section. His father is apparently a retired captain."

"He wore down your bowls and your chopsticks and you don't know where he is?"

"I didn't pay attention. I didn't want to know."

"The town is tiny, I won't be looking for long."

In one cyclo ride, Lam arrived at the workers' residence attached to the liquor factory. It was an old building on the south side of town, on the edge of a river black with the scum of the sewers and industrial waste. The stench of the garbage mixed with the warm, sweet smell of molasses used to brew the alcohol flooded the air. Every time the wind blew from west to east, the molasses smell spread, as heady as the smell of the country earth on festival days. When the wind blew from the sea, carrying the odor of salt, fish, and garbage, the air was nauseating.

A hasty coat of yellow lime-wash paint had just been slapped on the old dilapidated residence; you could still make out the crude brush-strokes on the walls. The residence was a sprawling, peeling, ramshackle assortment of crude apartments laid out like a military barracks, with badly installed windows still smeared with caulk, and lead gray doors. A long, narrow, common porch ran the length of the houses, and every five yards were plastic or tin pads spilling over with rotting garbage. Above the garbage pails hung pots of morning glories and butterfly flowers. Lam climbed stairs booming with loud music and thick with the smell of grilled mutton fat. He stopped, repelled by the smell. Before Liberation, their troupe had once accepted the grilled fat as a gift, but no one could stomach this popular Mongol dish, and they didn't even let their chopsticks so much as touch it. The authorities claimed it had been a gift from international donors who wanted to support the resistance, that in the West this fat was used to feed animals during the winter. It was the same for the powdered milk the government had imported from India, which was used to fatten up livestock during the birthing season.

Lam stopped a moment in front of the stairs to let the stench of the mutton fat dissipate, then continued, counting the numbers on the apartments, searching for "31," the address the guard had given him for Mrs. Ninh—also known as "the bearded guy's mother." He finally found it, but unluckily this was the source of the nauseating odor of mutton fat. Lam knocked on the door, and a man of about sixty, dressed in an old, patched Western suit, opened it.

"Hello, sir, I'd like to see the painter, Doan," Lam said.

"Yes, that's my son. Please come in," the man said politely.

Lam entered and sat down. The man served him tea, then said in a hesitant voice: "If you don't mind waiting, my son is sleeping."

"Of course. Don't worry."

"He was painting all night. He works really hard, doesn't sleep very much. When he sleeps, no one dares disturb him," the old man said, and sat down facing Lam. Surprised, Lam surveyed the room: It was small, no furniture of any value except for a nicely sculpted mahogany wood armoire. The owner must have bought it on the black market. In the middle of all the crumbling, worm-eaten furniture, and the unmatching teapot and cups, the opulent armoire seemed like a peacock gone astray in a chicken coop. A screen made of parachute canvas stretched onto a wood frame—it must have been the owner's creation—stood upright in front of a large bed, where "Doan, the unshaven guy with the disheveled hair" was spread out, fast asleep, in only his underwear, the tool he used to perpetuate the species erect as a masthead.

Ah! So that's the reason why little Vinh so hated and despised him more than the others. A pervert and a bit of a psychopath as well. Looks like he's the real boss in this house, not the mother and father.

The entire room bore the mark of Doan's domination. The luxurious mahogany closet wasn't piled up, as it was in other houses, with a tea set, various dolls and ornaments, but with an assortment of books on painting. On top of the closet, next to some relics from the altar to the ancestors, were two huge lacquered vases filled with paint-brushes. Paintings hung on the wall just behind the shrine honoring the ancestors and the household gods. Against the opposite wall there was an oil painting depicting a decapitated cow's head bathed in a pool of blood that turned from red to a lotus-blossom violet. Behind the cow's head, a pale crescent moon was sketched against a tortured sky hung with gray clouds. In the corner of the painting, Doan's curvy, snakelike signature was scrawled next to five fingerprints. On the wall opposite the entryway, the only door to the apartment, there was the portrait of a Westerner with a high forehead and aquiline nose, almost completely bald. A real dagger, attached to the wall with a little chain and two nails, had been thrust into the portrait, right through the man's throat. Under the portrait, a long white banner read: "Die Picasso! I'll be the man who digs your grave!"

"Hello sir, you've come to see Doan?" A woman's voice speaking in a pure Nghe An accent caught Lam's attention. He turned around. An old woman appeared from inside the kitchen, and with her the smell of burned mutton fat. This must be Doan's mother, Lam thought.

"Hello Auntie. I've got a matter I'd like to discuss with Doan."

"He's been asleep for three hours. He asked me to wake him in fifteen minutes." Like her husband, the woman spoke in a humble, courteous voice. And she too spoke of her son with the same reverence. She inspected a platter covered with a bamboo fly screen on her son's bedside table. Reassured, she went to sit with her husband, flicking a fan continuously in her hand. Lam suddenly realized that the room had just one Hitachi air conditioner, which rumbled at the foot of Doan's bed, while the old man and woman each did the best they could with bamboo fans. Lam stood the heat well, rarely needing a fan, but he admired the selflessness of the old couple, and the privations they seemed to endure for their son. According to the guard downstairs, Doan wasn't their only child; they had two daughters and another son, all married, all settled in the town of Vinh. Doan was the youngest. His parents had paid for him to study in Hanoi and he had almost finished at the Hanoi Academy of Beaux Arts, when he was arrested and imprisoned for raping a minor. He had spent seven years in prison, then returned to his native village with a few dozen painting books and a few old suits. But the town of Vinh, with its searing wind from Laos and its burning hot land, couldn't forgive him. With the criminal record of a rapist, he couldn't find work. His parents begged officials who came from Nghe An to help transfer Doan to the biggest town of the five provinces of central Vietnam, hoping he might find a more welcoming atmosphere.

"Please, have some tea." The old woman filled Lam's cup with green tea, then poured herself one and emptied it in one gulp—this was the way Nghe An peasants drank. She seemed sturdier than her husband, with her tanned skin and square face, her tiny, deepset, sparkling eyes. Having finished her tea, she moved toward the bed, gently shook Doan's shoulder. "Doan, wake up, it's time."

He didn't move. She pleaded with him. "It's time, my child, you asked me to wake you up." She spoke in the cajoling, tender voice you would use with children or dolls.

After her third call, he finally grumbled, shook his shoulders, stretched his arms and legs like a cat, and sat up. When he saw Lam, he quickly composed himself. Without waiting, Lam spoke up: "I've something I want to discuss with you."

At the tone of Lam's voice, Doan immediately sensed danger.

Lam continued. "Get dressed first. I'm not used to looking at cavemen.

Doan's face froze a moment, as if he were going to react, but then he hurried into a back room to get dressed. He came back a few minutes later in an old smock smeared with paint; it was a woman worker's blue uniform, borrowed from his mother. Doan's mother turned to Lam. "Give him time to eat."

Lam didn't have time to reply when Doan shouted: "Enough! To hell with the meal."

His mother fell silent, sat down on a corner of the bed, all her antennae out, suspicious as an old hen who senses a snake circling around one of her brood.

Lam gave Doan time to sit down. "Do you know who I am?"

Doan looked away, embarrassed, half-scared, half-irritated.

"I'm Suong's elder brother," Lam lied. "You know, the woman who jumped in the river to commit suicide thanks to your cruel joke. In fact, I shouldn't even speak to you, just tie you up like a pig and push your snout underwater so you touch the gates of hell."

The painter paled. He had his mother's square face but wild eyes that shimmered with a barbaric light, and the tanned skin and curly hair of the Katu or Ede minorities who lived in the highlands. His small, white teeth were as pointy as spears, like bat's teeth. Suddenly Lam understood why Doan had wanted to humiliate Suong, hurt her: She was the kind of prey he would never devour. His frantic, lecherous look revealed his soul.

Lam rose, opened his hands, and thrust them under Doan's nose. "Take a good look at my hands. They've killed at least a few men who were sturdier than you are. Lean over, go ahead, take a good look."

Doan's face went ashen, his lips trembled, hung open, jumping and twitching, exposing the dazzling white of his teeth.

Lam winced with disgust. Doan's mother rushed to the bed, gripped Lam's shoulder. "Please, if Doan has done anything, please tell us calmly . . . We'll make him understand."

Lam turned to her. "Are you sure you can educate your son?"

She froze, didn't dare reply. The father suddenly rose and did the only thing he could do: close the door so that the neighbors couldn't hear them. The room suddenly fell into an oppressive, shadowy darkness. Lam deliberately kept silent, waiting for the mother's reply.

"Please, please, I beg you!" she cried, digging her nails into his arm. "If you raise a hand against my child, I'll call the neighbors!"

Lam laughed, pushing the woman's hands off him roughly. "Scream louder."

The old woman stared at him, her eyes bulging, glistening with hatred. She clenched her fists in silence.

"Please, scream louder," Lam said slowly. A moment passed. Then he spoke again, measuring his words as if he were letting fish drop, one by one, into a basin. "I'm only afraid that you won't dare, that you'll never dare. This is a huge residence. Hundreds of families live here . . . and their daughters are still young. These people aren't going to defend a rapist."

The woman blanched, her eyes dazed, stricken.

I've struck her in the heart already. Poor woman. I didn't want to have to spit out the truth, but there wasn't any other way.

Suddenly, he shouted: "Shout, go ahead, shout!"

It was the final blow. She collapsed at Lam's feet, but then, after a few seconds, dragged herself to her knees. "Please, I beg you for mercy.

She pleaded, hands clasped, prostrating herself at his feet: "I beg you, beg you . . ."

Her husband remained glued to his corner, his head hung low. Doan, who sat motionless in a chair, didn't say a word, didn't even look at his mother.

The dog! He's never worried about his poor mother. A painter of such sublime talent! All he thinks about is his own life, that he alone deserves to live because he has talent, will bring fame and fortune to his family, to his country. His father, his mother, everyone around him, they're just tools, slaves to his talent, his success.

"I beg you, sir, if he has done anything wrong to you, tell us, we'll compensate you," the woman continued.

Lam asked her: "What is your fortune worth that you pretend you could compensate me?"

"We . . . we . . ." the old woman looked around the room with frightened, desperate eyes, her hands still gripping Lam's knees, continuing to supplicate.

"I beg you, sir, I bow my head and beg you sir." Tears streamed down the brown skin of her face, pooling in the wrinkles and pockmarks. Murky tears clogged with the dust and smoke of the kitchen, the smell of mutton for their miserable meal. Suddenly, Lam regained his compassion for her and pulled her up: "Please, sit down. I'm going to tell you everything. In any case, you're innocent, even if you did bring a devil into this world."

The woman sat down, wiped her eyes with the back of her sleeve.

"Where has your son been these last few months?" Lam asked.

"I don't know. He told me he had to give drawing classes at someone's house. He just came back here a few weeks ago."

"So someone hired him as tutor?"

"Yes," his mother nodded. But a shadow of doubt crossed her eyes.

"Your son wasn't a tutor. He lived like a parasite at someone's house. He's the kind who'd lick the plates at someone's house for a meal."

His mother suddenly understood. The father too. They lowered their heads.

Lam saw the old woman's knees tremble, her gnarled hands clench. The father's face slowly turned gray.

These are honest people. They feel shame when they're humiliated. But I can't stop myself from whipping their conscience. They're blind slaves to this bastard, and they're partly responsible for his actions.

The father's lips began to tremble just like the old woman's, and his face shriveled up, tears brimming at the corners of his red eyes, refusing to roll down his cheeks.

"You probably don't want to hear this, but your son doesn't just eat up other people's fortune, he tried to destroy a happy family, break up a marriage, make children orphans."

"My god, Doan!" the father moaned, incapable of holding back any longer. "Why didn't you stay at home and paint? Why do you humiliate us like this? Day in and day out, all we do is look after you, give you whatever you need." The old man wailed and hunched over, the veins in his neck throbbing. "Oh why didn't you just stay home?" In his pain and despair, the old man spoke in the Nghe An peasant accent.

Silent from the beginning, Doan jumped up now as if he had received an electric shock hearing his father's moans. Rage flashed across his wild eyes, his dirty, bushy beard seemed to tremble, and his lips and cheeks twitched convulsively. He kicked over his chair. "Damn you old bastard! Shut up! Take care of me, look after me, right . . . Do you think I can paint beautiful images fed on shit that's only good for pigs?"

He grabbed the platter and pulled off the bamboo cover his mother had carefully placed over it. A bowl of pickled cabbage, a bowl of tiny green eggplant soaking in *nuoc mam*, chilies, and a few garlic cloves. A red plastic box that used to be filled with soap powder.

His mother ran to him. "Doan, my child, every time there's meat, we save it for you. We've never dared touch our chopsticks to the dishes we save for you."

Doan stared at her, furious. "Meat? How many ounces do I get a week? Aside from rotten peanuts, what is there to eat in this house?"

He grabbed the red plastic box and threw it on the ground. The cover opened and shelled peanuts rolled out. He was right: they were stale, the kind people gathered from flooded fields, that cost five times less than good peanuts.

Lam surveyed the scene, indifferent, but he still felt like giving Doan a few slaps.

I had to make them taste the bitter fruit. Because they nourished it themselves, his selfishness, his cruelty. They dug the earth of their own garden to plant and raise this rotten bastard. Not just out of love, but because they were greedy for fame. They must have adored their son with the reverence of art lovers.

Lam waited until Doan's fit of rage had subsided, then got up and looked Doan straight in the eye. "You dog, how dare you insult your father and slap your mother around? You do whatever you want in this house. This is your kingdom. But don't you ever set foot in Suong's house again, or you'll pay with your life."

Lam strode toward the door, opened it, and then turned around, looking everyone over. "Art! Such a beautiful dream, too beautiful. You can paint your entire life, sharpen your pencils until you die, toil like an ant. But with cruelty and hatred in your soul, all you'll ever do is smear different colored paint for a few *dong*."

Doan's face twisted. His parents were mortified. All three faces were filled with doubt and despair. And for them, this doubt, this despair was more terrifying than death.

Poor people. They believed in their son's genius, were ready to sacrifice everything to this hope. Depriving them of it would be the same as throwing them into the boiling vats of Hell.

As Lam turned and left, he heard a cry from behind the door. "No, no, no!"

It was Doan, choking like a pig feeling the knife at his jugular.

II

8

The friendship between Vinh and Tan had begun suddenly. They had first met on a volleyball field, and a second time when Tan had gone with him to the hospital to visit Suong and witnessed his fight with Hung. Their third encounter came during a party organized by their high school. During the party, Tan sang a solo and he was the star of the show. Tall, handsome, witty, elegant, Tan had everything a young man could dream of. He dressed well, exuded self-confidence, and sang with the passion of a child who had never known cold, or hunger, or worries. Lost in the crowd of high school students, Vinh listened to Tan's voice, envious, filled with self-pity. Tan was two years younger than he was, but already he was preparing the final exams to graduate, while Vinh was still trailing behind as a freshman, one of a group they called "the old students." Disadvantaged by their background, late in their studies, most of them came from the countryside, and they arrived at school with their book bags, a bundle of inferiority complexes, and a yearning for revenge.

Vinh knew that Suong had sacrificed for him, that she hoped that one day he would fulfill their dead father's dream. At the beginning, Vinh thought studying was like a marathon; all you needed was strength and patience to reach the goal. When he lived with Mien in their hamlet in the mountains, he would lead the troupe of goats out through the barren hills, the steep valleys, all the places that the village children avoided, terrified. Their goat herd was the best in the region, reproducing the fastest. With his rough, callused feet that never tired, Vinh had wandered from hill to hill, not just to nourish the goats with the best leaves in the forest, but also to chase butterflies, dragonflies, and hunt for eggs in the nests of wild birds. But school had turned out to be a precipice to which there was no path up or down. In class, Vinh's eyes glazed over faced with the drawings of dinosaur skeletons. He couldn't remember the names of the bones in the claws, or those that linked the plexus to the neck, or head. He couldn't find any order in it all. Every time he tried to memorize a skeleton, his brain swirled with a gray fog that had nothing to do with the mist on the surface of the Trang Nguyen Lake of his childhood. The worst of all were the biology and math classes. Good god, all those figures, the letters of the equations a, b, c . . . linked together like the squiggled signs on some magic amulet.

$$(a + b)^2 = a^2 + 2ab + b^2$$

He had to rewrite that equation a hundred times on a piece of paper stuck to his desk, on the brick floor of the kitchen where he prepared their meals, in the palm of his hand as he walked to school, before he could learn it by heart. He felt weak with fatigue, overcome with sadness.

It's too hard. What's the use of learning this? It's harder than running across ten hills to bring back enough to feed the goats. What use is it, when the others do it as of it were child's play, and they're still a hundred times better than I am!

But he didn't dare tell Suong. Every day, he dragged his bag to school, preparing himself for the stinging slaps that awaited him, like a prisoner on his way to a torture session anticipates the whip, how the electric wires will be pressed to his body. Not just the pain but the humiliation.

That night, at the party, the applause roared for Tan, and a delegation of young girls ran up to him with a bouquet of flowers. Vinh felt his face burn with envy, jealousy, and humiliation.

"Vinh, are you in your class singing group?" A hand tapped him on the shoulder. The voice was gentle, soft, as if it questioned and answered at the same time. Vinh turned around. It was Tan in his stage costume.

"No, I don't know how to sing."

"That makes sense. One family with two star singers, what use would that be? Everyone has his own talent, it's better that way . . . do you want to stay and listen?"

"I don't know."

"I can understand. When you've heard Suong sing, all other singers must hurt your eardrums. Let's go out. The sky is beautiful tonight."

"How are we going?"

"As you like. If you want to walk, we can go on foot. Otherwise, if you like speed, I'll ride you on the back of my motorbike. We can get up to sixty-five miles per hour."

"Okay, let's take the motorbike. We're going into town, right?"

Vinh had wanted to go out on a motorbike for a long time, and whatever apprehension he'd had was quickly dissipated by the exhilaration of speed. Tan took them on a long ride down narrow streets, past scattered houses, crisscrossing the half-urban, half-country space, racing straight for the beach. It had been a long time since Vinh had drunk in the smell of the sea wind and the sand or listened to the rustling sighs of the night. The echo of the sea that had haunted his childhood brought him back to life, like a gulp of fresh air for someone about to suffocate. He forgot the interminable torture of the algebra equations, the chemistry formulas, the physics theorems. He forgot the stench of the chemistry lab, the stern, icy, disappointed looks of his teachers, all the struggles that had afflicted him for so long.

The two young men strolled on the beach until ten o'clock before returning to the town. Tan drove Vinh back to his house and promised to help him with his studies.

"I've studied longer than you, and I've got more experience. It's not that difficult," Tan said with modesty.

Vinh mumbled something, awkwardly. "If you like, but I don't want to bother you."

"What bother? We're from the same generation, aren't we?" Tan said as he left on his motorbike. He promised to come back and see Vinh two days later.

Why is he so kind? I don't have anything of use to him, do I?

Like all young people from the countryside, his suspicion, the habit of constant vigilance never left him. But he had to admit that Tan treated him well, and he seemed to have a good heart.

Tan's friendship helped Vinh progress somewhat in his studies. But it didn't triumph over the young man from the mountains. With each day, Vinh lost hope of ever winning the race, and the gate to the high school loomed in front of him, daunting, sealed off to his wild soul.

Why do I have to suffer like this? Tonight, it's definite, I'm going to tell Suong the truth. I'm not cut out to be a student. The pages of the book slide around my brain like rain off duck feathers. Why doesn't she find some work for me in one of the town factories? The factory director adores her, showers her with gifts. I like to pound a hammer, forge iron, see the sparks jump like flowers under the bite of the welding torch. I could become a welder, watch the blue and yellow flames spit from the welding sticks like water from a faucet. Why does she force me to suffer like this?

How many times had this thought landed on the tip of his tongue? But Vinh had never had the courage to spit it out, to say it. His sister's gaze was so trusting, so tender. Her voice seemed to echo in his brain.

Here, little brother, I've just bought you a new coat. This winter, you won't have to wear that old wool one to the high school anymore. Here, Vinh, I just bought you these study guides. Apparently they only distributed thirty in this town, because the Ministry of Education didn't print enough to put on sale. Here, Vinh, I got you some mint candies. Have some, it'll help clear your voice. Last night, I heard you were hoarse as you were reciting your lessons.

There was a whisper of hope behind her every gesture. And that hope didn't tolerate a refusal. Vinh, the only man in the family, had to fulfill the father's dream.

Vinh took his school books out of the closet, spread them on the table, opened them one by one. Each page seemed like a riddle without an answer. He closed them all and slumped on his bed.

It's all for my father. Why did he put me in this horrible situation? Suong only forces me to study because she loves him. In the end, I'm the one who is going to come out dirty and bruised from this fight. I could make every possible effort, as long as she wanted, and I would still lose.

The image of a mountain goat bounding up steep slopes covered with flowers and grasses was like a beacon of hope for Vinh; like the call of a pure stream, or a waterfall in the middle of the jungle, it was the promise of a wild, free life. And yet he felt strangled by an invisible rope around his neck, held tight by the fist of his father's power. That man—the first man in the family—continued to reign, refusing to yield his place to the second.

God, I'm still just a four-year-old boy, I'll always be that to him.

Urine suddenly seeped into his pants, not the almost odorless urine of a four-year-old child, but the nauseating urine of an eighteen-year-old. Vinh went to change. But the horrible feeling continued to haunt him. It reminded him of the stormy sky the day his father's coffin was lowered into the grave, of the buzzing of black flies, the scarlet red sun, the listless ripple of funeral banners in the sea wind, and the chants that wailed, incessant, the echo of a sad, dull life being dragged past the dunes to the open sea.

My son . . . I'm leaving. From now on, you're the only man, the pillar of the family.

Vinh remembered how the man had made a sign with his hand, gliding off into the distance, how his clothes had floated about him, as light and as transparent as a veil of silk. His eyes shot out barbs of flickering black light.

Now I'm going, really going. Try and live, my son, the only man, the pillar of the family.

Vinh's jaw had dropped, his throat parched, incapable of answering. The man disappeared, and Vinh ran after him in pursuit shouting like a madman.

You put a rope around my neck, but you still haven't yielded your place!

The old man hadn't replied, just flew up over the dunes covered with grass, toward the shore where the shells sang on the beach.

Vinh wept for a long time, then fell asleep, his head between the pages.

The waves of afternoon heat descended from the Truong Son Cordillera, crawling like snakes of flame through the town, through every room in every house, through Vinh's hair, the length of his back. The hot wind, like a boat, lulled the boy. Vinh saw his village, his childhood. His native land. A small village hanging between the mountains and the sea, between greenness and a dense cloak of violet that covered the rice paddies, the fields of manioc, tea, chilies, and pepper trees, growing darker and darker as it disappeared into the base of the mountains. On the stormy days, the waves howled and the wind screamed through the casuarina trees, filling the sky with their rage. On peaceful nights you could hear the roar of tigers coming down from the mountains. The sea and the mountain merged, trembling, crashing against each other in front of each house. At dawn, long processions of fishing people, groaning under the weight of their loads, filed down the sand paths that linked the provincial road to the village. Most of them were women, the kind tanned leathery by the sun, with muscles as firm as amboyna wood, dancing eyes, and voices as riotous as the waves. Their female scent, as heady as the steam off sticky rice, sent the men of the village scurrying back to their courtyards, or to the edge of the sidewalks, where they snuck desirous glances in their direction.

When he was five years old, Vinh had been deeply infatuated with a young fishmonger who must have been sixteen or seventeen. She used to carry two glittering black lacquer baskets full of fish on a bamboo beam over her shoulders. She wore a conical hat decorated with a sprig of myrtle and her blouse was always blue, like a beetle's shell. As soon as he saw the blouse flicker through the hedge of squash, Vinh would run out of the house. "Ma, Ma! Come buy some fish!"

His mother liked to spoil him and always bought a few fish, even when the larder was full. Vinh used to stare at the young woman's eyes, as liquid and black as a duck's. The more he looked, the more fascinated he was by the soft, tender light of her eyes.

Once, he was looking at her, transfixed, when he heard someone shout, "Vinh, come here!" It was his father, his face red, his eyebrows furrowed into a dark mass over his nose. Vinh's mother and the fishmonger were startled too and looked up at him. Then they rapidly concluded the transaction, and the fishmonger grabbed her baskets and ran out the gate. His father paid no attention to the women, dragging Vinh into the garden. Under an old honey locust tree, he shook the young boy's tiny shoulders, looked him straight in the eyes, and said: "Vinh?"

"Yes, father?"

"What were you looking at?"

Vinh said nothing.

"What were you looking at on that fishmonger whore?"

The little boy's tears began to fall. Had it been fear? Perhaps, but also out of pity for the young fishmonger with the liquid eyes who had just been called a whore. He dug his feet into the hot sand, his face burning under his father's fiery gaze. Furious, the veins on his neck swollen and pulsing, the old man shouted at him. Vinh had never seen his father so angry, and he trembled, panting, thinking that his father's huge hands might strangle him. But the old man just pounded his fist against his palm with each word.

"I forbid you—do you hear me—I forbid you from looking at that whore, or any of her kind." Then he gave his order. "You will stand here until dusk."

Then his father turned and stalked back to the house, saying to Vinh's mother: "From now on, my gate is closed to that whore in the blue shirt. Fish! That witch is drinking the boy's soul!"

His mother nodded, lowering her head obediently, slipping a

pained, pitying look toward Vinh. He met her eyes for an instant, but didn't dare call her. Tears flowed now, glistening with sunlight. He felt as if he were dying slowly, his body shriveling up like a cicada's on the branch of a honey locust tree, the tree's tiny flowers raining down on his corpse in the monotonous hum of cicadas, beetles, and maybugs. The melodious sound of the insects echoed through the hills, down the paths, over the dunes, and out to sea. Sirens carried this lament to the Heavens. And the Heavens performed a miracle, bringing him back to life, helping him emerge from the shell of a cicada to become a powerful giant who could strap his own father to the foot of the honey locust tree. And this stocky woodsman, like the guardian of the law at the pagoda, had to bow his head faced with the giant's infinite strength and hold out his hands, surrendering to Vinh and allowing himself to be tied to a tree with the same thick ropes he had used to bind tree trunks and drag them behind the water buffaloes. Then, right in front of him, Vinh greeted the fishmonger girl with the blue blouse, welcoming her to their house and staring into her eyes forever.

This dream lasted past noon, into the evening.

Vinh slept, his tiny body curled at the foot of the honey locust tree. His father picked him up in his arms and carried him inside. Vinh only woke when dinner was served.

The clock struck four in the afternoon when Vinh woke, dazed, remembering his dream of twelve years ago. He still didn't understand why, on this afternoon filled with the suffocating Laos wind, this dream had come back to haunt him. His father was dead now, and the deep pleasure he had felt in the dream was the pleasure of a man obsessed with the desire to kill his father. Vinh knew that of all the crimes of his life, this was the worst.

Steps echoed behind him. Vinh turned around and saw Suong, who had rushed into the room.

"Is Hung back?"

"I don't know. I fell asleep. Where did he go?"

"He left yesterday morning while I was with the troupe."

"Did he take the keys?"

"No, he left them with Auntie Tuong."

"He didn't say where he was going?"

"No." Suong shook her head and ran up the staircase. Vinh followed her in silence, saw her open the linen closet, fumble around for a long time. The more she rummaged, the paler she grew, like a drowned person, as if she had fallen into the river a second time.

That bastard Hung must have taken her savings, the money she was going to use to buy clothes for the girls and a refrigerator. My poor sister! Every night, she wanders like a ghost in the kitchen, making ice cream to sell to round out the ends of the months. And now that bastard husband has taken it all in one fell swoop.

"Well?" he asked, his voice heavy, half-mocking, half-interrogating. Suong slumped down into a chair.

"I told you," Vinh said. "Was I wrong?"

Suong said nothing.

"With someone like that you've got to always keep an eye out."

She still said nothing.

"You should never have made peace with him. You should hate him, hate him!"

"Please, Vinh, Please!"

"Oh, now you're asking me for mercy? You should ask yourself."

"Stop, Vinh," Suong begged. Her eyes filled with tears that spilled down her cheeks. "Vinh, let's go and look for him."

"I'm not going, I can't stand him."

"I know it's his fault, but he's Da Hai and Phuoc Hanh's father and he's my husband."

"So go and find him. I don't have the energy . . ."

"Okay, then I'll go alone." She went into the bathroom to wash her face, then she changed and went out with her bicycle. Vinh watched her, filled with a mixture of pity and satisfaction.

A slight breeze rippled through the hedge of white and yellow ylang-ylangs. In the rustling of the wind, Vinh saw his father appear again in front of the gate, silent, motionless. He could only see above the old man's knees, the funeral clothes—white pants, a tunic of green silk gauze. His father's thick, unkempt hair covered his ears, ran down his shoulders like black seaweed. He didn't say a word, just looked at Vinh for a long time, sad, melancholy. And hopeless.

9

Happiness always returns to port, like a lost boat remembers the old banyan tree by the shore, the sway of a wood bridge over the mirror of the water in the glow of dawn, the strains of a bamboo flute, a kite floating over the dikes with village children scampering after it as it rises and dips, fragile, in the wind. Happiness comes back to port like a man in a foreign land trembles faced with the storms, his heart filled with homesickness, remembering his country, his house, the peace of a quiet evening with children chattering around a meal under the lamplight.

Thanks to Lam, happiness had returned to their home after Suong's failed suicide. Before leaving town Lam had found Hung a small job and made him swear to make peace with Suong. Hung obediently went to work, despite the monotony of the task. The town had organized artisans cooperatives to make bamboo products for export—exotic objects from the tropics to add some spice to the banal, comfortable atmosphere of European living rooms. Bamboo was brought in from the mountain districts, cut into thin strips, polished with semimechanized tools, and then assembled into screens with a special dark yellow thread streaked with a green bamboo sap. The artisans painted tropical landscapes onto these screens according to models or commissions from customers: a weeping willow over a lake, the One-Pillar Pagoda, awkward copies of Chinese-style landscapes with rocks and trees, an old man seated on the rocks next to the water, fishing. Hung had never learned to draw but he had an artistic sense and he could use colors to perfection. In very little time, he earned the title of "the worker with the golden pair of hands," as the men and women who led the cooperative put it. They wanted to nominate Hung as a "progressive worker" but had to abandon the idea because of his "bad" dossier. Every day, Hung went to work at the cooperative, and at the end of the month he received a modest salary that contributed to their household expenses. Suong couldn't really believe that her husband had resigned himself to this kind of life, but she thought he would try and forget his position with the troupe for the sake of their happiness, the future of the children. One day, she came back home, a huge bouquet of flowers in her arms. Naively, she told Hung that she had just participated in an evening for visiting representatives from the Party Central Committee. Flowers had been brought all the way from Hanoi to offer to the guests who had in turn presented them to her as a gift. Hung examined each bouquet. Red, white, and pink gladiolas, velvety roses, scented pansies, dazzling white chrysanthemums as large as the moon that only grew in the cold, humid, fog-shrouded earth of the north. He admired each bouquet in silence while she changed and washed up.

When she returned, he said: "I'm sure they all wanted to kiss you and offer you flowers, didn't they?"

"Yes," Suong said, then asked, "How did you know?"

"Because I know the mentality of high-ranking officials like village kids know all the different kinds of toads and frogs. Because I'm a man too, though I must say in that domain I've had more success than they have."

Suong was stunned. Hung slowly explained. "I've been lucky in love. For them, it's the opposite. Like eunuchs, they have to suppress and destroy all carnal desire so they can fight and conquer to win their place at the imperial court. But you can't destroy their desire so easily—it's still lying there, inside them, like kidney stones in a sick man. Every time they meet an actress it's a chance to use flowers and perfume to slake their lust. A whiff of your powder and lipstick, even if it's cheap, is better than the stink of their wife's bed, her bizarre mix of Tiger balm, sweet-smelling soap, and mentholated oils. Your dazzling *ao dais,* your bras as transparent as grasshoppers' wings give the old geezers a real thrill. They might not be able to undress you, but they can always imagine it, and though they're idiots, their imagination flourishes when they see you in your paper-thin tunics, the idea of each layer leading to another . . ."

Suong kept silent.

This had never even occurred to her, though it was probably all true. But this truth was like a mirror that reflected her own image, and she suddenly felt insulted, just like she had by his drinking companions who had called her "the little peasant condemned to herding sheep her whole life if it hadn't been for Hung."

Suong's face burned. She lowered her head. Hung continued, his hands still fingering the bouquets piled on the table.

"Beautiful! Why, each one of these flowers is worth a prisoner's life. Did I ever tell you what the young women students from Saigon and Danang—young, intelligent women with bodies of pure jade—were forced to do in the camps?"

Hung's eyes darkened, plunged in a dark, shadowy world, a cold, damp place filled with blood and tears. At that moment his face was like it had been the night he had found the dirty knapsack from the camp, the one she had wanted to throw out. He had sealed off a part of his life, a secret, melancholy, resentful life. A life without her. A life that opposed her.

Suong shivered. She waited for Hung to mount the stairs, then carried the flowers over to Auntie Tuong's house. The next evening, she left a handful of calling cards and the flowers in Dam's office.

"What's the matter, Suong?" Dam asked.

Suong couldn't tell him what had happened, but she just said: I don't want to make him sad."

Dam nodded. He took a few drags on his cigarette. "Is he still going to work?"

"Yes."

"Do they pay him well?"

"Enough for now."

"The salary isn't the problem, is it?" Dam let his words hang there, then he opened a closet, pulled out two packs of cigarettes and handed them to her. "Here, please give them to him from me."

"No, keep them for yourself. He won't accept them. You know how he is."

"Tell him I've stopped smoking, that he's my only friend in town."

"Okay. Thanks."

"I'll see you off." He saw her all the way back to the house, but stopped at the gate. "I'll be going now."

"Thank you, Dam."

"Be gentle, patient with him. No one else can help him right now." Dam's eyes were lit with compassion; Suong could see that. She had tried to fulfill Hung, to protect their happiness the way you protect a flame flickering weakly in the wind. Now she was the one who washed his hair, clipped his nails, who came back late at night after the performances and washed his clothes, fighting the urge to sleep and the pain in her wrists. Suong had grown up in the wild hills, in the middle of the pepper and chili plantations. She was used to hard work, and for a while, she thought the Heavens had taken pity on her, compensating her for her patience.

But then Hung had left, suddenly, without explanation for the Rose Inn, without a word. The night before, they had spent the entire evening playing with the children and then made love. The next day Suong had gone to work as usual, eating lunch at the canteen with the troupe. Dam had put together a new show. He had asked everyone to stay there for lunch so they could make good use of the rest time. The provincial government gave them the meal for free. That evening, Suong grabbed a sandwich with the other singers before performing in honor of the army's telecommunications congress. By the time she left for home, it was already late at night. When she arrived at Auntie Tuong's house, the old woman handed her the keys.

"Hung gave them to me. He left about nine o'clock this morning. He said he had some work to attend to."

Seeing Suong's surprise, she added: "The little ones are already sound asleep. Let them spend the night here tonight, so you can go home and get some rest."

Suong went home. Vinh was already asleep, and had latched the door to his room. She climbed the stairs with the slightest of hopes, even though she sensed Hung wasn't there. The door to their room was wide open. When she turned on the light, the objects appeared in their usual places, the former owner's altar in its corner, Hung's desk in front of the window. She opened the armoire: one of the old knapsacks that Hung hadn't wanted to part with—his inheritance from the reeducation camp—was still there in the corner. Everything was as it had been, except Hung was gone. The room seemed enormous. A room without an owner.

All night, Suong tossed and turned, sleepless. Where had he gone? A hundred questions swirled in her head. The next morning, she went to the cooperative and they told her Hung hadn't been to work in two weeks, He hadn't given any reason, just promised to be back after he'd settled some "urgent business." Her mind racing, Suong returned to the theater, but she didn't dare say anything to Dam. She went on stage and finished two rehearsals with all the other actors. That night, when she went home, she hurried over to Auntie Tuong's house. She had no one else to confide in.

The old women listened, then said: "I wouldn't say he's right, but I don't dare reproach him, or insult him either. Men are like birds; they can't just live on food. You lock them in a cage and they'll waste away and die, even if you feed them on gold. Maybe he feels cooped up, stifled . . ."

"What can I do?"

"I can't help you with this. Go and look for him. And don't tell anyone. People today are short on compassion, but they've got cruelty to spare. Be careful. As for the girls, let them sleep here with me. Your life's not going to be easy from now on . . ."

That night, Suong wandered all over looking for Hung. She wore a solid color silk tunic so she would look no different from the waitresses in the restaurants and cafés. She combed the streets, the bars, the cafés, the clubs that attracted music fans, where students and young people went to dance and sing. Toward midnight, in a dense fog, she returned home, her legs swollen, stiff. The next day she woke up late. Vinh had already eaten breakfast and left for school. Suong climbed the staircase, her heart racing, hoping for a miracle: Hung would be there, she'd find him sound asleep, his wavy hair fallen over his forehead. But the room was empty.

A night passed. Then another. And yet another. The more she searched, the more desperate she became. Her face thinned, her eye sockets deepening like the two holes children dig in the ground to throw coins into. On the fourth day, in the morning, Dam called to her as she paced down a corridor at the theater.

"What's the matter with you, Suong? Look at yourself in a mirror. Don't forget that one of your duties as a professional actress is to protect your beauty."

Suong burst into tears. "It's Hung, he's left . . ."

"Left?" Dam said. Then he pulled her gently into his office, lowered his voice: "When did he leave?"

"It's been four days already. They told me he hadn't been to work for the last two weeks."

"Strange . . . where could he have been hiding for two weeks? He must have gone some place when you thought he was making screens at the cooperative. And we've got to find that place."

"But I've already been everywhere, all over town, even out to the suburbs."

"No . . . no . . . a woman won't find him. This is a man's task. Does Hung have a friend that we can trust absolutely?"

"Yes, Lam."

"You mean the clown? I heard he was very close to you and Hung during the war."

"Yes."

"Good. Tomorrow, take the day off and go find him. Take this scarf. It belonged to a woman who loved me and betrayed me. It's a bad souvenir for me, but it's a good scarf. Keep it to protect your throat. Don't forget, your voice is your only weapon in this life."

Dam saw Suong to the door, glanced suspiciously around. But his caution was useless. When he had ushered Suong into his office, the ears "of revolutionary vigilance" had followed them, listened attentively. The next day, Suong barely had time to get dressed when two uniformed policemen, rifles in hand, asked her to follow them to the station.

It was the same man, the same old face. Handsome, as hard as iron, as cold as money. "Where is your husband?" he asked.

"I don't know."

"Really? Or are you pretending?"

"No."

"How many days ago did he leave?"

"Four."

"Why didn't you alert the authorities?"

"I went to look for him first. I thought he would come back."

"Why did you think that?"

"My husband wouldn't abandon his wife and children."

"You think he'll come back, so you must know where he is."

"If I knew, why would I have gone searching for him the last few days?"

"If husband and wife don't know each others' whereabouts, then who does?"

Suong didn't reply, stubbornly kept her silence. To the left of the interrogator stood a crew-cut officer with a jutting chin and a glass eye that seemed to stare at her. The other eye, the real one, looked out into the courtyard.

I've got to learn to keep silent or they're going to kill me with this kind of question. Oh Hung, where are you now? Why do you make me suffer like this?

"Okay. You can go. If your husband tries to escape by boat again, the punishment is going to be three times as stiff as the last time. He may be your husband, but he's also a traitor. You're an actress, a cadre with a state salary, and it's your duty to denounce his counterrevolutionary behavior to the authorities."

She didn't reply, just got up and left. As she crossed the paved courtyard of the police station, she was startled to notice a man was watching her, but she felt neither curiosity nor fear. Her head lowered, she walked faster.

At first she thought she would go straight to the bus station to look for Lam, but suddenly she realized she was right in front of the Thanh Truc Café, where she had often stood waiting for Hung. The sign with the letters Thanh Truc was straight as an arrow, with blue neon lights on in full daylight.

The owner's son was one of his prison buddies. Maybe the mother could give me some leads.

Suong entered the café, but it was deserted. An old woman sipped coffee, spoonful by spoonful. Her wrinkled hands, covered with gold rings, lifted the tiny spoon with an elegant gesture, as if she wasn't drinking coffee, but measuring fragrant hair oils at a Tet bazaar.

Suong fumbled in her handbag to check that she had enough change so she could order a lemonade and wait for an opportunity to talk to the old woman. Once before, she had stopped in front of this café, but she had pulled down her hat to hide her face. She didn't like to talk to the townspeople, especially the women. She could never guess their intentions from the ambiguous way they talked, all their vague undertones and insinuations, and she never knew how they might react. But now she had to make an effort.

To capture the tiger, you've got to enter its lair.

Suong sat down at a table facing the old woman. The owner, buried in her account books behind the counter, looked up, a flash of recognition in her eyes.

"What will you be having?" the woman asked in a high, clear voice.

"Uh, a lemonade, please," Suong stammered, as if, faced with this woman, she had lost confidence in herself. Everyone said Suong was exceptionally talented on stage. Under the glare of thousands of lamps and candles, faced with thousands of spectators, she carried herself naturally, like a fish in water. And yet here, faced with a café owner, she didn't know what to do with her hands and feet, was so embarrassed she didn't dare meet the woman's penetrating gaze. The owner slowly prepared the lemonade and served it to Suong with a serene, graceful manner more like a hostess welcoming a guest than a shopkeeper.

"Enjoy your drink," she said, setting the drink down on a white saucer. She wiped her hands with a cotton towel.

Suong lifted the glass, then set it down without tasting it. "Excuse me, ma'am," she stammered, blurting out the question that had tortured her for days. "My husband, the composer Hung, he knew your son, didn't he?"

"Yes, by a twist of fate my son was in the prison camp with him."

"That's why I'd like to ask you a question: Would your son have tried to get my husband to leave with him again?"

"To go where?"

The woman stared Suong straight in the eyes. Suong felt her face blaze. *I've got to tell her the truth. At this point . . . after all, she's not going to eat me alive.*

Suong summoned all her courage and then said in one breath: "My husband left the house four days ago. He took all my savings. I don't know if he followed your son to leave by boat."

The woman searched Suong's eyes for a long time without saying a word. Suong was sweating profusely but she didn't think to use a handkerchief, just lifted the sleeve of her blouse to wipe her brow. Something about this simple gesture won the older woman over. To her, Suong was just another peasant woman, an unhappy wife in search of her husband, even if she was the star actress of a regime she hated.

"How much money did he take?" the woman asked.

"Uh, I don't remember, I had put money aside, little by little, for almost two years now."

"Okay, okay, but how many 'branches' of gold would it buy?"

"Just over one branch, ma'am."

The woman burst out laughing. A lighthearted, teasing, compassionate laugh. There was everything in that laugh. Suong blushed again, but she didn't dare ask another question, just waited in silence. Recovered from her fit of laughter, the owner asked Suong: "Do you know how many branches of gold you need to buy a place on one of the boats that flee this country?"

"No ma'am."

"Five branches. That's without the other costs. My family in Saigon had to pay one hundred and forty branches to get three kids out. You're surprised? It's not hard to figure out. You escape, they arrest you, you buy your freedom from prison with branches of gold. When you get out, you try again with a new boat. The unlucky ones get arrested as many as five times. But in the end, they always manage to get out.

"So, ma'am, you mean your son was also . . ."

"Yes, my son got out of the camp just three months after your husband. That's life. There aren't any laws here that don't bend under the weight of money. And it's always been like that," the owner said. She paused a moment, then lowered her voice.

"Don't you worry. The money your husband took would be barely enough to buy a bottle of wine to drink while they watched the others board the boats!"

"And what about your son?"

"Oh, he's left." She nodded emphatically to confirm this, then her lips pulled back in an ironic, contemptuous smile, as if to defy some invisible enemy. "Right now he's sitting in California. He's a sculptor working in a nice big apartment . . . that's good compensation after eating all that Communist prison rice."

Suong sat there, stunned. Her only hope had just evaporated. The owner's son had left. Hung didn't have enough money to buy a place on another boat. Where would she look for him now? Was his life at risk? If something happened to him, how would she find the money to pay for his funeral? Many times she had had to secretly sell off gifts that her fans had given her for a third of their value. The gifts they gave her were always expensive, destined for rich women who led lives of leisure. She would never forget her humiliation each time she had to sell the gifts, her naive, awkward attempts to hide her embarrassment, never forget the real life that she led, that people refused to believe. Her fans were used to seeing her in glittering costumes under the spotlights; in their eyes, the seductive curves of her body made her a kind of goddess of pleasure, a fairy who only appeared in this world to welcome them to paradise. They couldn't—wouldn't—imagine another Suong, the humiliated woman who served trays of food and wine to four debauched men, who scrubbed piles of dirty laundry in the bathtub, and who, pale and exhausted, measured flour and sugar late into the night, making ice cream to earn enough to feed her kids. At that moment, she finally saw all the indignities of her life, the irony of it all, and her eyes filled with tears, but she quickly wiped them with the back of her hand. She thanked the owner, paid, and left.

From behind the counter, the owner watched the singer go, then called to her. Suong came back, waited in silence, wondered if the woman was going to offer advice or if she would start to give details about the fugitives, the boat people.

"I'm going to give you an address," the woman said abruptly. "Do you still want to find him?"

" Yes, I want to bring him back home."

"He used to come here for coffee with my son after he got out of prison. Then he disappeared for years. Two or three weeks ago he came back with some men."

Suong looked at her, terrified, her heart racing, and asked: "Were they painters, poets . . . ?"

The owner nodded. "Yes, They used to come here, once. But I threw them out."

"You threw them out?"

"I can't stand noise and vulgarity. It's not your husband, but I don't have time to waste on the other hooligans. Customers here at the Thanh Truc are honest, polite people. I knew your husband had fallen in with a bunch of devils. But he's too old to listen to advice."

"So you know where he is now?"

"Like I said, probably in a place drinking while he watches others escape by sea. Not just drinking. I suspect they've been smoking too . . ."

"Smoking? But my husband has always smoked."

"Not tobacco. Opium. You don't know what that is, do you? Go and find him, then you'll understand." The woman ripped a leaf from a calendar hanging on the wall, scribbled an address on the back, handed it to Suong: *#79 Tran Phu Street, District II, The Rose Inn.*

"Thank you so much . . . thank you, ma'am."

Suong took the piece of paper, her hand shaking.

She had only heard about opium through the stories about thieves and robbers, the taverns and pubs where they met. And now her husband, the sweet man who had never even learned to shoot a gun, was mixed up in all this.

She decided to take a cyclo to find Lam at the bus station. When she reached the intersection, cars were coming at her from all directions. She hailed a cyclo from the other side of the street, and an old driver with a hat made of banana leaves made a U-turn with his cyclo right in front of another, screeching to a halt at the sidewalk where she was standing. "Where are you going, miss?"

"Take me to the bus station. How much is it, Uncle?"

"Five *dong* please."

Just then, a man's hand held out ten *dong*, right under Suong's eyes.

It was the young guard in the striped shirt from the reeducation camp. "Here, Uncle, wait a moment under the flame tree on the other side of the street. She'll be back in a moment."

After he had paid the man, he turned to Suong: "Where are you going in such a hurry? How have you been lately?"

"Thanks, I'm fine," she said curtly, recognizing the gaze that had followed her this morning at the police station.

Where was this guy hiding while I was in the café that he found me here? Why is he playing this game? Maybe he knows that Hung is hiding out somewhere and wants to use me, pressure me into paying something?

"This isn't a good place to talk, let's go into the café."

"No, no, I'm in a hurry. If you need something, talk to Lam."

"Stay calm. I'm not inviting you and Lam to perform. It's something else, entirely. And it only concerns you."

"No . . ."

"I know you're busy, but give me a few minutes. If you like, I can accompany you to the bus station to find Lam. Did I guess right?"

Suong couldn't say anything. She followed him into another nearby café. The place was huge and he chose a table right in the middle, not at all discreet. "There, right where everyone can see us, that's the best." He got up and ordered two glasses of manioc milk, then came back and sat down facing Suong. "Sister Suong . . ." He lowered his voice to a whisper. Suong had to bend her ear to hear him. "At the camp, we're really fond of you and Lam. Especially my boss. He's a sentimental man. He knows about your problems and he asked me to deliver a small gift to you."

The waiter brought over the two glasses of manioc milk. The young man took a few drags on his cigarette. He waited until the waiter had returned to the counter before continuing. "Don't be polite. Let me remind you, we adore you, and we respect you. We hope you'll come back someday to visit. Especially my boss . . ."

He fumbled in his pants' pocket and pulled out a notebook with a fake leather binding, set it on the table, and pushed it toward Suong.

Inside the notebook was a bulging envelope. Suong could tell it was filled with money.

"No, it's impossible . . . I thank you, but I can't accept this." Then she stood up: "Excuse me, but I've got to leave." Without waiting for his reply, she turned on her heels and walked out. Seeing her, the old driver, sitting under a tree on the opposite side of the road, pushed his cyclo toward her. "Take me to the bus station, please," she said.

She didn't turn around. She knew that the young man was still waiting calmly in the café. He would probably drink the two glasses of manioc milk before asking to pay and leaving. He had seemed calm, controlled. The old cyclo driver put his full weight on the pedals, suddenly lurching forward, and Suong felt the cool of the wind brush her face, as her mind settled. She remembered the look in the young man's eyes, the frank pride in his walk, his two hands thrust in his pockets. And behind this young man was another, the same man who had ordered him to come see her, who had gazed at her with a passionate look that transcended distance.

Why is he doing this? It's so strange.

But even as she asked this question, she knew why. She just didn't dare admit it to herself.

Lam had said they had a long-term debt with the prison camp, one they couldn't escape paying. Three months after Hung's release, Suong and Lam had returned to the camp to perform and the reception had been just as jubilant as the last time, but much friendlier. They put up the electric-powered spots again, flooding the night with light; laughter and joking had echoed through the forest and mountains. The commander was not as shy or as severe as he had been during the last performance. He personally came to inspect the preparations, refusing to leave this task to his deputy. The first night, when Suong was putting on her makeup in a room behind the stage, she had suddenly felt someone's warm breath against the back of her neck. She turned to see the commander standing right behind her.

"How's the makeup? I hope you weren't disappointed?" he asked cheerfully.

Suong lowered her eyes, not daring to look at the man's sparkling white teeth.

"It's excellent quality, better than what we had in the troupe," she replied.

He stared at her. "Allow me to offer you this makeup kit then."

"Oh, no, I couldn't."

"Please, don't be polite. You're the only one who deserves to use it."

The man's warm breath grazed her temples and cheeks, seeping through her skin into her flesh. She felt powerless, frightened. She shivered. In this man's mesmerizing gaze she sensed a wild animal, filled with desire, just waiting for a chance to slake his lust.

"I'm very grateful you came back. In the name of all the comrades in the camp, I thank you," he continued, with all the politesse of a diplomat. When he finished, he leaned his head toward Suong, his breath burning her earlobe, a part of her neck. Then he left.

The second night, the commander made the rounds to inspect the courtyard. Suong and Lam were already made up and were chatting with the deputy commander and some prison guards when the commander approached them: "Tonight, we're going hunting. Would either of you like to join us?"

"I would," Lam replied, who ever since his childhood had loved to hunt.

"Me too," the deputy commander said.

The commander laughed. "So we'll just desert the camp to go hunting and leave the prisoners to mutiny if they like? No, you stay here."

The commander turned to Suong. "Would the singer like to come along on the adventure?"

"No, no . . . thank you, but I can't . . ."

Lam spoke up. "Even though she used to live in these mountains, she's never been hunting."

The commander laughed: "So the nightingale with the crystal voice only knows how to sing in a crystal world, eh?"

And he strode off toward the barracks to the south of the courtyard, a torch bobbing in his hand. Suong didn't look at him, but all her senses were focused on the man. His smooth stride reminded her of the gait of a leopard; it was a stride that seemed to both challenge and intimidate her.

After she and Lam had left the camp, Suong had been swept up in daily life again, with all its myriad worries. Expecting a second child, she concentrated all her thoughts on saving money, preparing for the birth. And a new daughter, Phuoc Hanh, was born. The baby's clever, radiant, face fascinated her; it was as if the Heavens had sent this beautiful child to console her. But the happiness didn't last. Hung's friends had dragged her down, driven her to the brink of suicide. Time flew by, a rushing current. And now, the memory of this man made her shudder.

"We're here," the old cyclo driver announced.

Suong jumped down and walked toward the station, which was jammed with buses and wagons. She could see about twenty horse-drawn wagons, but not Lam's. One of the drivers told her that he had left the previous night for the high plateaus with a cargo of merchandise and wouldn't be back for two weeks.

Suong resigned herself to looking for another cyclo to go home. At that hour, all the drivers were resting in a corner or had gone off to eat lunch. Suong walked in circles, hoping to spot any arriving vehicle that might take her back into town, Before she could find one, she saw the young man in the striped shirt racing toward her on his Honda.

"Hello again! You can't find a cyclo back to town?" he asked, smiling like a man who had just won the lottery. Suong didn't even have time to reply. "Lam's gone, hasn't he? You really don't have much luck, do you? Well, hop on and I'll take you back home. And don't be polite, it's just like helping you across that stream."

Suong couldn't help laughing, remembering when he had helped her and Lam cross a wooden bridge suspended over a chasm to visit the sugar cane fields. In the middle of the crossing, he had teased her, made her scream in terror. Just as she thought she was going to fall into the ravine, he had pulled her back with a gentle, precise gesture. The young man drove Suong all the way back to the gate of her house.

"May I have a glass of water? I don't need tea or coffee, just water will be fine."

Without waiting for a reply, he continued. "Would the singer be so impolite as to dismiss her chauffeur without so much as a glass of water, a word of thanks?"

Suong laughed again, opened the gate, and invited him in. "I'll make you some tea. I'm not a connoisseur, but there's always good tea at our house."

The young man took her hands. "Sister Suong . . ." His soft, tender voice was almost inaudible. "We love and respect you. Don't be cold. Consider this gift a token of our gratitude for sharing your voice with us."

· The man's hands squeezed hers. His face was filled with warmth, compassion, without a trace of intimidation. She couldn't reply. She let the man hold her hands for a long time. Then Suong said: "Thank you."

He pressed her hands a last time, then let go. "Take care of yourself I'm sure there's still going to be lots of trouble ahead for you." He pulled out the fake leather notebook, placed it on the table and left. Suong didn't see him off. Less than a minute later, she heard the Honda roar down the street.

10

Hung had thought he could return to a normal, peaceful life.

After Lam left, Hung went off every morning to make bamboo screens. At first, this artisan's work distracted him, and he often changed the colors of his palette, sometimes by accident, sometimes on purpose. He found new harmonies in the old designs, the stereotyped models. The leaders would have a fit every time he changed colors, but they didn't react publicly, because they were afraid of him, or, more precisely, because they were afraid of losing their profits. Apprehensive, they would always deliver the merchandise discreetly. But every time, the change of color would bring even better sales. They compensated Hung with small "bonuses" and stopped thinking of him as the lowest of the low, a criminal that they had adopted out of charity to "contribute to the socialist renewal of the State." In the end, they considered Hung a genius who held the fate of eighty-seven other people in his hands. The artisans' cooperative was organized into three divisions and Hung worked in one with about thirty colleagues. No one said it openly, but as the days went by, they indulged him more and more. Hung didn't have to come to work on time, or work eight hours a day. He could leave and go off to the bar to have a coffee or a few drinks, and come back three or four hours later and no one dared reprimand him. The same artisans who had trained him to paint were now studying the art of color harmony and design with him. They were just simple artisans, and the design principles and drawing techniques Hung had learned in college were totally foreign to them, another world. At first, the only bond between Hung and the other artisans had been the struggle to make a living, but little by little, feelings deepened as polite chat gave way to heart-to-heart talks about their love affairs or various scandals in town. For the townspeople, these discussions were a source of spiritual fulfillment, and everyone ended up opening a small window on his or her own private life. In just a few short months, Hung succeeded in winning over his colleagues, and when he arrived at work, he often found a steaming cup of tea on his desk, or an American chocolate bar, a Havana cigar, and he knew they were gifts.

Life is sometimes so simple. A man struggles to make a living to find a bit of love to light his heart. He devotes most of his life to his wife and his kids. I have all that. Da Hai and Phuoc Hanh are the most beautiful works of my life, works born of Heaven's will, that we vulgar mortals are incapable of ever creating. There are so many rich, powerful people who can't have children or who bring monsters into the world.

Hung thought of the unhappiness of the people around him, the son of the provincial Party secretary who, on his twentieth birthday right before Tet Lunar New Year, had shot himself in the head. The daughter of the head of the militia, the deputy provincial secretary, who had become a nymphomaniac, sneaking past the guard to run after men in the street, howling after them like a cat in heat. Crushed by shame, her parents tied her up in her room, but they couldn't stop her horrible moaning. At night, the neighbors used to hear her desperate cries. The two unhappiest people in town were also two of the highest ranking officials. These stories consoled Hung, even though in his heart he never wished them harm. His life flowed by, peacefully, uneventfully.

We always need to complicate life, to romanticize it. In reality, people are simple, and their dream of happiness isn't an illusion, it's within their reach. Humanity has

been through Communism. May the gods spare us from falling prey to yet another
illusion.

Another sad, interminable rainy season passed, but Hung was no longer
haunted by the rain. Every morning he got up with Suong and they
made breakfast, drinking a cup of tea together before they went off to
work. At the intersection, Suong would cycle off toward the center of
town, while Hung would stop for a coffee before going to the cooperative. He remembered the "life in the new lights" that he had dreamed
of when they emerged from their underground shelter after the war,
sacks of rice and dried potatoes slung over their shoulders.

In the end, I've managed to light a lamp. Despite the pain, the humiliation, I've
found happiness. I've got you, my sweet wife, my children, a roof, and a garden in the
shade filled with the sound of birds. That's all a man needs.

But in the midst of these thoughts, the scent of the yellow ylang-
ylang flooded his soul, waltzing in a dizzying circle, and he found himself singing aloud a melody that he had hidden from even himself:
Forget, forget, forget.

Then one day, suddenly, he saw it again, the fetus forcibly ejected
from a uterus, wriggling in a pool of blood. The two tiny legs kicked
in a red pool amidst the floating veins of the placenta. He didn't want
to die, he demanded his fragile, miserable life.

He could see his house fading, then flickering out, like a mirage.
Trees, the indifferent faces of loved ones, the shade of leaves, birds
singing—everything receded, slipping off the edge of the horizon. All
that was left was a thin blue wisp of smoke that hovered and undulated,
linking the bottomless sky with the face of the earth, an eery, melancholy chant, calling forth melodies from a strange land, a world he had
never known. He held his breath, reached out his hands to grasp it, but
it danced and dipped in front of him, inviting, provocative. A painful
thirst crushed his heart, seeped into his nerves, his muscles, preventing
him from working as usual.

Art is humanity's whore; she fools me with her powder and her makeup, her daz-

zling clothes; she invites me to some paradise, then makes me lose my wits en route. Then she strips me of the morals it took my ancestors and my parents millennia to create. Oh, she gives me pleasure, no other woman in flesh and blood could. But afterward, she leaves me with a blight no medicine in this world can cure. Even if she is a whore, I'd gladly die in peace after sleeping with her. I've got to dare . . . Think of poor unhappy Schubert, the musician with the face of a gorgon, a sad, lonely soul. Now he was unhappy: no family, no wife, no children, no lovers. He went almost his entire life without women. Then, one day, the miserable soul, tortured by desire, walks into a brothel. But even there, he was unlucky; he had barely tasted pleasure when he came down with syphilis and died in a public hospital. But Schubert left humanity with timeless melodies. And me, I just gesticulate like a buffoon, conducting folk songs, glorifying heroes and historic deeds. All the same, I'll never be able to give up music, art. I've got to set foot in the promised land, even if I die there.

You silly man! You sit here and mix your dirty pot of colors to earn your daily rice, smearing screens day after day. Poor worm, you wolf down two meals and a bowl of noodles a day, fulfill your conjugal duty each night, gulp down a cup of coffee every morning, and you don't really know why you're alive, do you? You're just a number among millions of other numbers, an anonymous being among millions and millions of other anonymous bipeds that call themselves human beings. How will I ever be happy with such a pitiful existence?

Hung closed his eyes, straining to grasp the melodies that danced in a dreamy blue smoke. But they escaped him, slipping from him like sea eels.

Hung knew that he had already lost. He had lost the deepest source, the wellspring of his inspiration, the raw material with which he had built his spiritual life. Now he saw clearly that his spirit was like an old wall, and at the first gust of wind, it would collapse into a pile of broken bricks.

As he walked out the door of the cooperative in silence, no one asked where he was going.

Hung had left in search of a cafe. It had been a long time since he had been back to the Thanh Truc Café, the fatal place where he had met the young man who had saved him from death on the beach. Destiny had linked their fates: first on the boat, then in a cell, and finally around a café table, drinking, discussing art for an entire rainy season.

Hung remembered the young man's clear, rabbitlike eyes, his moist, almost feminine lips, his long, white fingers, yellowed at the tips by cigarettes. Their conversation had seemed endless, flowing with the rain, drowned out by the rush of sudden showers.

"Do you really want to create art?" the young man asked.

"Why do you ask?"

"Out of friendship, I guess."

"I've always loved art," Hung said. "Ever since I was a child. I grew up with that love, lived and breathed it. Then studied it, to the extent I could."

"Loving is one thing, but creating is another," the young man replied. "Loving art doesn't demand anything. But creating art imposes rigorous conditions. That's not my observation. I myself am incapable of . . . my mentors taught me this."

"Keep going, I'm listening." Hung said quietly.

"Art demands three fundamental conditions: freedom, leisure, and material comfort. Here, I don't see even one of those conditions. Maybe it's cruel to say it, but you've got to make a clean slate of everything you have created up to now. You northerners, you've always considered yourselves the real artists."

"And those from the south?"

"Just a bit better, but on the whole, the Vietnamese people can't create art worthy of being called art because we've never been free." The young man shook his head, fell silent, looked at Hung.

"You create art when you write from your heart. There was a time when we lived with that inspiration."

"Oh, I know. Forgive me . . . I know you succeeded in creating things during the war because your inspiration happened also to coincide with that of the Communist Party leadership. But if someone hadn't shared that inspiration, do you think for a minute that he'd be allowed to live in peace, to produce songs denouncing the war like Trinh Cong Son?"

Hung couldn't reply. The young man was right. And he was twelve years younger. At their last meeting, he had looked Hung in the eye and said something honest, but cruel: "The heroic epic is just a primitive form of art. Centuries have gone by since *The Iliad* and *The Odyssey* were written. Our country is like a stagnant pond lagging behind other civilizations. The works you wrote during the war are like fragments of epics, but watered down—a little local color, a bit of bamboo, a backdrop of tropical forests."

Hung remained silent. The young man's ruthless words resonated in his brain, a flash of lucidity, the same insight he had had on the beach that night before he was dragged out to sea with the boat people. Hung studied the young man's mouth, the way it reminded him of a ripe fruit. He felt terribly sad.

He sees everything as clearly as springwater, coldly classifies each pebble. He speaks the truth, and in that truth, I see the humiliating fate of our people. What we thought was a temple was just a mud shack by the side of the road. No . . . no more illusions. We can't build great works of art and civilization with war. If all that is possible here, it's only now that they can truly begin.

Hung glanced at the window in the door, saw the wrinkles on his cheeks, the gray in his hair, the shadows under his eyes that were once so seductive.

"Well, do you live for art?" the young man asked. "I mean, do you really mean to create art?"

"Why do you repeat this question?"

"You should leave this country."

"I've never even dared think about it . . . And I'm not even free, I'm tied to my family."

"That's a shame. No one can climb to the summit of two mountains."

The two men fell silent, watching the rain fall, smoking their cigarettes.

Finally Hung asked: "When are you planning to leave?"

"Soon, very soon . . . the time it takes them to let down their guard . . . for the dogs prowling around here to tire."

"Are you going South?"

"Of course."

"You won't worry about your mother?"

"No, it's my mother who is forcing me to leave. She's stronger, more decisive than a man. She's the one who gathered the gold necessary to pay for my escape, who made the contacts with the networks, met the people you could trust, made the introductions. In short, she organized the whole thing; I just followed her instructions."

"How much does each attempt cost?"

"Five branches . . . a pretty hefty sum."

Hung laughed sadly: "Five branches of gold, five lumps of metal you can trade for money. Once my mother used to have a chest full of those branches. Now, my wife's annual salary wouldn't buy one of them. Material wealth. That's one of your three conditions for art, isn't it?"

A few days after their conversation, Hung came back to see the young man, but he had left for Rach Gia to flee by boat. Since then, he hadn't been back.

What wind brought Hung back to this place again? Nostalgia for a faraway friend, or the passion for art? Hung couldn't say. His feet had led him here. His soul still echoed with old conversations and the rain. Now it was beautiful out. Thin silvery clouds crisscrossed a clear, brilliant blue sky, but the memory of the rain still drummed inside his head.

The café owner noticed him immediately. "It's been a long time since I've seen you. You've been depressed, haven't you? Have a drink with me. It's on the house."

Since fate had linked their lives, they had become friends. The owner had often listened to the conversations between Hung and her son, silently refilling their glasses at the right moment.

"Any news from your son?"

"Not regularly, but often enough not to worry."

"Everything going well for him?"

"Fine . . . Just fine." She sipped a bit of cognac, then smiled. "He's doing what he wants to do, living the life he wants to lead."

"Are you planning to join him?"

"No . . . no, I'm not going to lug my old body halfway around the globe. Each to his own fate. I've already sufficiently lived mine. Now it's his turn. I leave him free to do what he wants."

"Here . . ."

"You're going to say my life here is hard, aren't you?" She smiled. "This particular regime isn't my choice. But who can have everything in this life? I'll survive whatever happens. I'm not an artist like you, or my son. Ordinary life is fairly easy for me." She raised her glass. "To your health? And to my son's success. He just had an exhibit in a gallery over there."

"In California?"

"That wouldn't be worth drinking to. No, the exhibit was in New York . . . my son was the first Vietnamese to set foot on that territory, where the competition is stiff."

Her eyes sparkled, pride etched on her fading lips. Hung congratulated her. He knew that her son was her only hope, the meaning of her life, her work of art. And it was a work more sacred than the Holy Land for the believers.

The cognac she served them was a luxury, but its amber-honey color made him sad. Hung imagined the young man walking around a gallery in New York, a town that he would only ever know by name, in another land, under another sky. A young man who, not long ago, had faced him across the table, savored a glass of wine with him, shared a cup of coffee, listened to the rain, talked about life. The young man had entered the temple of art while Hung decorated bamboo screens with cheap paint. Between them lay an ocean.

"Ah, hello big brother!" A tiny voice whispered in Hung's ear. It was a familiar voice, but he couldn't place it. "What fine wine! Fucking Western civilization! The devil himself is laughing at us poor miserable bastards here."

With those words Hung guessed that the man who had just uttered those vulgar words was Doan. He turned around, furious. "I want you to leave this place . . . I never want to see your face again."

Doan said nothing. He pulled up a chair, sat down facing, Hung. Fortunately for Hung, the owner, after toasting with him, had gone out into the courtyard to take down some laundry.

Hung slowly repeated himself: "I don't want to see you anymore. Get out!"

Doan just snickered. "We're in a bar. They sell here, and I've got a right to buy," he replied, smacking his lips, his cat's eyes riveted on the glass in Hung's hand. His skin was a light chicken yellow, his eyes sunken in their sockets. A long, straggly beard covered his gaunt cheeks, drowning his emaciated face. He was young, but his Adam's apple stood out, pointy, in the middle of his thin neck.

"Give me a sip," he said in the same rasping voice, and he grabbed Hung's glass. "Oh just a sip . . . don't be selfish now" he said in a lewd voice, his fingers curling around it, refusing to let go. But the owner entered and Hung was afraid she would see this ridiculous encounter, so he resigned himself to letting go.

Doan emptied the glass. None of this—Doan's famished look, his dirty clothes—escaped the owner's notice. She let Doan set the glass down, then picked it up calmly and returned to the bar. The painter watched her, then said to Hung, "How about treating me to a drink, for old time's sake, in honor of our friendship."

"You're no friend."

. Doan shook his head. "It's useless to lie to me. I know everything about you, how your house is furnished, where your bed is, the closet, the broom, all the rags. There's only one thing I don't know yet: How many pubic hairs your wife has!"

"You bastard. I've never met . . ."

"Someone like me, right? But you did, and you meet me again today, in this bar."

Hung got up and sat down at another table. Doan followed him, pulled up a chair facing Hung, then turned to the owner: "Where did you find such good booze? How much is a glass of that stuff anyway?"

"This café only sells coffee, no liquor. Mr. Hung is a friend. I offered him a drink from my private stock."

"Well, I'm a friend of this old fallen composer guy, so will you offer me a glass?"

The owner smiled, contemptuous. "I'm sorry, I don't know you."

Doan chuckled, squinted his cat's eyes: "Ah, my old beauty, my eternal old beauty, why so shrewish?"

A cold, lead gray lit the woman's eyes.

Hung got up and shouted, "Shut up!"

Doan sat up, guffawed with laughter. "My, my such vulgarity? I thought you were from a good family, that you spoke politely?"

"You get out of here. Just get out."

"What right do you have to throw me out? The owner herself doesn't have the right. Cafés and markets are like whores; they spread their legs to whoever's got the money."

The owner laughed, then spoke up in a polite voice: "My café sells coffee. Do you have enough money for a cup or not?"

"Why wouldn't I?" he replied, sticking out his beard, his cat's eyes darting toward the door. Hung knew that he never carried a *dong* on him, that he was used to begging even a bowl of green tea or a cup of *nhan tran* juice.

The owner chuckled again. "Well in that case, you pay first. Your appearance doesn't inspire confidence in us shopkeepers."

Doan got up, fumbled in his pockets, stared the owner down, and left.

"Forgive me . . . I didn't expect to meet him here," Hung said.

"That kind of man can't touch me. But he's going to make trouble for you, I can see that."

Hung sighed.

It's true. I'm a weak man, I let other people take advantage of me. Even Truc Son, that naïve poet, noticed it. Why did I even let Doan enter my house?

Hung remembered their first meeting. They were drinking and munching on green guavas in the room of an old bachelor named Trong Cang. This unemployed playwright belonged to the Cultural Service and had vegetated there for at least ten years. Once, Hung only saw him in meetings. They greeted each other out of courtesy and then each went his own way. Hung was one of the "three heroes" of the Service—the three trusted men who had talent and power. Trong Cang, an old cadre, had been gathering dust for a long time and he just received a small salary, no special subsidies, just enough to fill his daily rice bowl. The man used to wash his own clothes with cheap hand soap; his clothes were patched all over. He had a wife and two daughters in some remote district of Thanh Hoa province, but they had either abandoned him, or he them, more than twenty years ago. He lived alone, incapable of finding a woman. The State had given this unemployed playwright half a warehouse as housing. The other half was used to stockpile old signs waiting for a new coat of paint. The former playwright's kingdom was tiny, just big enough to fit a single bed, a termite-eaten dresser for his clothes, a huge chest filled with rice, noodles, fish sauces, and various condiments picked up here and there, in the groceries and markets. When Hung was released from the reeducation camp, he once saw Trong Cang pass by outside, and when the man saw him, he entered the café without hesitation.

"How are you, Hung?"

"Thanks, just so-so."

"Still composing?"

"For what?"

"For yourself I wrote three new plays, did you know?"

Hearing the man boast like this, Hung was intrigued: Once he had considered Trong Cang beneath him, outside his world. He didn't understand people like this, how they led their dull, petty, resigned lives, like worms. For many years he had never heard Trong Cang utter a single interesting phrase, or take a position that might impress others. Hung thought incompetent people just acted like this because they couldn't survive if they were ostracized. What would Trong Cang do, live on without his pitiful salary from the Service? He didn't know how to farm, or work with wood, or make bricks. He didn't even know how to cut out letters to spell slogans on a banner, or paint a pedestal for an exhibition hall. Now this useless being was telling him that he was a writer? Three new plays? Did his resigned look hide a secret talent?

"Really? Well, I admire you."

Trong Cang ordered. "A coffee please, ma'am." Then he rummaged in his pocket and pulled out some change, counting out each *dong*, and neatly slipped the tiny bills under the ashtray. Hung watched the way the man meticulously set the money down, shivered. *So that's what a man becomes when he has no money. I've always wasted money, opportunities to make it. But thank God I've been lucky and haven't had to count out each dong like he does.*

"Put it away. I'll pay for it all later."

Trong Cang looked at him, stunned. "But you don't have a salary, or subsidies."

"Yes, I'm an outcast . . . but I still have enough to offer you a cup of coffee."

As they drank and smoked, the playwright talked about the plays he had just written. Hung listened to the drone of Trong Cang's sad, gloomy voice, it was like a stream of urine against a wall. He stared at a black birthmark the size of a mung bean on the man's nose.

It's only now that I'm no longer one of the three heroes, that I don't have any power anymore, that I can finally bear to see these people rotting in their corners. They're like castoffs; old, useless objects that because of some bad luck have become refuse. So they are their own bitterness. And they've sighed a thousand times that "if only . . ." This man is the first in the entire Service who has dared talk with me. The others, after their hurried greetings, always slip away fast, afraid the security police will spot them.

Hung felt a twinge of remorse. "One day, when I'm free, I'll come by and see you," he promised Trong Cang.

"Then I'm taking that as a promise."

"Good. But aren't you afraid? The deputy chief of Service hates me, everyone knows that."

"He wouldn't even come near the stinking warehouse where I live. And he's never considered me a worthy target. And now I hear he's busy sharpening his knife against a new opponent."

"Who?"

"A cadre the central administration sent us as reinforcement."

Two days later, Hung went to visit the old man in his warehouse. The poet, Truc Son, was waiting for him there too. A sweet but horribly dirty man, always drunk on alcohol and poetry. The two old men were drinking pure rice wine—what they called "national contraband"—that had been distilled from potatoes or corn in some village. Each held a green guava in his hand. After reciting a verse, the poet would dip his guava in the source and perfume of his inspiration: a bowl of sugared *nuoc mam* set in front of them. The playwright would dip his guava into the bowl with each nod of his head, as if the salt of the fish sauce stimulated his neurons, sharpened his senses. When they saw Hung arrive, they applauded.

"Welcome, welcome, composer friend." Truc Son took him by the shoulder, forcing him to sit down with the half-friendly, half-tottering gesture of a drunken man.

"Sit down, dear brother . . . We're all artists here, belong to a class of artists. The solidarity that has united us is more glorious even than the solidarity of the proletariat, the one that old bearded Marx invented. Have a seat, I'm going to read you a magnificent piece of poetry."

The old man stood up between Hung and Trong Cang, his pants caked with dirt, two flies stuck to them. He must have sat down on a shelf of rice noodles, or some other dried food to have brought back these souvenirs stuck to the seat of his pants. Hung tried to hide his disgust at the stench from the poet's stinking clothes and body. He glanced furtively at Trong Cang, who seemed to share his discomfort, but he didn't want to make his friend lose face, so he didn't dare say anything. Poor Trong Cang, so fastidious about his hygiene, had to lean backward, and in this position he looked like a potbellied man whose bum had been displaced to the side.

Truc Son closed his eyes, searching for inspiration, then cleared his throat, shivered, wriggled his back like a snake, furrowed his brow, and moaned:

> *O, beloved void, I love you infinitely*
> *My half moon*
> *Half moon of a shattered sky*
> *Your blouse shivers*
> *streets streets streets*
> *O, deceitful slip of a moon*
> *that slices through my soul*

The poet composed himself, and then, to patch up his sliced soul, he gulped down five or six tiny cups of rice wine before opening his eyes.

From outside, a voice echoed: "Trong Cang, are you there?"

"Come in," Trong Cang replied. Then he turned to Hung. "I met a young painter. He's vulgar and cynical and well . . . a rogue, to tell the truth. But he's intelligent. I have to warn you. Now if he's impolite, please just let it go. Truc Son and I, we're used to him."

The playwright stopped speaking and glanced at the door. A young man entered, dark, short, with a beard and dirty clothes. Tiny, deep-set cat's eyes. He swaggered toward the host, not looking at anyone, and without waiting to be introduced, he turned to Truc Son and said, "I heard your poem from the door. Great! But I'm not quite satisfied. It's as if I hadn't emptied a glass before setting it down. Stand up and read us the next part."

The poet was delighted. "You really heard it?"

"Don't forget, I'm a devil. I've got the eyes of a lynx and the ears of a dog. Come on, read on, for Mr. Trong Cang and your new guest."

Truc Son turned toward the master of ceremonies and Hung, who nodded. Moved, the poet rose, pulled up his baggy pants, closed his eyes, and after a few seconds' pause began to recite:

> Tear at my soul
> Make rags of my life
> Your numb lips
> The wine of love's despair
> I prostrate myself
> May the grass be green green green green
> grass of exile
> over there . . . in the other land

"Bravo! Bravo! Bravo!" Doan's noisy applause put Trong Cang and Hung ill at ease. They sat stricken, embarrassed, looking at each other. Doan cried out in a husky, cloying voice: "Magnificent, extraordinary . . . Lamartine would have thrown down his pen; Apollinaire would have closed his notebook and retired. Do you see? The world is blind! To think that a talent like yours has been buried in this pit, that they ask you to glorify their irrigation projects, their contraception campaigns! But don't be sad, artists aren't mere mortals; they rise above circumstance, transcend their times. One day, the name Truc Son will shine in the pantheon of poetry."

Mesmerized, Truc Son stammered: "Thank you, thank you, young man." His moist eyes were riveted on Doan. "You too, you'll be an artist who will defy time. Such ambition, such courage. It would be hard to find a match . . ." Truc Son panted, groping for words. Breathless, he turned to their host. "Dear Trong Cang, what a splendid reunion . . ."

Doan said. "All reunions are splendid. Let's raise our glasses, but not with cheap booze and green guavas. One can't write beautiful poetry while eating food fit for dogs. How about getting us some of that nice grilled squid from that old fat shrew around the corner?"

"Grilled squid? Uh, sure . . . okay, okay . . ." the poet said. He rummaged in his pocket, brought out a wad of torn, dog-eared bills. He flattened them, one by one, his hands shaking, then pushed the money out in front of him. "It's all there. I'll go and trade it for a few mustachioed fish and relive the scent of the ocean."

Doan watched the poet leave, chuckling. When Truc Son had disappeared, he turned to Hung and Trong Cang. "What an idiot! A bit of flattery and he'd eat chicken shit straight from the coop if you asked him to. I guarantee it, he's just given up a week of breakfasts. Tomorrow, he'll go and beg the accountants to give him an advance on his salary."

He laughed, exposing his tiny rat's teeth. Hung shuddered. He had never met such a cynical bastard, and it terrified him. Cynicism was a force outside his ken; he could neither understand nor oppose. He had inherited his respect for others and his contempt for money from his father: Both attitudes were the fruit of a comfortable, aristocratic childhood. But Hung was weaker than his father. He had let Doan into his house even though he knew, from the very first day, that he was the worst of devils.

The clinking of glasses tore Hung from his reverie. The café owner came and sat down next to him. "That beggar has left. How about another glass on me?"

Hung realized that she had changed the glasses.

She's really meticulous, She even refuses to use a glass that bastard's lips just touched. To think that I let that guy sleep under my roof, week in and week out for months on end, let my wife feed him . . .

"Have a taste . . . It's a very fine port. You'll like it." She served the Portuguese wine. The bottle was a rough, dark green, almost black, reminding Hung of the surrealist paintings he had seen when he was a student at the Music Conservatory. This time, it wasn't the color of the wine that saddened him but all the memories it rekindled.

"Do they still let your wife onstage?" the owner asked.

"Yes."

"I once heard her sing. The Heavens certainly endowed her with an extraordinary voice. Strange, how so many famous singers were all small women . . . Edith Piaf . . . Mireille Mathieu."

"Do you like music?"

"Oh those are the names of my time. Everyone has their day." She got up, went out into the next room, and brought back a plate of fried chicken. Hung realized that this woman desperately wanted to console him. Her attention made him feel like a leper faced with a nun, as if he were mentally ill, or some kind of war invalid. She was giving charity to a living corpse, a pilgrim whose skeleton was drying in the desert but whose eyes were still turned toward the Holy Land.

He took a sip of wine, felt the sun of a strange land spread in his blood, a place where scales beckoned to him like waves on a sea of glass. He emptied his cup. The blazing sun showered his heart with a dazzling light, warming every cell in his body. Tides rocked, lulled him. He floated, bobbing and pitching like a boat without a skipper. It was a sweet feeling, though tinged with fear. *We need strong sensations to explore our emotions, like a miner digging for coal, we sift through human feelings. Who said that? One of the great Western writers, someone well-fed, comfortable. A brief stay in a reeducation camp would give him his fill of strong sensations. But why drift off with these dark memories? Where are the melodies that once moved my heart, that haunted my soul?*

He had emptied his glass to keep floating on those waves. But the miraculous tide had receded, and all that was left was an empty desert, all the way to the horizon. And above it, a sinister wisp of blue smoke, twisting, undulating, like the melodies now beckoning to him.

Suong was the person who supported the family. But she never left Hung without money, so he would have to ask her for it. She regularly put money into a small fake leather purse shaped like a chicken gizzard, which she put away in the left drawer of her linen closet. Hung could always dip into the purse when he needed to. Since he had begun working at the cooperative, he no longer used this money. But in a week of drinking at the Thanh Truc café, he had spent the last of his salary.

That morning, before leaving on his bicycle with Suong, he had had to dip into the purse. He didn't think about where he would find money once he had spent this sum. All he could think about was getting out, away, meeting someone, anyone, talking, forgetting the sorrows that crushed his heart.

A provincial capital is a provincial capital, and this one was as small as a village pond. After wandering in circles for a while, Hung came back to the Thanh Truc Café. Here, he had an oasis of peace, a place filled with nostalgia that could dull his suffering. His back against the wall, he gazed at the street through the thin green bamboo curtain, watching people file past the door, pulled by the shadows of their lives. Here, he could guess at their hopes and dreams, let his imagination roam, ferret in the corners and back alleys of life, forget for a moment the longing that gnawed at him.

From time to time, the owner would come over to chat with him, but she was usually serving other customers, especially regulars like the ridiculous old woman with all those precious rings on her fingers, and that piercing voice. Shaken from his thoughts by her voice, Hung's face flushed red with anger. Just as he was getting irritated, Trong Cang entered the café in the company of the poet Truc Son, and from their gait Hung could tell they had been sure they would find him here.

"How did you know I was here?" Hung asked, as they approached his table.

"I met you here once before," Trong Cang replied.

Hung shook his head. "That was a long time ago, and you don't usually come down this street."

The two men looked at each other, embarrassed.

"I know who told you that you could find me here," Hung said. The two men said nothing. "And I never want to see that guy's face again," Hung added.

"Look, I'm really sorry about what happened at your house. All in all, it's my fault. I introduced him to you. And I joined in when he started his disgusting, malicious challenge. Frankly, even if you hadn't forbid me to ever set foot in your place ever again, I would never want to face your wife."

"So that's why you came to find me? What's the problem?" Hung asked.

The two men fell silent. Their pitiful silence made Hung even sadder.

Why interrogate them further? I've read to the very bottom of their poor souls. It would be cruelty toward the weak, the desperate. They live in peace in their boring lives. They've never tasted the heights of success, or the pain of falling into the abyss. Let them enjoy their ordinary happiness in peace. I don't have such luck. Once you've tasted the joy of creating, all other joy seems like a poor wine.

"Whose house were you at when Doan told you to come and find me? Yours or Truc Son's?"

The two men looked at each other sheepishly, neither daring to speak up. Hung continued in a calm but weary voice. "Doan's hungry. He knows I have money. It's as simple as that. As for you two, you're still that bastard's allies." He laughed painfully. "And me, even against my will, I have to ally myself with you because I'm sad. I'm just a loser, a weak man, who can't stand loneliness."

"No, no, you're too bitter," the poet said warmly. "We're artists bound in the spirit of . . ."

"The international proletariat, right? Is that it? Okay, where are we going?"

"A wonderful inn. Good wine, good cheap food. We can gaze at the sea. After all, the sea has always been an inexhaustible source of artistic inspiration.

"That's good. But let's wait until we get there before you start reciting poetry. Where is it?"

The playwright signaled to Truc Son to keep quiet. He fumbled in his pocket for an address, pulled out the metallic paper of a pack of cigarettes, unfolded it, and handed it to Hung: "Here, it's the Rose Inn, number seventy-nine . . ."

As the owner passed by, the old man stopped speaking, his shoulders hunching over like someone with tuberculosis.

"Have you ever heard of the Rose Inn?" Hung asked the owner.

"Yes, I've heard of it."

"It's a wine bar?"

"Oh, they have all kinds of merchandise. Have you ever read the great Chinese novels, the cloak-and-dagger kind? Well, imagine it like that, a kind of rendezvous for adventurers, one of those black inns they describe."

Hung shivered. But at the same time another thought crossed his mind.

My God, this woman must take me for some kid that still smells of mother's milk. Black inn, black inn . . . that's all very romantic. In any case, it can't be more horrible than my life. Maybe this black inn will lead me to something interesting, lighten the weight on my soul. Let's go, you forty-year-old man, follow Nietzsche's example. From now on, we should live dangerously, like artists. So let's go, artist, take up the challenge, play the game.

These thoughts were like a slight intoxication, as if in place of the coffee, he had just drank some wine flavored with sun and wind, the perfume and passion of Portugal. He settled the bill, smiled, said good-bye to the owner, and left. The two older men trundled behind him, surprised by his sudden high spirits.

The Rose Inn was at the end of a narrow alley in the suburbs. The number "79" was actually painted on a whitewashed strip of bamboo hung on a plantain tree outside the building. An awkward, vulgar hand had traced the 79 in tar. Back here, the streets and sidewalks weren't paved or covered with pebbles, but with sand, seashells, broken bricks, and garbage. Hedges of prickly acanthus rose on both sides of the inn, and beyond, tiny shacks with thatched or tin roofs with low wood doors. A few of the doors had windows opening onto a food stall with an assortment of snacks: shrimp crackers, a jar of peanuts, some moldy strips of mung bean candy. The Rose Inn overlooked the sea, dominating the other buildings on the same strip. A big, dark red rose was painted on the side of its brick wall, and underneath the flower, some twisted writing, also red: *Always remember the red rose!*

"The owner of this place must have sung in one of the renovated theater melodramas, eh?" Hung said, joking with his companions.

A man appeared from inside the inn. "Yes, we sang in the Ngoc-Khanh troupe."

Hung laughed, surprised that his hunch was correct. The man looked like an actor, but he was mostly just a wily tavern owner who hid his laziness with glib, unctuous chatter, and charmed his clients with jokes and flattery instead of the cleanliness of the place, or the quality of the food. Just looking at the place was proof of that. Supplies and personal belongings were piled up, tossed pell-mell into a large glass cabinet against the wall—bottles of wine, the owner's wife's sanitary napkins, candies and peanuts, shrimp crackers, a jar of salt, several bunches of dried onions, and various condiments. A stack of music tapes was propped up against a jar of pickled chilies in vinegar, and a broken old *kim* instrument had been tossed in a corner next to a teetering pile of dusty bowls, evidence that the owner must once have tried unsuccessfully to sell bowls of *pho* or rice noodles.

"What do you feel like having, gentlemen?"

"I'll have a beer, to start." Truc Son replied instantly. He was a natural glutton.

"Anything to eat?"

"Of course," the poet said, but he turned to Hung and scratched his ear. "Uh, what should we order? I don't know how much your wallet weighs tonight."

"Order whatever you like," Hung replied. The poet turned to the innkeeper and said in a grandiose voice: "To start, grilled dried squid and a plate of stir-fried meat and vegetables. Then a whole chicken. We'll eat that with wine, after the beer."

"Right away!" the innkeeper said, and turned to shout inside: "Thien Nga! Where are you, Thien Nga?"

Hung shot a curious look into the back room. *Odd, another woman with the name "swan," that famous love tragedy. When I saw Swan Lake in Hanoi, I was still an enthusiastic young man. Now my hair is speckled with fog and I've seen the desert strewn with pilgrims.*

They didn't wait long. The woman named Thien Nga appeared, not from the back room but through the door, behind them. She replied to her husband in a low, husky alto voice: "I'm here."

The innkeeper turned to her: "Prepare some food for these gentlemen."

The woman nodded, greeting them, not with the hurried manner of an ordinary restaurant owner, but politely, coldly. She was tall and thin, with huge, sad eyes, which had an odd, troubling glow that seemed to swallow her bony frame, hiding other flaws. Her thick hair was pulled back into a tight chignon fixed to her head with a single buffalo horn pin; a few stray, wispy hairs floated at the nape of her neck. In her drab, solid colored clothes with tiny white specks, she seemed to come from elsewhere, estranged from everything here, even the innkeeper with his slick hair greased back over his temples and ears.

The men, seated on the terrace of the restaurant, shaded from the sun by the thick foliage of the plantain tree, could look out at the sea. They were just a few yards from the waves, could see them dancing all the way to the horizon line.

Hung chose a chair directly facing the sea, where no one could hide it from his view. He reached down and picked up his left foot, rubbed the nerve on the sole to keep it warm, and stared out at the sea, leaving the two men to drink beer and nibble at the snacks, to savor pleasures that now bored him. He didn't hear them, or listen anymore, though the two men still tried to talk with him, remembering that he was the one who was paying, and that without him they would never have been able to enjoy these delicacies. The two old artists had been through a dry spell since Hung had chased them out of his house, so they now had a keen understanding of deprivation. From time to time, Hung would grumble, nod without knowing what they were saying, or what they were toasting with all the raising and lowering of their glasses.

Time flowed by in the constant rush of the waves, in the tide of his thoughts that mixed, and tangled, and crashed, exhausted against each other. Hung didn't notice that the sun's shadow had marked noon on the plantain tree. The innkeeper brought out huge mugs of beer, set out cups made of crude china for the wine, and following the grilled squid and stir-fry, a huge steamed chicken.

"Serve yourselves . . . eat the chicken while it's hot!"

"Come on Hung, have a drink with us. You haven't touched the beer. I had to empty your glass for you."

The two men lifted their chopsticks and bowls, motioning for Hung to join them.

"Son of a bitch, you old bastards are eating here too!" The insult echoed behind Hung's back. It was Doan. The man's sudden appearance interrupted Hung's memories: He realized that his tolerant attitude toward Doan had been a mistake.

He turned around, looked straight into the man's yellow, bearded face. "Leave this table, and if you like . . ." Hung spat out his words, pointing to the inn, "ask the innkeeper to seat you somewhere else."

Doan's face seemed to turn even yellower, and he lowered his voice. "Don't be so angry, elder brother. We're all brothers here, aren't we?"

"I'm no brother to you."

"Well I ask for your forgiveness. We young people aren't anything to fear, just a bit more debauched than the previous generation," Doan said, almost breathless. Just one look at Doan's face and Hung could tell that Doan had to muster all his intelligence and will not to beg for something to eat.

They say everyone in his family is poor. Why should I humiliate a man who is hungry? Poverty isn't a crime. My parents taught me this: Even if the Heavens curse you, try not to humiliate the hungry by flaunting food.

"Please, elder brother, forgive me."

When Hung heard Doan beg for the second time, then laugh obsequiously, he turned away. But his anger had subsided and he didn't have the heart to watch a hungry man reduced to grovelling.

Oh, Mother, in my situation what would you do? Would you kick this miserable bastard out or hand him a pair of chopsticks and offer him a seat at your table?

Behind the men, past Doan's shoulder, Hung suddenly saw a wispy apparition, the image of a woman as supple and as resistant as bamboo.

The beloved shadow of his mother. Hung closed his eyes, savoring the softness of this vision, the sun filtering through the leaves of the plantain tree, scattering in shards as fine as needles. As those shards shot rays of rainbow-colored light, Hung let himself go, gliding, floating with the colors.

While Hung dreamed, Doan quietly sat down at the table, picked up a pair of chopsticks and a bowl, and buried his face in the food.

11

The Rose Inn became a regular haunt for Hung. The innkeeper had learned to set out a table for him at the foot of the plantain tree, so he could gaze at the sea for hours on end. In the sea's vastness, Hung found the freedom of the horizon just as he lost his own. Day after day, he sat by the sea in the frail hope that someday the strains of music would rise from the waves like a mermaid and carry him off to his lost paradise.

Every morning, he would leave with Suong, bicycle in hand. She would cycle off to work with the troupe, and he would go and sit by the sea. There, he felt himself come alive again in the silence of the wild sand beach and the carefree waves, under the blue indifference of the sky and the ceaseless rustle of the wind. Sometimes other failed, hungry artists would pester him, tortured by the need "to talk and exchange ideas," as they put it. Hung didn't pay much attention to their conversation, but sometimes they were a nice distraction. Heaven hadn't blessed them with success, but it had endowed them with a talent for appreciating life's small pleasures. That too was a way of consoling themselves, of forgetting their lot. Often, after having downed a dozen glasses of the innkeeper's herb wine, they would discuss the Chinese art of drinking.

"Brother Hung, do you know how many ways there are to drink in this world? The ancients taught us that there are three classes of men, and three classes of animals. In fact, there are hundreds of categories of men and hundreds of animal species. There are as many ways to drink as there are types of men: magicians, sages, poets, not to mention the kings, mandarins, peasants, water buffaloes, and demons. Of all these methods, only one caught my attention: the manner of the poets. The tragic destiny of poets forces them to seek out strange sensations and for each of these there is a different wine. If you want a heart of ice, need to feel the assassin's lust for blood, then you drink a wine macerated with bitter herbs, from the gelatin of an old tiger's bones. If you want to be a Don Juan, make love to seven women every night, and make love to an eighth before dawn, then you've got to drink strong spirits brewed with tiger fetus and ginseng. That'll fire up your blood."

But after all these heroic speeches, they would collapse and fall asleep on a big wooden bed behind the inn. Poetry, music, and art having flown, they were no more than an unkempt little flock. Since it was hot, they would take off their pants, leaving them in their underwear, their T-shirts rolled up to their necks, exposing their rough, dirty skin. Hung shuddered to think that he had once welcomed this group into his home out of some fellow feeling that Truc Son had compared to Marx's "class solidarity."

One day, a brutal, torrential rain fell and Hung couldn't stand being alone, so he joined the group, taking full part in their drinking bouts. Conversation drifted about in an alcohol-induced haze: the art of rhyming in traditional poetry; the way the people who live in the highlands prepared sticky rice; the role of oracles in folk culture; women, all the various feminine types and faces; the art of face reading. And of course, their own unhappy fate.

Hung felt the pain rise in him, as if his heart was breaking into small pieces, and from his empty soul rose the cry of some devil trapped at the bottom of a cavern, banging his head against the stone walls.

"Hung, say something to us. We were talking about the theory of yin and yang, of Doan's sun and moon."

"Yes," Doan piped up. "We were discussing the difference between yin art and yang art, the feminine and the masculine. Yin art gives birth to women as lithe as jellyfish, that suck up man's vital energy at night, breathing poisonous fumes into his soul, ruling him with the diabolical blue light of the waxing moon. Yin art gives birth to flowers that bloom in shadow, to nocturnal breeds of worms, insects, and green snakes. Me, I'm a moon worshiper, a yin art man. As for the sun and its stark, vulgar light, that can only create second-rank artists, musicians for the travelling singers, admirers of *luc bat* poetry and two-stringed violas, to painters who spit colors they've licked off someone else's palette. But we were elected by heaven to create an eternal art, so we have to reject solar, yang art. Our art lies in that instant when the yin couples with the yang, when man unites with the devil feminine. Androgyny is the art humanity has dreamed of, the art of the future."

Hung smiled sadly. *This pervert can be a brilliant orator, but if I offer him a wad of bills, he'll be only too eager to prove that I'm right to spit on his own theory. He'll suddenly argue that solar art is the only authentic, eternal art, that only yang art can save humanity.*

Outside, the patter of raindrops fell heavier, and the roar of the sea mixed with the rumble of the rain. In another room, the innkeeper, seized by some sudden inspiration, sang a verse or two. The plantain leaves, shaken by the rain, shuddered, bending and rising, infinitely patient, resisting the downpour. But some were ripped and broken, torn from their branches, and they spun frantically on the sand. Hung couldn't take his eyes off these leaves. They were a desolate, translucent green, as if the days of sun had evaporated from each leaf into an intense green halo, then scattered into fragments on the ground, like pieces of cloth torn from a funeral shroud. These leaves touched some mysterious, fragile nerve in him.

"There's neither yin art nor yang art in this country, Doan," Hung snapped. "Wasn't it you who said that no one can compose beautiful poetry when you're fed on food good for dogs? So how can you discourse on art, yin or yang? You can only create art when you live with dignity, in a free society. Even a slave knows how to put pen to paper, or mix colors on a palette. But a cowardly, servile, hypocritical soul can never create art."

"Oh, so we're just a bunch of slaves and this society doesn't belong to us?" Doan retorted.

"That's what I said."

"So this society isn't free, and it doesn't allow men to create art?"

"That's already clear, isn't it?"

"So we're just temporary residents here, and if we want to make art we've got to find our own country, is that right?"

Hung laughed. "Why are you asking me such stupid questions? You know I went to prison, and not even for a crime like yours, but because I just happened to be on a beach the night that a bunch of boat people were fleeing this country. And at the time, I had no intention of leaving. Now I dream of leaving, but it's an impossible dream. I don't know where I'd find five branches of gold to buy a place on a boat."

"Oh, what a pity!" Doan said in his soft, sarcastic voice, laughing. He smiled, baring his pointy rat's teeth.

A few minutes passed in silence. Then, a loud clicking sound in the silence. Truc Son looked up, startled. "What was that noise?"

Trong Cang and Hung hadn't noticed, but Truc Son repeated his question: "Something clicked, like a chopstick snapping. Didn't you hear it?"

Doan jumped up, pulled the innkeeper's tape recorder out of an old beer case, rewound the cassette and pressed the play button. Their entire conversation had been recorded. At the end of the tape, Hung could hear his own voice clearly, and in his terrible words all the repressed anger he had hidden inside himself. Now each word echoed through the inn, even against the torrential rain outside. Trong Cang turned to Hung with a pale, defeated look. Then he jumped up and grabbed the tape recorder, opening it to pull out the tape, but Doan pulled it back.

Realizing what had happened, Truc Son began to whimper: "Oh Doan, we're all artists, brothers. How can you play this dirty game?"

Doan stepped back, stuffed the tape under his shirt. He pointed at Hung's face. "Listen, you idiot, now you're going to respect me like your old man. Yes, me, the beggar, the thief, the rapist, the shameless leper." He cackled, his eyes sparkling. "Now I'm *your* old man, Hung. I've got power over you, so don't cross me. You've been to prison, so you know that it's not a very pleasant place."

"You sold yourself to the police?!" Truc Son screamed. "You scum, you informer, there have always been people like you and . . ."

"And they're always held in contempt, right? I've been to prison, had a lot of contempt. Now the only thing I need is money. One day when I'm famous, have left Matisse and Picasso in the dust, spat on Salvador Dali and Chagall, the whole world—including you—will be at my feet, having licked me from the testicles to the soles of my feet." Then Doan slipped out of the room and began to run fast.

Rain, still rain. Water and more water, white sheets of it, as far as the eye could see. In a flash, Doan had disappeared.

"Oh misery and damnation! Oh god, oh god . . ." Truc Son wailed.

Trong Cang just stood there, stricken, his pale face twitching. After a moment, he began to weep, then silently wiped his tears with a clean handkerchief folded in a neat square. Hung said nothing.

The innkeeper's wife came out of the back room, picked up the tape recorder, and asked in a dull voice: "Which one of you lent him my tape recorder?"

The men looked at each other in silence. The woman repeated her question in a low, hoarse voice. "I asked you: Who gave it to him?"

From the back room, the voice of the innkeeper: "I did." His voice seemed choked, as if he had been asleep.

"Why did you give it to him?"

"He's a customer, I can't . . ."

"And these people? Aren't they customers? After all, who pays every time? How dare you give him one of my old tapes!"

"He didn't have a *dong* in his pocket. How could he buy a new one?"

"What debt do you have with him?"

"I'm scared. He works with the security police. You know we couldn't operate here without their permission. If we upset them, where would we go?"

"So for that you hurt other people?"

The man didn't reply.

"Do you know how despicable that was?"

Still, he made no reply.

"Answer me!" the woman screamed.

Then there was the sound of a violent slap. "You're just a coward . . . you've always, always been a coward," the woman's voice sobbed. "I've stood by you, but you'll never be anything but a coward."

Suong would never forget Hung's face the day she and Dam went looking for him on the beach. The inn by the sea that the woman who owned the Thanh Truc café had called "a devil's nest" wasn't as horrible as she had imagined. A crude brick house, sparse and dusty like all the buildings on the outskirts of town. A bushy plantain in front of the door and a few chairs in the shade created a peaceful atmosphere. A tarpaulin hung out over the veranda billowed in the wind. Inside, she could make out a glass cabinet filled with bottles of snake spirits and other alcohol, but none of the horrible skulls and skeletons that she had imagined in the Chinese adventure novels.

The inn was deserted, except for a man with a big head and a mangy head of hair, parted in the middle, who sat playing a guitar, humming a tune.

"But there's no one here," Suong said, turning to Dam.

"Let's go inside, we'll see." Dam replied, led her inside, and walked up to the innkeeper. "We're not customers," Dam said abruptly. "And we're not interested in booze or girls. We're looking for a man." The innkeeper's eyes opened wide, he studied Dam, perplexed, unsure of what attitude he should take. Dam didn't wait for his reply, just thrust a certificate from the People's Committee under the man's nose. "Read this."

He let the innkeeper finish reading before continuing. "Where are the customers who stayed here last week?"

The innkeeper shook his head. "We don't have rooms."

"Really?" Dam retorted, snickering.

The innkeeper tensed up, raised his voice defensively: "Why are you harassing me? We're a tavern, not a hotel."

Dam replied calmly. "I spent some time with the town police before coming here. I know that this inn doesn't just sell wine. You sell a lot of other things too, and you may not advertise rooms, but you have them if a customer asks. You also have a whole apparatus of hammocks and folding cots to service other customer requirements. Do I need to go into more detail?"

The innkeeper paled. Dam let a moment pass, time for the innkeeper to get scared, and for him, too, to steel his nerves.

"Where are they?"

"I'll take you there," the innkeeper replied. He put his guitar away in a corner and opened the door to his room. "Thien Nga, Thien Nga!" They heard the call fade, as if the man had gone out into a garden to call his wife. Dam and Suong waited ten minutes before they saw him return. A woman followed him, a tall, thin woman with a cold face, her hair tied back in a chignon. The man turned around and said to his wife in a frantic, hushed voice: "You stay here, I'll be back right away."

The woman stood silently, her thin lips pursed, her eyes following some lost boat on the horizon. "I'm going now," the man said. The woman said nothing, slowly sat down on a chair, leaned back on an old cushion, folding her hands behind her neck.

The man lowered his eyes and led the way, hesitant. Dam and Suong followed him to the left of the inn, through a field of casuarina trees that stretched the length of the shore, all the way to a rocky beach at the foot of the mountain. The beach was covered with tide pools filled with fish that had been trapped there when the tide withdrew. Here and there were huge boulders shaped like kneeling elephants, as white as rock salt. The forest behind them was filthy, strewn with tin cans, old food wrappers, old condoms, beer bottles, and piles of broken snail and crab shells. All this lay baking in the sun. Nauseated by the sight and stench, Suong turned her head away.

What is Hung doing sneaking off to a place like this? Why? I'd rather find him in the black inn, some remote mountain crevice. I'd even rather find him in prison.

She remembered the dull, numbing pain she had felt watching the prisoners walk by Indian file in the courtyard on that first morning at the camp. The sallow, thin, defeated faces had broken her heart, and it was that pain that had revived her love for Hung. But now that feeling had vanished.

Suong had asked Dam to come with her when she hadn't been able to find Lam, and that night she had slept peacefully, liberated from her anxiety. But now, the further she plunged into this horrible forest, the more her soul cooled. After walking a half mile, the innkeeper stopped, pointing his finger at a wooden shack about a hundred yards away.

"Over there . . . you just go over there. They haven't left yet."

Dam looked at the man in silence.

The innkeeper continued: "I can't go any farther . . . they're customers. Please understand." He turned and raced back to the inn.

"Let him go! We don't need him as a witness." Dam said, leading Suong further. A few minutes later, as they neared the shack, they could make out graffiti scrawled in tar on the wall—five fingers, a heart pierced by an arrow, vaginas, phalluses . . .

"Oh Dam, this is too horrible, too disgusting. Go ahead, I'll wait for you here." Suong said.

Dam looked at her. "I know all this horrifies you, but you've got to get over it to save Hung. Only you can do that."

"I can't, Dam."

"You've got to. Try to get a grip on your emotions, the fear as well as the shame." He held out a hand. "Come on, let's go."

Suong took his hand, but her fear didn't subside. She turned away from the sordid graffiti and her face no longer burned from shame, but she knew that unhappiness loomed inside the shack, a danger that wasn't aimed at her or at Hung but at something between them. A premonition told her she was about to plunge into a swamp hidden by a coat of grass like a peaceful carpet over a sea of mud. As soon as she set foot in it, the mud would pull her into the abyss.

"What's the matter?" Dam asked, turning back. Suong's fingers had gone icy, her face white. She was panting, breathless.

"I'm afraid, Dam, I'm so afraid." she said, her voice breaking.

"It's not as bad as you think," Dam said. He laughed, thinking she was scared by the graffiti, the ravages of opium. He grasped her hand firmly and pulled her forward. Suong's heart jumped; in another moment, she would see him, she would come face to face with disaster. When they reached the door to the shack, Dam looked in first, then turned back to her: "They're here."

Suong moved forward mechanically, peering through the window on the low door that barely came to her nose. The sight of the men lying on torn, weather-beaten fishnets reminded her of the nests of mice she used to find in their garden—tiny red mice, blind, naked pieces of crawling flesh.

"Hung!" Dam shouted.

Lying on the floor of the shack, his face against the wall, Hung sat up, looked outside. He had woken up a long time ago, but didn't expect anyone to call him. Suddenly he recognized the small woman standing next to his friend. "Suong!" A single cry and then he fell silent, as if choked.

The other men struggled to their feet, flabby as old rags.

Suong felt numb, paralyzed. She didn't reply. Her brain echoed with the clear, icy words: *So it's over . . . there's nothing left . . . nothing at all.* The moment Hung called out to her, looked up at her, she saw both a guilty child and a drowning man up to his neck in mud. In the space of that moment, her love had been snuffed out like a fire extinguished by a sudden rain. Not even an ember was left. Her sun, her devoted master, her passionate lover, her tender husband, were all dead.

Seeing Suong motionless, without a word or a gesture, Dam felt ashamed for Hung and urged her on. "Suong . . ."

But she didn't move.

Dam turned to Hung: "I think it's time you left this devil's nest. Or are you going to wait until she takes your hand and pulls you out?"

Hung remained slumped, inert on the pile of nets.

"Are you deaf?" Dam shouted.

Hung pulled his legs from the nets, struggled to extricate himself from the tin pans, glasses, syringes, packets of food. He staggered to his feet, crossed the shack, his back hunched over, and walked out the door. He didn't notice the stunned, stricken, distant look in Suong's eyes, or her tears. Dam tried to console her, taking her by the shoulder. "Don't cry, Suong, don't cry. Everything will be okay . . ."

Hung slipped past them, walking in front of his wife, his head low, devastated by shame.

Sweet wife, little woman from the mountains, I've tortured you for too long. If heaven gave me three lives it still wouldn't be time enough to repay my debt of love, to erase the suffering I've caused. I swear that from now on I'll resign myself, lead the honest life of an ordinary man, give up my crazy dreams, everything that has pushed us to the brink.

Suong let her tears wash over her face. He was there, walking right in front of her. All she had to do was reach out a hand to touch him. But he seemed far away, blurry as a shadow. The handsome man with the graceful walk and the tender, mocking chestnut eyes . . . this ghost from the past that walked ahead of her now was a sordid criminal, a repulsive being who crawled on all fours through fishing nets, who blinked his eyes, blinded by the sun, his lips parched and shriveled.

Tears streamed down her face. But she knew she wasn't crying from despair, or pity, or joy. She was mourning a love. A dead love, whose corpse was slowly growing cold in the chill sea wind.

Suong brought Hung back home, but the next morning she took five branches of gold over to Auntie Tuong's for safekeeping. The terror she had felt when she opened the armoire and found that Hung had taken the money she had saved for the family hadn't left her. Anxiety about how she would feed the family and assure their survival was like a deadweight on her heart. And now that she no longer loved Hung, she no longer felt guilty about mistrusting him. The money that the young man from the prison had given her was a huge sum, a fortune. She had bought twelve branches of gold, buried seven in a corner of the kitchen, like peasants used to bury their urns of silver coins, and had taken the rest over to the neighbor's house.

When she handed it to Auntie Tuong, the old woman sighed, reluctantly taking the leaves of gold that Suong had wrapped in an old towel. "Don't be sad. Women have always had to watch over the home, keep accounts, mind keys."

Suong shook her head. "You're trying to console me. Who has to hide their keys and savings from their own husband?"

"Be generous, Suong. Forgive. He's in pain, and there aren't many people who can understand that pain."

Suong said nothing. She knew that the old women would always defend Hung. *Fate has spoiled him. Hung will always find supporters, people to defend him without his even having to plead his own case.*

She suddenly remembered the jealousy that had consumed her their first night together during the war, when she had gone to find him. How jealousy of the shadow of a tall woman she had glimpsed leaving his underground had turned her into a woman. That night, in the shadows of his underground, she had grabbed his neck and embraced him like a madwoman, shouted deliriously *I love you I love you I love you*, carried away by the desire to possess. She had wanted him to belong to her. Only her. Always. She had dreamed of banishing all the other women from his life like a general evicting foreign invaders. The memory came back, the echo of some forgotten song.

Suong stood motionless, silent for a moment, then turned to Auntie Tuong. "Please take what I owe you from the five branches. I'm so busy I haven't had time to settle with you for all you've spent on the girls."

"No," the old woman protested. "What I give the girls is what I give you. That's the way I want it to be."

"But Auntie, I don't want you to be in need."

"We all end up under the ground someday and as long as I live, I'll protect you, help you and your children. Your mother and father are dead. I have no children, no relatives. Our meeting was a boon from the heavens."

The old woman got up and walked toward Phuoc Hanh's crib; the little girl had started to cry. Da Hai was playing on the neighbor's bed, pretending to be a shopkeeper. Soon she would be old enough to go to kindergarten, and Auntie Tuong had already bought her school clothes. Suong wanted to send her to a kindergarten run by Catholic nuns. The government had just given them permission to open schools and to use the funds for a lepers' camp isolated in a seaside village about six miles out of town. The kindergarten was located on a boulevard next to a row of villas surrounded by well-kept lawns and orchards, where the air was filled with the sound of organs and choirs. Above the entrance gate, on a column of fake marble, was a sign that read: *Saint Theresa's Kindergarten.* The yard behind it had a lawn and playground with a carrousel that had seats shaped like animals and cars. Crowds of children were always playing and climbing on it.

Every time Suong passed in front of the kindergarten, she dreamed of the day Hung would take Da Hai to school there, in the world of this happy crowd. That moment, so long desired, was approaching. But her little girl wouldn't know the happiness of other children. *My poor baby, my poor girl. Who would ever have thought this would happen?* She hugged and kissed her daughter, haunted by the idea that this child was a fruit born out of season, of a love that had died.

• • •

By the time she got back to the house, Vinh had already left for school and Hung was still asleep. She mounted the stairs, gently opened the door so as not to wake him. She gazed at him. The man lying on that bed had become a stranger. Why? She didn't know, but since she had stopped loving him, she had stopped wanting him. And this left her both troubled and indifferent.

Hung couldn't read Suong's thoughts. He was tortured by withdrawal even though he had barely tasted the dangerous pleasure of opium. He slept a lot, but every time he got up, his bones ached, a dull throbbing pain, and his limbs seemed wobbly, as if they were made of the clay they used to model tiny animal figurines at the Tet markets. Day after day he felt a desperate hunger cry out from the marrow of his bones, in each cell of his body, echoing through every pore of his skin, every inch of his flesh. The hunger for a wisp of brown smoke. He remembered the euphoric moments lying on the nets, listening to the sea, the eery melodies behind the regular, insistent beating of the waves, how they had fluttered around him like clouds. The sad, dusky pink of dawn, the wistful violets of dusk, the harsh blue of the void, the distant, untouchable white of final separations. These colors had swirled in the fog, enclosing him in a tower of sweet memories, a jumble of dim images, and the more they faded, the more intimate they became. He had lived wonderful moments. If only he had died right then! But then a voice had risen from the other side of the mountain, the distant voice of an ancestor—or was it the voice of his mother, his father? He couldn't tell, but that voice made other sounds echo in his brain: the quivering din of gongs; the dry tick tock of a wooden tocsin; the haunting wall of a trumpet rising from a night of mourning, long ago, during the conquest of the south. These sounds seemed to stab at him, like so many needles in his gut.

Hung walked out into the garden, wandered under the ylang-ylang trees. Their terrifying perfume murmured in his ear, conjuring up a distant, fog-shrouded land that he couldn't see clearly. Under the vault of leaves, he suddenly heard the laughter and chattering of his children, a sound that hurried him back to a forgotten love. He went over to the neighbor's house, played with the girls, listened patiently to their silly stories. He played horsy with them, gazed at their sparkling eyes, wondering how such beautiful beings could have slipped from his consciousness without a trace. He pinched himself to see if he was really there, or if he too was just a dream drifting on the river current. But the pleasure only lasted a moment before the frantic, crazed hunger ripped through his flesh again, tearing each muscle and nerve. He found himself writhing on the bed, rearing like a psychotic tortured by nightmarish visions. He resisted, struggling to free himself, trying to sweat it out as the doctors had advised. He gulped down a glass of cold water, then collapsed like a bunch of wilted cabbage. At those moments, he realized that since he'd come home, he hadn't made love with Suong, had forgotten it entirely, as if the desire had gone. And Suong hadn't said anything. *Why? Have I become impotent? Has she found another body to fill the void?* But this doubt rapidly dissipated as endless waves of mute, eery cries from all sides pulled him out to sea.

I'm like a river weed now, drifting through this floating life. I'm no longer worthy of being human. Just flotsam, a weed buffeted by the current.

Lucid now, Hung contemplated his fate, laughing darkly. But he knew he couldn't stop living like this.

Every day, Suong went to work. She hadn't urged Hung to go back to work. He was the one, the very night he had come back, who had promised to do it. He said he would rest for three days and then go back to work, make sure that their family life returned to normal. When he tried to explain why he had taken the savings, she dismissed him with the wave of a hand, saying: "What's past is past. You taught me that. Let's just get back to work, we'll earn it back."

They should have made love that night. But they hadn't. Why? Suong had brought their two daughters back to see him, and while Suong did the laundry, Hung and Da Hai had fallen asleep in the room upstairs. Suong had slept downstairs with Phuoc Hanh. During the following days, she had worked hard. He had been tortured by the opium withdrawal. *Well, there's nothing abnormal between us. It's just the opium. When I'm cured, I'll make love to her again like I used to.*

One morning, someone called Suong out of a rehearsal. "You've got a visitor!"

Suong looked puzzled. "Who's looking for me at this hour?" That morning she was rehearsing with the orchestra. They had just been sent two new violinists and a pianist, and the dress rehearsal was coming up soon. At the very best, she would have two mornings free between now and the performance.

Seeing her hesitate, Dam stepped in. "Go ahead, take the afternoon off. I'll postpone the rehearsal until tomorrow morning. The orchestra can rehearse with the actors today."

Suong thanked him and left. Maybe it was Lam, or Vinh? But waiting for her in the lobby wasn't either of them, but the young man in the striped shirt from the prison camp.

"How are you?" he said, smiling warmly.

"Fine thank you," she said, intrigued.

Dapper in his light green shirt and white gabardine pants, he looked like a student who had just graduated. The gold cap on his pen stuck out of his pocket, as if to flaunt his taste and culture. Suong knew that he had completed university before working at the camp.

"So you're rehearsing a new show? Sorry to disturb you."

Suong nodded. "Yes, we were going to rehearse with the orchestra this morning, but the director just gave me the day off."

"Ah, just our luck!" the young man cried, unable to hide his joy. "I'd like to invite you out. Let's go somewhere else." He pulled the Honda out of the courtyard, remembering to wink at the doorman, who waved back. A military wave, but friendly. They crossed an expansive courtyard, walking between rows of poincianas and jacaranda trees. The poinciana flowers were fading, but the trees were in full bloom and their petals had covered the path with a light, cottony pink carpet.

"Sister Suong, our commander is in town today," the young man said.

Suong didn't reply, but her heart raced. The strong, vigorous man was here, right in town. It hadn't taken much for her to imagine him, his breath on her skin, her flesh, and the strange, unsettling feeling she had felt in the reeducation camp a few years before.

"The boss came to work with the provincial government, the committees that oversee the national detention system. He's finished with business now, and he'd like to see you again.

"To see me? Why?" Suong asked, hearing her own voice crack. The young man walked silently by her side, pulling his heavy motorbike. He walked slowly, gracefully. The Honda must have weighed over two hundred pounds, but it seemed as light as a toy in his hands.

"Elder sister Suong," he said softly, as if she hadn't heard him. "Our boss is a sentimental man. He has admired you for a long time. Whenever we go hunting, he always brings along a tape recorder so he can listen to your songs."

"I'm flattered, but . . ."

"You can't imagine how such a sensitive man, cooped up in the forest and the mountains, can attach himself to such feelings."

"I know, but I . . ."

"We others in the camp, we're younger, don't have as much experience, but I've never met someone as true to his word as the commander. With his subordinates, he's very generous, very attentive."

"I'm really very grateful to the commander, but . . ."

"The day I started working at the camp, he immediately took me under his wing, trusted me, didn't even check my C.V. or my dossier, never asked me to prove myself. We became friends almost instantly. You don't meet a man like that every day. He's at least a gentlemen, if not a hero."

"I . . ." Suong knew that her words carried no weight in this exchange, that the young man said what he needed to say. She replied with stupid, awkward phrases that she didn't believe in. *Why shouldn't I go and pay my respects to this man? I should at least show I've got good manners, don't forget my debts.*

They left the garden, and the glistening path of pink petals gave way to a gray asphalt road. The young man revved his motor. "Have a seat. Hold on tight so you don't fall, I don't know how I'd be made to pay for your death. Ten thousand townspeople would tear me to pieces."

He drove her down a narrow street to a one-story house. The building was half-modern, half-classic, but gracious. Behind a wrought-iron gate covered with climbing bougainvillea, a courtyard was filled with pots of chrysanthemums and roses from Dalat. The brown doors and windows and the pale yellow walls to the house gave it an understated elegance. A huge lock and chain hung around the iron gate, which had been painted white. The young man took a key out of his shirt pocket, opened the gate, leaving a gap just big enough for one person.

"Please, you go first." Then he hung the chain back on the gate and locked it. "I'm going to get some refreshments. Don't worry, I'll be back soon," he explained, seeing Suong's suspicious look. He laughed, waved to her, and was off on his Honda. After the roar of the motor had faded, the alley fell back into the silence. Suong could hear the bougainvillea leaves falling, the bees buzzing around their nests in the wall that separated the house from an orchard filled with custard apple trees. Suong glanced around, not understanding why she had followed the young man here, wondering about her own naiveté. But the bougainvillea leaves fluttered to the ground, creating a tranquil, safe, secure atmosphere that dissipated Suong's anxiety.

"Hello Suong," said a soft voice behind her. She stood petrified in the middle of the courtyard, incapable of replying, her mind just conscious enough to feel the excitement that ran through her body to the rhythm of the man's breathing, just strong enough to resist turning around, to resist the urge to let her own breathing fall in sync with his like iron in a magnetic field.

"Hello Suong," the man repeated, his voice muted now like a storm that subsides to a whisper, like a light wind through the reeds. *I have to reply, I have to reply.* But Suong stood mute, transfixed under the bougainvillea.

"Let's go inside." A warm hand took her arm, pulling her gently, tenderly through the courtyard, up the stairs into the house. Suong walked forward, as if bewitched. She hadn't even turned around to look at him. They walked up a gleaming ebony staircase, through a door, entered a room paved with white stones. The man showed Suong to a velvet armchair.

"Suong." His voice fell like drops of wine overflowing a glass. She had to look up.

"Suong, I love you. I've loved you for a long time. I'm sure that you know this." He took her face in his hands. She could see him now, the man who had made her tremble. His rosy skin glowed with health, his eyes sparkled like stars, and his teeth were like white jade. Waves seemed to spring from his eyes, rising and falling like a river in the flood season, washing over her. His thick, dense hair fell over his forehead, which was beaded with sweat.

"Suong," the man repeated. His sensual lips, as red as ripe July fruit, quivered. Suong could make out each shiver, each wrinkle. I love you."

The man's lips pressed against hers. *No, you have no right!* The voice echoed again in her brain, but her lips had already lifted to meet his. Time shuddered on their lips, the life span of an entire love affair for other couples. The commander got up, his eyes sparkling. "Darling, darling."

Suong fell back, dizzy, into the velvet chair. The commander suddenly walked quickly to a corner of the room, picked up a vase filled with roses that had been set on a porcelain stand. He tore the petals off the roses and scattered them on the bed, as if he were covering the white sheets with scarlet flames. Overcome by passion, he carried Suong to the bed, smothering her with kisses, repeating over and over again: "Darling, my love, my dream."

His feverish, awkward hands fumbled and groped at her Chinese blouse. Finally he undid a button at the top. These gropings only made him more frantic, more impatient. "Darling, darling, I've waited so long, I've waited for you."

Suong gazed at the man's strong neck, the pores of his skin, at a beauty mark. She shivered with terror, passion. She felt the cool, velvety rose petals against her back. Then her thoughts took flight, carried on the wind, into the void. All that was left was a naked woman on a bed of crimson flowers, pinned under a firm, corpulent body that raged like a volcano.

12

The entire town was crazy about Dam after the new show. Even the deputy chief, who had been consumed in a battle with his new enemy, had to show a forced smile to congratulate him on his success. This exile to central Vietnam had, in the end, some advantages, Dam thought, as he toasted with everyone, thanked the town and provincial leaders for their praise. After the rush of enthusiasm, he retreated, alone, to the shade of the jacaranda trees. He thought of Hung, remembering his colleague, the man whose shadow had haunted the red velvet curtains on opening night.

He should have been up there, on the podium of honor. He should have been the one to get the bouquets of flowers, to shake hands with all those officials, congratulate the actors, have the joy of inaugurating the palace that he built. He was born for the stage lights. Me, I'm like a horse gone astray in fate's cynical game. I never wanted to grab the banner from Hung.

Dam thought about his unfinished book, still waiting for him. Putting on a new show had meant dealing with a whole array of personnel and financial issues, suffering through interminable meetings and introductions. Then there were the piles of dossiers he had had to plow through before finding a theme for the show. The whole process had consumed him, dragged him into a whirlpool of bureaucracy. The book that he dreamed of finishing during his rustication to the central provinces hadn't advanced a single line.

Dam suddenly remembered the passion that had gripped him, crushed his future between two huge millstones. Had it been love or desire? Had he confused them or had it been both at the same time? In Asian culture, no one had really analyzed, or made a distinction between these two ideas. If he hadn't loved this woman, he could have spent his time and energy writing books about Vietnamese music, retracing the tragic, heroic history of his country, meditating on the people who, threatened by their neighbors to the north, had invaded the peoples of the south. The icy wind of the Dinh Ho Gorge had blown at the backs of the immigrants, echoed with the strains of a flute mourning final separations and uprootings, the loss of childhood and the ever-receding dream of a peaceful life. The wail of the icy Dinh Ho wind that had born the frantic melody of a people crazed with hunger and fatigue, numbed by the horror of all the heads that had rolled, all the blood spilt. It was the melody of a people who had trudged south through thick, impenetrable jungles where the panting of stones echoed the rumbling streams, the stench of corpses mingling with the hypnotic perfume of tropical flowers, where dusk dyed the plains the dark, unfathomable hue of sadness. Yes, if he hadn't wasted so many years on his love for a woman, he might have plumbed the depths of traditional music in the rich motifs of the *quan ho,* or in the popular love songs, or the lyrical *loi lo.* In the mirror of that pure spring, he might have seen his country's tragic history unfurl its shadow, read the message behind each refrain, each melody. He might have distilled the essence of the music of the ancient Viet people, tinged with the vibrancy of the Cham soul and the icy Red River winds, the burning winds that swept in from Laos over mountains littered with corpses and dead horses. Yes, he could have, if he had been less passionate. He would have traded all the anxious waiting, all the feverish embraces, the secret lusts, to create a life's work. But who can know where the "ifs" would have led? And then Dam suddenly thought of Hung. *If only he had known the "ifs," perhaps he wouldn't have let his life be swept away by destiny.* From the day he had gone with Suong to find Hung on the beach, Dam had been terribly busy, but he had thought that with a woman like Suong, everything would slowly return to normal. Now, freed from all his work, he remembered that morning, how Suong had clutched his arm, her hands icy, her breathing choked. *As if there were something wrong, something I couldn't read, some unforeseen disaster looming for them.* This thought worried him and he decided to go over to their place immediately. It was after seven o'clock. He hailed a cyclo, his mind too troubled to take a motorbike or a bicycle through the crowded streets. Even in this provincial town, the traffic was dense and chaotic, and accidents often happened at intersections or sharp turns, especially turning down the narrow streets. Since Dam had left Hanoi, he hadn't taken a cyclo, and he suddenly felt the need to relax. The cyclo that he hailed was new, and its wheels turned quickly, clicking. Just twenty minutes later, he arrived at the gate to Hung's house. He rang the bell. It was Vinh who came to open it.

"Hello Elder Brother!"

"Are your sister and your brother-in-law at home?"

"Yes," Vinh replied, opening the doors to the gate to let him in. Dam strode through the courtyard strewn with ylang-ylang blossoms. In the crackling of the dead leaves under his feet, he sensed a chill. The heady scent of the flowers hung in the air, stuck to his lungs, hung on his heart with the weight of a malediction. This was the first time he had noticed this scent, and it seemed to sharpen an unnamable anxiety in him.

"Suong? Are you there?" he called as he walked through the door. "Here, I'm coming, wait a second." Her voice echoed in the courtyard behind the house. She had been doing the washing. She appeared, her arms wet. "Why didn't you tell me you were coming?"

"It's not important. Where's Hung?"

"Upstairs."

"He stays up there all day?"

"Yes."

"You bought the medicine he needs to get over the addiction?"

"I did everything you told me to do."

"And he's willing to take the medication?"

"I think he's still drinking it."

"Has he been at home since we went to get him?"

"I think so."

"What do you mean you think so? You've got to make sure, Suong."

"Yes, there are three sets of keys at home. I take one of them, Vinh has one, and the third I've given to my neighbor Tuong. Hung has never gone to get that set, so I think he's never been out."

"How's his appetite?"

"He doesn't eat much, almost no meat. Every morning I make breakfast for the family, buy a sticky rice or a *pho* for Hung's lunch. I only call up to him for dinner, after I get back from work."

"I'd like to go up and see him."

"Okay."

Suong showed Dam the way. The door to Hung's room was wide open, as if he had been expecting a visit. Wind blew through the window, rippling the curtain in front of the altar to the ancestors like a funeral banner. Hung was seated, facing the wall, as if he hadn't heard footsteps on the stairs.

"Elder brother, it's Dam, he's come here to see you," Suong said. She had to repeat herself three times before Hung turned around and threw the covers off his stomach.

"So you're free tonight?" Hung asked.

"I've wanted to come see you for a long time, but tonight was the first night I could find the time. How's your appetite?"

"As usual."

"Suong told me you weren't touching meat."

"That's true. Meat and fish disgust me. It must be some sickness. There are people who suddenly can't stomach rice. Others become allergic to streets and cities, go live in the jungle. There are as many ills as there are living species. It's normal, don't worry."

Suong had returned with two glasses of water. "Since he's been back, Hung doesn't drink tea anymore. And Vinh and I aren't really tea drinkers."

"Don't worry. You can leave us alone for a moment. Men like to talk about strange things sometimes."

"Fine, then I'll go finish the laundry." Suong went out, closing the door behind her. Dam waited a moment, then hearing her footsteps fade down the stairs, he asked: "What are you planning to live on?"

"I've got to think for a while. That's a difficult question."

"Suong told me that you promised to go back to the cooperative."

"That's a promise I made sincerely, the night I came back from the beach. But promises are like feelings, they tend to slip away like the shadows of the clouds."

"Hung, I don't want to be giving you advice. But we both have responsibilities to people who are close to us, linked to us. Don't you realize that you can make Suong happy?"

"I made her happy. And I want to continue making her happy. But what people want is one thing. Have you ever really put yourself in someone else's place?"

"Not fully, I don't think, but I try to understand people who live around me."

"Imagine you're a beggar, they tie you with the rope of responsibility and ask you for ten pieces of gold every morning."

"No, I'm not in the mood for that music. I want you to understand me, Hung. I came here, to your native lands, with the soul of an emigrant, an exile. All I wanted to do was to spend my days at the library finishing my book. Fate forced me to take the banner from your hands. It's not been easy. Try putting yourself in my place, then maybe you'll understand."

"I can understand, in part. Honesty is a great luxury. Maybe it will kill us before the knives or sicknesses finish us off."

"Dying with a clear conscience is a pleasant death, because a man needs a conscience. But let's come back to our problem. Are you going to tear yourself away from that gang you were hanging out with? Can you kick the opium habit?"

"I'm trying. Since I've come back, I haven't been out once and I'm taking all sorts of medicine. But if you ask me to tell you what I'm going to do tomorrow, who I'll hook up with, who I'll abandon, that's difficult. I don't want to lie to you, Dam. The night I came back, I promised to go back to my job. But when the time came, I couldn't. Partly because of the opium habit, partly because I couldn't go back to a place I had left. Not because of face, or pride. Because I just couldn't. You may think I'm lazy, cowardly. You can insult me, call me a worthless human being. For me, words are all the same, like a whore that sleeps with someone today before fucking another tomorrow. You know, they once called me 'the soul of the troupe, the devoted soldier for art in the resistance against the Americans to save the nation.' Now, they call me a 'traitor,' accuse me of 'sullying the honor of the Party and the State.' And it's always the same language to talk about the same subject: me. I lived through prison, Dam, and it was good soil for cultivating other plants, for killing the flowers of illusion. Remember, I'm the one who went to prison, not you. We don't speak the same language, even if you are good and you do try to understand me."

Hung stopped talking, raised his glass of water, gulped it down, his long, pale fingers shaking. Dam gazed at those hands, fascinated. They had traced such beautiful melodies on paper, gathered the instruments of a frail orchestra with such talent, breathed such soul and life into inert, unconscious notes. Listening to the melodies that Hung had composed during the war, Dam understood why musicians of their generation in Hanoi couldn't write such music. What distinguished Hung's music was that something you might call the soul of music. Hung had lived deeply, sincerely, with real, profound emotions. No technique or training could compete with that. You had to pay for your art with the value of your own life.

Drops of water trickled down Hung's chin. Dam shivered.

So a man can age this quickly? In a few days, a few weeks, a summer. That's all it takes. An upheaval in life. A turn on the path of fate. He's right, whatever sympathy I have for him, I can't understand.

Dam wanted to reach out and wipe Hung's chin, but he didn't dare. He felt powerless, ashamed. The wind whistled through the room, mussing Hung's hair. The neon ceiling light illuminated the wrinkles on his pale forehead. The drops of water kept falling from the composer's chin onto his shirt. Dam had to restrain the urge to run out of the room, so he looked out at the sky.

"Well, it's late, I've got to go. You take care of yourself."

"Thank you. Good-bye."

They knew that they were going through the motions, like officials going about their administrative duties. Hung pulled the covers back over his stomach, looked out the window. When Dam reached the bottom of the stairs, he said to Suong: "Tomorrow, stay at home, take care of him. He's taking the medicine, but he's so depressed. I feel powerless. You're the only one who can help him back to a normal life."

"Does that mean you're giving me the day off?"

"Yes. We've been performing for a week. Tomorrow, the actors need to rehearse and correct some errors in the play, improve the set. You rest . . . I've got to go now." Dam practically ran out into the courtyard. Suong had to race after him to see him off at the gate.

13

After Dam left, Suong went to get the children from Auntie Tuong's house, even though they were already sound asleep. The old woman scolded her: "Why do you have to tear them out of bed? It's not as if you're short on company over there, are you?"

"Auntie, it's been so long since they slept with us, and I miss them. Also, Hung seems more lucid tonight, I wanted him to play with the kids, to distract him."

Taking her eldest daughter by the hand and the little one in her arms, Suong brought the children back home. Vinh was studying in his room. The room was lit, but the door was closed. Recently, he seemed to have grown thinner, but whenever she asked him about it he just shook his head. "It's nothing, nothing." His character had changed; he had become more taciturn, aloof from people, even the two girls. Suong thought she could detect his voice deepening, that he was becoming an adult. Da Hai asked where Uncle Vinh was and Suong put her finger to her lips to be quiet."

"Go up and see your father." Suong urged Da Hai up the stairs. Hung turned around and caught Da Hai's eyes on him. Clear, dreamy chestnut eyes as tender as the dawns that used to break over the veranda at his mother's house, before the war. Back then, he too must have had those eyes. Everyone said that Da Hai looked like him.

My little girl, who knows if looking like me will bring you luck or misfortune. People like me aren't cut out for normal life. We're like plants that only grow in shadow, that only bear flowers as fragile as soap bubbles. If you're like me, you won't be able to stand hardship, your own passions will sap your energy, your capacity to accept life.

His daughter wrapped her arms around her father's neck. "Papa! Why didn't you come play horse with me?" Hung buried his head in her lap.

"Daddy was sick. Will you forgive me?"

Da Hai kissed his head, consoled him. "Daddy be good, eat well so you can get better. I'll let you build me temples and pagodas." Her tiny hands fiddled with his hair, his neck, his forehead, just like his mother's soft hands.

My little girl, now you're consoling me too. When did Daddy stop being a father, the pillar of this family, and turn into some fragile being that even you have to protect?

This bitter thought made him smile contemptuously to himself. He looked up, gazed at his wife. She was holding the baby in her arms, at the edge of the bed, looking at him with dark eyes. He couldn't read her thoughts. All he could see was that she no longer gazed at him with her passionate, hopeful, trusting look. Now her eyes were mute, empty. She bent over to kiss Phuoc Hanh, avoiding his gaze. She seemed to use the girls to erect a barrier between them, to flee an intimacy that he could have claimed.

Since I've been back, I haven't made love to you. That's abnormal, unacceptable. I'm your husband, and I love you, I have to prove that my love hasn't changed. But fatigue and depression, like any icy wind, had seeped into his bones and muscles, pulling them apart, crushing them. *No, no, it's not possible and it doesn't matter. I've loved you so many days, so many years. I'm not some young stallion that needs to prove itself on the first race across the plain.*

Hung lifted the little girl from his wife's arms, kissed her, then handed her back. "Here's your bundle."

He turned to Da Hai. "So tonight are you sleeping with me?"

"Of course Daddy."

He nodded. Suong stepped down the stairs, holding Phuoc Hanh in her arms.

It seems like that's all she was waiting for. As if she wanted to be free. Not a doubt, not a demand, not a single nagging word. These last few days have been unusual for our marriage. But she seems to accept it all with an odd silence. Or . . . maybe . . . no, no, the suffering I've inflicted has exhausted her. I've tortured you, made you lose your vivacity, your spontaneity. It's me who's the guilty one, who killed the happiness under this roof.

His daughter's tiny hands touched his head. "Daddy, why don't you say anything? Why are you so sad?"

Hung looked at her. "Who told you I'm sad?"

The little girl thought a moment before replying. "I see it on your face. Auntie Tuong said so too."

"When did she tell you that?"

"Yesterday, before yesterday, and before that, too. She says it a lot."

"What else did she say?"

"That I shouldn't bother you, that I have to love you because you're sad."

Her hands stroked his chin, grazed his beard, like a mysterious electric charge, filling his heart with both sweetness and bitterness. Hung suddenly hugged his daughter tightly, breathed her familiar smell, felt her heart beating.

The next morning, when Hung woke up, Da Hai wasn't in bed next to him. The clock showed nine-thirty. He could hear laughter and children playing over at Auntie Tuong's. He didn't know if Suong had left for work or if she was out in the courtyard. Still curled up under the blanket that barely covered his chest, he was remembering the warmth and softness he had felt holding Da Hai in his arms, when Suong appeared with a bowl covered with a cotton towel.

"Have some breakfast. I've got to go out for a bit."

"Are you going to rehearse?"

"No," she said, hesitating for a moment before adding: "Dam gave me the day off. But I've got some errands to do. Da Hai is going to go to kindergarten soon. I forgot to tell you."

"I should have taken care of that. But I've become an invalid, and you've got to pick up all the pieces."

"No, no," Suong said suddenly, blushing.

He thought he had hurt her. "I'm sorry if I upset you. But . . ."

"You . . . you have some *pho*, while it's hot." She urged him hurriedly, and without waiting for his reply she opened the medicine box, examining everything, counting the pills.

"You're almost finished. I'm going to get some more medicine. They say there's some new tonic out."

"There's no hurry. There's enough medicine for another three days."

Suong replied without meeting his eyes. "I'm going to get some more for you at the market. Eat the *pho*."

Hung smiled. "Don't worry. And remember to take the keys. I'll put the house in order."

She didn't laugh, just mumbled something, then slipped down the stairs.

That morning, before seven-thirty, Suong had taken the girls over to Auntie Tuong's. The young man from the prison was waiting, an enormous bouquet of scarlet roses under his arm.

"This is to wish you a nice day," he said. The roses startled Suong. She blushed, didn't have time to respond when the girls, who had spotted the flowers in this stranger's hands, began shrieking with delight. The young man bent down. "So you like flowers?"

"Yes."

"Well then, I'll give you some. Wait, I'll take off some of the thorns, or they'll cut your hands."

"That's what Auntie Tuong says: 'There's no rose without thorns,'" Da Hai said, proudly reciting a verse from a lullaby the old woman sang to her little sister. The young man opened his eyes wide: "Who taught you that? My, you talk like a little mama already!" He burst out laughing. "Like mother like daughter, and you seem even more mature than your mom."

He handed Da Hai a rose that he had stripped of its thorns. The little girl looked up. "Are you going to give one to my little sister too, Uncle?"

"Of course . . . this is your mother's bouquet." He handed the bouquet to Suong and lowered his voice. "The commander has invited you out for a stroll."

"I'm busy," Suong said. "Don't you see, I've got to take the children . . ."

The young man coldly ignored her words. "Do you want me to wait for you here, or should I send the jeep? The only problem is that it has government license plates."

"No, no," Suong said hurriedly. She started to panic, not knowing how she was going to get out of this invitation. She lowered her voice, as if to plead with him. "Can't you see I'm busy?"

The young man touched Da Hai's face. "She's so cute. Come on, take them over to the old woman's house. I'll wait for you here."

"No . . ."

The young man leaned over to the girls. "You kids go on over to Auntie Tuong's house. I'll be back soon and I'll bring you some presents."

He knows her name. He knows that the old woman is more trusted in our family than even relatives. He knows I don't have any reason to refuse.

Seeing the girls arrive, Auntie Tuong exclaimed, "Oh my girls, how I've missed you! Tonight I'm not going to let you go home with your mama Suong." The old woman hugged the girls in her arms right in the middle of the courtyard, as if she had been separated from them for ten years. Taking one girl by the hand and the other in her arms, she turned around to Suong. "Go ahead and do your errands, we'll be just fine."

Suong didn't know what to say, resigned herself to going out. The flaming bouquet of roses still in the arms of the young man standing in front of her door was both a reminder and an invitation. At this hour, if Hung got up, he would see the young man. Suong felt a shiver run up her spine at the thought.

"Are you coming?"

"No, no, please."

"I could come back and pick you up later?"

"No."

"Sister Suong, please, take pity on a man who is totally devoted to you, with everything he has, all his soul."

The wind seemed to amplify his voice, making it echo through the streets.

Panicked, Suong accepted. "Okay, okay, I'll come."

Her head lowered, she dashed into the house. Vinh had left for school, and Hung was still sleeping. She was lucky. She contemplated the bouquet: It was like a flame that cried out for remembrance. Just thinking about their affair fascinated and terrified her, and she both relived it and tried to erase it from her mind.

How could I have done that? Why? For so long, without admitting it to myself, I secretly loved that man. A criminal love. I can't keep it buried in my heart like some eternal debt. Maybe I was just moved by his generosity, so I behaved like someone who doesn't dare be an ingrate?

Suong couldn't find the answer. For three evenings running, she had seen the commander attend her performances of the new show. Every night the young dandy in the striped shirt walked up to the stage to hand her an enormous bouquet of red roses that caused whispers to ripple through the audience and sparked jealousy among the other actors. Suong had been careful to leave these bouquets at the theater, or in Dam's office. She never brought flowers home. It had become a habit.

"Do you know this man?" Dam had asked her.

"No ... I ... just met him ..." Suong stammered. Then, seeing Dam's inquisitive look, she explained. "He's the commander of the reeducation camp. We met when Hung was in there, when Lam and I went to take supplies and food to him."

"Ah! Now I see . . . So the guardians of hell can turn out to be terrible romantics." Dam laughed and went off. Suong didn't understand his mocking attitude, but by the next day no one mentioned the conversation. Dam was too busy researching a new part of the troupe's repertory. He spent his days poring over songs and plays, making new additions to the orchestra; he even sent an emissary to Hanoi to select more musicians. One day, he said to Suong: "I've just found an exquisite song, and your voice is totally right for it. When the new musicians arrive, we'll start rehearsing."

Suong thought he had forgotten the enormous bouquets of roses and the young man from the prison, and she sighed with relief. But during the evenings that followed, when she went out on stage, she slipped a look into the front rows of the audience, hoping secretly to see the man's face, his sparkling eyes, the desire quivering in the smile on his lips. *I'm a weak woman, a bad woman, I have no right to . . .*

Every night she reproached herself, looking for excuses to stay backstage. But every night she searched the audience, anxious, expectant.

The commander's attendance at her shows was a costly luxury for a man in his position. It had only been eight days since their first intimacy. *My God, he only went back to the camp for a few days. Already he's back. Like me, he's been swept up in the whirl of it. I'm just an ordinary actress, but he's a commander, he has social position, power. This passion is going to harm him. I've got to see him, persuade him to end it.*

Suong was genuinely concerned about this man, though he was still a stranger to her. She got up, washed an old dusty vase and arranged the flowers in it. Fresh, dazzling roses with long stems and thick thorns, lithe, cutting, full of vitality; they reminded her of the man who loved her. While she was arranging the flowers, she suddenly heard Hung coughing, but then he fell back asleep. Suong hurriedly mounted the stairs, opened the door, peaking into the room. Hung was sleeping peacefully, the covers pulled over his chest. The sun lit his wavy, disheveled hair, his pale forehead, the fine bridge of his nose. Pain shot through Suong's gut.

I've betrayed him. I've shamed him. The first man who loved me, who was so faithful, who gave me so much attention, so much love . . . after my father. He's done me wrong, but they were the ones who pushed him over the edge. And now I . . .

These thoughts tortured her. But another memory raised its voice.

The man I loved is dead. I can't love some filthy being reduced to crawling over fish nets in an opium den, his back hunched over like an old man, a face like a criminal. That's not the Hung I knew.

The clock on the wall struck nine o'clock. Suong's heart raced from impatience. Was the commander thinking about her, calling her, cursing her? She could see him, striding across the room, his graceful, powerful gait. How could such a man find the patience to wait for her? And yet he had waited for years, and he was still waiting.

A thorn pricked her finger, making it bleed. Suong pressed it with one of the petals, then quickly changed and put on her makeup. She still hadn't decided whether to go or not, but she was doing everything to make that happen. Hung woke up when Suong brought him a bowl of *pho*. As she checked the medicine box, she didn't dare look him in the eye. It seemed to her that his eyes had preserved the image of the man she once loved. And she feared that the old Hung might kill the wretch that crawled among the fishnets, and that he would reclaim his old power over her. Hung laughed. And his laughter seemed sharp, like a razor held to the thin fibers of a reed. She ran down the stairs, drenched in sweat.

Hung had managed to quit opium but he still hadn't returned to work. He stayed cloistered in his room all day, contemplating the ylang-ylangs, his arms hugging his knees. Leaning on his desk, he could gaze for hours at something in the bottom of a cup of tea gone cold. His skin was still pale, as if all tonics and foods were powerless to revivify him. He complained of difficulty urinating, an illness he must have gotten in prison. Often Suong saw him come out of the bathroom, his face white as a sheet, his lips twisted painfully, but she didn't dare ask questions. She just silently bought him diuretics, made him light meals. They still hadn't made love even though three weeks had gone by since his return. He treated her gently, spoke to her kindly, but he seemed absent. And he apologized over nothing. Only his sad eyes revealed a world of shadow and pain. A world that was closed off to her. Crushed by shame herself, Suong didn't dare look too deeply. She shrank when faced with Hung's gaze because her lips, hair, feet, and hands, every inch of her body bore the mark of another man. She dreaded the moment when Hung's eyes might leave his desolate world and begin to search her face and body. He would be able to name it, detect the trace of other lips. He was her master, knew her faults before anyone else. Like a schoolgirl who had cheated, Suong shuddered at the idea of being caught in the act.

"Do you feel better?"

"Yes, I feel better. Don't worry so much."

"You're not eating anything. You've got to eat to cure your illness."

"Thanks sweetheart, I'm trying."

"The sticky rice is on the table, and I'm keeping the *pho* warm in the kitchen. Don't forget to eat some later. The fruit basket is in the cupboard at the foot of the bed."

"That's fine, I'll remember. You don't need to remind me where the furniture is. Go off to the rehearsal, I'll be fine."

"I'm going. Don't forget to take the medicine."

Every day, the same conversation. Every day, Suong left on her bicycle, turning to look up at the window on the first floor. Sometimes, she saw a hand wave, his hair tossing in a familiar gesture, and it broke her heart. Sometimes, the window was empty, and she would feel a formless sadness envelop her.

One day she decided not to look up at the window anymore. But just a few yards past the door, out of some old reflex, she turned and looked up. Hung was standing there, a thin arm raised, smiling. His smile, that sad look in his brown eyes were like a silent reproach. *No, no,*

I can't think about it anymore. I don't love him. I don't have anything to reproach myself for. But then a moment later she remembered how the commander had made love to her, and she felt a pang of pity for Hung.

A few weeks later, Hung came down with a fever. Every time he went into the bathroom to urinate, he was drenched in sweat, trembling. He said he had a boil on his groin, but he refused to show her. When she placed her hand on his abdomen, she could feel the heat of his skin, his abnormally swollen penis.

"How could you have a boil there? I've never heard of anyone having such an illness."

"Neither have I," Hung said, gritting his teeth in a spasm of pain. Suong held his hand, not knowing how to give him some of her strength. Suong had heard of boils like this when she lived in the mountains. One of their neighbors, a hunter, had contracted something similar; a boil, the size of an egg, that had grown inside the muscle. The more it grew, the more his thigh swelled, until it was as hard as wood. The hunter couldn't put on his pants and had to stay inside all day with only a loincloth to cover him. He was always feverish, never ate anything, and he clenched a wood beam in his hands to get through the bouts of pain. But the boil refused to go away, and there was no balm or herb that could heal it. After three weeks, his family sent someone to the other side of the mountain to look for a young Chinese doctor attached to a military unit. After days of waiting, the doctor was free to help. When he arrived, he asked them to tie the sick man to his bed before operating. When he lanced the boil with his scalpel, the doctor screamed as a stream of blood and pus spurted forth, showering his white coat. He had to clean the wound for almost two hours; there wasn't much of the man's thigh left after the operation. The hunter had been strong and vigorous, and he had recovered.

But Hung was no hunter, so Suong would have to just wait until the boil popped by itself.

"I'll call a doctor," she said to Hung. "You can't bear this kind of pain."

"No, no," Hung said, sitting up in bed, taking Suong's arm. "No, it's not necessary," he said, his voice pleading, "Boils always end up popping. I can stand the wait."

Suong yielded, but the next day, she decided to come home for lunch and surprised Hung, who was going over to get the keys from Auntie Tuong's.

"Where are you going?"

"To buy some medicine," Hung said tersely. He was pale and drawn, his forehead drenched in sweat, the veins on his neck pulsing. Suong helped him back to the house. Without a word, she went in search of a doctor.

She had once met a doctor during a performance for a national congress of medicine. The doctor was supposedly "a man who had stayed in the country from the days of the puppet government" as the cadres liked to say. He was a polite, elegant man, who spoke with great modesty, his gestures as precise and rigorous as if they had been weighed in a laboratory. After the performance, Suong had gone out onto the veranda, where the doctor had gone out to smoke a cigarette. In his white suit and brown checkered tie, he seemed extremely neat, more graceful than those around him. During their meeting, he had bent over to listen to Suong, asking her questions with an affectionate, genuine concern and interest. His manner reminded her of another voice from her past.

Tell me, Suong. What animal left a track there? Don't answer right away, my child, look at the other tracks around it first. See that excrement at the base of that tree? Notice how the bark on that bush has been scraped away? That's a sign that a wild boar was trying to uproot it, and that's his excrement. A fox's would never be that size.

Tell me, Suong. The melody came back like a refrain as she remembered the doctor, how their conversation that night, after the performance, had made her happy.

The doctor had left her his calling card. Even though he had been with the southern puppet regime, they had given him a job in the medical division because he was a "bone in their throat" as he liked to say. "Couldn't swallow me, couldn't spit me out." Outside of his working hours, he continued to see old patients that he had followed from birth.

Suong hailed a taxi and went directly to the doctor's house. He was napping. His wife, a portly woman of about fifty, invited Suong in for a glass of fruit juice in their living room, which was sparkling clean. The woman asked Suong if she wouldn't mind waiting for her husband to wake up and handed her a comic book. While Suong flipped through it, the woman went back to reading the famous Chinese adventure novel *The Beauty Who Slew the Dragon.* At exactly one forty-five, the woman set her book down, mounted the stairs, and woke her husband. Five minutes later, he appeared in his gray suit, his attaché case in hand.

"What a pleasure! Mai Suong, the famous singer! Now I wasn't expecting to see you as my patient today," he said warmly, then turned to his wife. "Hey, Lan, do you know who this young lady is? The Edith Piaf of Indochina!"

The woman looked at Suong, surprised. "Oh, forgive me. I didn't recognize you. You're so wonderful on stage."

"Who would imagine that in real life you're just an ordinary person?" the doctor continued with a generous smile. "I like the simple way you dress. The stage is one thing, but life is another. Who do I have the honor of examining today? Yourself or your husband? Or one of your children?"

"Oh Uncle, I've come to ask you to help treat my husband."

"What are his symptoms?"

"Uh, he's had a fever for more than a week, and . . ." Suong didn't dare continue in front of the doctor's wife. Seeing her hesitate, he said. "Okay, let's go to your house, I'll examine him when I get there. On bicycle, cyclo, or by motorbike?"

"I came by cyclo."

"Okay, I'll drive you back on the motorbike."

"I don't want to bother you."

"Not at all, it's easy. And I'm not so old that I can't drive a Honda."

He turned around and instructed his wife. "If someone asks for me, tell them to leave their address so I can make a house call later."

The woman got up and accompanied them to the door, a ritual that must have been decades old. They said good-bye affectionately, as if he were leaving on some mission abroad, as if they wouldn't see each other for dinner.

Are they happy? There's nothing in their gay, polite words, in his wife's attitude, that would lead you to suspect their marriage might someday fall apart. But who knows where the snake makes its lair? Everyone, including Dam, thought we were a happy, harmonious, close couple. And yet I've betrayed Hung, and I'm the only one who knows it.

As she sat behind the doctor on his motorbike, this thought haunted her, gnawed at her for the length of the trip back to the house. She only forgot it when they arrived. She got off the bike and opened the door for the doctor, guiding him up the stairs.

The doctor entered the room. "So this is your sick husband?"

Lying in the bed, half asleep, Hung sat up, turning his gaunt face toward the doctor. "Yes, hello sir." He tried to prop himself on his elbows, but the doctor discouraged him. "No need. Stay lying down."

Hung was going to lie back down, but he glanced anxiously at Suong, hesitant. She waited patiently behind the doctor's back. Hung didn't dare ask her to leave, but he didn't dare let the doctor examine him in front of her. The old man understood immediately and turned to Suong: "You may leave us now. If I need anything, I'll call for you."

As Suong went downstairs, she realized she was famished. She had skipped lunch at the cafeteria, thinking she would buy Hung a bowl of *hu tieu* soup, or some *bun moc* with a plate of stir-fried eel that he liked so much. Hung must still not have had anything to eat. She turned and went back up the stairs to ask Hung if he wanted to eat after the doctor's visit. But the doctor's voice stopped her halfway up the stairs.

"Do you realize that, in doing this, you are endangering your wife's life?"

"I know . . . But I swear to you, I didn't touch her . . . not once."

"Can I believe that?"

"Absolutely, doctor. Not because I'm a saint, but because the circumstances haven't allowed us to have a normal intimacy, like other couples. I just went through a detoxification cure for opium. You're a doctor, you know that in that state a man doesn't have either the strength or the desire to make love."

"Okay. I believe you. But I have to warn you again: You must control yourself, avoid all sexual contact while you're sick. Your wife is also the mother of your children. An honest woman doesn't deserve to pay such a terrible price for your behavior."

The doctor's harsh, biting words so totally clashed with his usually gentle, polite manner that Suong was stunned. She stepped back, silently, down the stairs. Her hunger was gone, she couldn't even think about food. She sat down on a chair, waiting.

About fifteen minutes later, the doctor came down. Suong met him at the base of the stairs: "Uncle, what does my husband have?"

The doctor didn't reply, just glanced around. "Could you bring me a pan of hot water and some soap?"

"Right away." Suong went into the bathroom, poured the boiled water from a Thermos bottle into a pan and brought it to the doctor with some soap. The doctor scrubbed his hands meticulously, drying them with a towel he carried in his briefcase. Then he sat down facing her. "I know it's embarrassing for women to discuss a subject like this, but it is my duty to ask you a question. Please answer me honestly: Have you and your husband stopped having sexual relations?"

"Uh . . ." Suong felt her face burn, her ears redden, but she replied clearly. "Since he has been back, we've slept in separate beds. He's been on medication to help him with the detoxification."

"Search your memory. These are natural acts, it's not a sin. There's no reason to be ashamed. Did you make love, even once?"

"No . . . in fact . . ." Suong remembered a night, not long ago, when Hung had wanted to make love, had led her upstairs. Though she had just been with the commander and was exhausted, she felt guilty and decided to make love with Hung. But just as they started, little Da Hai screamed. She had just had a nightmare and was sobbing, calling for her mother. Suong had run down the stairs, picked up the child, and sung her a lullaby. A half hour later, Da Hai finally fell back asleep, and

Suong dozed off between the two girls, didn't notice Hung when he came to find her. Seeing them all fast asleep, he had given up.

"Yes, in fact, we almost did, once, but I was too tired and the girls were crying. That night, the old woman who was watching the girls had gone to the pagoda, so I had them at home."

The doctor nodded. "Well, if that's true, good. I had to ask you because this concerns your health and the future of your children. Your husband has a disease that we call Korean syphilis; it's a venereal disease that soldiers transmitted to prostitutes."

So that's it. Korean syphilis. I've heard people talk about it, but I always thought of it as a sickness for sinners who lived in another world. How could I have thought of it here, under our roof? And Hung telling me it was an infected boil!

Suddenly Suong felt tricked, and the anger rose in her, choking her. *To think that I washed the towels he soaked in cold water to sooth the pain, that I emptied his chamber pot, cared for him, tended to him, exhausted myself.*

The doctor continued: "You mustn't have any sexual contact with your husband during the treatment. Avoid everything that touches his body. For example the towel he uses to wash his penis: If you use it, you could go blind. The microbes from Korean syphilis are resistant to antibiotics. And the most important thing is that you've got to keep him away from the little girls. And there's another thing . . ." He paused for a few moments, hesitating before he continued, then decided to go on.

"Fortunately, you've got two children. From now on, you and Hung can't have any more children. If you do get pregnant, you'll give birth to abnormal children, with deformities."

Suong nodded.

"I've given him a shot and left some medicine for him to take tonight. Tomorrow, I'll be back to give him a second shot. Don't forget to tell him to take his vitamins and to eat well so he won't exhaust his bone marrow." The doctor sighed and lowered his voice. "I'm so sorry. This is an unexpected tragedy for you. But I couldn't hide the truth from you. I want you to protect your own health."

"Thank you, Uncle."

"I'll be going now." The doctor lifted his arm, looked at his watch. Suong noticed his starched sleeve, smooth, without a crease, as if it had been cut from marble.

Suong saw him to the gate, then watched as his Honda 50 turned into the intersection and disappeared into the distance. She stood on the sidewalk for a long time after he had gone, not knowing what to think, what to do. Passersby turned to look at her, curious. A few school kids were hanging about, excited to see this famous singer without makeup, simply dressed like other women. Suong stood there, motionless, until she sensed someone behind her. She turned, saw Hung's silhouette framed in the door to their house.

He's been there, standing there, for a long time, watching me. What does he want to say now? An explanation, an excuse, some lament?

He was a stranger to her now, alien, repellant.

To think that I was tortured by remorse.

She went back into the house, collapsed on the bed. Her tears didn't flow anymore, her heart no longer raced with anxiety. She just lay there, motionless, staring at the ceiling, her brain and soul empty. After a long time, she felt Hung touch her feet.

"Suong . . ." He knelt beside the bed, stammering through pale, drawn lips. "Suong . . . I beg you to forgive me . . . I'm not worthy of your love, your devotion."

Suong sat up.

Hung continued, the wrinkles on his forehead tightening, who knew whether from the pain, or the illness. "You can forgive me . . . or not . . . it's all up to you. I don't dare ask you for anything for myself. I just ask one thing: Never tell the girls. Now or later. Whether I'm dead or alive. They're innocent. They need to think of their father as a good man. Ever since they were born, I've always wanted to be worthy of their respect, to live well by them. It was a moment of weakness, of error . . . forgive me for that moment. Just for the children. I don't dare ask you for anything more. From now on you're free . . ."

Suong wept. But in her soul another voice rose, a voice full of hate and bitterness. *I didn't wait for your permission. I gave myself that freedom. And I deserved it.*

In the days that followed, Suong went back to see the commander, made love to him with all the passion of her pent-up desire. She was no longer like the closed jar of the first few days.

The man was first stunned then overcome with happiness. "I know, it's only now that you really love me. Only now am I really in your heart. I didn't wait in vain."

Rose petals littered the floor, the carpet, the bed, the tiles of the bathroom, reddening space, making the walls blaze. After they made love, the commander would bury his head in Suong's arms. "I'm thinking of the moment I'll have to leave you, and then the moment when I'll return . . . happiness is so short."

"Yes, I know. It's sad for you to live in the mountains, but it's sad for me here too," Suong said, stroking his hair. She remembered the long bumpy road that seemed to stretch forever between the town and the thick jungle he had crossed to reach her. She imagined the dawns shrouded in fog, the dark nights without the slightest light when he took his troops out to hunt, to kill the time. On those remote paths amidst the tall reeds, he thought of her, missed her. His imagination endowed their love with an unusual beauty.

"I love you, Suong, did you know that? I've loved you ever since you set foot in my office, with your pale cheeks and your blouse covered with the dust of the roads."

"How could I know?"

"Now you know, you must know." Suddenly he stretched out his arms, pulling her to him.

14

There are days here without rain, without sun, when the wind on the mountains blows day and night, not the wind from Laos that roasts everyone in its furnace nor the icy wind of the gorges thick with mist, but a wild, ominous wind, neither hot nor cold, that doesn't howl, doesn't murmur, but drones, recalling gaping, unending memories. Carried on the wind, clouds of termites appear out of nowhere, invade the sky, flood the small towns, swarm through the cities, weaving a net above people. They crash into cars, falling thick and fast to the ground. Their corpses litter the streets, the sidewalks, drifting on the trickle of sewers, sticking to the surface of the bogs, rustling among the dead leaves near the canals, settling in drifts on the rooftops, the arching porticoes of the public gardens. Propelled by this sad, dismal wind, clouds drag their tattered coats through the sky, curling in leaden spirals, as if to build a Co Loa Citadel, that funereal city that presaged betrayal and despair. In this desolate wind, no one can help stopping for a moment, gripped by the need to search for roots, some future vision, some simple, dignity above the oppressiveness of religion or morality.

On a day like this, Hung, seated in his room, his knees clutched in his arms, suddenly realized that he felt nothing: no sadness, no pain, no regret, no desire. He watched the termites swirl in the air, crash against each other, falling onto the crests of ylang-ylangs, wave after wave of them at the same speed, with the same euphoria. As if suicide were their only aim, their supreme goal, as if each of these tiny creatures had been created by God to fly to their death, tracing majestic, solemn circles in the sky with those beautiful, gossamer wings, executing to perfection a ritual for which they had been created. Hung contemplated their vertiginous flight, their sudden fall.

Could they be images of men? After all, they rise to conquer unknown, distant, open space, they soar up just to reach freedom—to free themselves if even for one moment from their shadowy dens on earth. They don't know they will die for it. Even insects don't have the courage to greet the end of their existence with joy. As soon as they trace the first circle of freedom in the air, the angel of death is already gathering them in its vast net. They will only glimpse the bottomless space for an instant before being swallowed in the abyss. Isn't man offered happiness on the same terms? Light is only visible against a background of darkness; the shadows of the abyss loom, always lurking for human beings intoxicated with happiness. This is the law of life. Once you have accepted it, what is there to regret?

Hung felt lighter, freed of a heavy burden. But after a fitful sleep, other thoughts resurfaced like mud stirred from the bottom of a basin. *No, it's just a cowardly way of justifying oneself: to destroy life, escape responsibility. I've already lived a useful life. At those moments, life appeared to me in a different light. When did I fall into this abyss?*

Remorse tortured his conscience, just as powerfully as the consoling gentleness of the termites dancing in the air. *No, I'm not alone, millions of men and women know that life is ephemeral. Other fathers would throw their bodies to the tigers before they would deliver their children to the lords of the jungle. Other husbands would have jumped into the river before they'd let their wife throw herself to the demon of the waters. I'm just a selfish coward. Me, the intellectual, the one who reads all the books, the words of the sages, who knows all the moral lessons, I've unloaded my burden on the shoulders of my own wife, stolen the money she saved for our children. Nothing can excuse it . . . nothing.*

Hung felt his body go limp. The day this catastrophe had befallen him: What had it been like? Had it been rainy or sunny? Had the sky been tormented, filled with fleeing gray clouds, like today? Or had it been a clear blue summer sky? He had lived days and months of unhappiness, but the most horrible had been that day of pouring rain at The Rose Inn. He had fallen in Doan's trap, become his prisoner. And when the man had fled, clutching the hat to his chest, Hung had been paralyzed, his head empty. A few days later, terrifying memories of his prison days had come back to haunt him. The fetid odor of his cell, dank with fear and hatred, reeking of the shit that piled up in the gutter in the corner. The sallow glow of the oil lamp, not just a glow but the mirror of their hellish existence. The moaning of men wracked with pain, gasping as they tried to expel their shit; the insults of the other prisoners.

Hung saw them all again: their bodies, their wrinkled, scarred thighs; their groins covered with sores, oozing with pus; their penises, dangling, limp and shriveled as black worms; the translucent skin of their shaved heads. He saw those horrible instruments they called spoons stirring that insipid fluid they called soup, the shit that still clung to the roots of the water spinach, the dead bugs floating on top. He saw the jungle fade into dusk, the smoke and fog, heard the long, heart-rending cries of a dying young prisoner, echoing all night, every night, over and over again, hurled against the stone wall of the mountains.

He remembered the faces of the political prisoners, condemned to solitary confinement, kept at the bottom of a ravine, or isolated, one by one, in underground shelters built into the mountains on the other side of the sugar cane factory. One day, those ravines echoed with shots, rounds of gunfire. The other men told him that they had just executed one of the six prisoners he had met the day before during hard labor. The same man who had picked up a rock and smashed another prisoner's skull for stealing six shrimp. Starving, the prisoner had eaten them raw—six tiny shrimp, the ones you fished out of streams. He had paid for them with his life, the horrible, animal life they had led. Hung couldn't stand it. His heart had always beat to the delicate, subtle emotions of music, couldn't bear the shocks of such a barbaric existence.

No, no, that bastard Doan isn't going to put me back there. I'll never set foot in that hell hole again.

Trong Cang and Truc Son shared his fears. They urged him to compromise with Doan. *Your life is too precious, your talent as an artist mustn't go to waste for some useless sacrifice. Retreat, step back; you'll have a future . . . you'll have time and space to create again, to write music.*

So he had surrendered, given Doan half the money he had stolen from Suong. That madman had shrieked with joy; he had never even seen a tenth of this money. He ran out and bought expensive paint, silk canvases. Ecstatic, he proclaimed that these new materials had inspired him: Now he saw visions, portraits, landscapes of life in a new light, and he would create masterpieces that no one could equal, not all the lousy painters in this lousy S-shaped country, not even those famous blue-eyed white painters.

No one dared contradict him. Artists were crazy, weren't they? But there was another, more compelling reason: They were terrified of him. He was "with the police." Just those words gave him a mysterious, shameful power, and yet made him somehow imposing, almost regal; because, after all, who isn't afraid of prison? But after a few days of inspirational work, Doan went back to look for them at The Rose Inn, which had become home to Hung and the two failed artists. He proposed that they go in search of something to rouse the muse of poetry.

Why shouldn't we taste pleasures others enjoy? We creators, the purest of the pure of human society, we belong to a superior class, we're not part of the crowd that ekes out an existence, or the puppets who follow the regime's orders, or the norms of their ancestors, that bunch of rotting corpses. They lead banal lives, not so different from worms and insects. And yet these second-class citizens, these lackluster idiots enjoy all the pleasures of life, while the rest of us who save humanity with our art are condemned to living like village hermits.

Doan, the painter-informer, could be a real orator. During the first few days by The Rose Inn, Hung had gazed absently at the sea. He ignored Doan's speeches to Trong Cang and Truc Son, just saying tersely: "I wouldn't mind, but I don't know where I'd steal the money to pay for your excellencies'. I barely have enough to cover my daily two bowls of rice vermicelli and shrimp."

But one day, Hung couldn't stand his dull, secret existence any longer.

A life of insects and worms. Why live like this? I can't go back to my wife and children. I can't compose beautiful music anymore. I don't want to prolong the life of a body that they call a man. One of God's failed, neglected creations. Like they say, the value of a life isn't measured by its length, but by the quality of each of its moments. Doan is right. We should enjoy life's pleasures. Who knows, maybe the muse of music will return. And if she doesn't, well let's at least enjoy the experience. Because in the end, everyone has to die. At least I won't go to the gates of hell as some idiot who never knew or understood the back alleys and corners of human misery. My wife and girls will go on living their lives. Suong earns good money, everyone adores and dotes on her. She has everything. She'll find a way to provide for the girls like millions of other women.

As evening fell, Hung asked the innkeeper: "Do you have any brown smoke here?"

"No," the innkeeper replied, shaking his head. "I'm not that brave, but I know where you can find it."

"Is it far?"

"Not very. But I've never seen you have any."

"What a man hasn't done yesterday, he'll do tomorrow. Let's go."

Hung's two companions didn't dare say a word. They considered this particular pleasure to be a temptation from the devil. Naturally gentle, they were accustomed to living in misery and they didn't even dream of this forbidden fruit. Hung's unexpected decision both tempted and terrified them. They followed him, two silent shadows.

The innkeeper led them along a row of casuarina trees at the edge of the beach, to the left of the inn. A fiendish light lit the sky. A crescent moon, planted like a scythe in gray clouds as thick and spongy as sea foam. The wind whistled through the trees with its ancient, mournful refrain. Sand poured into their slippers, itching their feet, and now and then, the spines of tiny wildflowers pricked their legs. After about ten minutes, ghostly shadows emerged from the night. But these ghosts weren't clad in elegant, perfumed robes, like in the legends. They wore tight, clingy blouses of thin, see-through fabric with plunging necklines and cheap perfume that smelled like the bleach used to clean hotel bathrooms.

"Come here, honey . . ."

"Hi sweetheart, come with me, come on, over here."

"Come enjoy darling, the beach over there is sooo cool."

The innkeeper barked at them: "Not now! Scram!"

These female shadows lurked around the men for a few minutes longer, then disappeared, scampering back into the field of casuarina trees. The innkeeper led Hung and his companions into a shack filled with fishnets. He went in first, fumbling around for a gas lamp, then set it down on a wooden crate. The light flickered weakly, like the light of fireflies.

"Come on in! Watch your heads! The ceiling is low, so you've got to bend down to get through."

They entered one by one. The innkeeper pulled a reed mat off one of the beams of the roof and unfurled it over the nets. "Have a seat on this. There's more than enough room on these nets. Sometimes as many as six men come here to smoke and no one feels cramped."

The innkeeper went out, carefully surveyed the surrounding beach, then paced around the shack several times before stepping back inside. He knelt on the ground, dug in the sand like a fox, then pulled out a wooden box almost as large as the kind actors used for makeup, tightly bound with elastic bands and copper wires. He carefully unraveled all this, lifting off the cover: a set of opium pipes. He pulled out a piece of cloth and wiped the tray, skillfully cleaning the necks of the pipes, then laid it down on the fishing nets.

"What will you have? First, second, or pure?" He asked Hung.

"What does it mean?"

The innkeeper raised an eyebrow. "You've never done this?"

"No, that's why I'm here."

"There are different varieties of opium. First, there's the pure. Then, by diluting the paste, you get the first quality. When you use this a second time, you get what's called the second water. It's like producing plastic. There's the pure, then the recycled . . . once, twice . . ."

Hung smiled. "Clearly this is a refined, arcane pleasure, one that requires great skill. Like art. Works of art can be classified in the same manner."

The innkeeper continued. "Of course, the price depends on the quality. The pure is obviously the most expensive."

"Well, then give us the pure. There's no need to bargain: We're not coming back for a second round."

The innkeeper smiled, reached into his pocket, and pulled out a mint candy box. It contained a black paste wrapped in a small plastic packet and a scoop made out of a finely polished clam shell, as tiny as a shirt button.

"One scoop each? Who starts?"

"Mr. Hung?"

"No, I'd like to watch before smoking. You try first, Truc Son. After all, you poets are the avant-garde, aren't you?"

Truc Son stretched out on the mat and the innkeeper served him the first opium pipe of his life. He coughed and choked on the first draught, but after each cough, he inhaled the smoke more deeply. After half a dose, he held the neck of the pipe between his teeth. His eyes glazed over slowly, as if he would fall asleep whenever he let go of the pipe.

At least it will be a sweet slumber. Half of humanity has been seduced by this smoke because it yearns to dream. I'll join them. I no longer have any place here, in this wretched life. I'm going in search of dreams now.

These thoughts swirled in Hung's brain, blurring the filth that he had felt as he crossed the forests of feathery casuarina trees to this stinking hut. Hung felt his heart race, his blood run faster in his veins.

The brown smoke was truly magical, steeping him in colored dreams, a vast, serene space, a peaceful sky filled with the flight of birds in search of shelter, where kites danced, flutes sang toward all horizons. In these chants, he found the awe and excitement of his youth, saw himself advancing toward a future on an endless, sun-dappled road that called him toward the future, compelled him. He felt the blood rush back into his heart, the desire to love, to create surging back into him. A myriad of emotions, like the countless streams that trickled, gurgling in the crevices of rocks—all he had to do was listen and they would feed into a single stream, become music.

Strange! That a man could be saved from self-destruction by this wretched ball of matter. No mysterious or divine force, no profound thought of some sage, just brown smoke from the sap of a vulgar plant.

Hung asked the innkeeper for a second pipe. The man had waited there, watching them like a vulture surveys a flock of chicks, sure of capturing his prey. This time, the brown smoke gave him wings, sent him straight to the sky, inspiration gushing forth, soaring up the steep mountains to the genie of music and then plummeting to the green pastures of the flesh.

A woman: I need a woman to release the sap within me, to smash the barriers of my heart, break the dike that holds back the waves of my inspiration. I need a woman. Angel or devil, she is the face of my destiny, she will bring me what I desire.

He turned to his companions: "Shall we turn to other games?"

The poet looked at him with bleary eyes. "What now?"

Hung stated in silence at Trong Cang. The old man flushed, lowered his head like a young virgin. "As you like," he replied, his voice choked, tremulous.

Hung chuckled. "We've lived our entire lives in fear. For once, let's live. Why not express your desires? Of all of us, you two need it most."

Truc Son finally understood. "Wait, I'm not afraid! No, no . . . I . . . I'll try. For so long I've wanted to make love with a real woman, in flesh and blood, not just some poetic muse. But I'm shy, and I'm broke. However, if you're paying, I gratefully accept."

The poet turned to the innkeeper: "Can you provide them?"

The innkeeper smiled. "That too exists in three categories. You want the pure, the prime, or the second class?"

Truc Son turned to Hung. "Hung, for once let's die with dignity."

"The pure," replied Hung, as drunk as the poet.

The innkeeper slipped outside and scampered down the beach, barely visible under the pale moon. A violent slap of sea wind swept through the hut, lifting the reed mat; Hung shivered. The wind had sobered him. An image flashed through his brain: Suong, her full, naked belly against a brown plastic tarpaulin, legs spread wide like the open arms of a compass, as livid as the full moon, like the one here tonight, the sea howling nearby. Her cries had been drowned out in the roar and bellow of the waves. Seeing her pale thighs, her naked stomach, he had shuddered, that terrible night when Da Hai had come into the world.

Oh, my wife, where are you now? Are you asleep with the children? Are you out here, looking for me? While I spend the money you saved singing yourself hoarse to buy the body of another woman.

He felt his brain, his face burn, but another flame licked at his flesh, set his nerves ablaze.

No . . . at this very moment, the mandarins are raising their glasses, enjoying the game they control, at which they are always the winners. Me, I've been excluded from the game. As they delight in the glare of the spotlights, why shouldn't I enjoy the dull light of the moon, on a deserted beach littered with garbage? On the Buddha's lotus throne, even an ant has the right to live.

My wife? A famous woman who at this very moment is probably toasting with those pigs in their priestly saffron robes. Every night, they shower her with flowers, pressing their stinking faces to hers. She's become their idol, the icon of my enemies. Even unconsciously she's stepped over the line, to their side.

Darling, life has tilted the balance, done justice by letting me waste your hard-earned money. All in all, you're the one born under the lucky star. But who helped you up the steps to fame? Me . . . and you let me fall, alone, into this abyss. Your beauty, your intelligence are beyond compare, nothing like these poor, wretched boat people that I met in prison. Don't reproach me, lucky one, my little nightingale with the crystal voice. I don't want to betray you, but I want justice.

Exploded like lava in his brain, these thoughts called forth other images, the faces of women detained as political prisoners, locked up with common criminals. A wall of coarse brick, just two or three yards high, but ringed with barbed wire up to the roof had separated their cell from the men's. Every sound echoed distinctly through the walls, from cell to cell—the fights, the whispers, even the farts. Obsessed with sex, the men recounted perverted, salacious stories, using words to slake their lust. On the other side, some of the women, the common criminals, had their own equally diabolical tales; their dialogue could make anyone with a bit of dignity shiver in horror. So in the end, the devils on both sides of the wall found a way to buy and sell sex. The men agreed to pay a ration of boiled manioc—the dish most coveted by the prisoners, a creation of the prison warden—in exchange for the right to fondle the vagina of one of the women. They ground manioc they found in the terraced fields perched high in the mountains into a fine powder, kneading it into a dough that they rolled into small balls filled with green mung bean paste. Then the whole thing was wrapped in a banana leaf and steamed in huge pots. Every time the male prisoners increased their yield, or got ahead of schedule with the harvests of corn or sugar cane, the cooks would make this snack as a reward. The male prisoners, with the exception of those whose stomachs had shrunk, were always hungry. And so the old hags among the prisoners would prostitute the younger women to get those cakes. When the jailers had gone to eat in the kitchen, the older women would force three young women to climb the wall between the cells and straddle it, their hands gripping barbed wire to keep from falling. They had to stay there while the men fondled them, let them do anything they wanted to slake their lust. And they couldn't come down until the pimp prisoner had shouted: "Okay!" Then the men would throw manioc cakes over the wall, through the barbed wire, and three other young women would take their place. Unforgettable: the pain on the faces of those women who had to expose their genitals to the gaze of these depraved men, to submit to their perverse tortures, even bleed for it. Once a young women refused, and one of the pimps pulled her off the wall and beat her so badly her liver was ruptured. They finally took her to the infirmary, but she died two days later. Another girl, who couldn't bear the humiliation, had hung herself.

Unhappy young women who shared my lot. Like me, society has expelled you, crushed you. You cannot return. There is no bridge . . .

And there you are, Suong, glorious, on the other side of the abyss, next to the men with the power and the money. Me, I'm here, on this side, with the condemned. Don't be angry. This is fate.

Ten minutes later, the innkeeper returned with three young women. Hung pulled the palest into his arms. She had dark circles under her eyes, high, bony cheekbones, wet, indigo lips, as if bruised by some wound.

Come to me, little girl. Haven't we met before? Back in the camp, separated by just a cement wall, a coil of barbed wire?

Hung spoke as in a dream. Tears in his eyes, he kissed her young lips, her scrawny shoulders, and it was as if he had loved her in a past life, waiting for this moment to find her again, at last.

Oh river without a bridge!

Hung had read this verse when he was young, and it had never slipped from his memory. Now, it seemed to have foretold the course of his own life. His life with Suong was beyond salvation; now they stood on opposite banks of a river without a bridge.

The intoxication of the smoke had started to fade, and he felt a throbbing pain in his groin. About two or three days later, it burned every time he urinated. He suddenly knew he was going to have to pay a high price for that moment of pity and desire.

Either the Heavens are torturing me again, or I must carry the seeds of evil inside myself. Every time some depraved passion touches me, her steel bands strangle me, choking all resistance, leaving her deep scratches on my body. People have smoked opium for years without becoming as addicted as I am. Debauched men have slept with all kinds of prostitutes and managed to keep their bodies intact. Me, I just barely touch the infernal jungle and I collapse with the most virulent strain of syphilis. Maybe I was an assassin in a previous life and I'm expiating past crimes.

He remembered the prostitute with the moist, red lips, the dark circles under her eyes. That night, had he really made love with her, or had it been just pity and desire for some fellow being crushed by life? He couldn't say. All he could remember were those blood red lips, how her ribs stuck out like those on the Buddha at the Tuyet Son Pagoda, and how, behind the excitement of pleasure, there lurked infinite pain and sadness. And the spiritual pain had left a ruthless scar, a sickness that exposed the carrier to the humiliation and contempt of everyone around him.

You left me a painful souvenir. Your shame, your worthlessness. Now it's my turn to suffer the contempt, my turn to lose my dignity, even if I don't lurk in that sordid forest of filaos, waiting for clients. But I don't blame you. This is my fate.

Hung talked in silence to the young woman with the thin shoulders as emaciated as the skeleton of death in the first throes of agony.

Every morning, after Suong left, he would lock himself in his room, take off his pants, and examine his penis. From the outside, there were no visible signs. You had to look closely to see that it was swollen. But inside, the rot was spreading. Every day he stayed curled up for hours and hours, trying not to scream, to resist the pain. He felt like a steel blade or a trickle of lead was slowly crawling through his urethra, burning here and there, without any clear direction, but each day more ruthless. The external inflammation didn't get worse, but inside the illness seemed to gnaw at his flesh. After two weeks of incubation, the pain now came not only when he urinated, but all the time. He didn't dare move around too much. Every time he went to urinate, he felt like he was mounting the guillotine. At night, he took a double dose of sleeping pills with the excuse that his body, now used to medication, needed more than just the normal dose. Suong went to the pharmacy, buying more and more sleeping pills and a passion flower syrup. Meanwhile, Hung furtively searched the house, hoping to find enough money to buy antibiotics that could treat venereal disease. But his searches were in vain: The fake leather purse was in the armoire, but it only held electricity and water bills. The day Suong had brought him back to the house, he had already spent all the money he had stolen. Suong even had to pay the innkeeper the equivalent of three months of her salary to settle his debts. Hung and Dam were there when she pulled this sum out of her purse. Hung, suddenly lucid, felt shame cover his face like a crust of mud.

Sometimes Hung had thought of borrowing money from Auntie Tuong, but he didn't have the courage. He gritted his teeth and endured the pain as it mounted with each passing day.

One night, the suffering erupted with the return of his desire. Hung was lying on the bed, his hands crossed on his stomach. He lay motionless, trying to endure the pain, fighting himself. It was about nine o'clock. Suong was downstairs with the children. Auntie Tuong had gone to visit some remote pagoda and planned to stay the night with the other pilgrims. Vinh had gone camping about fifteen miles out of town. All evening they had played with the children. Suong had the day off because the troupe was preparing a new show. It had been a long time since they had had dinner together. The girls played, scampered around. They were at home, and yet they explored everywhere, enthusiastic, curious, as if they were visiting a neighbor's house. Da Hai searched through the tea chest, getting out boxes of tea, cakes, mirrors, Japanese and French dolls. These objects that she had played with for a long time now seemed new.

The children babbled in their angelic language and he listened to the sound of it without needing to understand its meaning. He felt dizzy for a moment, as if he were crossing a narrow monkey bridge. He belonged to them, these angels, and yet that he was excluded from their warm, innocent world, the world of the family.

If one day my daughters learn that I'm a sinner, will they still took at me this way? If one day they discover how horribly I behave, will they keep their silence or judge me?

The girls kept playing, and now they were pretending to be a thief and a policeman. They suddenly fell into his arms, their bodies clambering all over him. Their familiar smell seeped into his heart. He hugged them, covered them with kisses. Suddenly, he felt the pain shoot through him like a needle. He froze, rigid in his chair, trying to hold back the pain until the girls climbed off him to continue their game of hide-and-seek, then he retreated in silence up the stairs.

The pain had barely subsided when he felt a wave of desire break inside him. Lying there on the bed, on his back, motionless, he crossed his arms over his stomach, listening carefully to the echo of laughter and games from downstairs, the murmur of the trees outside in the garden. For a long time, the whispering of the leaves had been his only conversation with the world, bringing him comfort.

Together we've crossed the sea. Our boat sank. All that's left is driftwood. Now we're on opposite shores.

He couldn't bear this naked, horrible truth. He would soon dissolve into dust, like garbage on the streets of life. Suddenly, a memory, like a flame, singed his heart, the memory of the underground where Suong had first come to find him during the war. How he had carried her in his arms, with her breasts as small as two areca nuts, her velvety, fearful eyes in the shadow of her dark lashes, her ebony hair browned by the sun. His little girl from the land of exile, the crystal flower he had plucked from a village. He had made her a woman even before she had left adolescence, had showered her with love and passion, performed a miracle only the gods were capable of: transforming a bud, in the space of an instant, into a flower, compressing time in the density of a kiss, forcing the arrival of spring before the end of winter. *No, I can't leave her, the perfect being I created.*

Exalted by these memories, Hung felt his hand tense as desire stretched like an arch through his body. *I must make love to you, make love to you . . . you're mine. You must share my joy, my pain. You don't have the right to stand there on the opposite shore and watch me drown. You don't have the right to be so heartless.*

Hung stood up, glanced at the clock on the wall. Ten-thirty. Downstairs, all was silent. The children were sleeping. He tiptoed down the staircase, approached the bed, put his hand on Suong's breast. She opened her eyes at this signal.

"I'm so tired," she said. "But if you want to . . ."

She sat up on her elbows, gently extricating herself from the girls. They were lying by her side, one holding her arm, the other with her leg flung over Suong's stomach. She pulled the covers back over the girls and followed Hung up the stairs. He looked her in the eyes, but she only met his gaze for an instant, then lowered her eyes. She stared into the distance, into the emptiness behind him.

"I love you Suong."

She said nothing, waiting

"Suong, I love you."

Still, nothing.

"Do you hear me, Suong?"

"Yes."

She doesn't love me anymore. She just submits to her conjugal duty. The woman I loved is dead. But you won't die alone. We'll die together. You can't stand there, alone on the shore, while I . . .

Hung unbuttoned the back of Suong's nightgown. She helped him slip it over her shoulders, then threw it to the bottom of the bed, let him pull down her panties. Just at that moment, Da Hai screamed: "Mama! Help me, Mama!"

The little girl was screaming as if someone were attacking her. Suong sat up, threw on her nightgown, kicking off the underwear that Hung hadn't had time to take off and that still dangled from her ankle. She ran down the stairs in her bare feet.

"Mama! Mama!" Da Hai kept screaming. Her cries pierced Hung's brain like a knife. *My children, my poor children! I almost put your mother's life in danger, I almost plunged you into unhappiness too. My poor girls.*

He had sensed then what the doctor later confirmed. Hung remembered lying motionless in the bed, listening to Da Hai stammering, explaining her nightmare. Suong had comforted her, and finally the child's long hiccups faded into sleep. These hiccups reminded Hung of other sobs. He felt a damp, icy wind slip through his eyelashes, and behind this wind, the full moon spread its cold, damp light the length of the beach, a long, long time ago.

Hung and the troupe had just performed for a special unit of People's Army soldiers who were training to cross the Truong Son Cordillera. They performed their show for almost two weeks, then packed to go. Instead of taking the main road, they preferred to travel the length of the beach. The previous day, bombers had attacked a fishing village. The napalm had set flame to anything made of wood—the beams on the houses, the planks of the fishing boats, casuarina tree trunks scattered on the beach. The stench of corpses mixed with the smell of dead fish and seaweed trampled underfoot. You couldn't make out anyone's face anymore in the swirl of shadow and smoke. Everyone was ragged with exhaustion. They all dragged their feet through the sand, their rubber sandals slipping and sliding. Every time the napalm flashed it illuminated someone, a ghostly, emaciated face. No one dared talk or predict how long their strength might last before they collapsed, fell on their faces. The waves roared, drowning out their thoughts. Now and then, the shimmer of a dead fish, phosphorescent as a butterfly in the sudden, sinister flare of the napalm.

"Oh God, oh God!" an actress screamed, jumping aside.

"What is it?" Hung said, turning around.

The actress staggered forward, trembling. "I just tripped on a leg."

Hung cupped his hand to mask the light of his torch, illuminating the ground. She was right. In a tangle of dense seaweed, the beach cleaners had left behind someone's severed leg. Ordinarily, they only missed shreds of flesh scattered in the bushes and reeds, buried in the sand, or forgotten in inaccessible corners where they ended up decomposing, the wind and the rain finishing off their work by dissipating the stench. But they rarely missed a limb, or a skull. No one in the troupe had the strength or the patience to stop and bury the leg, "It's terrible, but we've got to keep moving," Hung said, pushing the woman gently forward and retreating to the back of their group. Hung could see Suong now. She looked so pale to Hung in the glow of the moon and the flicker of napalm, it was as if she had been sculpted from marble. Panicked, he put a hand to her face. It was icy, drenched in sweat. She clung to him, panting. "I can't walk anymore . . . I can't . . ."

Had the time come? Hung's heart raced. "Where's the nurse?" Hung shouted.

His shout stopped the entire troupe. The nurse came running back from the front of their line, her medicine case on her shoulder. She was still padding through the sand when Suong suddenly screamed. "Oh God! Oh, help me!"

Trembling, Hung held his wife in his arms, massaged her back, the length of her spine. "Try and bear it." She grabbed his arm with her hands, sinking her nails into them. Hung kept imploring her, frantic. "Try and stand it, just a little longer darling, please."

Suddenly she pushed him away, violently. "I can't, it hurts so much, oh my God, oh Father . . ." Collapsed on the sand, delirious, she began ranting and screaming in her native dialect, weeping. Hung dropped to his knees, held her in his arms, incapable of saying anything. The troupe huddled around them. The nurse stood motionless, as stiff as a millstone, waiting for Hung's orders. After a few moments, his calm returned. "Do you know how to deliver babies?" he asked her.

"No, I only know how to do bandages, tourniquets, injections."

"Shit shit shit!" Oddly, as Hung swore his lucidity came back to him, his fear faded. Energy surged forth in him, giving him unusual confidence and strength. He got up and said, "I'm going to help my wife give birth. The nurse will stay here and help me. You all should keep going. It's almost time for another round of enemy bombardments and one stray mortar could wipe us all out."

The troupe didn't move. Hung lifted his arm, looked at his watch. The fluorescent hand was nearing the fatal hour. He raised his voice. "It's an order! Everybody back in file, get out of here!" The actors muttered then, one by one, they left in Indian file, trudging ahead down the beach.

Hung helped the nurse spread a nylon mat on the sand at the edge of the waves. There, in the light of the phosphorescent seaweed, she could sterilize the surgical knife with alcohol to cut the umbilical cord. Hung lifted Suong in his arms and laid her down on the mat, then he rolled up his sleeves and plunged his hands into the salty sea water.

Oh Heavens, I pray to you, may our child be born safely! May your grace save us from the bombs and the mortars! Help us return safe and sound to the underground shelters!

Hung prayed to the heavens three times as he washed his hands in the sea. He returned to Suong. The nurse had taken off Suong's pants, and her thighs and stomach, naked in the light of the moon, made him shudder, but he kept standing. Suong's cries became more and more terrifying. In the distance, from the dark horizon, a machine gun could surge at any moment.

Lucky or unlucky, the heavens will decide. I don't have the right to be afraid right now. I've got to bring our child into the world. Its life is in my hands. I'm its father.

Hung knelt on the sand, stroked his wife's stomach, remembering the lessons of the midwives he had overheard as a child. The heavens answered his prayers. Da Hai came into the world without any problem. The artillery on the American gunboats, drunk with sleep, still anchored out at sea, had spared them. After he cut the umbilical cord, Hung asked the nurse to wrap the baby up while he went to bury the placenta in the dunes. After he finished, he took off his shirt, wrapped the baby in it for extra warmth, and handed her to the nurse. Then he dressed Suong and carried her on his back. They walked for about an hour and a half before they found the closest hamlet. Just as they plunged down into an underground shelter, the artillery started to strafe the ground. Circles of flame harrowed the ground, shredding and tearing it, while in the underground, Suong, the nurse, and the baby fell sound asleep. Alone, too alert to sleep, Hung watched the furrows of mortar fire. After the ordeal, he was totally lucid. And as he watched the enemy bombs rip through the sky, a new strength grew inside him, making him into a different man, braver, mature, more confident, as if a new current flowed in his veins.

Now these memories kept Hung from sleep. His heart twisted as if some sadistic hand clutched it in a stranglehold, releasing it, just time enough for him to come back to life, then squeezing it over and over again. Downstairs, the lights were still on. Suong was sleeping again, a child on each arm, like a branch bearing two fruits. Only her long eyebrows seemed to frown in her sleep, the uncomprehending, irritated expression of a schoolgirl faced with a question to which she didn't know the answer. He stood there a long time, transfixed, gazing at his wife and children, the tightness in his heart easing. And yet the old sea kept murmuring, whispering inside him.

We lived them all together, the ultimate moments in life, loved each other as much as two people can. My girl from the mountains, is there still a place for me in your soul? Even if you have cast me out of your life, what we had, what happened between us will live on, and that is art.

After that evening, Hung couldn't stand the torment of the sickness any longer. He had tried to borrow money to buy medicine, but fate had already hung a cord around his neck. He had barely arrived at Auntie Tuong's door when Suong returned. That day, the last bridge that could have linked them had collapsed. He became a wandering shadow on the first floor, spending his days taking medicine, giving himself injections, wordlessly swallowing the meals that Suong still conscientiously prepared for him in silence. They only exchanged a few words when necessary.

"The doctor is off duty today. He told me to tell you you should take the same medicine as usual. Tomorrow morning, he'll come by at nine-thirty. Make sure you listen for the bell to let him in."

"Don't worry, I'll remember."

"Another thing, a car is coming by early to pick me up. I won't have time to make your breakfast. Have some with Vinh or go to a restaurant. There's money in the medicine box on the table."

"I know, don't worry."

"Have a bit of bouillon. The doctor said you should drink lots too."

"I've had enough, thanks."

Behind these polite, gentle words, a void, a river without a bridge or a ferry, even a quay. Vinh, though he was simple by nature and didn't feel any sympathy for Hung, could sense this too. Sometimes Hung thought he could see in those wild eyes, in certain brusque gestures, a touch of pity. *Look at me, reduced to accepting pity from a teenager. On top of it my wife's little brother. So the hero of modern times survives thanks to the people's charity.*

Hung remembered the protagonist, Pessorin, in Lermontov's *A Hero of Our Time:* A typical Russian man, proud, generous, sentimental, who committed crimes with the innocence of a child, driven by a desperate desire.

Why not just put an end to it now, right now? I don't have any more reason to live. People often enter history intelligently and leave it like idiots. They don't know how to leave the palace with dignity; instead, they let lackeys chase them out the back door.

Hung paced back and forth in the room, counting and recounting the tiles on the floor, spinning in circles with his thoughts.

One day, while he was cutting his nails, Vinh ran into the house, his face dark, his eyes flashing with menace. "Hung!" he shouted. An odd hoarseness in Vinh's voice made Hung put down the nail clipper. "What is it, Vinh?"

"Get up! Look out the window!"

Hung got up and looked out into the garden. He saw Suong standing in front of Auntie Tuong's house in the company of Vinh's friend Tan, the handsome student who had visited her in the hospital. Tan was on his motorcycle, the latest luxury model. Hung didn't care, but Vinh had told him all these details. Now the young man was helping his wife take Da Hai to kindergarten. Suong had her back turned to him, so Hung couldn't see her face, but he recognized the sparkle of love in the young man's beaming face. What were they saying to each other while little Da Hai played, wriggling with delight on the back seat of his motorcycle?

"You see that! Look!" Vinh snapped, furious.

Hung turned to him and laughed. "He's helping your sister by taking your niece to kindergarten. Where's the problem?"

Vinh shot him an angry look. "What did you say? Are you blind?"

Hung shook his head. "Calm down. Why are you talking like this?"

"Because I'm not blind like you! If this guy comes to take Da Hai to school it's not because he likes her, but he . . ."

Hung smiled, feeling a twisting in his gut, but a new, icy calm had almost reduced his heart to silence. He replied slowly. "So what if he is in love with Suong? That's his right."

Vinh stared at him, his lips contorted. "So you don't care if your wife falls in love with him? Don't you see how she already likes him, then . . ."

Hung put his hand on Vinh's shoulder. "Even if it was the case, I don't have the right to forbid her. She's your sister, and she's my wife, but she's also a free woman, and she still has all the rights of a free being. That's something I myself have acknowledged."

Vinh glowered at Hung, his eyes wild, furious, frantic. Suddenly he bellowed: "You're just a coward! You're worthless as a husband!"

Hung stepped back, sensing that Vinh wanted to slap him, but the young man had caught himself in time, turned, and run up the stairs.

Hung sat down in a chair, heard the door slam. Vinh had locked himself in his room. Hung looked at his nail clippings, the white dust that covered the table.

Could Suong be in love with that boy? Apparently. No, no, absolutely not. This young man's love just confirms her value, flatters her. Yes, I am worthless. But Vinh isn't much better. Even though he hates me, he's my ally, shares the same fate: living off a woman.

Hung knew that Suong had invested a huge amount of money in Vinh's studies, but that the more he studied the further he fled the world of learning. Vinh had locked himself in his room every night, to memorize his lessons, but that still hadn't opened the door to the university.

In practical terms, this young man Tan is useful. He helps Suong bring back heavy goods, takes Da Hai to school and her mother to the doctor's office. An educated, handsome, elegant boy, like that has everything you need to seduce young women. Why wouldn't he move her heart? It's natural, even banal.

A drop of blood fell on the table. He realized that he had just cut the flesh of his own finger. Another drop. But Hung didn't get up to get cotton to stop the bleeding, he just sat there, watching the drops fall. The cold serenity of his intelligence had abandoned him. He was in pain. And jealousy went hand in hand with this pain that had to hide its face, that became even lonelier, more violent, more destructive. In spite of everything, he still loved Suong, the woman on the opposite bank of the river. The river without a bridge.

15

Vinh had quit school more than a week ago and Suong still hadn't noticed a thing.

In the morning, he ate his bowl of Chinese noodle soup with her, then tucked a few books under his arm and left. After Suong had gone to work, he would come back to the house, go to his room, lock the door, and lie down on the bed. At noon, he let Hung eat the lunch of *pho* or sticky rice that Suong bought for him before he went down, ate by himself, and washed the dishes. After that, he'd lock himself in his room all afternoon like an ascetic. In the evening, he waited for the couple to finish their meal before he ate. Then he would clear off the tray and wash the dishes. Aside from these unavoidable encounters in the kitchen, he tried to avoid Suong. His door was always closed. She had tried many times to talk to him, to make peace with her brother without really knowing why he was angry at her. Vinh just kept his sullen, inscrutable face.

My little brother must be in the throes of adolescence. I have to be patient, wait until he gets through this and matures.

Suong was by nature a simple person, and this is how she thought. But one day, she happened to bump into the main professor for Vinh's class in the street. The woman told her that Vinh had been absent for over a week, that she guessed he must have had to return to their village to settle some unexpected matters. Stunned, Suong went home that same evening and knocked on Vinh's door.

"Vinh, I need to talk to you."

Vinh had done the dishes and he had just disappeared back into his room. But he stayed lying down, his face buried in his pillow, pretending to be asleep.

"Vinh, open up," Suong repeated, raising her voice. "Vinh!"

She distinctly heard him move inside, "Vinh, get up!" She was almost shouting, her voice quavering. But her little brother remained motionless, indifferent, as if deaf.

Shaking with rage, she pummeled the door. "Vinh open up!"

He jumped up and pulled the latch from the door, which suddenly opened. Suong almost fell on her face. She staggered for a moment and grabbed the curtain to regain her balance, then slumped down on a chair. Meanwhile, Vinh had retreated to a corner. He stared at her with cold, wild eyes. *Why are you looking at me that way?* Panicked, Suong leaned back in the chair, as if searching for some support. The soft, padded chair rotated on its axis; it was the most comfortable chair in the house. To find it, she had had to search through the stores on several long summer afternoons, drenched in sweat, her eyes blinded by the sun.

"Sit down, Vinh."

Vinh stayed standing in the corner. He looked at her, unblinking, his lips still tightly pursed.

"Sit down, little brother, I want to talk to you," Suong said, swallowing her rage, patiently trying to soften her voice.

"No need. I can listen to you standing," Vinh snapped. He kept staring at her. These weren't the loving eyes of a brother but those of a leopard, a metallic gray, full of hatred and defiance.

What have I done to deserve his hatred? I've exhausted myself trying to make enough to raise him, to pay for his studies, I've bought him the best clothes in town, paid for tutorials with the best teachers. At Tet, I knocked on every door in this town bear-

ing gifts in the hope that I'd win everyone's sympathy, the devotion of his teachers. And now he looks at me with these hateful eyes.

"Vinh, why did you give up school?"

Vinh said nothing.

"Vinh, you've been absent all week and you didn't say a word to me? Why?"

Still, he remained silent.

"Vinh, why have you given up? I'm the one who's raising you. Whether you like it or not, you have to answer me."

Hatred flashed from his eyes. "I abandoned my studies because I don't want to study anymore!" Vinh shouted. He clenched his jaw, gritted his teeth. Suong could see the muscles in his jaw tense, his neck shivering. He was afraid, but his anger stopped him from retreating.

Suong shouted back, her voice like a slap in her brother's face. "You have no right to answer me like that!"

"That's all I can say. If that upsets you, well shut up and don't ask me any more questions."

Suong sighed. Her anger and her courage were fading. She stayed silent for a long time, then, almost in tears said: "Vinh, how can you speak to me like this? I had such high hopes for you! None of us ever had a chance to study. Sister Mien and I, we put all our hopes in you. Can't you understand that?"

Vinh's eyes gleamed like a drunken tiger's and he roared at her in a harsh voice she had never heard before. "Who asked you to put your hopes in me? Do you think I wanted that? Do you think I'm happy? You answer me! Answer me!"

He almost screamed these last few words. Suong thought her brother had suddenly gone mad. His frantic gestures terrified her. She got up and left the room.

Vinh stood there, frozen, panting like a boxer who has just stepped down from the ring. After a long time his anger subsided, he stretched out on the bed, his face buried in his pillow. Tears streamed from his eyes, wetting the cotton of his pillow that his sister had made with her own hands. Like she had bought him the jeans, the striped and flowered shirts, like she had dreamed of educating the only son of the dead timber man.

Soaked in tears, the pillow felt cold. Calmer now, Vinh composed himself.

I shouldn't be angry with her, she loves me. She forces me to study to please our father, so his descendents can rise in society. My father! Why didn't he study himself? Why does he force me to satisfy his hunger for learning? I'm the one who has to pay the debt. A plus B squared! This horrible debt is shattering my brain. My own father sentenced me to this torture. I didn't need to know these complicated equations, these laws of Archimedes, of Newton, these crazy chemical formulas . . . no, my life is elsewhere.

The rolling green hills surfaced from his memory, unfurling like images from a film. The hills of his past, where the goats grazed lazily through the grass and leaves, where dusk fell in the branches of the trees, in the ferns and the myrtle, back when Suong used to take him in her arms. The tiny young woman who replaced his mother used to sing him lullabies when evening fell, the enchanted melodies of his childhood.

> *Hungry, I nibble half a myrtle fruit, sip half a bowl of water*
> *I leave in search of my love*
> *Oh my love, my love!*
> *I leave, my heart filled with longing, waiting*
> *And if you're faithful, I'll still be waiting a hundred years from now*

A hundred years . . . a hundred years . . . these clear, vivid sounds had crystallized in his heart, flowed into his blood. Vinh had once believed he could sleep in that little woman's arms for a hundred years. Then one day, she suddenly left in a rickety wagon pulled by a water buffalo, on a dusty red road. And this red dust mingled with his tears, blurring his gaze.

During those long years of separation, when evening fell, as he herded the goats into the barn, he watched that road, the road to the village, secretly hoping that a fairy with a magic wand would make his sister appear, her shovel slung over her shoulder, her pockets filled with ripe rose myrtle fruit. After the last goat had scampered into the barn, he would pull the latch and wander around, waiting. Sometimes he didn't go back to the house until the road, lit only by the glow of sunset, had slipped into the shadows of dusk. That night, he slept with Mien, but she didn't hold him in her arms, didn't sing him lullabies like Suong had. Exhausted by a long day of farm work, she slept like a log. Sometimes, when she heard him whimpering in the darkness, she would give him little taps on the back. "Go to sleep, come on, let's sleep." And she would fall right back to sleep in midsentence. One night he sat up and pummeled Mien's back with his little fists.

"Call Suong home! Call Suong home for me, quickly, quickly!"

Mien woke up, wiped the tears from his eyes. "How can you say something like that? You've got to let her go. Later, when she's succeeded, she'll come back and take you with her. If you make her stay here, what's going to become of us?"

Then she took Vinh in her arms and waited until he had fallen asleep. That was the only time he could remember sleeping sweetly, tenderly. And from then on he had waited for what seemed like forever for the day when she would come back and take him with her.

That day came in a clatter of wooden clogs in the courtyard, with the appearance of the strange and yet familiar face of Lam the clown. He took Vinh in his wagon along the dusty red road that Suong had disappeared down six years earlier. Vinh couldn't sleep along the trip. Night and day, his eyes were wide, his ears open, alert. Everything seemed new and exciting. Finally, his little mother had come back to take him with her, like Mien had promised.

The first days, despite the unhappiness that crushed Suong, Vinh had felt happy. He had found his lost love. He was proud that she still loved him like she used to. In his sister's voice, her laughter, her gestures, he found the woman who had held him in her arms and sung him lullabies as night fell. His own sister had become a famous artist, the most adored of all women in the five central provinces. Vinh saw his own shadow right beneath the halo of his sister's glory.

But the joy didn't last. Every day he saw that his sister had become another man's slave. A man that she called by all kinds of names: my teacher, my husband, the father of my children. Hung was welcoming, tolerant, simple. And yet Vinh thought he could detect a touch of pity in his brother-in-law's slightly mocking, protective smile. Hung always defended Vinh when he accidentally offended people with his crude peasant's behavior and taught him about life in town. But Vinh secretly continued to detest the man who had stolen his kingdom. When he ate with his sister while Hung and the gang of artists drank and feasted on the first floor, he listened carefully to their stories, the flood of words that he didn't understand, thinking bitterly that he belonged to another world and that there was no road to the universe where these useless men reigned. Many times he had berated Suong: "Why do you support him? You're the one who brings the money home. Why don't you kick these dogs out? What are you afraid of?" But each time, she replied in a soft voice, "You don't understand. It's thanks to Hung that I've become who I am. It doesn't matter what happens, I'll always be grateful to him, respect him." After these quarrels, Vinh had fallen into dark, depressed thoughts.

I'm not wanted here. I'm just a parasite. The only thing I can do is to study hard so I can make it into the world of letters. These dogs had their chance before I did, but they're old already. I've got my youth and all the time in the world to take their place.

Armed with this resolution, he recited his lessons aloud every might like a *quoc* bird. He dragged his books to tutorials that Suong arranged for him, invited Tan over to help him. At night, according to an old tradition, he wrapped seven frangipani flowers gathered at the temple gate in a handkerchief and slipped them under his pillow, praying for success at school. These efforts brought him some meager progress, but the more he learned, the further the world of learning receded. The more he studied, the more he found himself lacking stamina, like a drowning man who finds himself sinking deeper into the water, seeing clearly the moment when life will melt into the algae and scum, the mud of rotting corpses. At school, the teachers watched him, talked about him, shaking their heads, convinced that with a student like that their efforts would be like water off a duck's back.

Of course Vinh was hardworking, clever. In gymnastics and at all the sports meets; on the camping trips, he was a star thanks to his talent for finding wood, lighting fires, and cooking rice using just sugar cane husks for fuel. He helped everyone raise their tents, get their boats across the rivers. At those moments, he was likeable, confident, attractive. His agility, warm laugh, and twinkling eyes made him a kind of Robin Hood. But after these physical exploits, he would always fall back into his prisoner situation at school, the terrifying land that he didn't dare leave. Every day he trudged there, like a shadow, to wander and suffer.

Little by little, not just at night, but all day, the longing for the hills surged in this young man's soul like a strong wind heavy with the scent of *tetracera* flowers, fragrant herbs, daisies, wormwood trees, and the buds of wild basil he used to like to crush between his fingers. He even missed the stink of the goats after a long hot day when they scampered back into the yard. He began to dream of his return to their native land. Sometimes, he could see the rolling hills, like ocean waves, the mountain peaks that enclosed them, the camphor trees, the dark green grasses. And in the spring, the soft mauve of myrtle flowers snaking through the loud violet patches of *mua* flowers as if they had been embroidered on the quilt of the hills. He saw the green fields of pepper trees, places he and Suong had once slipped under the fence to weed. At noon, dripping with sweat, they would go and swim in the stream. She always finished her bath first, and while he dove and splashed in the water, she would gather dried herbs and roast potatoes and manioc. Nothing in this horrible town could compare to the taste of those grilled roots.

The cock crowed, announcing the third watch. Vinh fell asleep on his tear-soaked pillow. The next morning, he woke up at noon when Suong came back from her rehearsal and knocked at his door. The dream had taken shape in his heart like dregs at the bottom of a wine barrel. He waited until she questioned him to pour out his resentment and his pain. But Suong didn't ask, she just said: "I've got the afternoon off. It's too much trouble to cook. Let's go out to a restaurant and have some roast pork with rice noodles."

He didn't have time to answer. Already she was mounting the stairs to call Hung. They all went out together, walking down the street to the restaurant.

Vinh kept his silence all week. Suong did the same. Neither spoke to the other. Between them all, Hung managed to maintain an almost normal atmosphere at home, saying a few words to one, asking a few questions to the other.

Many times, Vinh had been on the verge of telling her but each time, when he found himself face to face with Suong, a strange knot formed in his throat. He realized that he couldn't say it, not just because he was attached to his sister and couldn't leave her so brutally. There was another reason: He had a hard time opening his mouth to ask her for money. Money . . . Ah, it wasn't easy to find it. Living under his sister's protection, his nose buried in his books, he didn't know where he would find the money to replace the cash that his sister slipped in his shirt pocket or between the pages of his books. Suong's salary as a star singer barely got her through two weeks of household expenses. To provide for the last two weeks of every month, she had to sing for conferences and congresses, in cabarets. Vinh also sensed that she was getting money from another source. When Hung had taken her savings, Suong must have cried all night for a week. She didn't dare complain to Vinh, but just one look at her ravaged face told him that she was tortured with anxiety. Yet a few days later, she was back to normal. She even started turning down the extra invitations to work so she could rest. She slept a lot and began spending more liberally. She put on some weight and her complexion improved. Once, she returned from a shopping trip with dozens of summer and winter outfits for Vinh and the children. She didn't bring home the bouquets of flowers they offered her, but she bought a new crystal vase. She sold the old refrigerator to a store and replaced it with a new one that had an ice-box that could hold up to twenty pounds of food. She had the house repainted, and another day she changed all the curtains, even the fabric in the screen. Vinh's pocket money grew. Sometimes, she left the enve-lope with her bonus on top of a book left wide open on his desk. *This has got to come from somewhere, from someone.* He guessed who, but said noth-ing. Now these details flooded back from memory. He realized how naive he had been. If only he had set aside some money, he could at this moment grab his knapsack, head for the bus station, and buy a seat on a wagon back to his mountain hamlet.

I'm an imbecile. Why didn't I follow my bastard brother-in-law's example? He made off with a year of Suong's savings. I only need a fraction of that sum, and not to buy a place on some boat, or to smoke opium, but just to go home. She's the one who has trapped me in this suffocating existence. She doesn't have the right to reproach me.

Satisfied with this logic, Vinh started fumbling in the drawers, through the closets. But Suong didn't keep her money at home any-more. He rummaged in vain. Once, Hung caught him sifting through papers that Suong had stored in her old handbag. Hung didn't say a word, just withdrew in silence, climbing up the stairs. Stung by shame, Vinh ran after him, grabbed the back of his shirt on the stairs.

"You look down on me, don't you? Why didn't you say anything?"

Hung didn't turn around, just said slowly. "Why would I look down on you? We're allies, both powerless." He smiled derisively. Vinh let go of his shirt and sighed, discouraged.

"Why don't you ask Suong for money?" Hung asked.

"You didn't, did you?"

Hung shook his head. "I couldn't. But that was different. You're her little brother. You can ask for things I can't."

"Easy for you to say," Vinh muttered.

"You want to go back to your hamlet, to the mountains, don't you? Do you want me to talk to Suong about it for you?"

"Naww. She wouldn't let me go. She wants me to die behind my desk at the high school."

"Maybe she doesn't understand. But someday she will."

"She'll never understand. Stop dreaming. She only knows how to obey, to bow down, nod her head to the dead old man's wishes," Vinh said bitterly and stalked off.

Days went by. Every day the road home beckoned to Vinh, the longing for it wrenched his gut. His desire to find the money to pay for the trip burned inside of him as if he had a hot coin stuck in his throat. He wandered through the garden, paced around in his room like an ant crawling around the rim of a white-hot pot. When Suong was home, he could see her seated in front of the window, staring out at the garden. Beyond his sister's gaze, lost in the distance, behind the shadow of the ylang-ylangs was the vision of a man. Vinh was sure of that, and he felt anger explode inside him.

Who is her gaze turned toward? A man whose face I don't know, or that kid who is two years younger than I am? My sister doesn't have the right to sully herself like this. Whatever happens, Hung is the father of her children. He was the one who got her out of the mountains. Whether I like it or not, he deserves to be her husband.

The longer Vinh imagined the stranger who preoccupied his sister, the more pity he felt for the brother-in-law he had hated for so long. For the first time, he noticed the goodness and spontaneity in Hung's smile, his maturity and experience. And in that look, there was a sadness the young man didn't understand, could only sense, and that gave Hung a gentleness, like a shaft of light from some other world beyond his reach. Vinh remembered his first day at school, how nasty town kids had bullied and mocked him, the stupid peasant boy. He had challenged them to a fight in the courtyard, and the town kids had lured him into a trap, beat him until his face was bruised and puffy. Hung had just been released from prison. He went to each of the kids and talked to them, won them over. From then on, they had left Vinh alone.

Or another time, when the young man was careless and had short-circuited a transformer that Suong had just bought. Vinh had been ashen with fear, but Hung pretended it was his fault. These patchy memories came pieced together and formed a whole, making Vinh unhappy at the idea that he could have hated Hung, once prayed that his brother-in-law would drown or be run over by a truck.

One morning, Vinh went out to sit in the garden, brooding over his thwarted dream. About seven o'clock, Suong ran over to Auntie Tuong's to get Da Hai ready for school. She had just finished dressing the little girl and got out her school bag when Tan arrived on his motorcycle and stopped just in front of the gate. When he honked, Suong ran out holding Da Hai by the hand. They chatted for a moment by the cactus hedge.

"Hey Suong!"

"Hi Tan, that new suit looks nice. Why are you all dressed up?"

"Oh, these are just everyday clothes. I wear them to school, or to go out."

"For me that's luxury."

So they call each other by their first names, chatter about nothing. This handsome playboy is courting my sister. He's gone straight for his goal for a long time. He got close to me on the volleyball court so he could visit her at the hospital. He even helped me with my math homework to get past the door of the house, to win the heart of a woman who is the mother of two kids!

"Da Hai? Have you greeted your Uncle Tan?"

"Hello Uncle Tan."

"Da Hai, can you recite the poem I taught you the other day?"

"Oh yes. Mama is a wonderful woman, the most beautiful fairy in my life."

"Bravo! You're a smart girl, Da Hai."

"Drive safely, now," Suong said.

"Wait, just a moment. Let me stay a few more minutes. Don't chase me away so fast," Tan pleaded.

Vinh could hear Suong laugh, happy but slightly embarrassed. Their conversation hummed with a certain giddy, excited tenderness.

That bastard, he dares to court my sister in front of the little girl. I'm not going to just stand here, petrified while this Don Juan plays his games.

Vinh leapt over the cactus hedge and in three strides he was face to face with the couple. "Uh, hello Vinh," Tan said.

"Who asked you to come here?" Vinh snarled, instead of returning his greeting.

Tan paled slightly and smiled. "Hey, that's not a very welcoming way to talk. I've come to take Da Hai to school."

"That's not my question. I'm not blind."

"So what do you want to know?"

"Don't play your games with me. You know what I'm talking about."

"I have no idea what you're talking about," Tan said politely but coldly, looking off into the distance.

Vinh suddenly shouted: "Who gave you permission to court my sister? Don't you see she's married, has two kids? Don't you see that you're just a rotten bastard?"

Tan stood paralyzed. He hadn't foreseen that this discussion would take such a nasty turn. Vinh's vulgar peasant language stunned and disarmed him.

"I . . . I . . ." Tan stammered, searching for words.

Vinh continued to roar. "I'll smash your rotten face in and you'll understand right away." Vinh suddenly punched Tan in the left eye. The young man still managed to hold onto the motorcycle, balancing it between his two hands. He didn't dare let go, afraid it would slide and throw the child onto the ground, so he took the punch full in the face.

"Vinh! Vinh! Have you gone crazy?!" Suong shouted, running over to protect Tan. The second punch struck her in the jaw, and Suong collapsed on the ground, and grabbed her brother's legs. Da Hai screamed in terror. Auntie Tuong ran out into the courtyard with Phuoc Hanh in her arms. Vinh stopped, looked at his sister. She had used all her strength to protect that playboy, a kid younger than her own brother! His sister's eyes looked at Tan with the same compassion and tenderness that they had looked at him, every time he fell, when the neighborhood kids tried to beat him up. That same look. Once it had belonged to him alone. Tan hadn't even tried to defend himself; it was as if he knew that Suong would use all her strength, even her own body to protect him. *He's happy. Happy to take my blows. He's the winner, not me. I lost. I'm nothing anymore.*

Suddenly Vinh felt like crying, screaming, shouting for his mother, cursing the heavens, rolling on the ground, burying his face in the grass like he once did. But he couldn't. He grabbed Suong, stammering. "You bitch! My God! You bitch!" And he slapped her with all the violence of his pain and bitterness. By the time the neighbor had reached the scene, he had leapt back over the cactus hedge. He ran toward the house, his face drenched with tears. He didn't bother to wipe them, just grabbed his clothes and stuffed them in an old canvas sack that he had brought from the hamlet. He threw in his flashlight, diary, photo album, seashells and souvenirs from summer camp, and a ball of parachute thread to pitch tents—and left.

That day, Hung had slept late. The previous night he had wandered in the garden until three in the morning, unable to sleep. A strangely calm, serene night. The town seemed mute. You couldn't even hear the street vendors' cries as they hawked their hot bread and sticky rice cakes at dawn. They must have left for the train station, unless the sinister scent of the ylang-ylangs had drugged them all, left them crumpled and silent in some forgotten corner of the town. Inside, Suong and Vinh were sleeping, their lights out. Only the lamp in the courtyard shone, but instead of emitting light, it seemed almost to darken the shadows hidden in the foliage of the trees, tracing weird shapes in the night sky. The perfume of the ylang-ylangs wafted, snakelike through the crisscross weave of light and shadow. Hung paced around the garden for hours, like a water buffalo chained to a millstone. At least he could smoke, constantly reviving the glowing tip of his cigarette as he touched it to his lips, then exhaled the smoke, turning his face to the sky. Bats darted above his head, intoxicated by his cigarettes, the smell of the flowers. After he had quit opium, he went back to strong cigarettes made from a special black tobacco cured with sap, like they used for water pipes up North. The tobacco gave off a special, pungent smell that seemed to numb his senses. Sometimes he told himself that this smoke had sealed his heart the way a spicy dish filled with chilies coats the tongue, numbs it. For hours on end, he watched the smoke rise, curling and spreading in front of his eyes in an endless, imaginary tide. Each wave carried off a chapter of his life: the joy, the pain, what he had received, what he had lost, the hopes, the despair. Everything slipping softly, silently away like a wisp of smoke, without a trace.

This parade of the senses has no meaning. It's like a chess game. You need all the pieces to start: the king, the castles, the elephants, the canons, the horses. Or a game of dice where the different sides follow each other, one two three four five six. If I had remained a student at the Music Conservatory I would still be following my old illusions; if I hadn't known solitude, sickness, exclusion, unhappiness, it's not certain I would be any happier than the lonely man I've become. No one wants to suffer, but maybe it helps a man grasp the essence of life, the reality of his destiny? And to understand that life is not a possession you can buy. You have to pay for it with blood and tears, sometimes with your own life. But what is my life? Something my parents created in a moment of passion, or conjured from the embers of a sacred dream? The dream of love has something fanatical, like the faith of a pilgrim who will cross oceans and deserts to set foot in the promised land. My parents lived to see their dream come true; they died fulfilled. At least, while they were alive, I showed them a finished product. An obedient son. A brilliant student. A generous young man always ready to help his neighbors, his relatives. Now their creation has degenerated, no longer has a reason for living. I was born from the void of the dream, and to this void I'll return. Perhaps, when my body decomposes into dust, my soul, lighter than air, will be free, soar to the skies. At least that flight will be perfect, beautiful. Perhaps I'll meet those who gave me shape, who gave me a life on this earth. Yes, a man must be brave enough to take leave of history, to know when to go. The most important thing is to choose the right moment. Who should I pray to? Buddha? Christ? Or to my parents that they may bless the moment their fruit returns to the earth?

These gentle thoughts, as luminous as sea waves at dawn, danced through his mind. Hung continued to blow smoke into the sky, watching each new wisp replace the one that had just vanished. He lit cigarette after cigarette, his soul light, free from his body, floating high in space, above the dark crown of the yellow and white ylang-ylangs, the bats that darted after their prey, above the bewitching perfume of those diabolical blossoms floating in the air of the garden like clouds of invisible butterflies, for even this perfume had a weight and density.

About three in the morning, his hair and shoulders damp with fog and dew, Hung went back inside to his room. He didn't dream at all, felt no torment. Before falling asleep, he saw translucent waves flood the sandy bank of a mountain stream. He was surprised. *How in the flood season can the stream be so pure, so clear?* An idyllic sleep. In the morning, he was awoken by Da Hai's crying. He stayed lying down, under the covers. Suong must have denied the little girl something; Da Hai rarely cried, but when she did, she cried for a long time, stubborn, inconsolable.

Oh my darling little girl! If your grandparents were still alive they would be surprised to see that their child produced a second being, almost identical to their own. They would be so happy because you are the exact replica of their love, and they continue in you.

He smiled, happy, curled back under the covers, enjoying the feeling of well-being that suffused these moments between sleep and waking, when the soul hesitates on the bridge between the foggy shore of dreams and the sunlit bank of reason. Here, in this state, lay the roots of primitive images and melodies. It had been a long time since Hung had felt this way. He lay motionless, mute, trying to penetrate the ancient, primeval forest, searching for some trace of beauty.

But his daughter's crying hurt his ears, accompanied with other cries. "Mama! Mama!" He heard other cries behind his child's cries, shouts from some violent argument. In a flash he recognized Vinh's crude, brutal voice. Hung sensed something abnormal in the quarrel, and he got up quickly and threw on his jacket. On his way down the stairs, he heard Vinh run into the house and slam the door to his room. A few seconds later, Suong appeared. She ran after her brother, bumping into Hung at the foot of the stairs. She burst into sobs, threw herself into his arms. Her face was red, bore the mark of a slap. Hung held her, stroked her swollen cheek as it turned from red to violet. It had been so long since he had held her in his arms, and her familiar smell troubled him. He hugged the slim shoulders of this tiny woman as she shuddered in wave after wave with her sobs.

Why does this feel so sad? And yet nothing has happened. I've held you in my arms a thousand times, made love with you through so many nights, so many days. I know every hair on the nape of your neck, the size of the beauty mark on your back, the exact length of your menstrual cycle, when you will stop singing to catch your breath. There is nothing new or strange that could upset me so deeply like this.

He massaged Suong's cheek, looked at the tiny beauty marks under her eyebrows, the fine downy hair at her temples, felt her bosom rise with each sob. Her lips were dry, bitter. Hung tried to say something, but it only made her weep more violently. Her tears wet Hung's chest, drenching his coat, soaking through his cold, damp shirt. He fumbled in the pocket of his pants and jacket, but couldn't find a handkerchief. Now she cried like a child, her face smeared with tears and saliva, and he let her wipe it on his sleeve.

Mountain girl from the virgin forests. Who would know you're a mother of two girls? It's as if you never really lived your adolescence, that you are claiming it now, that lost piece of your life.

He stroked her hair, lifted it from the tangle on her neck, patted her on the back and shoulders with the gentle, tender gesture of a father or an elder brother. They stood at the foot of the stairs for a long time, without speaking. A man happy to be able to console a woman. A woman happy to be consoled, making it last by weeping harder, her head buried in his shoulder. By noon, Suong's throat was hoarse, her eyes puffy. Still she clung to Hung, letting him carry her upstairs to sleep.

EPILOGUE

More than five years had passed since the end of the war between the two halves of the country. The date of the ceremony in honor of the victory had been fixed six months in advance, and the city's artistic troupe had received the order to prepare a performance "worthy of the great work of national liberation and its historic significance," as the deputy secretary of the provincial Party committee had announced to the conference of high-ranking cadres. Dam, as the director of the troupe, had also been invited, and he arrived in a tailored wool suit that he had brought back from Hanoi. The suit had belonged to his grandfather.

This suit will either be the perfect introduction to their ranks, or expel me across the dividing line. But one shouldn't disdain clothes; after all, if it had been unimportant, our ancestors wouldn't have taught us the adage: The art of dress is one of the highest virtues.

Dam's youth had fled, wasted unjustly, a pure loss of war. His grandfather was dead. But the rites and rituals of his childhood had remained alive in his soul, so when he left Hanoi he had taken some of his grandfather's old suits—they were about his size—and tossed them in his suitcase before boarding the train.

There is a time for everything, even men.

These were his grandfather's words. Everything stayed with Dam: Like pebbles in a streambed, his grandfather's words had laid there in silent repose and slowly, depending on the situation, Dam would find them again. He couldn't help smiling as he put on the suit he had inherited.

Some objects have a second life.

Dam knew that when he entered the conference room, all the Party mandarins would stare at him with envy, coveting his expensive suit. After a half-century, the old styles had come back in vogue, and they were all the more seductive now that cadres had gotten rid of their Mao suits or their uniforms, studiously training themselves to wear Western suits and ties, squeezing their rugged feet into leather shoes, and making every effort to chew with their mouths closed during receptions so as not to spit in the face of a guest across the table.

Dam's calculations were on the mark. He was only the director of an artistic troupe, much lower in rank than the Party cadres, the heads of services, or the mayors of cities, but an attention to the rituals of life had given him an elusive power, and the fact that its value had not yet been publicly acknowledged made it all the more effective. More than fifty cadres were seated around a large oval table in the center of the conference room, everyone dressed according to their means and esthetic standards and visibly making a great effort to catch up with the fashions of the cities. One of the cadres still wore a stiff, high-colored Sun Yat Sen suit, but with a Western tie; another had matched Maoist-style pants with a checkered shirt. Others experimented with leather jackets and striped scarves, or Western suits and berets. In the middle of these bizarre, ridiculous combinations, despite these heroic efforts by people raised outside of urban culture, Dam shone like a peacock; he was also blessed with height, a majestic bearing, and a handsome face. Aside from these advantages, his grandfather's suit had created an instant sensation. For the first time, he noticed that jealousy between men is no less vicious than between women: furtive stares, icy, surprised looks that strained to conceal their envy. But their curiosity was impossible to mask. Dam enjoyed his urbanity with feigned indifference. Sometimes, he had to lower his head so as not to smile.

Now, in the first part of the conference, they're going to recite banalities about the spirit of the ceremony. I'll stage my battle in the second act. An offensive is going to be necessary; I mustn't miss my call.

He waited. About nine o'clock, after the provincial Party secretary's speech on the ceremony, during the break, the dignitaries rushed out to the veranda for refreshments. They clamored around Dam, admiring and noisily complimenting him on his suit. Seizing the moment, Dam fraternized with everyone, delivering an introductory fashion lesson that he recited, almost by heart, from his grandfather's teachings. The new chief of the Cultural Service participated in this lively discussion. He was from the central provinces, but had spent more than twenty years in the north. Now, he had returned and pushed out Hung's enemy, the deputy chief of the Service: The man was retired "early" and had apparently opened a scrap metal store. The new chief was at the stage in his job where he was trying desperately to surround himself with new talent, faithful followers. He treated his potential collaborators with great attention, sensitivity: He was the one who had proposed inviting Dam to attend the conference. When the new chief accepted, Dam realized the occasion would be the perfect opportunity to realize his goal. After a round of tea and cakes intended to rouse the mandarins from their post-lunch stupor, they started the second half of the conference.

Dam asked the chief of the Service for permission to present his program for the performance. The most controversial aspect, Dam explained to the assembled cadres, was a reorchestration of the works of the composer Hoang Hung, "the man who was once considered the soul of the provincial artistic troupe, a commander on the spiritual front of the war against the Americans to save the country. . . ."

The chief of security police cut him off in the midsentence: "Comrade Dam, you must not praise past virtues. You forget the present situation of this Hung character. At present, he is the only cadre among us to have tried to flee the country by boat. Whether you like it or not, he has betrayed the revolutionary mission. This man is currently under strict surveillance. I'm afraid it won't be possible to use his work."

The other participants clammed up like grains of paddy rice. Of all the cadres, the chief of the security police was the most powerful. He who held the guns held the power; hadn't that always been their logic? Even the Party secretary, the Party vice-secretary, had to keep quiet, not to mention the heads of the lowly cultural departments. Everyone here was a local boy, and they all had family who depended on the favors and protection of the security police. No one, not even the secretary and his deputy, could claim that the members of his family, or his clan, were all clean, honest people, or that they would be spared the prison gates.

But I'm an outsider, only a temporary resident here. No one will have any problems because of some family link to me. Dam glanced around the table, scrutinizing the fifty faces to gather material for an experiment in the art of physiognomy, savoring the privilege and safety he alone enjoyed. After a few minutes of this, he spoke: "I waited, but since no one took the floor . . . I'll have to speak up, even though I'm one of those people who prefers to save their saliva."

Dam's haughty, provocative introduction startled them. They kept silent, waiting. He spoke slowly, choosing his words, intentionally prolonging the construction of his sentences in order to take stock of the game, identify the minefields all around him.

"Our comrade, the chief of police, has spoken with great candor, on a firm and indisputably revolutionary position. This position, in my opinion, was justified—about five years ago. But if we put this old suit back on, we may find ourselves striking a false note. Instead of imparting a positive, artistic spirit to the ceremonies, I fear we'll end up with negative results."

Dam paused, seeing the jaws of the chief of security police clench and flush scarlet. The man shot him a quick, incendiary look, then lowered his eyes, swirling his cigarette lighter on the table.

Ah-ha! Right on target, your excellency, Mr. All-powerful Chief of Police. You thought you'd reduce me to dust between your fingers, cast me into the tiger's cage, piss and shit on my head, me, a nothing who dares mock you, disagree with you. Think carefully.

Dam took a sip of water, continued in a neutral, indifferent tone: "Revolutionary principles must also evolve if they are not to become obstacles to the revolution. Five years ago, the dictatorial spirit of the Comrade police chief was quite well suited to the demands of the revolution. We had a war to fight and an enemy that faced our mortars, our rifles. But five years have gone by, the country has been reunified. High-ranking Party and State leaders themselves raised the flags of national unity to rebuild the country. Among those who were reintegrated into our national community, there were people who fought on the other side. But Hoang Hung is a man who fought side by side with us in the war, an important cadre. I know he has made mistakes. But he has already been dismissed from his position, his ration tickets have been cut off; he's been excluded, exiled from the life of the community. For a man who gave his youth and his talent to the war effort, to the country, this seems like excessively cruel punishment, ruthless . . . dare I say, inhuman? I think each of us, at least once, should put ourselves in the place of others. If we don't understand our people, their lives, how can we hope to govern them humanely? So I propose that we devote ten minutes to that. For the first five, let's put ourselves in the place of the composer Hoang Hung. And in the other five, let's consider our other compatriots who have just been reintegrated into this national community. Think of them as your neighbors' children; they are standing at the door to revolutionary power. Do you think these people will dare cross the threshold, rejoin this extended family as adopted children when they see the ingratitude and barbarism with which we treat the real children of the revolution? This elementary method of reasoning is called deduction;

it's fairly simple, and when applied properly it can clear our vision of a problem."

Dam stopped speaking. He poured himself a cup of tea, sipped it slowly, his gaze turned toward the window where the lace curtains glowed in the sunlight. The room was silent, the faces sober, as if their thoughts were taut as antennae.

"I'm not from this region . . ." Dam said suddenly, his voice hurled like a stone onto the stagnant surface of a bog. He didn't meet anyone's eyes, addressed no one in particular. "I'm not from central Vietnam, you see. That puts me at a certain disadvantage, but it also gives me a certain objectivity. The composer, Hoang Hung, is one of your own. His compositions, inspired by your native lands, are almost the only compositions of any artistic value in the entire province. Soon, you will be celebrating the fifth anniversary of the victory. The principal theme you have chosen is the glorification of the sacred resistance of our people. All in all, our people don't have much to be proud of aside from their warrior heritage. No other composer can do this theme justice like Hung can.

"Comrades, you have the power to decide whether or not we use his work. As a musician, allow me to repeat: For the purposes of this performance, using Hung's work is not a choice, it's a necessity. If we don't, I'll have to copy a few numbers produced by central department and the performance will look like one of those song and dance groups from Hanoi. The glorious history of the struggles of this province will leave no trace on the stage of this city's theater. It will be a flop. And in this case, there's no need to spend a lot of money on some trivial spectacle. You'd do better to organize some dragon dances, some tightrope walkers, and a few rounds of gunfire . . ."

Dam took a drag on his cigarette, turned his face up to the sky, and exhaled the smoke, as if he didn't care what any of them thought.

The secretary spoke first. "Okay, if you have to, use his work. But I would ask you not to use his name. Use the compositions, but under some kind of pseudonym, whatever you like."

Should I accept this? Yes or no? Yes or no?

"If we use Hung's work under another name, we're breaking the law. In other words, we're illegally profiting from a man's work. In spite of it all, to ensure the success of the performance, I'll try to convince him. But an artist's work is like his child. And as you know, the singer, Mai Suong, is his wife. She is the one who will interpret his songs. I think that he will accept for this reason."

The chief of police cut Dam off, opening his jaws like a snake: "Comrade Dam, you lack judgment in talking like this. Hoang Hung is a traitor to the revolution. If we use his work we're doing him a favor, an honor he doesn't deserve. There's no need to ask his permission."

Dam burst out laughing. "Respected Comrade, let's suppose a man makes a mistake. Society excludes him, forbids him from earning his living, prevents him from making use of his talent, denies him all means of livelihood. Then suppose he has to depend on his wife, simply because he hasn't had the courage to put a rope around his neck, that he spends his time pacing around his house like a rat in a sewer. Then, one day, society needs his music, uses it under a false name. Do you think that he will applaud this news with joy, acknowledge it as a special favor? Respected chief, I thought that a man of your position might have received a minimum of training, a few courses in basic psychology, if not at university perhaps at the high school level."

Today's little game has really been worth the wait. For these Party guys, I'm just a pawn at the bottom of the heap, but as an outsider I hold the wild card: the strength of the void.

A long moment passed. Dam stared down the chief of security police, waiting for his reply. He was expecting a blow, but it wasn't going to be delivered here. Dam tried to be cheerful, joking, but it barely hid his defiant, ironic attitude. The entire assembly was mute with awe. There are times when the spectacle of another's humiliation consoles men for resentments that they have had to mask for too long.

The chief of security police was stiff, utterly disoriented. He never imagined something like this would happen. Dam's words were simple, like well-aimed blows too difficult to parry. With no talent for repartee, the man stared at Dam, his eyes bulging, his mouth agape like a clam on a barbecue.

The provincial Party secretary began to speak again: "Comrades, let's wind up these discussions. Our decision has been made, now let's move on to another subject." He leaned over his notebook, flipped a few pages, and then looked up in Dam's direction. "I personally entrust you with the task of finding a pseudonym. It should be a relatively optimistic name, say Red Light, or Sunlight, or Red Dawn, for example. The goal of this ceremony is to glorify the revolution, to celebrate victory over the Americans. So the name must be chosen in this spirit."

The chief of the Cultural Service rushed to speak: "Yes, sir, absolutely, we understand, sir. We'll talk about it amongst ourselves after the meeting."

Head lowered, the chief of security police spun his cigarette lighter violently on the table and didn't say a word until lunch.

That evening, Dam asked Suong to come to his office and told her that they would use almost all of Hung's compositions in the upcoming show to celebrate the victory. He would rearrange certain compositions since the orchestra was three times as big as the one Hung had used.

"I'll tell him when I go home. I'm sure he'll be very happy."

But Dam dismissed the idea. "No, absolutely not. I want to surprise him. I'll invite him to sit in the row of honor for the premiere. We'll see if they dare and banish me from town for it."

"No, Dam don't do that," Suong pleaded. "It's too risky."

Dam shook his head. "What do I have to lose? Nothing. If they accept it and shut up, I'll continue my work here. If they chase me out, I'll just pack my bags and go back north. In this season, the light up there is beautiful."

Suddenly Dam burst into song.

Oh, Hanoi! I didn't wait for the chill of autumn
To intoxicate myself on you with those first summer nights
On West Lake, the smell of lotus blossoms, sweet in the wind . . .

As he sang, he marched around his desk. Suong watched him, curious, until the end of the song. He stopped, turned to her. "Did I sing well?"

Embarrassed, Suong didn't dare reply. He roared with laughter, wiping his tears with a handkerchief. "This morning I had a lot of laughs. But enough; the time for laughing is over. You've got the evening off, but be back tomorrow for the rehearsals! And don't forget, it's going to be hard. Your mission is to recreate a whole past era, a world that belonged to all of you, especially to you and Hung."

Suong lowered her head. Dam saw her to the door. By the time he got home, it was late. On his desk sat a bottle of cognac, a few packets of dried beef jerky—liquor and snacks he had bought and kept for the day he would invite Hung for a drink. *You don't drink good wine alone. Let's go to sleep. I'm sure I'm going to sleep like a log tonight.* Dam put the bottle of cognac away in a closet and turned out the light. Shadows cloaked the room. In the window frame swayed a branch of jacaranda, like a painting.

How many poets have immortalized the quivering shadow of flowers in a window frame? From all ages, from the poetry of the Sun dynasty to the Tang, and all the way through the songs of my youth. "The plum tree has just flowered, its branches sway in the wind, dance in the glow of the waning moon." The woman I loved used to sing that song.

Dam pulled the covers over his stomach, closed his eyes. But sleep wouldn't come. The branch of jacaranda kept swaying in his mind. He imagined it thrashing, saw its delicate flowers fall and scatter like threads of silk. And behind them, he saw the skies of his adolescence, the ramshackle roofs of the old quarter in Hanoi, heard the cries of the snack vendors late at night as they cycled down the deserted back streets in the rain. And beyond all that, he saw the surreal silhouette of a woman cloaked in evening fog, in a swirl of smoke from firecrackers on a fragrant spring day.

Why am I suddenly so hopelessly sentimental? I should sleep, regain my strength for tomorrow. I've got to read all those files, I've got to . . . Never mind. You've got to let yourself enjoy the small pleasure left behind in these disparate memories, these modest dreams.

A melody rose in him. He remembered the old gramophone that belonged to his grandfather, how when he was a little boy he used to get up on tiptoe and reach his tiny hand out to touch the shiny chrome arm. In his imagination, when he was just a three-year-old child, the voice of the singer emerged from this metal stem shaped like a goose's neck, and he wanted to hold the melodies in his little hand.

The impossible dream of childhood. The one that leads us to other dreams, equally impossible, of our adulthood. When the last days fade, when the game is over, we look back at our life and see a vast cemetery littered with the dreams that died. A chaotic assortment of untended graves. Each life unfolds and creates a graveyard for its own hopes and aspirations, whether modest or grandiose. Why on this happy day, a day of success, can't I sleep? Why do I feel so sad? It's not logical.

Dam threw off the covers, got up, turned on a light and put on a tape of Schubert. This composer's tormented, tragic sky covered his mind with orphan clouds. His back propped against the wall, Dam listened. A half hour later, he couldn't stand it anymore and rummaged in the drawers for a cigarette. He had quit smoking, but tonight, like this morning, he didn't have the courage to resist. In his desk drawer, he found half a pack of 555s and a pack of Marlboros. He didn't know why, but the image of the American cowboy stirred something in him, and he opened it. *Schubert, Schubert . . . like a fate I chose when I was a student at the Music Conservatory. It's brought me bad luck. A different kind of bad luck than Hung's. He liked Schubert too, as I remember.*

Dam remembered that he still had to choose a pseudonym for Hung, so that the audience would swallow the infidel's music. The name couldn't be too provocative for the authorities, the officials who held power, but it also had to be a name that wouldn't betray his friend. He sat down at his desk, scrawled the names that the provincial Party secretary had given him in a column: Red Light. Sunlight. Red Dawn. All names that were supposed to evoke the soul, the quintessence of the Party. *The Party opened my eyes, my heart.* Dam suddenly drew an X through the names. Then he wrote another list of names in another column: Hung Nam, Viet Hung, Anh Hung, Hung Anh. *No, these names make too explicit reference to Hung. All you have to do is read them once to think immediately of Hoang Hung, of the land that gave birth to him.* And he drew another X over the words he had just written, set down his pen, and got up. Schubert's melodies still swirled through the room. In the window frame the jacaranda branches seemed to shiver, moved by the beauty and the sadness of the unhappy artist's music. Dam opened the window, lit another cigarette. He contemplated the space outside, the garden of jacarandas in the amber light of the street lamps. Behind the low walls, the roofs of the town and the church tower rose like a black mass against the backdrop of the sky. He stood there a long time, motionless, inhaling the smoke, watching it vanish into the air. Suddenly, a name came to him: *Hai Ha, Oceans and Rivers.*

Ah-ha! The dream of the oceans and the rivers, the dream of our youth. Of all human dreams, that was the greatest, the most perilous. A beautiful name. Don't his two girls have names like that? Why couldn't I use them to designate their father? They are his flesh and blood, his lost future. That's it, that's the best way to both name and hide the man.

Dam snuffed his cigarette out in an ashtray and rummaged through a closet, looking for the notebook that held the actors' curriculum vitae. He quickly located the names of Hoang Hung's two daughters under Suong's dossier: Da Hai, Phuoc Hanh. He combined the names to come up with Hai Hanh. It was a cacophonic name, but full of meaning: This was the wish that Dam would secretly send to Hung.

I can do more for Hung. After the show, I'll invite him to collaborate with me on the next show. He's a talented composer. They don't have the right to use a political sentence to kill his career, to use one error to exclude him forever from public life. The new head of the Service will have to support me. If not out of decency and goodwill, out of self-interest. He needs to consolidate his power.

Dam lit another cigarette, his heart racing with enthusiasm. Unable

to contain himself in the room any longer, he went out into the courtyard. The town was asleep. Alone, his mind spinning with ideas, he
strode down the path of jacarandas, puffing on his cigarette. In the
cold night sky, the smoke was strangely seductive; it made him feel
younger, more pensive, more passionate. From time to time, a jacaranda
blossom fell, grazing his cheek. Petals covered the ground, light and
fluffy as cotton, and as he walked his toes touched their smooth, humid
softness. With each breeze, the scent swirled, a light, delicate perfume.
Lighter and gender than air. So it bobbed in air, waiting for the wind
to stir, to touch the face of the passerby like a silken thread from
heaven, like a mirage.

The evening Dam told Suong they would use Hung's compositions in
the performance commemorating the victory, she felt dizzy, as if someone had slapped her. Riding her bicycle back to the house that night,
her head buzzed. Dam's news had stirred a long chain of melodies,
songs, and, behind them, the months and years past that she had
thought dead and which now, suddenly, threatened to spring to life
again. That was another life, another world. And in that world she had
been just a fragile child, living under Hung's protection, a ball of wax
in the hands of a magician. A magician who had transformed her, Mai
Suong, the shepherd girl from the mountains, into "Suong, the diva of
the entire central region." In that world, Hung had reigned like a god,
and the memories and objects and sounds that rose from that world
threatened to metamorphose into judges who would stand to interrogate and accuse her. And she knew, too, that an even greater danger
lurked for her, because another accuser, even more ruthless, more
intransigent, lay in wait at the bottom of her own soul.

Suong arrived at the house, opened the door. Things seemed to
have eyes, to watch her: These inert objects, without conscience or feeling, seemed to have acquired a soul, to stare at her with irony, contempt. The electric lamp cast a harsh, naked light. Each object revealed
itself in minute detail: glass beads in a glass vase; old dolls, lined up in
the tea chest; faded, silk flowers in a wicker basket; the golden rims of

the glasses she had found in the stores near the market. *There they are, in their places, the same as always, and yet they seem to stare at me, mocking: What are you looking for in our boring lives?* The window panes, like hollow, vacant eyes, cast cold, diabolical looks at her. A wail rose from the murmur of the leaves: Was this cry human or did it belong to some malevolent wandering soul? She froze in fear, called to Hung. He came running down the staircase, startled. "What's the matter?"

She shook her head. "Nothing. I must be tired today . . . Let's go have a *pho* in town."

He climbed back up the stairs to change. She followed him with her eyes. For a long time now he had lived like a nomadic shadow up there, counting the days by the tiles on the wall, marking the passage of time by the swish of the trees, brooding over thoughts she couldn't know, didn't want to know. And now she had stopped LOOKING UP TO HIM, stopped LOVING him. The morning her little brother had punched her, Hung had come back, and she had fallen into his arms, slept by his side. In the pain, the humiliation, she had taken refuge with this tender, generous soul. Then she had woken up, found her strength, her confidence. Once the anxiety had gone, she no longer needed solace, protection, and the hatred and contempt for his illness flooded back to her. She extricated herself from his arms, without explanation. And he had accepted this in silence, with a sad smile, resigned, acting as if nothing had happened between them. That night, at dinner, he asked her: "Don't you think you should give Vinh some money? I think he's going to need some to buy a ticket back to the hamlet."

"No," Suong replied curtly.

But after the meal, she said. "It's not that I don't want to give him the money. I just don't want to see him again."

"I could go find him, give him the money. Whatever happens, he's your flesh and blood. You were the one who brought him here."

She shot Hung a suspicious look. But he added: "Don't worry, I'm not going to run away on you. You can't bathe in two streams at the same time."

He fell silent a minute, then smiled. "And if I do go, it will be very far. You won't have to waste time looking for me." He spoke slowly, his gaze lost in the distance, far away, as if he was wandering in other lands. And those lands didn't belong to her.

Hung took the money, and the following evening he informed her that he had found Vinh working for a truck driver so he could earn a ticket back to the hamlet. Suong listened, then went back to the kitchen in silence, set the table without even a word of thanks.

Why am I so cruel, such an ingrate? Of course he made me suffer, but I betrayed him. I was the first one who turned my back on him.

Hung changed, then went downstairs. The couple had locked the house and gone out to eat a *pho* in town. Suong had poured a spoon of chili sauce into Hung's bowl. She saw his lips crease into a smile. A smile full of meaning that she could no longer decipher.

The next morning, Dam handed Suong a bound notebook filled with songs. They were all Hung's songs, but reprinted on sparkling new white paper. Once, Hung had helped her rehearse songs that he had composed on scrap paper with notes and lyrics scrawled in the margins, or in ragged old notebooks with covers that looked like they would fall off.

"When they are compiled, Hung's compositions make an extraordinary body of work. It's hard to imagine one man producing this much. You reread and rehearse these songs this morning. I'll be back early this afternoon to listen."

Suong bent over the pages of the notebook. The scales were like unfinished roads that carried her back to her native lands, down the old paths, through the fields and trenches, the underground shelters, and familiar streams. She could almost see flames flickering in the mountain hamlets, the ladybugs crawling on the leaves of the pepper trees, and the dusty red road she had taken to follow Hung's call. She could see the falls at the mountain spring where he had carried her, pregnant, on his back when she could no longer walk. She remembered how the hair on his chest had frightened her when they made love for the first time in broad daylight. These images still haunted her, clamoring at the walls of her heart.

When Dam came back to find her that afternoon, he noticed her eyes were puffy, but he didn't say anything. "Do you feel ready to sing?"

She nodded.

They started to work.

Day after day, the rehearsals carried her back, deep into the mountain lands she had forgotten. An entire world of the past reappeared on the horizon, each day more vast, more luminous in the splendor of memory. And Suong advanced toward the light, unsteady, hesitant, pained. Memory projected its light into the corners of her soul, and she recognized the face of regret. Dam discreetly watched her, but said nothing. She knew it, remorse stuck to her skin like a coat of indelible paint. Back at home, Hung had no idea that these were the thoughts that haunted her. He had entered the role of the dead man a long time ago, and now he lived alone with that death. Often, she wanted to say something to him, but she couldn't find the words. As for Hung, though he would smile at her, talk to her, look at her with gentleness, he seemed absent. She knew that after her cruelty, when she had torn herself from his arms, she had destroyed the last link between them. Since then, he no longer expected anything from this life. *He doesn't need me anymore. Now, it's not just me who has stopped loving him. He no longer loves me.*

Hung's indifference felt like a red-hot stake that had been thrust into her heart. She longed for him, began to want to reconquer the lost citadel. And with each passing day, the songs she rehearsed only heightened that yearning.

The rehearsals had gone on for more than three weeks. One morning, the guard came right in to the stage to announce that Suong had a visitor.

"Who is it?" she asked.

"One of your acquaintances," he said, winking at her. She knew who he was alluding to and felt her ears burn.

"Don't you see that we're busy rehearsing to prepare for the victory show?"

The guard, surprised by her anger, stood stunned for a few minutes, then said softly. "Your visitor has been waiting for half an hour. I wouldn't have come if I had been able to chase him away."

"I can't leave right now."

The guard stood motionless, refusing to go. Suong realized she had no choice but to follow him. She told the orchestra that some urgent matter had come up and to continue with the other actors. She left the stage and followed the guard.

The young man from the prison was reading a newspaper in the waiting room; she recognized him even from the back. As soon as she entered the room, he got up, looking at her with sad eyes.

"How are you?"

"Fine thank you," she said, without meeting his gaze, and in an irritated voice: "As you can see, we're very busy rehearsing and . . ."

The young man bowed his head, interrupted her. "The troupe is preparing the show for the fifth anniversary celebration of the liberation of the country. I understand that you are very busy. Other people know too. But an unexpected matter brought me here to find you."

He greeted the guard before taking the steering wheel of his Honda and pushing it through the courtyard. She followed him, mechanically, knowing she couldn't refuse. They crossed the row of jacarandas, reached the sidewalk. The young man finally turned to her. "The commander has just received orders to take charge of a large reeducation camp up north. He's leaving on the first plane tomorrow morning."

Suong didn't reply. She didn't know why this news both saddened and relieved her, how she could feel these two emotions at the same time. She had loved the commander. But this love had burned out like a straw fire, and she could see the ashes clearly now.

She climbed on the back of the Honda, asking the young man. "Are you going with him?"

The young man sighed. "I don't know. He asked that they transfer me with him, but the Service hasn't granted permission yet."

"You want to follow him, don't you?"

"Yes. We've sworn lifelong loyalty to each other," he replied, as if it was obvious.

Suong fell silent. Friendship between men is simple, solid, she thought. This young man is faithful to his boss, and the commander is no doubt sincere with him. She had once truly loved the commander. But this love had burnt out, consumed by itself. She didn't want that to happen, but it had all been beyond her control. That awkward, passionate man had loved her with a persevering, yet passionate love. He had longed for her, adored her, admired her, pitied her. This guard of the gates of hell had kept a romantic love burning in his wild heart. The sincerity of that love had attracted her. What's more, the commander had provided for her materially, giving her the means to lead a more comfortable life than her colleagues and yielding to this temptation had not left her without a certain arrogance. The rose petals that had been crushed under their backs so many times, and the scent of the expensive perfumes he bought her wafted through the house where they met to make love. She remembered his rough hands, how they had awkwardly caressed her elbows, the waves in her hair. His face would suddenly beam with a naive happiness when she laughed, or delighted in some new gift he had given her. The ecstasy on his face whenever he heard her sing made him look more like a huge child than a man in love. They saw each other almost every day, but just when the commander thought he had imprisoned her forever in his heart, she began to doubt, to flee him.

Their lovemaking no longer terrified or intoxicated her like it had the first day. She felt him become stranger and stranger to her. When they saw each other, all they could say was the eternal refrain, the melody that he repeated without ever tiring of it: *I love you, I love you, I love you.* Sometimes, his startled eyes, frozen in adoration, scared her. It was as if he were some kind of mythical animal who had just been transformed into a man, yet who couldn't forget the behavior and the habits of his bestial life. Once, he fell asleep on top of Suong after they made love, almost crushing her under his weight. She had to shout and shake him, thrash about for a long time before he awoke. The ruddy complexion that had once attracted Suong had slowly begun to frighten her, for sometimes it turned a shade of purple as if a torrent of blood was rushing right beneath the surface. Everything in this man was strange, out of proportion. That troubled her. What's more, she knew nothing about him aside from what he himself had told her. He had married early. His wife was eight years older and had borne him two daughters. Just as he entered the prime of life, she had aged. He hadn't been back to his village for many years, except on special occasions or to obey his mother's wishes. But that's all Suong knew and she didn't dare ask questions for fear of upsetting him. But every time they made love, she felt as if she were embracing the genie of the mountains, some bandit, a tiger or a lion disguised as a man. This huge mass of flesh would never become her flesh and blood, would never merge with her. And when she felt this, she remembered Hung, her first love, her unhappy husband. She remembered the safe, secure happiness that she had found in his arms, when their bodies mingled, when each cell of her body had vibrated to the passionate echo of his, when she had felt that she was inside him, belonged to him, and he to her, so close, inseparable.

The Honda came to a halt. Suong realized she was in front of the familiar house at the end of the alley. Bougainvillea littered the ground, rotting there. Not a single flower was left on the trees. The wind had swept away the last of the roses, tossing them over the high walls whose rims were spiked with broken glass.

"Go ahead in," the young man said. Not waiting for her reply, he revved the motorbike and disappeared back down the alley. Suong stared at the open gate, waiting. Suddenly she found it all strange. *Why? Why?* A few seconds later, she pushed through the gate into the courtyard, tapped in the code as usual. *It's nothing. Nothing. It's the last time. Tomor-*

row, he flies to the North, and me, I'll go back to Hung. He is still my husband, the
father of my children. No one will ever know about this affair.

She moves toward the threshold of the door, conscious that behind the window, a man watches her with eyes still flaming with passion and longing. She walks, counting the tiles in the courtyard, imagining still waters. The water of Lake Trang Nguyen in her native village. How she used to go there to play. When the children skipped stones, or rock shards, shivering rings of water spread to form larger circles within circles that effaced each other, and finally the surface of the lake became smooth, silent again. The love between her and the commander had been like a pebble tossed by some mischievous boy into that lake. The circles of time would slowly fade and the surface of the lake would grow still and mute again, masking forever the secrets that lay buried in its muddy depths.

Twilight flickers out, dies. The last rays of sun in the garden vanish. City lights, like stars, illuminate the skyline. Only this house is without fire or light. Long shadows wash over the garden, creeping, one by one, into the rooms through the open doors. From the courtyard, he contemplates his home: Windows loom like silent eyes of time, screens across which flash the ghostly shadows of days past: sweltering days crushed by torrential rains; clear blue days; stormy cloud-ridden days; shattered, ragged days of thunder and lightning; days of happiness as frail as dragonfly wings spinning in the wind; lonely, mute days; tortured days as dark as the alley that led to the gates of prison hell. Shadows glide up to him, as through the silent windows of a silent film. He contemplates them, serene, detached, as one would the fate of a passerby, or that of a character in a novel. Parade of the faded days, the months, the years; why so gentle, so calm? This too, comes unexpected.

That afternoon, after her rehearsal, Suong hands him an invitation in Dam's writing:

In celebration of the fifth anniversary of the liberation of the south of Vietnam and
the reunification of the country, we cordially invite the composer Hoang Hung (or "Hai

Hanh") *to do us the honor of his presence at the performance. Your presence will be the pride of the artistic troupe of our province.*

He picks up the invitation, holds it for a long time in his hand, disoriented. He studies the curves of Dam's handwriting: *"Dear Hung, you must come. I'm expecting you. We have so much to talk about."* He turns to Suong: "What does he mean by this?"

"Just that he wants you to see the new performance, wants your opinion," she says. Then she takes him in her arms. It's been a long time since she's done this. He freezes, stunned. Her warm, tender lips take him by surprise, a brief, unexpected intoxication. And then she leaves, after the kiss, her eyes moist. "I've got to go." He nods, accompanies her to the door, as usual.

Why are you crying? What pain do you have to hide from me? Have you let yourself fall madly in love with this young man? Is this what seems to help you pity me? I know, I know, I've become a beggar for love, first yours, now the girls'.

Still holding the invitation, he sits down on the bench in the shade of the yellow ylang-ylangs. He reads and re-reads the lines of golden letters, the tiny italic script, Dam's elegant handwriting on the back. He doesn't understand. Why is he suddenly being invited to a theater he's been forbidden to enter for the last five years? The authorities organize dozens of commemorative ceremonies so they can polish their coats of arms, like a woman feverishly applying layers of powder to cover her sickly skin. But Dam had never invited him to participate before; perhaps his friend hadn't wanted to reopen an old wound that would cause them both pain.

But now it's all behind me. Whatever happens, it won't change anything.

He spends the afternoon seated in the yellow shade of the ylang-ylangs, until the city lights flicker on.

Leave my house in silence, in darkness. Sometimes, night is the most tender presence; like water, it soothes; like reeds, it rocks the nooks and crannies of the heart, kindling memories . . .

These romantic thoughts make him laugh. In a few minutes his house will plunge into the long shadows of the garden. Night will swallow the rooms in a dark fog, hang its mysterious canvas, projecting images of the past. He watches the procession, utterly lost. Peals of bright, girlish laughter echo through the window; his daughters are having fun at Auntie Tuong's house. This afternoon he bathed them while she kneaded the rice paste to make cakes. Their shiny hair, the downy softness of their skin, their sweet, warm perfume still hover about him.

My little girls, blood of my blood, flesh of my flesh: You have grown up so fast, to be more beautiful than I ever imagined.

And again, a procession of images sweeps him away, like a tide. He too fades into a long film, into scene after scene of his life: A summer's dawn at the base of a ravine; a stormy beach in autumn; birds singing in the blistering heat of an afternoon in the camp; the patter of wounded soldier's urine into a chamber pot near his bed, one night in a military hospital.

There is no link between these images: The tide of mud and scum, water lilies, decaying corpses of animals, rotting leaves, garbage, *lim* seeds. Half asleep, half awake, he drifts on the floodwaters of memory. He has forgotten Dam's invitation, is about to fall asleep when the clock strikes seven. Chimes echo through the garden.

Oh God. Were did I have to be? The performance, Dam's show. I have to go, if only not to disappoint a friend. He has no debt to me, and yet he has been kind . . . now that's something precious in life, unexpected, unhoped for.

He returns to the house, turns on the lights to change. Too late for dinner. He grabs a few crackers, runs out to the street.

Dam is waiting for him at the gate to the theater; he seems taller to Hung, more handsome than ever in his white suit and satin blue tie flecked with tiny purple flowers. Dam takes his hand and pulls him into the theater, escorts the composer to a place of honor in the first row, a seat ordinarily reserved for the provincial Party secretary or his deputy.

Looking at Dam, he shakes his head. "Taking this seat gives me no pleasure. They're all the same, just as long as you can see the show."

"It's not just a show," Dam says. "This is an experiment, and this chair you're seated in is like a vaccine to test the antibodies."

"Why?"

"Once in awhile, a man has to dare, even if it goes against his self-interest. Only businessmen measure their lives by profits and losses."

"You're crazy, Dam."

"I try. For example, the pseudonym I chose for you. The provincial Party secretary wanted something symbolic of revolutionary enthusiasm. But I combined the names of your two girls. They're your flesh and blood, and that eased my conscience a bit. In a moment, every big shot in the province will hear that name. I'm waiting for their reaction—waiting to see how they feel when they find they're seated next to a boat person, a traitor to the revolution." Dam bellows with laughter, and it is infectious.

Hung laughs too. "Tell me, why do you attach such importance to a fake name?"

But Dam doesn't have time to reply; a man is approaching. "Have a seat, Hung. I've got to go," he says, gets up, calmly climbs the stairs to the stage, and slips behind the curtain. The shiny velvet of the curtain is much more opulent than anything Hung had when he ran the theater. Everything seems new. They have replaced the spotlights, replastered the building. The walls are no longer smeared with dust. Only the armchairs remain as they were after the war. He remembers the day he and the troupe first entered the theater, how the actors had shrieked with delight, bounced and wriggled around in these chairs, stroked and poked them. The troupe members have probably forgotten this embarrassing scene. But he remembers.

Memory can be a torturer: Its horses have been trained to canter down the old roads, forcing us to retrace our steps, to balk at new lands. If only I could have rid myself of it, turned to new passions. Who knows, perhaps I could have had a peaceful, happy life, could have been an artisan lacquering screens with gold. On holidays, I might have strolled with my wife and daughters in the public gardens. If only I had been able to forget this longing, this hunger, I might have been a model husband, a good father, found a home in the oyster of domestic happiness, like any other mortal.

My tragedy is that I can't forget. I never learned how. My memory has become too heavy. Why can't I cross the line between dreams and resignation? Go ahead, drink the water of the River of Oblivion, forget everything and you'll have another destiny. But how can a man who drinks this brew remain human? In the legend, our ancestors ordered us to paint it on the palms of their hands before they died: "Never drink the water of the River of Oblivion, never eat the porridge of forgetting." Human beings have always taken pride in memory, bearing the burden of consciousness, of previous lives, as they step toward the future. These people, these ordinary folk who led ordinary lives, they had the courage not to forget. They too were artists, weren't they? A cold, yet lucid memory; that is what it means to be human. How could I flee?

He wanders alone among his thoughts. A bell rings, familiar to his ears, announcing the curtain. This sound that he has been estranged from for years explodes in him now like a challenge. All around him, the high-ranking provincial party dignitaries; It is impossible to guess who is who, secretary from deputy secretary; they all have the same solemn faces, eyes riveted on the stage. He doesn't have time to gauge their attitude toward his presence. Indifferent, distracted, he retreats, crouches back into his shell, ignoring the entourage. The first bell has barely finished when the second rings out, shriller, more insistent. Slowly, the curtain rises. His heart twists. The stage, there, in front of him; the small, square space that he had possessed for so many years, where he had built an entire little world, his own and one that had captivated people. He had lured them into that labyrinth, made them laugh or cry, feel joy or remorse, taste feelings alien to their long, boring lives. Here it is, his old dominion, his dream, the life he had chosen, and that they had taken from him.

Ah, now Dam is reading the inaugural speech. What is he saying? . . . Platitudes . . . glory and miracles and history and time . . . The historic significance of the ceremony . . . what next? The holy war of our nation. Artists who gave their youth, their lives to the struggle . . . Tonight's performance . . . the most important compositions of Hai Hanh, the man who trained the province's artistic troupe, who guided and transformed it into an elite commando group for the holy war! *What is he saying? How can he play this game with them—it's a slap in the face, some-*

thing I wouldn't even dare imagine. The program will begin with a chorale: The Truong Son March. Music by Hai Hanh, soloist Mai Suong.

The curtains slowly close. In the space of the pause, his gaze hangs in space. He can hear his own breathing, feel his heart throb. Something has suddenly changed: He feels dizzy, faint. He senses, vaguely yet clearly, that he is now at the center of the theater. Thousands of eyes will turn and fall on him if he makes even one misplaced gesture. He must sit up straight so the crowd won't recognize him, so that the men seated all around him can pretend to ignore his presence, as if he were a statue, or a nobody.

The curtains open slowly amidst a roar of applause. The singers on stage are in Western dress, the native land of the genre.

There was a time when this troupe trudged through the mountains, waded through the streams; pale men and women, crippled by hunger and malaria. Who would have imagined that they would one day look so elegant, so opulent? The power of money and a director's talent. Dam is an artist, after all.

The applause subsides. Dam appears from behind the curtain, the conductor's baton in hand, stunning in his conductor's traditional black. Hung flushes, envious, humiliated.

The egotistical dwarf in you just reared its head. For the first time in your life, you feel envy. You were always one of a kind; now you face your brilliant disciple from the north. Forgive me, Dam, I'm just a man, after all. A sick man.

These thoughts flicker out when Dam lifts his baton. The first phrase of the chorus begins; it isn't the strains of the trumpet, but a quartet accompanied by a piano.

Stupefied, he listens to the music he had written as if it was some unknown work written by someone else. Yes, he had composed the score one night in the middle of the jungle, trembling with fever. The scales traced in his notebook had rippled like the mountains all around them. Delirious, he had seen a vision of a yellow sky. The previous night, his detachment had crossed a bombarded zone, marched all day and night through villages and hamlets, across a countryside obscured by smoke, down roads lined with corpses. A narrow road, bordered by two irrigation canals. The corpses had been laid out vertically, a few inches apart, like waxy black mannequins. A moonless, starless night. No fireflies, not even the phosphorescent glow of rotting leaves. The light from a torch covered with parachute silk was the only thing that kept them from trampling the dead. It had been like stepping through hell. He remembered choking, lifting his face to the sky from time to time to gasp for breath, like a fish coming to the surface for air. Sweat had streamed down the back of his shirt, trickling over his thighs. Numb with fear, his companions shuffled along in silence, plodding, heavy steps, as if those corpses pulled at their feet, held them back. No one dared say a word. They marched that way for half an hour before leaving the field, then crossed clearing after clearing for two hours until dawn. In the twilight they could just make out the fringe of the forest, the huge heads of bears lumbering about in the undergrowth. Everyone sighed with relief. In the end, the light had saved them, slowly dispelling the terror that had congealed in their souls. Everyone had stepped up the pace. It was time to have a cigarette. Suddenly, the cook cried out: "Listen, footsteps. Hear them?"

The detachment stopped. He recognized the sound of footsteps, the march of a unit of soldiers. Footsteps echoed louder and louder, in wave after wave, beating in his heart as if they were no longer just footsteps but the rhythmic chant of rebirth, of the immortality of the soul. This chant lifted the icy corpses of the night, transforming them into immortal soldiers that pressed on, continuing their endless march toward the front. He felt a new energy surge in him: He was the corpses of the night lying in the fog the length of the road; he was the soldier that marched, singing in the dawn. In a flash, through this prism of shattered consciousness, he saw it: His strength and his people's stubborn, painful will to survive. He listened in silence, shivering in wait for a melody, sensing in the monotonous drone of the soldiers' steps an invisible tide that flooded his soul. He stood there, motionless, for a long time. His companions, impatient, had pressed him back to the road.

They marched for four hours, arriving about nine o'clock at a base camp. No one had had the strength to eat. They collapsed on bamboo mats, pulled the covers over their heads, and fell asleep. In the middle of the night, he woke up, his body on fire, sweat dripping down his back, the length of his spine. His throat was parched. He gazed up at the sky outside: It was yellow, as luminous as if a storm was about to break.

"Comrade, what color is the sky?" he asked the soldier on night watch, a young man who looked at him as if he had gone mad. "The sky . . ." Hung had repeated: "What is it, the color of the sky?"

The man shook his head. "Strange question, Comrade . . . there's no rain, no wind, no storm. What color would it be, aside from blue?"

The camp chief arrived and shook his head at the man. "Young man, wait a minute before raising your voice!" Then he turned to Hung. "You see a yellow sky, Comrade? Then you've got jungle fever. Tonight, you mustn't eat anything. I'll tell the cook to prepare you an infusion."

They made him a glass of hot sugar water with crushed ginger. He drank the burning, pungent liquid in small sips, his heart filled with love, tenderness, gratitude, forgiveness. Now, he saw them all again: The ignorant young soldier; the camp chief; the cold, stiff corpses lining the road; the soldiers marching that morning; the faces he would never know, whose footsteps he had heard. All this merged in him, into a single body, a single blood, a single pain. It was all the same loss, the same resignation, the same hope. And it had taken shape in a vague form that they called the people. His people. This people that had crossed the Truong Son Cordillera on foot.

The sky had turned brighter and brighter yellow. Black clouds of mosquitoes flew in all directions, and from this shadowy cloud rose bizarre purple, green, and gold flowers. But the hallucinations of his sick mind didn't dampen his inspiration; the strains of a melody, a mysterious voice still called to him. He had opened his knapsack, pulled out a notebook and traced wavy scales of music, writing the Truong Son March in a single feverish night.

The memory of it lived again, danced before his eyes, flooded back into his heart. He sees it again, the phosphorescent yellow sky, tastes the pungent, scalding water, the ginger on his palate, remembers the emotion that once washed over his soul, the happiness that had sprung from the gut of fear and death.

Did you really live those moments? Did you really, once in your life, cross the threshold of creation? Or was that just a masquerade, an illusion created by the magical hand of an orchestra conductor?

The chorus stopped.

One, two, three, four, five . . . I remember. There, I paused for five beats. Dam has kept them, remained faithful to my original. I recognize the trace of that old jungle road.

He lets himself fall, savors the silence that slowly engulfs the room, that slips over his head in a silky flutter of wings. He listens to the mute flow of time rush in the depths of the jungle with its sun-warmed paths, its ravines fragrant with the scent of wildflowers, the streams cooling the rocks. The jungle where he left his youth.

Suddenly, a woman's voice soars, taking flight through space. A voice like a knife in his heart. *The nightingale from the lands of exile.* He opens his eyes: Suong. She had appeared on stage for her solo. He hadn't seen her under the stage lights for five years. Now, finally, this woman who is his wife, here in the space that had held their love. How she shines! She is no longer his protégé: She is a diva. She moves now in her own halo of light, conquering the audience, captivating them with gestures that look effortless but that command them utterly, as they forget the outside world, focus all feeling on the spot that lights her face, waiting for that voice.

You have lost your spontaneity, Suong, your lovable fragility . . . you should have held onto that . . . my love. But you still have a rare voice that quivers with the passion of millions, that has carried men to the summits of happiness, and shown them the depths of their powerlessness. Yes, heaven gave you a timeless voice.

He contemplates his wife. Her makeup heightens the infinite, sad seduction of her eyes. She clutches a panel of her silk *ao dai* embroidered with silver sequins as if to brace herself, to keep from being swept away. Pearl earrings dangle from her ears, near the fine down at her temples.

So she lets her hair fall over her shoulders now, just like the Hanoi women do.

He remembers those earlobes, white and round like pieces of a game of Go. How he would bite them when they made love. His wife. She is here, before him, a few steps away, and yet so infinitely far. These last weeks, from time to time, her eyes have been teary; like this afternoon, when she held him, kissed him. Now, he understands. The music had breathed again in her, and like a wind, swept away the ashes over the last smoldering embers. Her love had been rekindled by this performance. Thanks to this glorification of the war effort commissioned by the Party apparatchiks, Dam had worked a miracle.

Suong falls silent, steps to the back of the choir as it opens the second movement. He doesn't try to analyze the orchestration. An image that just flashed through his mind continues to haunt him: *Ashes dispersed by wind, a few embers flare in the waning light. The rage of a dying light. Like one final lie before the numbing cold of winter. Like money won at roulette. A gambler's streak always comes before a fall.*

Again, Suong moves forward. The color of the spotlight changes: An eery, silver stream illuminates her face. In this new light, her features are distinct. She lowers her eyes, suddenly looking into the first row, searching. For the space of an instant, their eyes meet, link. Stunned, uncertain, his eyes freeze over; hers are stricken with sadness.

Dam lifts his baton. Suong's voice takes flight. She isn't looking at Hung anymore; her eyes are lost in the void, and in the void she draws images. Her voice seems to hold sighs, words she could never utter to him. Tears fall from her lashes, stream down her cheeks. Miraculous tears that call forth others, and now the audience weeps with her, choking back sobs.

There is no hoarseness in her voice; it is dense, nostalgic, seeps into the marrow of your bones, distilling the suffering, all life's injustices.

He tastes salt on his lips as he gazes at his wife. A voice echoes in him, half ironic, half tender. *Oh why are you weeping, my love? There is noth-*

ing for you to weep about, diva of the night, of every night, the nightingale with the crystal voice, whose arms tire under the weight of flowers, whose ears burn with the praise of admirers. Thousand of men have secretly loved you. Your vanity has been sated, your pockets filled. Like other women, you have children, a husband. But more than all of them, you have a freedom, a fame that they never will. Tears become you; even weeping, it seems, has become part of your art. Forgive me, my love, my soul is filled with bitterness and the man who deserved your trust is dead. Forgive him, in the name of all we have lived for.

He wipes the tears from his chin, remembering how he had once wiped hers. She had been pregnant, vomiting up everything she swallowed. But the troupe was on tour; she couldn't rest. Livid, drawn, she still didn't miss a single rehearsal. Onstage she had the energy of a young girl, but after the performances she would come back to their underground bomb shelter and collapse. One night, that night, he had carried her back, propped her against a wall to calm her down. She was afraid she would die. She wept, asked him if he would marry another woman? Would he mourn for her three years? Would he remember her? Don't be ridiculous, he had said. Don't worry. This too will pass. I love you, I'll always love you, all my life. He had wiped her tears, not with a handkerchief, but with the back of his hand. Like tonight.

Why does this memory make me suffer? It's nothing. Love has always been an illusion. The eternal illusion. The old myth of fidelity. How many millions of couples had sworn it and then betrayed each other? Now, in a moment of passion, she replays for her lover the scene of their old vows. Life, the ceaseless river, flows on. Why does this break my heart? And I thought I had become accustomed to bitterness. Not so, not so. No, I've never denounced the lights that lit my sky: to create, and to love. My sacred illusions: it's only now that I see you clearly, like each blade of grass, each splash of sun on the old path. The gray rocks, the wildflowers in the mountain ravines, the remote jungle where I spent my youth. Everything comes back to me now, all at once. All I've lived, experienced, accomplished, in art and in love. Aside from that, my life is a desert. Yes, it's time to leave now. Here, at the summit of this life that has been mine.

He rests his head on the sleeve of his jacket to dry the tears. He rises slowly, slips past the spectators, head lowered in respect for the crowd. No one notices his departure. The spectators are all in tears. Even the doorman's eyes are closed as Hung pulls aside the curtain to leave.

He hails a cyclo.

Home. He turns on a light, fumbles through the house, unable to find a rope thick enough. He mounts the stairs. It is even harder to find one in his room; Suong has thrown out his useless keepsakes, his odds and ends, replaced them with new furniture. The room is as clean as a hair salon. He goes downstairs, remembering a closet in the kitchen where she keeps things she hasn't had the heart to throw out. An old rusty lock. He enters the kitchen, searches for a knife, hurls it at the lock, which falls to pieces. He laughs to himself, realizing he still has something left in him. Inside he finds his old war knapsack; it is moldy, covered with spider webs, hanging on the door. He picks it up, but the filth stirs something unpleasant inside him; he too feels dirty. He opens the sack, searching for the ball of parachute cord: It's still there, in the middle of his things.

The last memory of my past. The only thing I can trust in this life.

He walks to the bathroom, carefully washes his wrists, his fingers, the cord, shaking it out to dry. He turns out the light, mounts the stairs to his room. The light is on. He turns it off, lights a candle, sets it in the corner. There, he finds another dirty knapsack, a souvenir from his prison buddies.

Ah, there you are! I'd almost forgotten you! Well, in the end, it's better that I forget you. What use . . . a little hatred to spice up the festivities, the right mix of lemon and chili pepper.

He looks down, watches the red wax of the candle dripping, drop by drop onto the tiles. He closes the door, leaving only a thin ray of light. He sets the chair on the veranda in front of the stairs, climbs onto it, fastens one end of the cord to a branch of white ylang-ylangs. The old gnarled branch scratches his wrist, makes it bleed. He goes back into the house, searches for the medicine kit, swabs the scratch with iodine, returns. One last time, he looks up at the sky, the city teeming with lights, the bats darting about in the darkness. He gazes at the patch of light in Auntie Tuong's window where his daughters are sleeping. A drop of water falls on his heart, like icy dew onto a leaf. He checks the knot around the ylang-ylang tree, slips it over his head, pulls slowly on the cord, and jumps off the balcony into the void.

A few seconds pass. Church bells are ringing. Who knows if it is to announce the beginning of the nuns' prayers, or end.

The Twelfth Day of the Year of the Water Buffalo
(February 18, 1997)

About the Author

Memories of a Pure Spring is set amidst the tremendous and disorienting material and psychological changes the Vietnamese faced in the 1980s after three decades of war. While the central character, a talented composer who runs afoul of the Communist Party authorities, is fictional, the broad lines of his fate—disillusionment with the Party, imprisonment, and ultimately, internal exile—closely parallel the author's own life and current predicament in Vietnam. Like her hero, Duong Thu Huong is a veteran who spent ten years in the tunnels and air-raid shelters of central Vietnam, the most heavily bombarded front of her country's "American War." She too was the leader of an artistic troupe and youth brigade sent to "sing louder than the bombs." One of just three survivors of that brigade, Huong emerged after the war as one of the most talented and widely read novelists of her generation, her first novels selling hundreds of thousands of copies. But when her best-selling novel *Paradise of the Blind* scandalized the Party authorities in 1988 by depicting the disastrous Maoist-style 1953–1956 land reform, Huong was publicly criticized and the work suddenly withdrawn from circulation. Again, like her hero, Duong Thu Huong found herself transformed overnight from patriot to pariah: Expelled from the Party, out of a job as a screenwriter, and unable to find a publisher who would dare to publish her novels, she became a kind of exile in her own land. In 1991, after sending abroad the manuscript of her *Novel Without a Name*—the first novel by a northern veteran to chronicle widespread disillusionment with the war effort and the Party leadership—Huong was imprisoned for seven months without trial on trumped up charges of "sending state secrets abroad." Though she has not been allowed to publish any of her novels in Vietnam since her release, almost ten years ago, she continues to live and write in Hanoi.

—Nina McPherson

A PENGUIN READERS GUIDE TO

MEMORIES OF A
PURE SPRING

—————

Duong Thu Huong

A Raft Perfumed and Rudderless:

An Introduction to Memories of a Pure Spring

*"Humanity has been through Communism. May the gods spare
us from falling prey to yet another illusion."*
(Memories of a Pure Spring)

Youthful ideals can provide guidance, inspiration, and resilience,
but once betrayed or corrupted they linger as bitter reminders of
past glories and present failures. In Duong Thu Huong's novel, set
during Vietnam's "American war," a well-known composer named
Hung leads a performing troupe through jungles bloodied by war.
The troupe's mission is one of artistic inspiration: to revive the
revolutionary fire in the soldiers' flagging spirits—to inspire with
art. Not actually raising any weapons or contributing directly to the
fratricidal carnage of the war, the performing troupe by its very
nature is an embodiment of high-minded ideals and a reminder
of the war's purpose. The performers' song is an uplifting response
to the eternal question: Why are we fighting?

While thus employed in a war-torn Vietnam, Hung meets a
beautiful young peasant girl with an exquisite voice, Suong, who
incites his passion and becomes both his wife and the star of the
troupe. As the long years of the war draw to a close on April 29th,
1975, when the last Americans leave Saigon, we find Hung and
Suong in love and ennobled by their struggles, both famous for
their talents and both full of promise.

However, as the postwar regime consolidates its power, cynical compromises and petty acts of revenge proliferate the political landscape. The noble ideals of the war have vanished all too quickly, persisting only in memories that harshly illuminate the current state of affairs. And it is, now, in their nation's victorious mundaneness that Hung and Suong must suffer—and they do suffer.

In a Vietnam richly brought to life with its flowers and fruits, cafés and teahouses, pho and chè, Duong Thu Huong uses dramatic external events—imprisonment, suicide attempts, love affairs, blackmail, opium addiction—to set the stage for the sensitive ruminations that form the lyrical core of *Memories of a Pure Spring*. Through the many artists that populate the book she explores artistic creation—its fragile preconditions, its awesome powers, and its frightening demands—as well as its soul-numbing substitutes. Through the book's central lovers she charts the Janus face of a love that is simultaneously ephemeral and eternal. Through the many deprivations and compulsions that shape her characters' lives she ponders sexual desire with its blinding drives and seductive pleasures. Through filial and familial relationships she investigates both the tender empowerment and the oppressive rigidity of family. Through the apparatchiks and officers of the Communist Party she illustrates the ignorant cruelty of the doctrinaire and the petty parochialism of the self-serving.

Throughout the novel, the memories of the past serve as the characters' touchstone as they attempt to navigate safely the shoals of success and flattery, chaos and desolation, love and desire, disillusionment and despair. Reading *Memories of a Pure Spring* forces unanswerable questions upon the reader: Is memory enriching or poisonous; a "pure spring" inspiration or an albatross?

ABOUT DUONG THU HUONG

Duong Thu Huong, one of Vietnam's most popular writers, was born in 1947 and raised in a loyal Communist household. In 1967 she—like Hung, the protagonist of *Memories of a Pure Spring*—volunteered to lead the Communist Youth Brigade, a troupe of singers and actors who traveled the country entertaining North Vietnamese troops at the front in jungle camps. She experienced first-hand the horrors of war: out of the volunteer group of forty, she was one of only three survivors. During China's 1979 attack on Vietnam, she became the first woman combatant present at the front to chronicle the conflict.

After the North Vietnamese victory in 1975, a journey to Saigon brought her face to face with the distortions of Communist propaganda: rather than the official North Vietnamese image of a Saigon oppressed and crying out for liberation, she found instead an affluent city full of laughing citizens and well-stocked bookshops. Thus began her disappointment in and reappraisal of Communist ideals as well as her long and vocal advocacy for human rights and democratic political reform. Though she had won several state prizes for her screenwriting work with the Vietnam Film Co., Duong Thu Huong lost her job there for speaking out against censorship. Undaunted, she continued to critique the social injustices of postwar Vietnam and began to write the novels for which she is justly famous both abroad and at home, including *Paradise of the Blind*, which was the first Vietnamese novel ever translated into English, published in the United States, and shortlisted for the Prix Femina; and *Novel Without a Name*, which was nominated for the IMPAC Dublin Literary Award. She was expelled from the Communist Party in 1989, imprisoned for seven months without trial in 1991 for sending the manuscript of *Novel Without a Name* abroad, and had her passport revoked by the government in 1995. All of her writings are effectively banned in Vietnam, where she continues to reside.

Penguin wishes to thank and credit the following article for information on the life of Duong Thu Huong: David Liebhold, "Lives Reshaped by History," *Time Asia*. April 17th, 2000, Vol. 155 No. 15.

QUESTIONS FOR DISCUSSION

1. The structure of *Memories of a Pure Spring* is marked by constant chronological shifts and frequent extracts from the internal musings of the characters? How does the author use the theme of memory as a structuring device? Is it effective?

2. In a moment of remembrance, Lam recalls the legends that explicitly note the ylang-ylang tree as a representative of the dark side of sexual desire:

> Why do those ylang-ylang blossoms in the garden frighten me? My father used to tell me that white ylang-ylang should only be planted in the pagodas, mausoleums, or altars—places protected by the spirits of pure men, masters of their fate, free of the mud of the world. He who is tempted by flesh is still chained to the infernal cycle of ambition, anger, passion. If you cultivate white ylang-ylang, you attract demons and create your own downfall.

Ylang-ylang and its seductive scent course through the novel (making a dramatic and meaningful backdrop to the last scene). What attitude toward sexual desire does the frequent recurrence of the ylang-ylang make manifest? What other figures and episodes in the novel serve as tropes for the menacing nature of sexual desire?

3. The purpose of art, the figure of the artist, and the struggle of artistic creation are all shown from many different points of view:

- Suong herself as the diva of central Vietnam and "the nightingale with the crystal voice,"
- the dissipation of Hung's debauched artistic friends,
- the viciousness of Doan's sham superiority,
- the inspirational role of the revolutionary troupe during the war,
- Hung's bitter struggle with his lack of inspiration, and
- Dam's impassioned advocacy for Hung's music as the only true expression of central Vietnam's character.

In the last analysis, what is the novel's "verdict" on these matters?

4. "People often enter history intelligently and leave it like idiots." With such observations, Hung, in his reminiscences and reveries, often contrasts the high-mindedness and sacrifice of the war years with the servility and mean-heartedness that reigned after the war. What other means does the author use to illustrate the same point?

5. Compare Vinh's father's severe reaction when he sees the young Vinh looking at the fishmonger girl with teenage Vinh's own implacable hatred of Hung for the sexual incident between Suong and his artist friends.

6. How does the conflict between illusion, melancholy, and sham, on the one hand, and "true art" on the other play itself out? Are these two poles presented as antagonistic opposites or as mutually dependent? Where does Hung fall in relation to this divide? Are his ruminations on Schubert instructive on this point or do they merely serve as foreshadowing?

7. Vengeance and struggle are constant themes, for example in Vinh's fulminations against Hung as well as the deputy chief's

settling of scores after the war. Does the author intend this specifically as a comment on life under a Communist regime or as a mark of human nature in general? How so?

8. While Lam is at heart a rustic, happy to be a porter in the countryside, Dam represents the urban sophistication of Hanoi. Discuss the parallelism and similarity of their respective roles that is hinted at by their similar names.

9. Hung brashly and forthrightly sums up his view of the place of the individual and the artist in Communist society with the passage:

> You can only create art when you live with dignity, in a free society. Even a slave knows how to put pen to paper, or mix colors on a palette. But a cowardly, servile, hypocritical soul can never create art.

Compare this with Doan's rebellious "yin theory of art" and his relation to the Communist authorities.

10. Vinh longs for the countryside. Hung waxes nostalgic for the war years. Suong feels bereft and rudderless without the love and respect she used to have for Hung. Many think back to the promise of "life in the new lights." Do these "lost objects" represent the "pure spring" of the title? What are the negative examples of purity used in the novel and how do these relate to memory's darker role? What are some of the novel's negative examples of memory? How do these relate to the occurrences of the insistent refrain, "Forget, forget, forget"?

11. At one point Dam says to Suong, "Your voice is your only weapon," yet her voice is always referred to as a crystal voice with unifying powers—a voice with which the many different people of

central Vietnam can relate, whether they be peasants, prison guards, or intellectuals. Discuss how Suong herself views her own voice and the uses to which she puts it.

12. Why and how does the seeming resolution of Hung's and Suong's difficulties lead to the book's dramatic last scene? Is this conclusion inevitable? Is it an act of passion? Discuss the possibility, or the lack thereof, of redemption in the novel.

PRAISE FOR DUONG THU HUONG

Paradise of the Blind

"Astonishingly powerful . . . a simple and beautifully told story of a civil war within a family." —*Los Angeles Times Book Review*

"Draws back the curtain on postwar Vietnam. . . . A literary jewel dripping with political nitroglycerine." —*Entertainment Weekly*

"Duong Thu Huong describes the problems of ordinary people and the contradictions of political reform openly. . . . *Paradise of the Blind* is a daring work of fiction." —*The New York Times*

"Duong Thu Huong is a social panoramist who writes with a tight focus on individual consciousness and personal relations . . . putting into print what the people of Vietnam know, that the way things are is different from the way they are supposed to be." —*The Nation*

"The first major woman's voice to reach our shores from all of Asia . . . will take your breath away and invade your dreams." —*Mademoiselle*

Novel Without a Name

"Reminiscent of *All Quiet on the Western Front* and *The Red Badge of Courage* . . . a breathtakingly original work."

—*San Francisco Chronicle*

"A poetic, painful, and universal story of the real spoils of war: horror, death, and the corrosion of the soul."

—*The Asian Wall Street Journal Weekly*

"If it is a crime to take an unflinching look at the reality of war and of life under a totalitarian regime, and to do it with great art and mastery, then Duong Thu Huong is gloriously guilty."

—*The New York Times Book Review*

"Extraordinary and profoundly tragic." —*The Boston Sunday Globe*

Also available from Penguin:

Paradise of the Blind   0-14-023620-1 $12.95
Novel Without a Name   0-14-025510-9 $12.95

For information about other Penguin Readers Guides, please call the Penguin Marketing Department at (800) 778-6425, e-mail at reading@penguinputnam.com, or write to us at:

Penguin Marketing Department CC
Readers Guides
375 Hudson Street
New York, NY 10014-3657

Please allow 4–6 weeks for delivery.
To access Penguin Readers Guides online, visit Club PPI on our Web site at: http://www.penguinputnam.com.

FOR THE BEST IN PAPERBACKS, LOOK FOR THE

In every corner of the world, on every subject under the sun, Penguin represents quality and variety—the very best in publishing today.

For complete information about books available from Penguin—including Puffins, Penguin Classics, and Arkana—and how to order them, write to us at the appropriate address below. Please note that for copyright reasons the selection of books varies from country to country.

In the United Kingdom: Please write to *Dept. EP, Penguin Books Ltd, Bath Road, Harmondsworth, West Drayton, Middlesex UB7 0DA.*

In the United States: Please write to *Penguin Putnam Inc., P.O. Box 12289 Dept. B, Newark, New Jersey 07101-5289* or call 1-800-788-6262.

In Canada: Please write to *Penguin Books Canada Ltd, 10 Alcorn Avenue, Suite 300, Toronto, Ontario M4V 3B2.*

In Australia: Please write to *Penguin Books Australia Ltd, P.O. Box 257, Ringwood, Victoria 3134.*

In New Zealand: Please write to *Penguin Books (NZ) Ltd, Private Bag 102902, North Shore Mail Centre, Auckland 10.*

In India: Please write to *Penguin Books India Pvt Ltd, 11 Panchsheel Shopping Centre, Panchsheel Park, New Delhi 110 017.*

In the Netherlands: Please write to *Penguin Books Netherlands bv, Postbus 3507, NL-1001 AH Amsterdam.*

In Germany: Please write to *Penguin Books Deutschland GmbH, Metzlerstrasse 26, 60594 Frankfurt am Main.*

In Spain: Please write to *Penguin Books S. A., Bravo Murillo 19, 1° B, 28015 Madrid.*

In Italy: Please write to *Penguin Italia s.r.l., Via Benedetto Croce 2, 20094 Corsico, Milano.*

In France: Please write to *Penguin France, Le Carré Wilson, 62 rue Benjamin Baillaud, 31500 Toulouse.*

In Japan: Please write to *Penguin Books Japan Ltd, Kaneko Building, 2-3-25 Koraku, Bunkyo-Ku, Tokyo 112.*

In South Africa: Please write to *Penguin Books South Africa (Pty) Ltd, Private Bag X14, Parkview, 2122 Johannesburg.*